THE
CARYATIDS

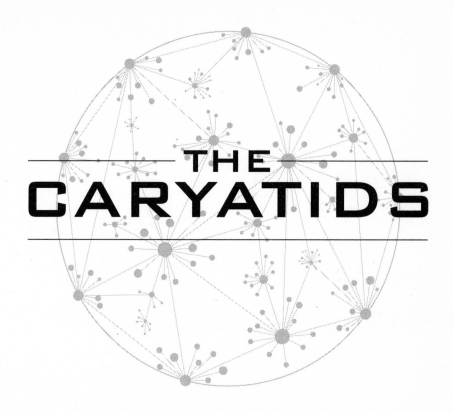

THE CARYATIDS

BRUCE STERLING

BALLANTINE BOOKS

NEW YORK

Copyright © 2009 by Bruce Sterling

Published in the United States by Del Rey, an imprint of The Random House Publishing Group, a division of Random House, Inc., New York.

DEL REY is a registered trademark and the Del Rey colophon is a trademark of Random House, Inc.

Library of Congress Cataloging-in-Publication Data

Sterling, Bruce.
The caryatids / Bruce Sterling.
p. cm.
ISBN 978-0-345-46062-2 (alk. paper)
1. Human cloning—Fiction. I. Title.
PS3569.T3876C37 2009
813'.54—dc22   2008051828

Printed in the United States of America on acid-free paper

www.delreybooks.com

1 3 5 7 9 8 6 4 2

First Edition

Book design by Christopher M. Zucker

To Jasmina

PART ONE
VERA
THE ADRIATIC

POISONS, PUMPED DOWN HERE at enormous pressure, had oozed deep into the water table. The seamy stone was warped and twisted. All around her, toxin miners scuttled like crabs.

The toxin miners pried the poisoned rock apart, slurped up toxins with busy hoses, then deftly reassembled the stifling walls in a jigsaw mess of glue. In their exoskeletons and filter suits, the miners looked like construction cranes wrapped in trash bags.

The miners were used to their work and superbly good at it. They measured their progress in meters per day. They were subterranean bricklayers. Cracking blocks and stacking blocks: that was their very being.

Vera thought longingly of glorious light and air at the island's sunny surface, which, from the cramped and filthy depths of this mine, seemed as distant as the surface of Mars. Vera had made it a matter of personal principle to know every kind of labor on the island: forestry, reef restoration, the census of species . . .

These miners had the foulest, vilest redemption work she'd ever seen. The workers were a gang of grimy, knobby ghosts, recycling sewage inside a locked stone closet.

Her helmeted head rang with a sudden buzz of seismic sensors, as if her graceless filter suit were filled with bees. Tautly braced within their shrouds and boneware, the miners studied the tortured rock through their helmet faceplates. They muttered helpful advice one another.

Vera loaded the mine's graphic server. She tapped into the augment that the miners were sharing.

Instantly, the dark wet rock of the mine burst into planes of brilliant color-coding: cherry red, amber yellow, veins of emerald green . . . A dazzling graphic front end for this hellhole.

Using their gauntlets, the miners drilled thumb-sized pits into the dirty rock. They plucked color-coded blasting caps from damp-stained satchels at their waists. They tamped in charges. Within a minute came the blast. Vera, sealed within her suit and padded helmet, felt her teeth clack in her head.

With a groan and squeak of their boneware, the miners wrestled out a cracked slab the size of a coffin.

A stew of effluent gushed forth. The bowels of the Earth oozed false-color gushes of scarlet and maroon.

"You can help me now." Karen beckoned.

Vera chased the software from her faceplate with a shake of her head. Vera's sensorweb offered sturdy tech support to anyone who might redeem the island, but the mediation down this mine was in a terrible state. These miners were plumbing the island's bowels with bombs and picks, but when it came to running their everyware, they never synchronized the applications, they never optimized the servers, they never once emptied the caches of the client engines. Why were people like that?

Badly encumbered by her filter shroud, Vera clambered to Karen's side through a cobweb of safety supports. The carbon-fiber safety webs looked as useless as dirty gossamer. Strain monitors glowed all over them, a spectral host of underground glowworms.

Vera found her voice. "What do you need me to do?"

"Put both your hands up. Here. And over there. Right. Hold all that up."

Vera stood obediently. Her exoskeleton locked her body tight against the ceiling.

Karen's boneware creaked as she hefted her power drill. She studied the rock's warping grain through the mediation of her faceplate, whistling a little through her teeth. Then she probed at a dripping seam. "This part's nasty," she warned.

Her drill spewed a tornado of noise. Vera's guts, lungs, and muscles shook with the racket. It got much worse as Karen dug, jammed, and twisted. Within her boneware, Vera's flesh turned to jelly.

Karen handled her massive drill with a dainty attention to detail, as if its long whirring bit were a chopstick.

Gouts of flying rock dust pattered off Vera's helmet. She twisted her neck and felt the helmet's cranial sensors dig into her scalp.

Two miners slogged past her as she stood there locked in place, hauling their hoses and power cables, as if they were trailing spilled guts. They never seemed to tire.

Stuck in her posture of cramped martyrdom to duty, Vera sourly enjoyed a long, dark spell of self-contemplation.

Like an utter idiot, she had allowed herself to be crammed into this black, evil place . . . No, in a bold gust of crusading passion, she had grabbed her sensor kit and charged headlong down into this mine to tackle the island's worst depths. Why? To win some glow of deeper professional glory, or maybe one word of praise from her boss?

How could she have been that stupid, that naive? Herbert was never coming down here into a toxin mine. Herbert was a professional. Herbert had big plans to fulfill.

Herbert was a career Acquis environmental engineer, with twenty years of service to his credit. Vera also wore the Acquis uniform, but, as a career Acquis officer, Vera was her own worst enemy. When would she learn to stop poking in her beak like a magpie, trying to weave her sensor-webbing over the whole Earth? Any engineer who ran a sensorweb always thought she was the tech support for everything and everybody. "Ubiquitous, pervasive, and ambient"—all those fine words just meant that she would never be able to leave anything alone.

No amount of everyware and mediation could disguise the fact that this mine was a madhouse. The ugly darkness here, the grit, the banging, grinding, and blasting, the sullen heat, the seething damp: and the whole place was literally full of poison! She was breathing through micropored plastic, one filmy layer away from tainted suffocation.

Stuck in her rigid posture of support, Vera gazed angrily through the rounded corners of her helmet faceplate. Nobody else down in this mine seemed at all bothered by the deadly hazards surrounding them.

Was she living an entirely private nightmare, was she insane? Maybe she had been crazy since childhood. Anyone who learned about her childhood always thought as much.

Or maybe her perspectives were higher and broader and finer, maybe she simply understood life better than these dirty morons. Stinging sweat dripped over Vera's eyebrows. Yes, this ugly mayhem was the stuff of life for the tunnel rats. They had followed their bliss down here. This hell was their homeland. Fresh air, fresh water, golden sunlight, these were alien concepts for them. These cavemen were going to settle down here permanently, burrowing into the poisonous wet and stink like bony salamanders. They would have children, born without eyes . . .

"Stay alert," Karen warned her.

Vera tried, without success, to shrug in her locked exoskeleton. "Work faster, then."

"Don't you hustle me," said Karen merrily. "I'm an artist."

"Let's get this over with."

"This is not the kind of work you can hurry," said Karen. "Besides, I love my drill, but they built it kinda girly and underpowered."

"Then let me do the drilling. You can hold this roof up."

"Vera, I know what I'm doing." With a toss of her head, Karen lit up her bodyware. A halo of glory appeared around her, a mediated golden glow.

This won her the debate. Karen was the expert, for she was very glorious down here. Karen was glorious because she worked so hard and knew so much, and she was so beloved for that. The other miners in this pit, those five grumbling and inarticulate cavemen banging their rocks and trailing their long hoses—they adored Karen's company. Karen's presence down here gave their mine a warm emotional sunlight. Karen was their glorious, golden little star.

There was something deeply loathsome about Karen's cheery affection for her labor and her coworkers. Sagging within her locked boneware, Vera blinked and gaze-tracked her way through a nest of menu options.

Look at that: Karen had abused the mine's mediation. She had tagged the rocky cave walls with virtual wisecracks and graffiti, plus a tacky host of cute icons and stencils. Could anything be more hateful?

A shuddering moan came from the rock overhead. Black ooze cascaded out and splashed the shrouds around their legs.

Karen cut the drill. Vera's stricken ribs and spine finally stopped shaking.

"That happens down here sometimes," Karen told her, her voice giddy in the limpid trickling of poisoned water. "Don't be scared."

Vera was petrified. "Scared of *what*? *What* happens down here?"

"Just keep your hands braced on that big vein of dolomite," Karen told her, the lucid voice of good sense and reason. "We've got plenty of safety sensors. This whole mine is crawling with smart dust."

"Are you telling me that this stupid rock is *moving*?"

"Yeah. It moves a little. Because we're draining it. It has to subside."

"What if it falls right on top of us?"

"You're holding it up," Karen pointed out. She wiped her helmet's exterior faceplate with a dainty little sponge on a stick. "I just hit a good nasty wet spot! I can practically smell that!"

"But what if this whole mine falls in on us? That would smash us like bugs!"

Karen sneezed. All cross-eyed, she looked sadly at the spray across the bottom of her faceplate. "Well, that won't happen."

"How do you know that?"

"It won't happen. It's a judgment call."

This was not an answer Vera wanted to hear. The whole point of installing and running a sensorweb was to avoid human "judgment calls." Only idiots used guesswork when a sensorweb was available.

For instance, pumping toxins down here in the first place: That was some idiot's "judgment call." Some fool had judged that it was much easier to hide an environmental crime than it was to pay to be clean.

Then the Acquis had arrived with their sensorweb and their mediation, so everybody knew everything about the woe and horror on this island. The hidden criminality was part of the public record, suddenly. They were mining the crime. There was crime all around them.

A nasty fit of nerves gathered steam within Vera. She hadn't had one of these fits of nerves in months. She had thought she was well and truly over her fits of nerves. She'd been sure she would never have a fit of nerves while wearing an Acquis neural helmet.

"Let me use the drill," Vera pleaded.

"This drill needs a special touch."

"Let me do it."

"You volunteered for mine work," said Karen. "That doesn't make you good at it. Not yet."

" 'We learn by doing,' " Vera quoted stiffly, and that was a very correct, Acquis-style thing to say. So Karen shrugged and splashed out of the way. Karen braced herself against the stony roof.

Vera wrapped her arms around the rugged contours of the drill. Her boneware shifted at the hips and knees as she raised the drill's tip overhead. She pressed the trigger.

The drill whirled wildly in her arms and jammed. All the lights in the mine went out.

Vera's exoskeleton, instantly, locked tight around her flesh. She was stuck to the drill as if nailed to it.

"I'm stuck," she announced. "And it's dark."

"Yeah, we're all stuck here now," said Karen, in the sullen blackness. Toxic water dripped musically.

"I can't move! I can't see my own hands. I can't even see my mediation!"

"That's because you just blew out the power, Vera. Freezing the system is a safety procedure."

An angry, muffled shout came from another miner. "Okay, what idiot pulled that stunt?" Vera heard the miner sloshing toward them through the darkness.

"I did that!" Vera shouted. In the Acquis, it was always best to take responsibility at once. "That was my fault! I'll do better."

"Oh. So it was *you*? You, the newbie?"

Karen was indignant. "Gregor, don't you dare call Vera a 'newbie.' This is Vera Mihajlovic! Compared to her, *you're* the newbie."

"Well, it's a good thing I still have charge left in my capacitors."

Karen sighed aloud in the wet darkness. "Just go and reboot us, Gregor. We've all got a schedule to meet."

"Please help me," Vera begged him. "I'm stuck here, I can't move!"

"You'll have to wait for a miracle, stupid," said Gregor, and he left them there, rigid in the darkness.

"You made Gregor angry," Karen assessed. "Gregor's our very best rock man, but he's not exactly a people person."

Vera heaved uselessly against the silent pads and straps of her dead exoskeleton. Her boneware, which gave her such strength, grace, lightness, power, had become her intimate prison.

"Who designed all this?" she shrieked. "We should have power backups! We should have fuel cells!"

"Be glad that we can still hear each other talking." Karen's voice sounded flat and muffled though her helmet and shroud. "It's too hot down here to run any fuel cells. Gregor will reboot us. He can do it, he's good. You just wait and see."

A long, evil moment passed. Panic rose and clutched the dry lining of Vera's throat.

"This is horrible!"

"Yes," said Karen mournfully, "I guess it is, pretty much."

"I can't stand it!"

"Well, we just have to stand it, Vera. We can't do anything but stand here."

Claustrophobic terror washed through Vera's beating heart.

"I can't do it," she said. "I can't bear any more."

"I'm not scared," Karen told her. "I used to be very scared every time I came down here. But emotion is a neural state. A neural state can't touch you. I'm never afraid like I used to be. Sometimes I have fear-thoughts, but my fear-thoughts are not me."

"I'll scream!"

Karen's voice was full of limpid sympathy. "You can scream, then. Do it. I'm here for you."

SEEN FROM THE AIRY HILLTOP, Mljet was a tattered flag, all bays, peninsulas, and scattered islets. The island's scalloped shores held stains in their nooks and corners: the algae blooms.

The rising Adriatic, carrying salt, had killed a dry brown skirt-fringe of the island's trees.

The island's blanket of pines and oaks was torn by clear-cut logging, scarred black with forest fires.

And if the golden shore of this beautiful place had suffered, the island's interior was worse. Mljet's angry creeks had collapsed the island's bridges as if they'd been kneecapped with pistols. Up in the rocky hills, small, abandoned villages silently flaked their paint.

Year by year, leaning walls and rust-red roofs were torn apart by towering houseplants gone feral. The island's rotting vineyards were alive with buzzing flies and beetles, clouded with crows.

A host of flowers had always adorned this sunny place. There were far more flowers in these years of the climate crisis. Harsh, neck-high thickets of rotting flowers, feeding scary, billowing clouds of angry bees.

Such was her home. From the peak of the island, where she stood, throat raw, flesh trembling, mind in a whirl, she could see that the island was transforming. She could hear that, smell it, taste it in the wind. She was changing it.

Brilliancy, speed, lightness, and glory.

Millions of sensors wrapped Mljet in a tight electronic skin, like a cold wet sheet to swathe a fever victim. Embedding sensors. Mobile sensors. Dust-sized sensors flying like dandelion seeds.

The sensorweb was a single instrument, small pieces loosely joined into one huge environmental telescope. The sensorweb measured and archived changes in the island's status. Temperature, humidity, sunlight. Flights of pollen, flights of insects, the migrations of birds and fish.

Vera turned her augmented vision to the sky. A distant black speck resolved as a patrolling snake eagle. The Acquis cadres were extremely proud of the island's surviving eagles. The Acquis had tagged that bird all over with high-level, urgent commentary. The eagle cut the sunlit air in a haze of miscellaneous archives, the glow of immanent everyware.

This hilltop was sacred to her. She could vividly remember the first day she had fled here, reached the summit: terrified, traumatized, ragged, abandoned, and half-starved. For the first time in her young life, Vera had grasped the size and shape of this place of her birth. She had realized that her home was alive and beautiful.

Life would go on. Surely it would. Because, despite every harm, distortion, insult, the island was recovering. Through her helmet's faceplate, Vera could see that happening in grand detail. She was an agent of that redemption. She had an oath and a uniform, labor and training and tools. She belonged here.

Someday this wrecked and stricken place would bloom, in all tomorrow's brilliancy, speed, lightness, and glory. Someday a happy young girl would stand on the soil of this island and know no dread of anything.

Vera put her gloved hands to her helmet, clicked it loose, and logged out of the sensorweb.

The helmet released its rubbery grip on her scalp. She pulled it, bent her neck, and her head was freed. She suddenly heard the almighty host of cicadas creaking in the island's pines, the summer army of insect occupation. The insect screams were shrill and piercing and tireless and erotic.

Vera powered down. Intimate grips and straps released their embrace of her arms and legs. She plucked her hands from the work gloves. She tugged her bare feet from the boots.

Deprived of the presence of her body, the boneware downsized and collapsed.

Vera placed the tender soles of her feet against a brown carpet of pine needles. She sat on a slanting boulder, with furred patches of orange lichen the size of a child's handprints. The dense sea breeze up the hillslope smelled of myrtle and wild honey. It seemed to pour straight through her flesh.

Fitfully, Vera worked a comb through her loosened braids. Her eyes ached, her throat was raw from screaming. Her back hurt, her shoulders felt stiff. Her thighbones were like two hollow straws.

She rubbed the seven shaven spots on her scalp. Her mind was clearing, the panic had shed its grip. The sensorweb was invisible to her now, gone with the helmet at her naked feet, but she still sensed its permeating presence across her island. Vera knew that the sensorweb was here, processing, operational. She could feel it in the way that a sleeping face felt sunlight.

As an Acquis web engineer, she had labored on the sensorweb for nine years, and its healing power was manifest. Once the web had been an aspect of the island. Now the island was an aspect of the web.

Vera tore at her suspension clips, her webbing belt. She rid herself of her tunic and trousers. Her underclothes, those final skeins of official fabric, shivered and crumpled as they left her flesh.

Vera sniffed and spat, shook herself all over.

Naked, she was a native sliver of this island, one silent patch of flesh and blood. Just a creature, just a breath, just a heartbeat.

VERA'S BOSS WAS AN ACQUIS ENGINEER: Herbert Fotheringay. The climate crisis had dealt harshly with Herbert's home, his native island-continent. Australia had been a ribbon of green around a desert. Drought had turned Australia into a ribbon of black.

The Acquis was partial to recruiting people like Herbert, ambitious people who had survived the collapse of nation-states. The Acquis, as a political structure, had emerged from the failures of nations. The Acquis was a networked global civil society.

From the days of its origins in planetary anguish, the Acquis had never lacked for sturdy recruits. Herbert had been ferociously busy on Mljet for nine years.

Herbert awaited her at his latest construction project: another attention camp.

Attention camps were built to house the planet's "displaced," which, in a climate crisis, could mean well nigh any person at almost any time. Attention camps were the cheapest and most effective way that the twenty-first century had yet invented to turn destitute people into agents of a general salvation.

Mljet was an experimental effort by a technical avant-garde, so its camps were small in scope compared with, say, the vast postdisaster slums of the ceaselessly troubled Balkans. So far, the island's camps held a mere fifteen hundred refugees, most in the little districts of Govedjari and Zabrijeze.

The refugees in Zabrijeze and Govedjari were among the wretched of the Earth, but with better tech support, they would transit through their unspeakable state to a state that was scarcely describable.

Herbert's newest campsite was a six-hectare patch of scalded, sloping bedrock that had once been an island dump. The dump had leaked toxins and methane, so it had been catalogued and obliterated.

Vera walked into the camp's humming nexus of construction cranes, communication towers, fabricators, heat-pump pipes, and bioactive sewage tanks.

Seen with the naked eye—she wore no helmet today—the camp was scattered around her like the toys of a giant child. Their arrangement looked surreal, nonsensical. It was only through the sensorweb that every object, possession, and mechanism found its proper destination. One might say that the new camp was systematically networked . . . or one might say, more properly, that the sensorweb was becoming a camp.

Vera stared through the camp's apparent confusion, out to sea. Morning on the Adriatic. How pure and simple that sea looked . . . Although, when Vera had learned analysis, she had come to see that the famous "Adriatic blue" was spectrally nuanced with cloudy gray, plankton green, mud brown, and reflective tints of sky; that apparently "simple and natural" blue emerged from a wild mélange of changing cloud cover, solar angles, seasonal changes in salinity, floods, droughts, currents, storms, even the movements of the viewer . . .

The sea had no "real" blue. And the camp was no "real" camp. There was a mélange of potent forces best described as "futurity." They were futuring here, and the future was a process, not a destination.

Feeling meek and frail without her helmet and boneware, Vera quietly slid into Herbert's saffron-colored tent. Herbert was shaving his head with one hand, eating his breakfast with another.

Herbert was ugly, red-faced, and in his early fifties. The dense meat of his stout body was as solid as a truck tire. He ran a buzzing shaver over his skull, which bore seven livid dents from his helmet's brain scanner.

Herbert's exoskeleton, bone-white, huge, and crouching in a powered support rack, filled almost half his modest tent. Vera's personal exoskeleton was a pride of the Acquis and had cost as much as a bulldozer, but Herbert's boneware was a local legend: when Herbert climbed within its curved and crooked rack, he wore full-scale siege machinery.

The burdens of administration generally kept Herbert busy, but when Herbert launched himself into direct action, he shook the earth. Herbert could tear up a brick house like a man breaking open a bread loaf; he could level a dead village like a one-man carnival.

Herbert smiled on her with unfeigned loving-kindness.

"Vera, it was kind of you to come so early. There have been some important developments, a new project. I've had to reassign you."

Vera's eyes welled up. "I knew you'd pull me out of that mine. I disgraced myself."

"Well, yes," Herbert admitted briskly. Naturally Herbert had read the neural reports from all the personnel on-scene. Everyone felt regret, unhappiness, embarrassment, shame . . . "Mining work is not your bliss, Vera. A mishap can happen to anyone."

There was a long, thoughtful silence.

People who had never worn boneware had such foolish ideas about brain scanners and what they did. Brain scanners could never read thoughts. Telepathy was impossible. That was a fairy tale.

Still, neural scanners were very good at the limited things that real-life scanners could do. Mostly, they read nerve impulses that left the brain and ran the body's muscles. That was why a neural scanner was part of any modern exoskeleton.

Brain scanners also read emotions. Emotions, unlike thoughts, lingered deep within the brain and affected the entire nervous system.

Grand passions were particularly strong, violent, and machine-legible.

Acquis neural scanners could easily read ecstasy and dread. Murderous fury. Pain and injury. Lassitude, grief, hatred, exaltation, bursting pride, bitter guilt, major depression, suicidal despair, instinctive loathing, sly deception, abject terror, burning resentment, a mother's love, and unstoppable tears of sympathy.

Acquis neural tech was still a young, emergent field, but it was already advanced enough to create a vital core of users and developers. Herbert was one of those people. So was every other Acquis cadre on Mljet. Herbert was an Acquis neural apparatchik, a seasoned captain of the industry.

Vera was his lieutenant.

Heat prickled the back of Vera's neck. "There's no big debriefing for me, Herbert? You know as well as I do that I completely lost my wits down there!"

"Yes, you suffered a panic attack," Herbert said blandly. "It's one of your character flaws. We all have them. It's our flaws that give us our character."

Vera was now certain that there was something dreadful in the works for her. Herbert was much too calm.

Vera analyzed her boss's ugly face.

Why did she love him so?

When she'd first met Herbert, he had badly scared her. Herbert was old, ugly, foreign, and fanatical. Worst of all, Herbert had bluntly insisted that she stick her head into an experimental helmet that scanned people's brains. Vera knew that ubiquitous computing was very powerful: she did not want that technology applied inside her skull. Vera feared that for good reasons. She had seen her loved ones shot down dead, and she had feared that less.

Vera had obeyed Herbert anyway, because Herbert was willing to rescue Mljet. No one else of consequence seemed even willing to try. The Acquis were global revolutionaries. They got results in the world. They did some strange things, yes—but they never, ever stopped trying.

So Vera had swallowed the panic and let the machine swallow her head.

Vera had swiftly learned that wearing a brain machine was a small price to pay to learn the feelings of others.

Herbert Fotheringay was an ugly man, but he had such a beautiful soul. Herbert had a touching simplicity of character. He brimmed over with kindness and goodness. For those who earned his trust and shared his aims, Herbert was a tireless source of strength and support. Herbert meant every word that he had ever said to her.

She had joined his effort as a bitter, grieving eighteen-year-old, her home demolished and her loved ones shot dead or scattered across the world. Yet Herbert and his scanners had instantly seen beyond her fear and misery. The machines had sensed the depth of her passionate love for her homeland. Herbert had always treated Vera as the heart and soul of his Mljet effort.

Herbert had made himself her mentor. He set her tests, he gave her tasks. She had eagerly seized those chances, and they had done so well. They had accomplished so much, together, side by side. The wounded island was healing before their eyes. Innovation was coming thick and fast, amazing insights, new services, new techniques. Transformations were bursting from her little island that were fit to transform the world.

Yet every industry had its hazards. Herbert and Vera had been close colleagues for nine years. They were very close now—they were too close. It had taken them years, but now, whenever Herbert and Vera met face-to-face, there were strong bursts of neural activity in the medial insula, the anterior cingulate, the striarum, and the prefrontal cortex.

That meant love. An emotion so primal was impossible to mistake. Love was Venus rising from her neural seas, as obvious to a neural scanner as a match in a pool of kerosene.

Vera was very sorry for the operational burden that her love brought to Herbert and the cadres on the island. In the Acquis neural project, leaders were held to especially high standards. Since he was project manager, Herbert was in some sense officially required to suffer.

To win the trust of the other neural cadres, to coax out their best efforts, their boss had to manifest clear signs of deep emotional engagement with large, impressive mental burdens. Otherwise he'd be dismissed as a fake, a poseur, a lightweight. He'd be replaced by someone else, someone more eager, more determined, more committed.

There were people—especially the younger and more radical cadres on Mljet—who whispered that she, Vera Mihajlovic, should become the project manager. After all, she was twenty-six and had grown up within the neural system and the sensorweb, whereas Herbert was fifty-two and had merely engineered such things. Whenever it came to redeeming Mljet, Vera was burningly committed and utterly sincere. Herbert was older, wiser, and a foreigner, so he was merely interested.

Herbert had his flaws. Herbert's largest character flaw was that he was publicly in love with a subordinate half his age. Anyone who wanted to look at Herbert's brain would know this embarrassing fact, and since Herbert was in authority, everyone naturally wanted to look at his brain.

Such was their situation, a snarl that was humanly impossible. Yet it was their duty to bear the burden of it. So far, they had both managed to bear it.

Herbert gently drummed his thick red fingers on his folding camp table. Heaven only knew what labyrinth of second-guessing was going on within his naked head. He seemed to expect her to make the next emotional move, to impulsively spit something out.

What was he feeling? Had Herbert finally learned to hate her? Yes! In a single heart-stabbing instant, this suspicion flamed into conviction.

Herbert despised her now. He hated all the trouble she had given him.

He'd just claimed that he was "reassigning" her. He meant to fire her from the project. He would throw her onto a supply boat and kick her off Mljet. She would be expelled, shipped to some other Acquis reclamation project: Chernobyl, Cyprus, New Orleans. She would never proudly wear her boneware again, she'd be reduced to a newbie peon. This meant the end of everything.

Herbert touched his chin. "Vera, did you sleep at all last night?"

"Not well," she confessed. "My barracks are so full of dirty newbies . . ." Vera had tossed and turned, hating herself for panicking in the mine, and dreading this encounter.

"A good night's sleep is elementary neural hygiene. You need to teach yourself to sleep. That's a discipline."

She gnawed at a fingernail.

"Eat," he commanded. He shoved his soup bowl across the little camp table. She reluctantly unfolded a camp stool and sat.

"Breakfast will stabilize your affect. You've spent too much time in a helmet lately. You need a change of pace." He was coaxing her.

"There's no such thing as 'too much time in a helmet.' "

"Well, there's also no such thing as a proper Acquis officer skipping meals and failing to sleep. Eat."

She was dying to eat from the simple bowl that Herbert used. That big warm spoon in her hand had just been inside Herbert's mouth.

Herbert edged past her and zippered the entrance to his tent. This gesture was a pretense, since there was very little sense in fussing about privacy in an attention camp. People made a big fuss anyway, because life otherwise was unbearable.

Neither of them were wearing their helmets: not even neural scanning caps. Any emotion coursing through them would stay off the record. How dangerous that felt.

Reaching behind his polished rack of boneware, Herbert found an ancient, itchy hat of Australian yarn. He stretched this signature bonnet over his naked head. Then he scratched under it. "So. Let's discuss your new assignment. An important visitor has arrived here. He's a banker from Los Angeles, and he took a lot of trouble to come bother us. This man says he knows you. Do you know John Montgomery Montalban?"

Vera was shocked. This was the last news she had ever expected to hear from Herbert's lips. She dropped the spoon, leaned forward on her stool, and began to cry.

Herbert contemplated this behavior. He was saddened by the dirty spoon. "You really should eat, Vera."

"Just send me back down into the mine."

"I know that you have a troubled family history," said Herbert. "That's not a big secret, especially on this island. Still, I just met this John Montgomery Montalban. I see no need for any panic about him. I have to say

I rather liked Mr. Montalban. He's a perfectly pleasant bloke. Very businesslike."

"Montalban is that stupid rich American who married Radmila. Make him go away. Hurry. He's bad trouble."

"Did you know that Mr. Montalban was coming here to this island? It was quite an epic journey for him, by his account. He took a slow boat all across the Pacific, he personally sailed through the Suez Canal . . . Making money all the way, I'd be guessing, by the look of him."

"No. I have never met Montalban. Never. I don't talk to him, I don't know him. He isn't supposed to be here, Herbert. I don't want to know him. Not ever. I hate him. Don't let him stay here."

Herbert lowered his voice. "He's brought his little girl with him."

Vera raised her head. "He brought a child? To a neural camp?"

"That's not illegal. It's against Acquis policy for people in radical experimental camps to *have and bear* children. After all, clearly, morally—we can't put kids into little boneware jumpers and scan their brains without their adult consent. But it's not against policy to *bring* children here, on a visit. So Little Mary Montalban—who is all of five years old—came here all the way from California. She's here to see you, Vera. That's what I'm told."

Vera's shock lost its sharpness in her dark, gathering resentment. "That little girl is Radmila's child. Radmila sent her baby here. I was always afraid it would come to this. This is all some kind of trick!" Vera caught her lower lip between her teeth. "Radmila can never be trusted. Radmila is a cheat!"

" 'Cheat' in what sense? Enlighten me."

"You can tell just by looking at Radmila that she has no morals."

"But Radmila is your own clone. Radmila looks exactly like you do."

Vera shifted in her chair in anguish. "That is not true! The fact that we're genetically identical means *nothing*. We are very, very different. She's a cheat, she's evil, she's wrong."

There was no more "Radmila." Once there had been a Radmila, and she and Radmila had been the same. They had been the great septet of caryatids: seven young women, superwomen, cherished and entirely special, designed and created for the single mighty purpose of averting the collapse of the world. They were meant to support and bear its every woe.

The world had collapsed and the caryatids were scattered all over:

they were wrecked, shot, exposed, scattered and broken into pieces, their creator hunted and hounded like a monster . . . And in the place of beautiful Radmila, magical Radmila, that noble creature Vera had loved much better than herself, there was only the diseased and decadent "Mila Montalban." A rich actress in Los Angeles. Mila Montalban took drugs and dressed like a prostitute.

"Vera, why do you say such cruel things? Your brother George—he suffered like you suffered, but he would never say such demeaning things about his sisters."

Far from calming her, these words spurred instant, uncontrollable fury. "I hate Radmila! Radmila makes me sick! I wish that Radmila was dead! Bratislava died. Svetlana, Kosara, they died, too! I wish Radmila had died with them, she *should* have died! Running away from me, forever—that was only a foul thing to do . . ."

"I know that you don't really feel that way about your sisters."

"They're not my sisters, and of course I feel that way. They should never have existed, and never walked the Earth. They belong in the grave."

"Your brother George is alive and he's walking the Earth," said Herbert calmly. "You talk to George sometimes, you're not entirely isolated from your family. You don't hate George in that profound way, do you?"

Vera wiped hot tears from her cheeks. She deeply resented her brother Djordje. Djordje lived in Vienna. Djordje had disowned his past, built his shipping business, found some stupid Austrian girl to put up with him, and had two children. Nowadays, Djordje called himself "George Zweig."

She didn't exactly want Djordje dead—he was useful—but whenever Djordje tried to talk to her (which was far too often), Djordje scolded her. Djordje wanted her to leave Mljet, leave the Acquis, get married, and become limited and woodenheaded and stupid and useless to everybody and to the world, just like himself and his fat, ugly wife.

The existence of Djordje was a curse. Still, Djordje never gave her the absolute loathing that she felt in the core of her being at the very thought of her sisters. No one who had failed to know the depth of their union could ever know the rage and pain of their separation. And nobody knew the depth of their shattered union: not their tutors, not their machines, not even "George," not even their so-called mother.

"Herbert, please. Stop debriefing me about my family. That is useless and stupid. I don't have any family. We were never a family. We were a crazy pack of mutant creatures."

"What about that tough girl, the army medic? George seems pretty close to her—they speak."

"Sonja is far away. Sonja is on some battlefield in China. Sonja should be dead soon. People who go into China, they never come back out."

"Where does your other sister 'walk the Earth' these days?"

Vera shouted at him. "We are Vera, Sonja, and Radmila! Those are our names. And our brother is Djordje. 'George.' "

"Look, I know for a fact there are four of you girls."

"Don't you ever speak one word about Biserka! Biserka is like our mother: we never speak about that woman, ever. Our mother belongs in prison!"

"Isn't orbit a kind of prison?"

An ugly dizziness seized Vera. She felt like a vivisected dog.

Finally she picked up the idle bowl of cooling breakfast and drank it all.

Moments passed. Herbert turned on a camp situation report, which flashed into its silent life on the luminescent fabric of his tent.

"You're feeling better now," he told her. "You've been purged of all that, a little, again."

She was purged of it. Yes, for the moment. But not in any way that mattered. She would never be purged of the past.

Herbert's breakfast bowl was full of vitamin-packed nutraceuticals. It was impossible to eat such nourishing food and stay sick at heart. And he knew that.

Vera belched aloud.

"Vera, you're overdoing the neural hardware. That's clear to me. No more boneware for you till further notice." Herbert deftly put the emptied bowl away. "I don't want Mr. Montalban to see you inside your neural helmet. The gentleman has a squeamish streak. We mustn't alarm him."

Herbert's nutraceuticals methodically stole into Vera's bloodstream. She knew it was wrong to burden Herbert with her troubles. It was her role to support Herbert's efforts on Mljet, not to add to his many public worries.

"George was stupid to tell you anything about our family. That is dangerous. My mother kills people who know about her. She's a national criminal. She is worse than her warlord husband, and he was terrible."

Herbert smiled at this bleak threat, imagining that he was being brave. "Vera, let me make something clear to you. Your fellow cadres and I: We care for you deeply. We always want to spare your feelings. But: Everybody here on Mljet knows all about those criminal cloning labs. We know. Everybody knows what your mother was doing with those stem cells, up in the hills. They know that she was breeding superwomen and training them in high technology—the 'high technology' of that period, anyway. That foolishness has all been documented. There were biopiracy labs all over this island. You—you and your beautiful sisters—you are the only people in the world who still think that local crime wave is a secret."

Herbert smacked his fist into his open hand. "A clone is an illegal person. That's all. This island is manned by refugees from failed states, so we're all technically 'illegal,' like you. You can't convince us that you're the big secret monster from the big secret monster lab. Because we know you, and we know how you feel. We're in solidarity with you, Vera. It's all a matter of degree."

Vera chose to say nothing about this vapid pep talk. No one understood the tangled monstrosity that was herself and her sisters, and no outsider ever would. The Gordian knot of pain and horror was beyond any possible unraveling. Justice was so far out of Vera's reach . . . and yet there were nights when she did dream of vengeance. Vengeance, at least some nice vengeance. Any war criminal left a big shadow over the world. Many angry people wanted that creature called her "mother" pulled down from the sky. Whatever went up, must surely come down, someday—yes, surely, someday. As sure as rainstorms.

"Vera, your personal past was colorful. All right: Your past was a bloody disaster, so it was *extremely* colorful. But we all live in a postdisaster world. We have no choice about that reality. All of us live after the disaster, everyone. We can't eat our hatreds and resentments, because those won't nourish us. We can only eat what we put on our own tables—today. Am I clear to you?"

Vera nodded sullenly. Having put her through the emotional wringer, Herbert was going to praise her now.

"You have extensive gifts, Vera. You have talent and spirit. You are energetic and pretty, and even if you tend to panic on some rare occasions, you always fulfill your duties and you never give up. The people who know you best: They all love you. That's the truth about Vera Mihajlovic. Someday you will realize that about yourself. Then you'll be happy and free."

Vera lifted her chin. Herbert had been telling her these spirit-lifting things for nine long years. Herbert said them because he truly believed them. He believed them so heartily that sometimes she was almost convinced.

After all, the evidence was on his side. Mostly.

Herbert drew a conclusive breath. "So: As a great man once said, in times almost as dark as our own times, 'Withhold no sacrifice, begrudge no toil, seek no sordid gain, fear no foe: all will be well.' "

Maybe someday he would just put his arms around her. Not talk so much, not understand her so loudly and so thoroughly. Just be there for her. Be there like a man for a woman.

That wasn't happening. Not yet, and maybe not ever.

VERA PICKED HER WAY BACK to her barracks, bare-headed and bare-eyed. The broken road was heavily overgrown; the flitting birds had no sensorweb tags, the flowery bushes had no annotations. Without her boneware, her arms and legs felt leaden. She had a heavy heart about the new assignment.

She was to "guide" John Montgomery Montalban around the island. Vera knew what that meant—she had just become a spy. She was a spy now, pretending to be a guide. Something dark and horrible was transpiring between herself and Radmila.

Why was the Earth so small?

Radmila had sent her child and her husband here, so that her shadow would once again touch Mljet. Why did that woman exist? Radmila had no right to her existence.

Radmila's fool of a husband—how had that man dared come here? "On vacation," he had said. Montalban had told the island's project manager, told Herbert right to his face, that he was here as a "tourist."

Could Montalban possibly imagine that Herbert, an Acquis officer, would be fooled by that lie? Vera felt shocked and numbed at the sheer audacity of such a falsehood. People who lived without brain scanners thought that they could get away with anything they said. The fetid privacy of their unscanned brains boiled over with deception and cunning.

No wonder the world had come to ruin.

Maybe Montalban imagined that his story sounded plausible, because Mljet had once had tourists—thousands of them. Before its decay, tourism had been the island's economic base. And Montalban was an investment banker, specializing in tourism. He'd even said something fatuous about his child's "cultural heritage."

Montalban was rich, he was from Los Angeles—which was to say, Montalban was from the Dispensation. Montalban was from the *other* global civil society, the other successor to the failed order of nation-states, the other global postdisaster network.

Acquis people struggled for justice. Dispensation people always talked about business. There were other differences between the two world governments, but that was the worst of it, that was the core of it. Everything the Acquis framed as common decency, the Dispensation framed as a profit opportunity. The Dispensation considered the world to be a business: a planetary "sustainable business." Those people were all business to the bone.

Montalban had clearly come here to spy for the Dispensation, although global civil societies didn't have any "spying." They weren't nations: so they had no "spying" and no "war." They had "verification" and "coopetition" instead. They were the functional equivalents of spying and war, only much more modern, more in the spirit of the 2060s.

Vera wiped sweat from her aching brow. Maybe she could defy Herbert, put on her trusty boneware, grab that "coopetitor" by the scruff of his neck, and "verify" him right back onto his boat. If she did that—in a burst of righteous fury—how much real trouble could that cause? Maybe the cadres would sincerely admire her heartfelt burst of fury.

The Dispensation prized its right to "verify" what the Acquis did. "Verification" was part of the arrangement between the network superpowers—a political arrangement, a détente, to make sure that no one was secretly building old-fashioned world-smashing super-weapons. In practice, "verification" was just another nervous habit of the new political order. The news was sure to leak over some porous

network anyway, so it was better just to let the opposition "verify" . . .
It kept them busy. Montalban had already toured an island attention
camp . . . He was photographing it, taking many notes . . . Shopping
for something, probably . . .

Vera knew that the Dispensation feared Acquis attention camps. The
Dispensation had their own camps, of course, but not attention camps—
and besides, the Dispensation never called them "refugee camps," but
used smoothly lying buzzwords such as "new housing projects," "entertainment destinations," and "sustainable suburbs."

Attention camps were a particularly brilliant Acquis advance in
human rehabilitation. So the other global civil society glumly opposed
them. That was typical of the struggle. The Dispensation dug in their
heels about advanced Acquis projects that couldn't fit their crass, mate-
rialist philosophy. They scared up popular scandals, they brought their
"soft-power" pressure . . . They were hucksters with all kinds of tricks.

A bluebottle fly buzzed Vera's bare face—the pests were bad in summer. No, she wouldn't attack Montalban and evict him while wearing
her armor. That was a stupid emotional impulse, not coolheaded diplomacy. Vera had limited experience outside Mljet, but she was an Acquis
officer. The word got around inside the corps. There were professional
ways to handle bad situations like this. Annoying and slow ways, but professional ways.

When some Dispensation snoop showed up at an Acquis project to
"verify," the sophisticated tactic was to "counterverify." Fight fire with
fire. The big operators handled it that way. She could watch whatever
Montalban did, watch him like a hawk. Stick to him like glue, be very
"helpful" to him, help him to death. Get in his way; interfere; quibble,
quibble, quibble; work to rules; mire him in boring procedures. Make a
passive-aggressive pest of herself.

There was certainly no glory in that behavior. Spying on people was
the pit of emotional dishonesty. It was likely to make her into the shame
of the camp. Vera Mihajlovic: the spy. Everyone would know about it,
and how she felt about it.

Yet someone had to take action. Vera resolved to do it.

Through handing her this difficult assignment, Herbert was testing
her again. Herbert knew that her troubled family past was her biggest
flaw as an officer. He knew that her dark past limited her, that it harmed

her career potential in the global Acquis. Herbert had often warned her that her mediated knowledge of the world was deep, yet too narrow. By never leaving Mljet, she had never outgrown her heritage.

Herbert's tests were hard on her, but never entirely unfair. Whenever she carried the weight of those burdens, she always grew stronger.

VERA SHARED HER BARRACKS with sixty-two other Acquis cadres. Their rose-pink, rectangular barracks was a warm, supportive, comforting environment. It had been designed for epidemic hunters.

These rapid-deployment forces, the shock troops of the global civil societies, pounced on contagious diseases emerging around the world. The medicos were particularly well-equipped global workers, thanks to the dreadful consequences of their failures. This meant they left behind a lot of medical surplus hardware: sturdy, lightweight, and cheap.

So Vera's barracks was a foamy puff of pink high-performance fabric, perched on struts on a slope above the breezy Adriatic gulf. Out in the golden haze toward distant Italy, minor islets shouldered their way from the ocean like the ghosts of Earth's long-extinct whales.

Nearby, the derelict village of Pomena had been scraped up and briskly recycled, while its old harbor was rebuilt for modern shipping. A vast, muscular Acquis crane, a white flexing contraption like a giant arm, plucked cargo containers from the ferries at the dock. Then the huge crane would simply fling that big shipping box, with one almighty, unerring, overhand toss, far off into the hills, where nets awaited it and cadres in boneware would unpack and distribute the goods.

Next to the docks sat a squat, ratcheting fabricator, another pride of the Acquis. This multipotent digital factory made tools, shoes, struts, bolts, girders, spare parts for boneware—a host of items, mostly jet-spewed from recycled glass, cellulose, and metal.

Karen suddenly towered over Vera's cot, an apparition still wearing boneware from the toxin mine, ticking and squeaking. "Are you sad? You look so sad, lying there."

Vera sat up. "Aren't you on shift?"

"They're fabbing new parts for my drill," Karen said. "Down in that mine, they're so sorry about the way they treated you. I gave them all such a good talking-to about their insensitivity."

"I had a hard brainstorm. That was a bad day for me, all my fault, I'm sorry."

"It's hard work," said Karen. "But the way you ran up your favorite hill afterward, to feel your way through your crisis . . . ? Your rapport with this island was so moving and deep! Your glory is awesome this morning. It's because you find so much meaning in the work here, Vera. We're all so inspired by that."

"Herbert gave me a new assignment."

Karen made a sympathetic face. "Herbert is always so hard on you. I'll power down now. You tell me all about it. You can cry if you want."

"First can you find me a toenail clipper?"

Karen stared through her faceplate at the thousands of tagged items infesting their barracks. Karen found a tiny, well-worn community clipper in twenty seconds. Karen was a whiz at that. She commenced climbing out of her bones.

As Karen recharged her bones, Vera picked at her footsore toes and scowled at the bustling Acquis barracks. New cadres were graduating from the attention camps almost every week. They bounded proudly over the island in their new boneware, each man and woman heaving and digging with the strength of a platoon—but inside their warm pink barracks, their bones and helmets laid aside, they flopped all over each other like soft-shelled crabs.

The cadres shaved scanner patches on their skulls. They greased their sores and blisters. They griped, debriefed, commiserated, joked, wept. It often looked and sounded like a madhouse.

These were people made visible from the inside out, and that visibility was changing them. Vera knew that the sensorweb was melting them inside, just as it was melting the island's soil, the seas, even the skies . . .

Karen returned from her locker, swaying in her pink underwear. Karen had a sweet, pleasant, broad-cheeked face under the shaven spots in her black hair. Karen's sweetness was more in her sunny affect than in the cast of her features. Karen's ancestors were European, South Asian, African . . . Karen was genetically globalized.

Karen's family had been jet-setting sophisticates from upper-class Nairobi, until their city had imploded in the climate crisis. Australia: A very bad story, the world's most vulnerable continent for climate change. India, China—always so crowded, so close to epic human disasters—

catastrophic places. Yet disaster always somehow seemed worse in Africa. There was less attention paid to people like Karen, their plight always fell through the cracks. One would think that African sophisticates didn't even exist.

Karen had lost everyone she knew. She had escaped the bloody ruin of her city with a single cardboard suitcase.

Some Acquis functionary had steered Karen toward Mljet. That decision had suited Karen. Today, Karen was an ideal Acquis neural socialite. Because Karen was a tireless chatterer, always deep into everybody else's business. Yet Karen never breathed a word about her painful past, or anyone else's past, either. Vera liked and trusted her for that.

Life inside an Acquis brain scanner had liberated Karen. She'd arrived on the island so bitterly grieved that she could barely speak, but the reformed Karen was a very outgoing, supportive woman. She was even a brazen flirt.

"The boss never treats you like a woman should be treated around here," Karen told her. "I have something that will change your mood, though." Karen handed over a box with a handwritten card and a curly velvet ribbon.

"Karen, what is this about?"

"Your niece came here to our barracks this morning," said Karen. "While you were being debriefed. She's the only little girl on this whole island. She walked straight into here, right up that aisle, through that big mess piled there. Like a princess, like she was born in here. The place was full of grown-ups wearing skeletons. Tough guys. Changing shifts. You know. Naked people. She wasn't one bit scared! She even sang them a little song. Something about her favorite foods: soup and cookies!"

" 'Soup and cookies'?" said Vera unbelieving, though Karen never lied.

"The cadres couldn't believe that either! They never saw anything like that! That kid can *really sing*, too—you should have heard them cheer! Then she left this beautiful gift just for you."

Vera kept her face stiff, but she could feel herself gritting her teeth.

Karen, as always, was keen to sympathize. "We couldn't help but love that 'Little Mary Montalban.' I know someday she'll be a big star."

Karen bounced on the stainless pink fabric of her surplus medical cot. "So, do it! Open this gift from your weird estranged niece! I'm dying to see what she brought for you!"

"Since you're so excited, you can open that."

Karen sniffed the scented gift card and ripped into the wrappings. She removed a crystal ball.

The crystal ball held a little world. A captive bubble of water. It was a biosphere. Herbert often mentioned them. They were modeling tools for environmental studies.

Biospheres were clever toys, but unstable, since their tiny ecosystems were so frail.

Biospheres were pretty at first, but they had horribly brief lives. Sooner or later, disaster was sure to strike that little world. Living systems were never as neat and efficient as clockworks. Biology wasn't machinery. So, as time passed, some aspect of the miniature world would depart from the normal parameters. Some vital salt or mineral might leach out against the glass. Some keystone microbe might die off—or else bloom crazily, killing everything else.

A biosphere was a crystal world that guaranteed doom.

Karen peered through the shining bubble, her freckled cheekbones warping in reflection. "This is so clever and pretty! What do people call this?"

"I'd call that a 'thanatosphere.'"

"Well! What a name!" Karen deftly tossed the gleaming ball from hand to hand. "Why that big sour face? Your gift from that princess is fit for a queen!" Watery rainbows chased themselves across Vera's blanket.

"That toy comes from a rich Dispensation banker. He's a spy, and that's a bribe. That's the truth."

Karen blinked. "Rich bankers are giving you gifts? Well then! You're coming up in the world! I always said you would."

"I don't need that toy. I don't want it. You can keep it."

"Truly?" Karen caressed the crystal with her cheek. "Won't somebody get mad about that?"

"Nobody from the Acquis. Nobody that matters to us."

"Well, I'm so happy to have this! You're very generous, Vera! That is one of your finest character traits."

Now Karen was intrigued, so she really bored in. "I've heard a lot of stories about toys like this. Dispensation people are crazy for their fancy gifts and gadgets. They're big collectors' items, from high society! I bet this toy is worth a lot of cash."

Vera methodically ripped the gift box to shreds. It was lined with velvet, with slender walls made of some fine alien substance, like parchment. It smelled like fresh bamboo. "They call their toys 'hobjects.' "

"Oh yeah. I knew that, too." Karen clutched the ball. "Wow, Vera, I privately own a fancy hobject! I feel so glamorous!"

"Karen, don't manifest sarcastically. Only little kids take candy from strangers."

Karen was hurt by this reproof. "But Little Mary *is* a little kid."

"That toy is sure to rot soon. It'll turn dark and ugly."

Karen rolled the shining ball across the backs of her fingers. Karen's use of neural gauntlets had made her dexterous—if her boneware was much like a skeleton, her skeleton had become rather like boneware. "Now, Vera: What kind of dark, bleak attitude are you projecting at me here? This is a whole little world! Look at all this wonderful stuff floating around in here! There's a million pieces of it, and they're all connected! You know what? I think this little world has a little sensorweb built in!"

"Oh no," said Vera. "That would be perverse."

"This is art! It's an art hobject!"

Vera flinched. "Stop juggling it!"

Karen's brown eyes shone with glee. "I can see little shrimp! They're swimming around in there! They're jumbo shrimp!"

Karen's eager teasing had defeated her. Vera reached out.

The biosphere held elegant branches of delicate fringed seaweed, bobbing in a vivid, reeling, fertile algae soup. The pea-green water swarmed with a vivid, pinhead-sized menagerie of twitchy rotifers and glassy roundworms.

And, yes, the sphere also held a darting, wriggling family of shrimp. These shrimp were the grandest denizens of their miniature world. Majestic, like dragons.

The crystal of the biosphere was lavishly veined. Some extremely deft machine had laser-engraved a whole Los Angeles of circuits through that crystal ball. The circuits zoomed around the water world like a thousand superhighways.

"Americans will buy anything," Karen said.

The dragon shrimp swam solemnly above an urban complex of fairy skyscrapers. Glittering extrusions grew like frost from the crystal into the seawater. Complex. Mysterious. Alluring.

It was as if, purely for random amusement, some ship-in-a-bottle fanatic had built himself . . . what? Factories like fingernail parings. Mini-distilleries. Desalinators, and filters, and water-treatment plants. A pocket city, half greenish ooze and half life-support network.

Squinting in disbelief, Vera lifted the biosphere into a brighter glare. Half the glass darkened as a thousand tiny shutters closed.

This was a lovely gift. Someone had been extremely thoughtful. It was apt. It was rich with hidden meaning. It was a seduction, and meant to win her over. Vera had never seen anything in her harsh and dutiful life that was half so pretty as this.

With a pang, Vera handed the biosphere back to Karen. Karen rolled it carelessly toward her distant cot. "Vera, no wonder bankers are courting you. I think the boss has decided to marry you."

"I'd do that." Vera nodded. There was never any use in being coy with Karen.

"Marrying the boss," said Karen, "is too easy a job for you. Herbert never gives you easy jobs."

Vera laughed. Karen never seemed to think hard, but somehow Karen always said such true things.

"Did you know that Herbert has filed a succession plan?"

Vera nodded, bored. "Let's not talk local politics."

Karen stuck a medical swab in her ear, rolled it around at her leisure, and examined the results. "Let me tell you my emotions about this succession business. It's time that Herbert moved on. Herbert is a typical start-up guy. A start-up guy has got a million visionary ideas, but he never knows what they're good for. He doesn't know what real people in the real world will do with his big ideas."

Vera scowled at such disloyalty. "You never used to talk that way about Herbert. You told me Herbert saved your life!"

Karen looked cagey. This was a bad sign, for though Karen had deep emotional intelligence, she wasn't very bright.

"That was then, and this is now. Our situation here is simple," said Karen mistakenly. "Herbert found some broken people to work very hard here, repairing this broken island. We heal ourselves with his neu-ral tech, and we heal the land with mediation at the same time. Inside heals outside. That's great. That's genius. I'm Acquis, I'm all for that. Sweat equity, fine! We get no pay, fine! We live in a crowded barracks, no privacy at all, no problem for me! Someday it'll snow on the North Pole again. Men as old as Herbert, they can *remember* when the North Pole had snow."

Karen flexed her multijointed fingers. "But I'm not old like him, I'm *young*. I don't want to postpone my life until we bring the past back to the future! I have to live *now*! For me!"

Clearly Vera's time had come to absorb a confession. She restrained a sigh. "Karen, tell me all about 'now' and 'me.' "

"When I first got to this island, yes, I was a wreck. I was hurt and scared, I was badly off. Neural tech is wonderful — now that I know what it's for! Let *me* have those helmets. I know what to do with them. I'll stick them on the head of every man in the world."

Karen scowled in thought. "I have just one question for every man. 'Do you really love this girl, or are you just playing around?' That's what matters. Give me *true love*, and I'll give you a planet that's *completely changed*! *Totally* changed. I'll give you a brand-new world in six months! You wouldn't even *recognize* that world!"

"Your soppy romance love story has no glory, Karen!"

"Vera, you are being a geek. All right? You are. Because you live in-side your mediation and your sensorweb. You never listen to the people with real needs! I fell in love here. Okay? A lot. With every guy in this barracks, basically. Okay, not with all of them, but . . . I give and I give and I emotionally give, and where is my one true love? When do *I* get happy?"

"Your scheme is irresponsible and it lacks any practical application."

"No it isn't. No it doesn't. Anyway, things are bound to change here. Soon." Karen folded her arms.

"I don't see why."

"I'll tell you why. Because we will promote our *next* project manager from among the cadres, using an architecture of participation! That's the succession plan. And our next leader isn't going to be like old Her-bert. Our next big leader is bound to be *one of us*."

This scheme was new to Vera, so she was interested despite herself. In

Mljet, it was always much more important to do the right thing with gusto than it was to nitpick about boring palace intrigues. And yet . . . there was politics here, every place had its politics.

"Look," said Vera, "very clearly, we don't have enough clout here to pick our own boss. If anything bad happened to Herbert, the Acquis committee would appoint some other project manager."

"Oh no, they wouldn't. They wouldn't dare do that."

"Yes, they would. The Acquis are daring."

Karen was adamant. "No they wouldn't! They can't send some gross newbie to Mljet to boss our neural elite! The cadres would laugh at him! They'd spit on him! They would kick his ass! He'd have no glory at all!"

Vera stared thoughtfully at Karen, then at the teeming mass of barracks-mates. It occurred to Vera that Karen, as the voice of the local people, was telling her the truth.

Vera was used to her fellow cadres—she could hardly have been more intimate with them, since their innermost feelings were spilled all over her screens.

But to outsiders, they might seem scary. After all, the Acquis neural cadres on Mljet were survivors from some of the harshest places in the world. They wore big machines that could lift cars. Even their women were rough, tough construction workers who could crack bricks with their fingers.

And—by the standards of people not on this island—they all lived inside-out. They didn't "wear their hearts on their sleeves"—they wore their hearts on their skins.

They were such kind people, mostly, so supportive and decent . . . But—as a group—the cadres had one great object of general contempt. Every Acquis cadre despised newbies. "Newbies" were the fresh re-cruits. Acquis newbies had no glory, since they had not yet done any-thing to make the people around them feel happy, or impressed with them, or more fiercely committed to the common cause. All newbies were, by nature, scum.

So Karen had to be right. Nobody on this island would willingly ac-cept a newbie as an appointed leader. Not now, not after nine years of their neural togetherness. After nine years of blood, sweat, toil, and tears, they were a tightly bonded pioneer society.

If they ever had a fit about politics, they were all going to have the same fit all at once.

Karen had found a big bag of sunflower seeds. She was loudly chewing them and spitting the husks into a cardboard pot. "Herbert's succession plan is to emotionally poll all the cadres," Karen told her, rolling salted seed bits on her tongue. "Our people will choose a new leader themselves—the leader who makes them *feel* best."

That process seemed intuitively right to Vera. That was how things always worked best around here—because Mljet was an enterprise fueled on passionate conviction. "Well, Novakovic has our best glory rating. He always does."

"Vera, open your big blue eyes. Novakovic is our chef! Of course we all like the *chef*. Because he feeds us! That's not what we want from our *leader* here! We want brilliancy! We want speed! We don't need some stuffy, overcontrolled engineer! We need an inspiring figure with sex appeal and charisma who can take on the whole world! We need a 'muse figure.' "

Vera squirmed on her taut pink cot. "We need some heavier equipment and some proper software maintenance, that's what we really need around here."

"Vera, *you* are the 'muse figure' on Mljet. You. Nobody else. Because we all know you. Your everyware touches everything that we do here." Karen offered her a beaming smile. "So it's you. You're our next leader. For sure. And I'd *love* to have you as my boss. Boy, my life would be *great*, then. The Vera Mihajlovic Regime, that would be just about perfect for me."

"Karen, shut up. You're my best friend! You can't plot to make me the project manager! You know I'd become a wreck if that happened to me!"

"You were born a wreck," said Karen, her eyes frank and guileless. "That's why you're my best friend!"

"Well, your judgment is completely clouded on this issue. I'm not a wreck! It's the *island* that's a wreck, and I am a solution. Yes, I had an awful time when I went down in that mine with you, I overdid that, I was stupid, but normally, I'm very emotionally stable. My needs and issues are all very clear to everyone. Plus, Herbert taught me a lot about geoengineering. I am very results-oriented."

"Sure, Vera. Sure you are. You get more done around here than any-one else does. We all love you for that devotion to duty. You're our golden darling."

"Okay," said Vera, growing angry at last. "Your campaign speech is impossible. That is crazy talk, that isn't even politics."

Karen backed off. She found a patch of open floor space. Then she stood up, unhinged her shoulders, lifted her left leg and deftly tucked her ankle behind her neck. No one in the barracks took much notice of these antics. Boneware experts always learned such things.

IN THE AZURE EASTERN DISTANCE, Vera saw the remote hills of the Croatian mainland: a troubled region called Peljesac by its survivors. The arid, wrinkled slopes of distant Peljesac had been logged off completely, scraped down to the barren bone by warlord profiteers.

Dense summer clouds were building over there. There would be storms by noon.

Montalban had chosen their rendezvous: a narrow bay, with a long stony bluff at its back. The ghost town of Polace was a briny heap of col-lapsing piers and tilted asphalt streetbeds. Offshore currents stirred the wreckage, sloshing flotsam onto Mljet's stony shoulders: sunglasses, san-dals, indestructible plastic shopping bags, the obsolete coinage of vari-ous dead nationalities.

During Vera's girlhood, Polace had been the most magical place in the world for her. The enchanted world of her caryatid childhood was every bit as dead as this dead town: smashed, invalidated, uncelebrated, unremembered. Reduced to garbage, and less than garbage.

The forgotten tenor of those lost times, her childhood before this is-land's abject collapse—Vera could never think of that life without a poi-sonous sea change deep within her head.

The past would not stay straight inside her mind. The limpid, flowing simplicity of those days, of seven happy little beings, living in their com-pound all jammed together as a team and psychic unit, the house and grounds bubbling over with magic sensors and mystic computation . . . Learning, interacting, interfacing, growing, growing . . .

Then came the horror, the irreparable fracture, the collapse. A smashing into dust and less than dust: transmuted to poison. The toxic loss of herself, of all of her selves—of all her pretty, otherworldly other-selves.

Her childhood fortress home . . . when this town of Polace had lived, glittering with evil vitality, then her home was a blastproofed villa of ancient Communist cement, dug deep into a hillside and nestled under camouflage nets. The sighing forest around the children seethed with intrusion sensors.

The children often played in the woods—always together, of course—and sometimes they even glimpsed the blue shorelines. But they were never allowed to visit the island's towns.

Four times each year, though, they were required to leave the island for inspections on the mainland: inspections by their inventor, their mother, their designer, and their twin, the eighth of their world-saving unit, the oldest, the wisest, their queen. So Vera, and her sullen little brother, and her six howling, dancing, shrieking sisters traveled in an armored bus with blackened windows.

The big bus would rumble up and down Mljet's narrow, hazardous roads, thump and squeak over the numerous, rickety bridges, park for a while on the grimy, graffiti-spattered dock, and then lurch aboard a diesel-belching Balkan ferry. Locked inside the bus, screaming in feral delight with her pack of sisters, Vera had feasted her eyes on an otherworldly marvel: that marvel was this place, this dead town.

The town had a name: Polace. Its townsfolk were black marketeers. They were brewers of illicit biotech. In a place of great natural beauty, they were merchants of despair.

Their gaudy pirate labs were guarded by militia soldiers in ferociously silly homemade uniforms. The harbor town was a factory, a pharmacy, a tourist trap, a brothel, and a slum.

Polace was an ancient Balkan fishing village of limestone rock and red-tiled roofs. Old Polace had been built right at the water's edge, so the rising high tides of the climate crisis were sloshing into the buildings.

Except, of course, for the new piers. These piers had been jerry-built to deal with the swarms of narcotics customers, sailing in from offshore. The black-market piers towered over the sea on spindly pylons of rust-weeping iron and pocked cement. The piers were crusted all over with flashing casino lights, and garish, animated street ads, and interactive billboards featuring starlets in tiny swimsuits.

Multistory brothels loomed on the piers, sealed and windowless, like the drug labs. The alleys ashore were crammed with bars, and drugstore kiosks, and reeling, intoxicated customers, whose polyglot faces were neon-lit masks of feral glee and panic. The little harbor held the sleek, pretty yachts of the doomed, the daring, the crooked, and the planet's increasingly desperate rich.

National governments were failing like sandcastles in the ominous greenhouse tide. There was nothing to shelter the planet's populations from their naked despair at the scale of the catastrophes. Without any official oversight, the outlaw biotech on the island grew steadily wilder, ever more extreme. The toxic spills grew worse and worse, while the population, stewing in the effluent, sickened.

Then an earthquake, one of many common to the region, racked Mljet. The outlaw labs on the island, jimmied together in such haste, simply burst. They ruptured, they tumbled, they slid into the sea. The tourists and their hosts died from fizzing clouds of poison. Others were killed in the terrified scramble to flee the island for good. Polace had swiftly succumbed; the island's other towns died more slowly, from the quake, the fires, the looting. When the last generators failed and the last light winked out there was nothing human on the island, nothing but the cries of birds.

John Montgomery Montalban clearly knew this dreadful subject very well, since he had made this careful pilgrimage to see the island's worst ruins firsthand. The California real-estate mogul calmly assessed the drowned wreckage through his tinted spex.

He told her it was "negative equity."

Montalban, her strange brother-in-law, was a Dispensation policy wonk. He was cram-full of crisp, net-gathered, due-diligence knowledge. He was tall and elegant and persuasively talkative, with wavy black hair, suntanned olive skin, and sharp, polished teeth: big Hollywood film-star teeth like elephant ivory. His floral tourist shirt, his outdoor sandals, his multipocketed tourist pants: they were rugged and yet scarily clean. They seemed to repel dirt with some built-in chemical force.

No Dispensation activist would ever wear an Acquis neural helmet, so Vera could not know how Montalban truly felt about her and this dark meeting. Still, Montalban kept up a steady flow of comforting chatter.

Legend said that the raider ships of Ulysses had once moored in

Mljet to encounter the nymph Calypso. Montalban knew about this. He judged the myth "not too unlikely." He claimed that Homer's Ulysses had "means, motive, and opportunity to swap his loot from Troy."

Montalban further knew that Mljet had been a thriving resort island in the days of the Roman Empire. He was aware that "medieval developers" had once built monasteries on the island, and that some of those stone piles were still standing and "a likely revenue source if repurposed."

Montalban entertained some firm opinions about the long-vanished Austro-Hungarian Empire and its "autocratic neglect of the Balkan hinterlands." He even knew that the "stitched-up nation of Yugoslavia" had preserved Mljet as its stitched-up national park.

When it came to more recent history—years during Vera's own lifetime—Montalban changed his tone. He became gallant and tactful. Her native island had been "abducted," as he put it: as "an offshore market for black globalization." Montalban said nothing about the eighteen dark years that his own wife had spent on Mljet. He said nothing about Radmila whatsoever. Montalban was so entirely silent and discreet about Radmila that Vera felt dazed.

Moving onto firmer ground with a burst of verbal footwork, Montalban launched into a complex narrative, full of alarming details, describing how the Acquis had managed to acquire Mljet to perform their neural experiments. Vera herself had never known half of these stories—they existed at some networked level of global abstraction that she and her fellow cadres rarely encountered. The details of Acquis high-level committees were distant events for them, something like astronomy or Martian exploration, yet Montalban knew a host of astonishing things about the doctrines and tactics of both the global civil societies. Most particularly, Montalban seemed to know where their money went.

Vera felt grateful for the way events were turning out. Vera had no money—because Mljet had no money economy—but if she'd had any money, she'd have cheerfully entrusted it to someone like Montalban. Montalban was so entirely and devotedly obsessed by money that he had to be really good at banking.

Radmila's husband was nothing like she had imagined and vaguely feared. Met in the suntanned flesh, he exuded wealth like some kind of cologne. Montalban was clearly the kind of man that rich clients could trust to work through huge, intimidating files of complex financial documents. There was something smooth and painless and lubricated about him.

When he sensed that his ceaseless flow of insights was tiring her, Montalban busied himself with his camera. He adjusted its tiny knobs and switches. He deftly framed his shots. He beachcombed through the wild overgrowth of the shore, a dense shady tangle of flowering shrubs thoroughly mixed with tattered urban junk. The summer glare bounced from his fancy spex, and when he removed his busy lenses, he had darting, opaque black eyes.

Busily documenting the wreck of Polace, Montalban urged her to "go right about your normal labors."

This was his gentle reproach for the way she had chosen to confront him and his little girl: defiantly towering over them in her boneware and helmet.

She'd done that to intimidate him. That effort wasn't working out well. Vera pretended to turn her attention to local cleanup work, levering up some slabs of cement, casually tossing urban debris into heaps.

Montalban turned his full attention to documenting his child. He moved Little Mary Montalban here and there before the ruined city, as if the child were a chess piece. He was very careful of the backgrounds and the angles of the light.

Miss Mary Montalban posed in a woven sun hat and a perfect little frock, delicately pressed and creased, with a bow in the back. The garment was a stage costume: it had such elegant graphic simplicity that it might have been drawn on the child's small body.

Mary had carried a beach ball to Polace. That was the child's gift to this stricken island, carried here from her golden California: Mary Montalban had a beach ball. A big round beach ball. A fancy hobject beach ball.

Mary certainly knew how to pose. She was solemn yet intensely visible. Her hair and clothing defied gravity, or it might be better said that they charmed gravity into doing what their designers pleased.

This small American girl was some brand-new entity in the world. She was so pretty that she was uncanny, as if there were scary reservoirs of undiscovered dainty charm on the far side of humanity. Still—no matter what her ambitious parents might have done to her—this five-year-old girl was still just a five-year-old girl. She was innocent and she was trying to please.

Mary Montalban had met a twin of her own mother: not Radmila, but Vera herself, a bony apparition, a literal moving skeleton, towering, vibrating, squeaking. Mary did not shriek in terror at the dreadful sight of her own aunt. Probably, Mary had been carefully trained never to do such things. But whenever Vera stilted nearer, the child shuddered uncontrollably. She was afraid.

This fancy little girl, with her childish walking shoes, her pretty hat, and her beach ball, sincerely was a tourist. She was trying to play with her dad and have some fun at the seashore. That was Mary's entire, wholehearted intention. Mary Montalban was the first real tourist that Mljet had seen in ten long years.

Some fun at the seashore didn't seem too much for a small girl to ask from a stricken world. A pang of unsought emotion surged through Vera. Pity lanced through her heart and tore it, in the way a steel gaff might lance entirely through the body of some large, chilly, unsuspecting fish.

Vera worked harder, stacking the debris in the gathering heat of late morning, but her small attempts to order the massive chaos of this dead town could not soothe her. How much that child looked like Radmila, when Radmila had been no bigger, had known no better. How quickly all that had come apart. How sad that it had all come to such a filthy end. Like this. To rubbish, to rubble, to death.

But a child wasn't rubble, rubbish, and death. Mary Montalban was not the product of some Balkan biopiracy lab. She was just the daughter of one.

That collapse had been waiting for the caryatids; it had been in the wind all along. The collapse started slowly, at first. First, Djordje had run away from the compound, in some angry fit—Djordje's usual selfishness. Their latest tutor, Dr. Igoe, had vanished in search of Djordje. Dr. Igoe never came back from that search. Neither did Djordje, for this time his escape was final.

Two days of dark fear and confusion passed. Vera, Bratislava, Kosara, Svetlana, Sonja, Radmila, Biserka—none of them breathed a word of what they all sensed must be coming.

And as for their mother, their creator, their protector, their inspector . . . there was not a sound, not a signal, not a flicker on a screen.

Then the earthquake happened. The earth broke underfoot, a huge tremor. After the earthquake, there were fires all over the coastlines, filthy, endless columns of rising smoke.

After the fires, men with guns came to the compound. The desperate militia soldiers were scouring the island for loot, or women, or food. The compound's security system automatically killed two of them. The men were enraged by that attack: they fired rockets from their shoulders and they burst in shooting at everything that moved.

Then sweet Kosara was killed, and good Bratislava was killed, and Svetlana was also killed, with particular cruelty. Suddenly murdered, all three of them. It had never occurred to these teenage girls to run for their lives, for their compound was their stronghold and all that their mother had allowed them to know of the world. Seventeen-year-old girls who had led lives of utter magic — air that held drawings and spoke po- etry, talking kitchenware, thinking trees — they all died in bursts of gun- fire, for no reason that they ever understood.

Radmila survived, because Radmila hid herself in the dust, smoke, and rubble. Sonja fought, and Sonja killed those who killed. Biserka, howling for mercy — Biserka had thrown herself at the bandits' feet.

Vera herself — she had run away at the first shots fired. Just run, van- ished into the woods, like the wind. Vera had always loved the open is- land much better than the compound.

Lost in the island's forest, truly lost on Earth for the first time in her life, Vera had been entirely alone. The Earth had no words for Vera's kind of solitude.

Bewildered and grieving, Vera had gone to Earth like an animal. She slept in brown heaps of pine needles. She ate raw berries. She drank rainwater from stony puddles.

Her world had ended. Yet the island was still there.

Vera tramped the stricken island from one narrow end to the distant other, climbed every hill she could climb, and there was not one living soul to be found. She grew dirty, despondent, and thin.

Finally Vera heard voices from the sky. Acquis people had arrived with boats, and those rescuers had a tiny, unmanned plane that soared around the island, a flying thing like a cicada, screeching aloud in a brilliant, penetrating voice. It yelled its canned rescue instructions in five or six global languages.

Vera did as the tiny airplane suggested. She ventured to the appointed rendezvous, she found her surprised rescuers, and she was shipped to a rescue camp on the mainland. From there Vera immediately schemed and plotted to return to Mljet, to save her island as she herself had been saved. At length, she had succeeded.

And now, after all that, here, again on Mljet, at last, was the next generation: in the person of Mary. The idea that Mary Montalban existed had been a torment to Vera—but in person, in reality, as a living individual, someone on the ground within the general disaster zone, Mary was not bad. No: Mary was good.

Mary was what she was: a little girl, a little hard to describe, but . . . Mary Montalban was the daughter of a rich banker and a cloned actress, sharing a junk-strewn beach with her crazy, bone-rattling aunt. That was Mary Montalban. She had a world, too.

Mary was visibly lonely, pitifully eager to win the approval of her overworked, too-talkative dad. Mary was also afraid of her aunt, although she very much wanted her aunt to love her and to care about her. That knowledge was painful for Vera. Extremely painful. It was a strong, compelling, heart-crushing kind of pain. Pain like that could change a woman's life.

Remotely chatting in their lively, distant voices, the father and daughter tossed their big handsome beach ball. The girl missed a catch, and the ball skittered off wildly into the flowering bushes. In the silence of the ruins Vera heard the child laughing.

Vera turned up the sensors in her helmet, determined to spy on them. The ruins of Polace were rather poorly instrumented, almost a blackspot in the island's net. Vera gamely tried a variety of cunning methods, but their voices were warped and pitted by hisses, hums, and drones. The year 2065 was turning out to be one of those "Loud Sun" years: sunspot activity with loud electrical noise. Any everyware technician could groom the signal relays, but there wasn't a lot to do about Acts of God.

Montalban did not know that Vera was eavesdropping on him with such keen attention. His formality melted away. Montalban swung his arms high and low, he capered on the wrecked beach like a little boy.

Now Montalban was telling Mary something about Polace, pointing

out some details in the rusting, sour ruins. Montalban was summing it
all up for his daughter somehow, in some sober piece of fatherly wisdom. Montalban respected his daughter, and was intent and serious
about teaching her. He was trying to instruct her about how the world
worked, about its eerie promises and its carnivorous threats and dangers,
phrasing that in some way that a five-year-old might comprehend and
never forget. A fairy tale, maybe.

Thrilled to be the focus of her dad's attention, Mary twisted her feet
and chewed at her fingers.

Montalban had brought his daughter here to Mljet, all this way
across the aching planet, for some compelling reason. Vera couldn't
quite hear what he was telling his child. Whatever it was, it certainly
meant the world to him.

Vera sensed suddenly, and with a terrible conviction, that the two of
them had come to Mljet to get far away from Radmila.

Yes, that was it. That was the secret. Montalban had not come here to
spy on her, or the Acquis, or the island's high technology, or anything else.
Whatever those other purported motives might be, they were merely his
excuses.

Mljet was a precious place for the two of them—because Radmila
was not here. The two of them were here alone together, because this island was the one place on Earth that Radmila would never, ever go.

Radmila Mihajlovic, "Mila Montalban" in distant Los Angeles: Radmila was the vital clue here, Radmila was the missing part of this story.
Radmila had renounced Mljet, fleeing the distorted horror of her own
being, a refugee washing across the planet's seas, like bloody driftwood.

Somehow, Radmila had found this man. She must have fallen on
him like an anvil.

Remorseless as the rise of day, the world had continued, and now the
father and the daughter had ventured here in order to be together.

Montalban flung the child's beach ball high. He waved his hands at
the hobject, gesturing like a wizard.

Suddenly, startlingly, the beach ball tripled in size. It soared above the
shoreline, a striped and glittering balloon. The bubble hung there, serene
and full of impossible promise, painted on the sullen storm clouds.

The beach ball wafted downward, with all the eerie airiness of a dandelion seed. It fell as if rescuing them from their misery.

The girl screeched with glee at her father's cleverness. Montalban, his whole being radiating joy and mastery, waved his hands. The ball plummeted to Earth. It bounded off with rubbery energy.

The two of them gleefully chased down their weird toy in their oddly posh clothing.

Mljet's newest tourists were thrilled to be here. They were entirely happy to treat the dismal wreck of Polace as their private playground. No ruin less awful, less desolate, could suit them and their love for one another.

Vera turned her helmeted head away. Her eyes stung, her cheeks were burning.

She waded into the cooling waters of the sea.

A dead water heater, poxed with barnacles, lay pillowed in a deathbed of mud. Vera bent and fetched it up. With one comprehensive nervous heave, she threw full power into her boneware.

The wrecked machine tumbled end over end and crashed hard above the tide line.

The child stared at her in joy and awe.

Vera hopped through the sea, splashing. She found a submerged car. She tore the rusty hood from its hinges. She flung the bent metal to shore, and it sailed like a leaf. She put her boot against a submerged door and tore that free as well. She threw it hard enough to skip it across the water.

Mary ran down the beach, skipping in glee. "Do it, Vera! Do it, Vera! Do that again!"

Montalban hastened after his child, his face the picture of worry. He half dragged Mary away from the wreckage and to a safer distance.

Up went his beach ball again, sudden and bloated and wobbling. The bubble rose with a wild enthusiasm, its crayon-bright colors daubing the troubled sky.

Montalban ran beneath the convulsing toy, pretending to leap and catch it. The child clapped her hands politely.

Then the toy burst. It fell into the sea in a bright tumble of rags.

THE LOCAL ACQUIS CADRES took a keen interest in Vera's feelings. With the arrival of her niece on the island, the Acquis cadres were obsessed.

For years, the cadres had accepted the fact that their island society lacked children. That was the condition of their highly advanced work. They didn't need kids to be an avant-garde society, a vanguard of the future. Surely they had each other.

The Acquis had hard-won experience in managing extreme technologies. Mljet was typical of their policy: a radical technical experiment required an out-of-the-way locale. It had to be compact in scale, limited in personnel. A neutered society. A hamster cage, an island utopia: to break those limits and become any bolder posed political risks. Risks posed by the planet's "loyal opposition," the Dispensation.

The Dispensation was vast and its pundits were cunning propagandists with the global net at their fingertips. They were always keen to provoke a panic over any radical Acquis activity—especially if those activities threatened to break into the mainstream.

Radical experiments that might be construable as child abuse made the easiest targets of all. So: No children allowed on the construction site . . . yet the clock never stopped ticking.

John Montgomery Montalban had brought his own child to the island. This was a Dispensation propaganda of the deed. The shrewder Acquis cadres understood this as a deliberate provocation. A good one, since there wasn't a lot they could do about adorable five-year-olds.

Montalban was simply showing everyone what they had missed, what they had sacrificed. Sentiment about the child was running high. Vera thought that it must take a cold-blooded father to exploit his own flesh and blood as a political asset, in this shrewd way. But John Montgomery Montalban had married Radmila Mihajlovic. He had married Radmila, and given her that child. There had to be something wrong with him, or he would never have done such a thing.

Vera could literally track the child's path across the island by the peaks of emotional disturbance her presence created. Mary left a wake wherever her polished little shoes touched the Earth.

The local Acquis cadres were unimpressed by Montalban. They considered themselves bold souls, they'd seen much worse than him. They felt some frank resentment for any intruder on their island, yet Montalban was just another newbie, an outsider who could never matter to them on a gut level.

Little Mary Montalban, though, was the walking proof of the cavity in their future.

Vera knew that her own powerful feelings about the child had done much to provoke this problem. In an act of defiance, Vera had chosen to wear her boneware and her neural helmet to meet Montalban—although Herbert had warned her against doing that. It had seemed to her like an act of personal integrity. Personal integrity did not seem to work with Montalban.

So: no more of that. If Vera put her own helmet aside—from now until this crisis blew over—the trouble would end all the sooner.

She had been wrong to trust her intuitions. She needed help. Karen would help her. Karen loved children. Karen had a lot of glory. Karen always understood hurt and trouble.

JOHN MONTGOMERY MONTALBAN—through an accident or through his shrewd, cold-blooded cunning—had chosen a new, more distant site for their next meeting. Without her boneware, Vera had to hike there from her barracks, on foot.

Mljet's few remaining roads were reduced to weedy foot trails. People in boneware had little need for roads: they simply jumped across the landscape, following logistics maps.

Vera no longer had that advantage, so she had to tramp it. Luckily, she had Karen as counsel and company. Unluckily, Karen's stilting strides made Vera eat her dust.

Modern life was always like this somehow, Vera concluded as sweat ran down her ribs. Impossible crises, bursting potentials. Rockets and potholes. Anything was possible, yet you were always on sore feet. Always, everywhere, ubiquitously. That was modern reality. Modern reality hurt.

Vera coughed aloud.

"Shall I carry you?" Karen said sweetly.

Vera wearily crested a ragged limestone ridge. Her humble fellow pedestrians crowded the valley below her. They were women from the attention camps, hand-working the island with hatchets and trowels.

The camp women wore their summer gear, with their hair up in kerchiefs. Every one of them wore cheap, general-issue spex.

Karen broke into a stilting run, bounding past the camp women like a whirlwind. The women offered Karen respectful salutes, awed by her cloud of glory.

Vera trudged among the lot of them, panting, sweating, sniffling. The camp women ignored Vera. She had no visible glory. So she meant nothing to them.

Vera took no offense. It was a software-design issue. Proper camp design reflected the dominant camp demographics. Meaning: middle-aged city women. Most modern people lived in cities. Most modern people were middle-aged. So most modern people in refugee camps were necessarily middle-aged city women. As simple as that.

These attention-camp newbies, these middle-aged city women, were diligently laboring in the open fields of an Adriatic island. They'd never planned to meet such a fate. They'd simply known that, as refugees without options, they were being offered a radically different life.

When they had docked at Mljet in their slow-boat refugee barges, they'd been given their spex and their ID tags. As proper high-tech pioneers, they soon found themselves humbly chopping the weeds in the bold Adriatic sun.

The women did this because of the architecture of participation. They worked like furies.

As the camp women scoured the hills, their spex on their kerchiefed heads, their tools in their newly blistered hands, the spex recorded whatever they saw, and exactly how they went about their work. Their labor was direct and simple: basically, they were gardening. Middle-aged women had always tended to excel at gardening.

The sensorweb identified and labeled every plant the women saw through their spex. So, day by day, and weed by weed, these women were learning botany. The system coaxed them, flashing imagery on the insides of their spex. Anyone who wore camp spex and paid close attention would become an expert.

The world before their eyeballs brimmed over with helpful tags and hot spots and footnotes.

As the women labored, glory mounted over their heads. The camp users who learned fastest and worked hardest achieved the most glory. "Glory" was the primary Acquis virtue.

Glory never seemed like a compelling reason to work hard—not when you simply heard about the concept. But when you *saw* glory, with your own two eyes, the invisible world made so visible, glory every day, glory a fact as inescapable as sunlight, glory as a glow that grew and waned and loomed in front of your face—then you understood.

Glory was the source of communion. Glory was the spirit of the corps. Glory was a reason to be.

Camp people badly needed reasons to be. Before being rescued by the Acquis, they'd been desolated. These city women, like many city women, had no children and no surviving parents. They'd been uprooted by massive disasters, fleeing the dark planetary harvest of droughts, fires, floods, epidemics, failed states, and economic collapse.

These women, blown across the Earth as human flotsam, were becoming pioneers here. They did well at adapting to circumstance—because they were women. Refugee women—women anywhere, any place on Earth—had few illusions about what it meant to be flotsam.

Vera herself had been a camp refugee for a while. She knew very well how that felt and what that meant. The most basic lesson of refugee life was that it felt bad. Refugee life was a bad life.

With friends and options and meaningful work, camp life improved. Then camp life somewhat resembled actual life. With time and more structure and some consequential opportunities, refugee life *was* an actual life. Whenever strangers became neighbors, whenever they found commonalities, communities arose. Where there were communities, there were reasons to live.

Camp user statistics proved that women were particularly good at founding social networks inside camps. Women made life more real. Men stuck inside camps had a much harder time fending off their despair. Men felt dishonored, deprived of all sense and meaning, when culture collapsed.

Refugee men trapped in camp thought in bitter terms of escape and vengeance. "Fight or flight." Women in a camp would search for female allies, for any means and methods to manage the day. "Tend and befriend."

So: In a proper modern camp like this one, the social software was designed to exploit those realities.

First, the women had to be protected from desperate male violence until a community emerged. The women were grouped and trained with hand tools.

The second wave of camp acculturation was designed for the men. It involved danger, difficulty, raw challenge, respect, and honor, in a bitter competition over power tools. It acted on men like a tonic.

Like any other commons-based peer-production method, an Acquis attention camp improved steadily with human usage. Exploiting the spex, the attention camp tracked every tiny movement of the user's eyeballs. It nudged its everyware between the users and the world they perceived.

Comparing the movements of one user's eyeballs to the eyeballs of a thousand other users, the system learned individual aptitudes.

A user who was good with an ax would likely be good with a water saw. A user quick to learn about plants could quickly learn about soil chemistry and hydrology. Or toxicity. Or meteorology. Or engineering. Or any set of structured knowledge that the sensorweb flung before the user's eyes.

The attention camp had already recorded a billion things that had caught the attention of thousands of people. It preserved and displayed the many trails that human beings had cut through its fields of data. The camp was a search engine, a live-in tutoring machine. It was entirely and utterly personal, full of democratically trampled roads to human redemption. By design, it was light, swift, glorious, brilliant.

Vera had spent time in attention camps. So had Karen. This initiation was required of all the Acquis cadres on Mljet. At first, they'd been bewildered. Soon they had caught on. Within a matter of weeks, they were adepts. Eventually, life became elite.

The graduates of Mljet attention camps lived in boneware; they'd become human power tools.

"The camp people are happier today," judged Karen, consulting her faceplate.

Vera shrugged. It was prettier weather. Better weather was always better for morale.

Karen flexed her slender arms within their bony pistons. "I'll knock down that big patch of casuarina. Watch them worshipping me."

"Don't be such a glory hog, Karen."

"It takes five minutes!" Karen protested.

"Karen, you need to cultivate a more professional perspective. This is not an entertainment. Neural scanning and ubiquitous mediation are our tools. An attention camp is a trade school."

Karen stared down at her from the towering heights of her boneware. "Listen to you talking like that," she said. "You're so nervous about that rich banker, and his kid is driving you wild."

MLJET'S TINY GROUP of Dispensation people were a discreet minority on the island. They'd been living on Mljet since the project's first days.

The Dispensation people were a tolerated presence, an obscure necessity, imposed through arrangements high above. They never made any fuss about themselves or their odd political convictions.

Now, however, those quiet arrangements were visibly changing in character. The local Dispensation activists were highly honored by the visit of Montalban and his daughter. Their leader, and Montalban's official host on the island, was Mljet's archaeologist: good old Dr. Radic.

Archaeologists were always a nuisance on reconstruction sites. They fluttered around the sites of major earthworks like crows before the storm. There was no getting around the need for archaeologists. Their presence was mandated.

Dr. Radic was a Croatian academic. Radic diligently puttered around the island, classifying broken bricks and taking ancient pollen counts. While Vera had labored on the island's mediation, installing her sensors and upgrading everyware, she had often encountered Dr. Radic. Their mutual love for the island and their wandering work lives made them friends.

A much older man, Dr. Radic had always been ready with some kindly word for Vera, some thoughtful little gift or useful favor. Radic clearly viewed her as an integral part of the island's precious heritage. Vera was no mere refugee on Mljet—she was a native returnee. Knowing this, Radic had jolly pet names for Vera: the "*domorodac*," the "*Mljecanka*." The "home-daughter," the "Mljet girl."

Radic loved to speak Croatian at Vera, for Radic was an ardent patriot. When she strained her memory, Vera could manage some "ijekavian,"

the local Adriatic dialect. This island lingo had never been much like
Radic's scholarly mainland Serbo-Croatian. Whenever Vera knew that
she would encounter Dr. Radic, she took along a live-translation earpiece. This tactful bit of mediation made their relationship simpler.

In the nine years that she had known the archaeologist, it had never
quite occurred to Vera that Radic was Dispensation. As a scientist and a
scholar, Radic seemed rather beyond that kind of thing. Year after patient year, Radic had come to Mljet from his distant Zagreb academy,
shipping scientific instruments, publishing learned dissertations, and
exploiting his graduate students. Dr. Radic was a tenured academic, an
ardent Catholic, and a Croatian nationalist. Somehow, Radic had always been around Mljet. There was no clear way to be rid of him.

Montalban and his daughter were guests at Radic's work camp, an ex-
cavation site called Ivanje Polje. This meadow was one of the few large
flat landscapes on narrow, hilly Mljet. Ivanje Polje was fertile, level, and
easy to farm. So, by the standards of the ancient world, the pretty meadow
of Ivanje Polje was a place to kill for.

Ivanje Polje, like the island of Mljet, was a place much older than its
name. This ancient meadow had been settled for such an extreme
length of time that even its archaeology was archaeological. At Ivanje
Polje, the fierce warriors of the 1930s had once dug up the fierce warriors of the 1330s.

As an archaeologist of the modern 2060s, Radic had dutifully catalogued all the historical traces of the 1930s archaeologists. Dr. Radic
had his own software and his own interfaces for the Mljet sensorweb. As
a modern scholar, Radic favored axialized radar and sonar, tomographic
soil sensors, genetic analyses. Not one lost coin, not one shed horseshoe
could evade him.

DR. RADIC UNZIPPED AN AIRTIGHT AIRLOCK and ushered his guests inside to see his finest prize.

"We call her the Duchess," said Radic, in his heavily accented English.
"The subject is an aristocrat of the Slavic, Illyrian, Romanized period.
The sixth century, Common Era."

John Montgomery Montalban plucked a pair of spex from a pocket in his flowered tourist shirt. Vera had never seen such a shirt in her life. It flowed and glimmered. It was like a flowered dream.

"We discovered the subject's tomb through a taint in the water table," Radic told him. "We found arsenic there. Arsenic was a late-Roman inhumation treatment. In the subject's early-medieval period, arsenic was still much used."

Montalban carefully fitted the fancy spex over his eyeballs, nose, and ears. "That's an interesting methodology."

"Arsenical inhumation accounts for the remarkable condition of her flesh!"

Karen, looming in her boneware, whispered to Vera. "Why is Radic showing this guy that horrible dead body?"

"They're Dispensation people," Vera whispered back. She hadn't chosen the day's activities.

"He's so cute," Karen said. "But he's got no soul! He's creepy." Karen swiveled her helmeted head. "I want to go outside to play with his little girl. If you have any sense, you'll come with me."

Vera knew it was her duty to stay with Montalban. Those who observed and verified must be counterobserved and counterverified.

Karen, less politically theoretical, left for daylight in a hurry.

Radic's instrumented preservation tent was damp and underlit. The dead woman's chilly stone sarcophagus almost filled the taut fabric space. There was a narrow space for guests to sidle around the sarcophagus, with a distinct risk that the visitor might fall in.

Radic had once informed her, with a lip-smacking scholarly relish, that the Latin word "sarcophagus" meant "flesh-eater."

Vera had never shared Radic's keen fascination with ancient bodies. Her sensitive Acquis sensorweb had detected thousands of people buried on Mljet. Almost any human body ever interred in the island's soil had left some faint fossil trace there—a trace obvious to modern ultrasensitive instruments.

Since Vera was not in the business of judgment calls about the historical status of corpses, she had to leave such decisions to Dr. Radic—and this body was the one discovery the historian most valued. Radic's so-called Duchess was particularly well preserved, thanks to the tight stone casing around her flesh and the arsenic paste in her coffin.

Still, no one but an archaeologist would have thought to boast about her. The "Duchess" was a deeply repulsive, even stomach-turning bundle of wet, leathery rags.

The corpse was hard to look at, but the stone coffin had always compelled Vera's interest. Somebody—some hardworking zealot from a thousand years ago—had devoted a lot of time and effort to making sure that this woman stayed well buried.

This Dark Age stonemason had taken amazing care with his hand tools. Somehow, across the gulf and abysm of time, Vera sensed a fellow spirit there.

A proper "sarcophagus," a genuine imperial Roman tomb, should have been carved from fine Italian marble. The local mason didn't have any marble, because he was from a lonely, Dark Age Balkan island. So he'd had to fake it. He'd made a stone coffin from the crumbly local white dolomite.

A proper Roman coffin required an elegant carved frieze of Roman heroes and demigods. This Dark Age mason didn't know much about proper Roman tastes. So his coffin had a lumpy, ill-proportioned tumble of what seemed to be horses, or maybe large pigs.

The outside of the faked sarcophagus looked decent, or at least publicly presentable, but the inside of it—that dark stone niche where they'd dumped the corpse in her sticky paste of arsenic—that was rough work. That was faked and hurried. That was the work of fear.

The Duchess had been hastily buried right in her dayclothes: sixteen-hundred-year-old rags that had once been linen and silk. They'd drenched her in poisonous paste and then banged down her big stone lid.

Her shriveled leather ears featured two big golden earrings: bull's heads. Her bony shoulder had a big bronze fibula safety pin that might have served her as a stiletto.

The Duchess had also been buried with three fine bronze hand mirrors. It was unclear why this dead lady in her poisoned black stone niche had needed so many mirrors. The sacred mirrors might have been the last syncretic gasp of some ecoglobal Greco-Egypto-Roman-Balkan cult of Isis. Dr. Radic never lacked for theories.

"May I?" asked Montalban. He caressed the cold stone coffin with one fingertip. "Remarkable handiwork!"

"It is derivative," sniffed Dr. Radic. "The local distortion of a decaying imperial influence."

"Yes, that's exactly what I like best about it!"

From his tone, Vera knew that this was not what he liked best about it. He was Dispensation, so what he liked best was that someone had taken a horrible mess and boxed it up with an appearance of propriety. So he was lying. Vera could not restrain herself. "Why are you so happy about this?"

Montalban aimed a cordial nod at their host. "European Synchronic philosophy is so highly advanced! I have to admit that, as a mere Angeleno boy, sometimes Synchronic theory is a bit beyond me."

"Oh, no no no, our American friend is too modest!" said Radic, beaming at the compliment. "We Europeans are too often lost in our theoretical practices! We look to California for pragmatic technical developments."

Montalban removed his fancy spex and framed them against the faint light overhead. He removed an imaginary fleck of dust with a writhing square of yellow fabric. "Her body flora," he remarked.

"Yes?" said Radic.

"Are her body flora still viable? Do you think they might grow?"

"There's no further decay within this specimen," said Radic.

"I don't mean the decay organisms. I mean the natural microbes that once lived inside her while she was still alive. Those microbes have commercial value. This woman is medieval, so she never used antibiotics. There's a big vogue in California for all-natural probiotic body flora."

Vera found herself blurting the unspeakable. "Do you mean the germs inside the corpse?"

Montalban pursed his lips. " 'Germs inside the corpse.' That's not the proper terminology."

"You want to *sell* the germs inside this corpse?"

"This is a public-health issue! It's more than just a market opportunity!"

"He's right, you know," Radic piped up. "Archaeo-microbiology is a rapidly expanding field."

"At UC Berkeley," said Montalban, donning his spex again, "they call their new department 'Archaeo-Microbial Human Ecology.' "

"Very apt." Radic nodded.

"A whole lot of hot start-up labs around UC Berkeley now. Venture money just pouring in."

"Oh, yes, yes, it was ever thus in California," said Radic.

"Microbe work is huge in China, too. The Jiuquan center, reviving the Gobi Desert . . . Microbes are the keystone of sustainable ecology."

"I don't understand this," said Vera.

Radic shrugged. "That's because you're Acquis!"

The old man's tactless remark hung in the damp air. It died and began to stink.

"I would never dismiss the microbe technology of the Acquis," said Montalban, demonstrating a tender concern. "Acquis medical troops lead the world at public sanitation."

Vera felt her blood begin to simmer.

Despite his lack of accurate neural information about her emotions, Montalban sensed her discontent. "The skill sets differ within the global civil societies. We should expect that: that's a source of valuable trade."

"So, what do you call this business? 'Frankenstein genetic graverobbing'?"

Montalban contemplated this insult. He twirled the earpiece of his spex gently between his fingers. "I suggest that we break for lunch now. I'm sure Little Miss Mary Montalban is hungry." Montalban carefully placed his spex inside his flowered shirt.

"Don't you want to use your fancy spex to scan the corpse here?" said Vera.

"Yes, I do. Still, it might be wiser if we ate first."

"You make quite a fuss about your scanning capabilities."

Montalban lifted one suntanned hand and plucked at his lower lip. "No, I don't 'make fusses,' Vera. I'm a facilitator."

"How could you eat? How could you eat today, now, after staring at this rotten woman and her rotten flesh? And then planning to *sell it*? How can you do that?"

Now even Radic knew that somebody had put a foot wrong. "Please don't get angry at our foreign guest, dear Vera, my *domorodac*! After all, this is your heritage!"

"Are you always like this, John? You invent all kinds of lies, and big fake words, to cover up what you do in secret?"

Montalban was suddenly and deeply wounded. A flush ran up his neck. His face was turning both red and white at the same time, like a freshly sliced turnip.

Vera realized, with a giddy intuition, that yes, John Montalban was always like this. She wasn't the first woman to tell him that about himself. Because he was married to Radmila.

Vera had touched him on some sore spot that Radmila had lacerated.

Montalban had never yet breathed a word about Radmila, yet Vera could almost smell Radmila now. Radmila was very near to them. It was as if Radmila were lying there in the coffin somehow. Disgustingly undead.

That black intuition—so true, and so immediate—panicked Vera. She felt a strong urge to strike Montalban, to hit him right across his handsome face.

Dr. Radic looked from her, to Montalban, and back again. The old man was completely bewildered and alarmed. "I'll see to our lunch," he blurted. Then he hurried through the zipper of the airtight tent and left it flapping.

The two of them were standing alone with the dead thing in its coffin. Hair rose all over Vera's arms. Very soon, she would scream.

"Here," said Montalban. He gently handed her the spex.

Hastily, Vera jammed the Californian hardware over her eyes. A galaxy of sparkling pixels swarmed across her vision.

The sarcophagus glimmered before her. The coffin went blurry for just a moment, then snapped into sharp focus.

The ancient sarcophagus was shiny, polished, precious, and entirely new.

A stranger lay in state inside of it. A woman who was freshly dead.

Newly laid to rest within her stony casement, the stately Duchess looked as detailed as a celebrity waxwork. Her silken robe shimmered. Her linen was white and fine. Gray tendrils threaded her oiled black hair. Her golden earrings, two little bull's heads, gleamed aggressively. Her death-pale cheeks and eyelids had been brightly smeared with undertaker's colors: lead-white cosmetics, black kohl, rouge, and antimony.

"You have an augment," Vera said. "You brought an augment here."

"Indeed I did," said Montalban. "I brought a tourist application."

Montalban's Hollywood spex had two little rubbery blinders that had sealed tight around her eyes. Vera had never seen mediation reach such a peak of graphic artistry.

Montalban's spex erased the visible world and replaced it with a simulation. The spex were firing a trio of colored lasers deep into her eyeballs. All this seemingly natural light that struck her eyes was artificial.

But she could still see her own hands, and the fabric walls of the tent. The program was scanning the real world in real time, then generating a visual addition to that world with 3-D modeling, ray-tracing, and reflection algorithms. It sucked all the real light out of the world, filtered it, augmented it, and blew it into her eyes with a mediated overlay.

It was doing this amazing feat in real time. Brilliantly, speedily. Using just a pair of flimsy-looking spex, instead of an entire heavy Acquis helmet and faceplate.

"Your augment is really fine-grained."

"Thank you," said Montalban. "It's the state-of-the-art from UCLA's graphics school. We're rather proud."

Vera turned her spex-covered eyes in the direction of his voice. The augment faltered a bit, and then let Montalban pop into her view. Montalban looked particularly pleased with himself, and, if anything, handsomer than before. "Of course, your Dr. Radic was a lot of help with our little project."

Vera pressed the spex against the bridge of her nose. She rocked her head from side to side. Everything panned smoothly: no breakups, no freezes, no jitters. The world had turned into a movie. A special effect.

She stared at the dead woman again. Confronted with death, at last, the Hollywood fakery became obvious. Vera had seen plenty of dead people. This was the Hollywood special-effects version of a dead person: much too tasteful, too bright, too crisp and neat.

"She's so tiny! Why is she so small?"

"That's the size most people really were, in the Dark Ages. You know our Dr. Radic. That old gent's a stickler for accurate forensics."

Arms stretched for balance, with small, careful steps, Vera sidled around the sarcophagus.

The dead woman had a thick waist, and no bust, and short, crooked legs. Her mouth and her jaws had a lemon-sucking look, for she had lost some teeth young and had grown old without dentistry.

Her brow was creased with sullen menace and there was a practiced

sneer at the wings of her waxy nose. The Duchess was a vicious, imperious, feudal grandmother. She looked like her evil eyes might flick
open at any moment.

Vera reached out a hand. She saw her fingers appear within her field
of vision.

She reached out to touch the sarcophagus. Her fingers vanished into
the thick visual lacquer of the augment. Finally she felt her fingers contact
real stone. Not new stone. Cold stone, dead stone, eroded by centuries.

Vera jerked her hand back with a feeling of shame. She was suddenly
ashamed of her crude local Acquis sensorweb, with its corny visual tags,
its blurs of golden glory, its sadly primitive icons. She'd thought that she
understood mediation, but now she knew she was just a hick, a regional
peasant. Because this California augment was years ahead of anything
she'd ever used or built. It was otherworldly.

"I can't believe my eyes! This is so swift and brilliant! People would
queue up to see this, they would make long lines to see!"

"Yes, that would be the basic business plan," Montalban told her.
"Mediation is a key enabler for tomorrow's heritage economy."

"What?"

" 'The replacement of national sovereignty and class consciousness
by technically sophisticated yet ethically savage private cartels which
dissolve social protections and the rule of law while encouraging the
ruthless black-marketization of higher technologies . . .' That's what a
famous Acquis critic once said about this technology. Augmentation is
a little dodgy. I agree it's not for amateurs."

Vera couldn't understand this long rote-quote of his—Montalban
was a Dispensation gentleman. It was as if he were quoting classical
Latin at her. His chatter didn't seem to matter much. Not when confronted with this. "Did you say this is 'dodgy'? Mr. Montalban—this
isn't even supposed to be possible."

"I'm pleased that you appreciate our modest efforts," said Montalban,
with just the lightest hint of imperial sarcasm. "Would you care to step
outside this tent, and have a look around?"

Vera lurched at once for the flapping tent door.

She stood outside. The excavated soil of old Ivanje Polje had suddenly become a Slavic Dark Age village. The spex augment showed her
writhing plum trees, clumsy vineyards, muddy pigpens, a big stone-

fenced villa. The stone longhouse was half surrounded by squalid peasant huts, homemade from mingled mud and twigs. It looked insanely
real, like drowning in a glossy cartoon.

The sky above medieval Mljet was truly astounding, staggering: a
heartaching vista of pure fluffy clouds. That medieval sky was scarily
blue and clean. Vera had never stood beneath such a sky in her whole
life. Because this sky was not her own deadly Greenhouse sky, the sky of
a world in the grip of a global catastrophe. This historical sky had never
known one single smokestack. It was the natural sky of the long-vanished
natural Earth.

Vera took one reeling, awestruck step and tripped over her own feet.
Somehow, Montalban was there for her. He caught her arm.

"Are there people here?" she shouted at him. "Where are all the
people?"

"We didn't yet write any avatars for this Dark Age augment," Montalban told her, his calm voice close to her ear. "Our Dark Age plug-in is
still in alpha."

Vera plucked the clinging spex from her face. Karen appeared in the
flowering field, with Mary Montalban. Karen had both her bony arms
out, and she was laughing. The child was cheerfully climbing her exposed ribs.

"Watch me throw her high in the air!" Karen crowed.

"Oh my God," moaned Montalban, "please don't do that."

VERA FORCED HERSELF to pick at Dr. Radic's elaborate lunch,
for the old man had outdone himself in honor of his guests. This done,
they hiked on foot to the ruins of Polace, over a narrow trail that Radic's
people had taken some pains to clear. Montalban carried his daughter
on his shoulders. Karen was in a buoyant mood, bounding along comi-
cally and making the child crow with glee.

When they descended from the island's rugged backbone to the
northern shore, it was clear why Montalban had been so eager to visit
these ruins.

The augment for Polace simulated ancient Roman Palatium.
Palatium, an imperial Roman beach resort in the year zero.

The island's beaches had changed a great deal in the passage of twenty-one centuries. This meant a design conflict between strict geo-locative accuracy and an augment that everyday viewers might willingly pay to see. That controversy hadn't yet been settled, so much of imperial Roman Palatium appeared to be hovering, uneasily, over the rising Greenhouse waters of the bay.

Ancient Palatium was not ancient yet. Palatium was raw and new, a Roman frontier town. The island village featured sturdy wooden docks, and two wooden Roman galleys with their wooden oars up, and some very authentic-looking sacks of grain. It had one donkey-driven mill, and many careless heaps of scattered amphoras.

The village featured a host of makeshift wooden fishing shacks, and one small but showily elegant upscale limestone palace. Palatium also featured a public bath, a wine bar, a temple, and a brothel.

To Vera's consternation, Roman Palatium had some avatars installed. These ghosts strolled their simulated Roman town, moving in the semi-random, irrational, traumatized way that ghosts roamed the Earth. The imperial Roman avatars were rather sketchily realized: tidy cartoons with olive skin and bowl-like haircuts.

One particularly horrible ghost, some kind of Roman butcher in a stained apron, seemed to have some dim machine awareness of Vera's presence as a viewer within the scene. This ghost kept crowding up in the corners of her spex, with a tourist-friendly look, inviting user inter-actions that the system did not yet afford.

Vera handed the spex back to Montalban. She was powerfully shaken. "You've turned this dead town into some kind of . . . dead movie game."

"That's not the way I myself would have phrased it," said Montalban, smiling. "I'd say that we're browsing the historical event heap in search of future opportunities." He stooped suddenly. The tide was out, and he'd alertly spotted a coinlike disk by the toe of his beach sandal. He plucked it up, had a closer look, and tossed it into the bay.

"The Palatium project," he told her, "is a coproduction of the University of Southern California's Advanced Culture Lab and Dr. Radic's scholars in Zagreb. They've done pretty well with this demo, given their limited time and resources. Frankly, those USC kids really worked their hearts out for us." Montalban slid the spex into a velvet-lined case. "If this demo catches on with our stakeholders, we'll be catering to a top-end tourist demographic here."

"But you made it . . . and it's just a fantasy. It's not real."

Montalban rolled his eyes. "Oh, come now—you built that sensor-web that saturates this whole island! Radic gave me a good look at that construction. That's brutal software. I sure wouldn't call it viewer-friendly."

"The sensorweb *saved the life* of this island! You're *pasting fantasies* onto the island."

"We could waste our time discussing 'reality' . . . Or, we could talk real business!" Montalban sat on the sun-warmed, sloping edge of a broken piece of Polace's tarmac. He scattered salty dust with a handkerchief and offered her a spot. "Vera, I'm here from Hollywood! I'm here to help you!"

Vera sat. She knew from the look on his face that he planned to exploit her now. This was the crux: they had reached the crisis. "So, John, you want to help us? Tell me how you feel about that."

"I need to make the dynamic of this situation clear to you."

Vera posed herself attentively. It felt nice to watch his face, even as he lied to her. He really was remarkably good-looking.

"I have come to this island because, at this moment in the event stream, there's a confluence of interests." Montalban pulled a shiny wad of film from his pocket. He fluffed the film open and set it down before them. It flashed into life before their feet.

A pattern appeared in it: something like a plate of spaghetti.

"What's this?"

"That's a correlation engine running a social-network analysis. Using this has become part of due diligence whenever we're trying to wire together a merger-and-acquisition deal. When a map of the stakeholders is assembled—very commonly—some player pops from the background and turns out to be the sustaining element . . ." Montalban leaned down, stretched out a finger, and tapped one of the central meatballs within the spaghetti. "That would be you. Vera Mihajlovic. You are right here."

"You drew all this?" Vera said.

"Oh no." Montalban laughed. "No human being could ever construct a map this sophisticated. Investor-analysis correlation engines use distributive intelligence."

"Your map doesn't make any sense. It looks like a plate of spilled food."

"That's why I'm explaining it to you," he said patiently. "It's true that you lack any formal executive power here. Still, you're clearly central to what happens here, and this map shows it. The cultists here really look up to you: and I can guess why. First, you were born here. You were the last to leave the island, and the first to return to it. You're a motivating, legitimating factor for them."

Vera shrugged. "Can't you talk to me about how you feel? Just tell me what you want."

"You have star quality. That's the simplest way I can put it."

Vera cut him short with a wave of her arm. "All right: This is a beach, am I right? That's seawater. That's a rock. Those are the ruins. Do you see any 'star quality' here?"

Montalban drew a taut breath. "Of course I know that! Tell me what you saw in that microcosm that I sent you."

"What?"

"The hobject, the microcosm. That diplomatic gift I conferred to you. You know. The crystal ball."

"Oh. That bubble thing." Vera shrugged. "I'm too busy for hobbies. I gave it away."

His face fell in raw incredulity. "You did *what?*"

"Well, it was a gift, wasn't it? I gave it away as a gift."

"You didn't *explore* the microcosm? You didn't *engage* with its interface?"

"How would I 'engage' with a ball of seawater?" She paused. "I remember it had some little shrimps swimming inside. Were those supposed to be valuable?"

Montalban sat up with a look of pain, as if his back ached suddenly. He gazed out to the ruins in the sea. She realized that she had failed him in some deep and surprising way. Montalban was genuinely shocked by what she had done. It was as if he had cooked her a seven-course banquet and she had crassly thrown away the food and smashed all the plates.

He slowly tapped his fingers on his knee. He didn't know what to do next. He was completely at a loss.

She spoke up. "I see that I've hurt your feelings. I didn't mean to do that. I'm sorry."

"It's just . . . Well . . ." For the first time, Montalban was unable to speak.

"I'm sorry about it, John. Really."

"I knew this assignment would be difficult." He sighed. "I'm going to say this in the simplest, bluntest way I can. You love this island, right? This place means more to you than anything else in your life. Well, I came here to give it to you. It is my gift to you. That's what I meant to say to you. You will be the duchess, the queen of Mljet. I will put this place at your feet."

"You think you can do that, do you?"

"Yes, I know I can. Because I've done it before." A flicker of pain crossed Montalban's face. "I said that I am a facilitator. I'm good at my work. I'm one of the best in the world, and the world is a lot bigger than this island. If you want this place that you love so much, if you want this island to be your own island, then you can have it. That prospect is written in the stars, or rather, it is written in this very fine analytical map in the dirt here."

"What do you ask from a girl, when you give her a gift like that, Mr. Montalban?"

"I don't ask for anything. That's why it's a gift. If you will agree to hold up your part of this deal I want to arrange, then every other element will swing into place. That work will take me a while, but I know that deal can be done: the financing, promotion, production, residuals, a user base, everything. Everything that a modern tourist island needs."

"So you want me to go into business with you, in some way? That's what you want? I'm not interested in business. I already have a business. I'm very busy all the time." Vera stood up. "I think you should go back to California."

"Sit down," he demanded. She sat again.

"Look," he said, "your status quo is just not in the cards for you. You don't understand this yet, but your story here is already over. You and your Acquis people here, you are way past the stage where you can be just a little extreme techno-start-up on some private island where no one important will notice. That story is gone. Because you accomplished something amazing here. So you have been noticed. You had a big success. The Dispensation always notices big success. Always. So: If we don't arrange that as a win-win-win outcome for all the stakeholders, there's going to be friction."

"I think I understood that last part," Vera said. "That was a threat."

"That's realism. Things gets ugly when the two global civil societies clash."

"How ugly do things get, John?"

"Unnecessarily ugly. The Acquis is the Acquis, the Dispensation is the Dispensation, and the third alternative is chaos. It can be terrible chaos. Like the chaos on this island before you redeemed it."

Montalban looked down the beach, where Karen was cheerfully playing with his daughter. "The Dispensation and the Acquis are a stable, two-party, global system. But the world is in desperate shape—so we have to try extreme solutions. Most of them fail, because they are so extreme. But whenever they *work*—that's when the world *has* to take notice. The whole point of having our two-party system is to have a system for reality checks against the extremist groups." Montalban spread his hands. "In any place but Europe, they'd teach that in elementary civics classes."

"We're not an 'extremist group' here. We are rescue workers and geoengineers."

"Of course you're an extremist group. *Of course* you are! You've got mind-reading helmets on your heads! Look at those shaven patches on your scalp! You don't even *walk* like normal people here—you all walk like you could bend over backward like crabs! Plus, this island is covered with weird labor camps that practice sensory totalitarianism! Anyone from the outside world could learn all that in a day."

Montalban knotted his hands. "So: The reason the Acquis was allowed to work here is that the climate crisis is bipartisan. If the seas rise, then the ark sinks, and we will all drown. We know that. So when it comes to fighting the climate crisis, we are willing to allow *anything*. But when you *succeed* at what you try, that's *different*. Then the consequences come."

"Why don't you run along home and let us finish the job here?"

"That is not a reasonable option. Your little experiment here: It violates civil rights, it violates human rights, it exploits desperate refugees as indentured labor with no access to the free market . . . This place is scary. I can rescue you from all that. I can save you from all those consequences. Because I will make you its queen."

"I can't even understand what you're saying! What exactly do you want from me? Use some real words."

"Okay: Here's the elevator pitch. Instead of being a test bed for a weird neural cult, Mljet becomes what it should be: a tourist island. Mljet becomes a normal place. It's decent, it's noncontroversial. This island has been saved, redeemed, reconstructed. That work is over. The cult relocates elsewhere."

"Where do my people go?"

"We give them an assignment that's better suited to their talents and technologies."

"Where are you putting my people?"

"The Lesser Antarctic Ice Shelf."

"You're exiling us to Antarctica." Vera looked at the glimmering edge of her native hills. "All right, that part I finally understand. Thank you for finally telling me."

"*They* go, Vera. *You* don't go. You *stay*. You encourage them to leave this place and work on the ice, and you remain here under the new dispensation. Because we're not 'exiling' the cult to Antarctica: we're *promoting* the cult to Antarctica."

"Why would they go to a place like that? It's horrible there. It's flooding and melting, it's like death."

"Because they're very good at redemption work and someone *has* to go there. The Big Ice is the front line of the climate crisis. Now, listen: Your boss, the Acquis commissar here, he's a pretty hard nut to crack. But he can do a budget. He has ambitions. He's an engineer: so he wants new hardware. They always do."

Montalban bent and smoothed his pocket film against the ground. A monstrous apparition emerged on the flimsy screen.

This metal monster brandished a drill on one hand, a backhoe on the other, and its sloping feet were the size of two fishing boats.

"This is a neurally controlled continental reconstruction unit. It's a giant robot exoskeleton that's nuclear-powered and four stories tall. Every one of these psychotic things costs as much as a full-scale Mississippi mud dredge. They're airtight, they're fully heated, they've got interior life-support systems, they're basically Martian spacesuits with legs.

Building these crazy things for him: That's the price that he demands from us."

Vera stared. "That big robot does looks kind of . . . weird."

"This darling of his has been sitting on his drawing board ever since he was in graduate school. Frankly, no sane capitalist would ever finance such a thing. Because it's got no market pull at all. It's a wild, macho, engineer's power fantasy."

Montalban leaned back on his slab of tarmac and tipped his sun hat. "We have agreed to his terms. A monster machine like this makes no sense to me, but nobody thought his Mljet plan would ever work out, either. It turns out he was right, and we were wrong. We admit that now. He wins. Mljet is light, and speedy, and brilliant, and glorious. Your boss has proved himself to the smart money and the power players. He has won. So if your boss plays some ball with us, he gets whatever the hell he wants."

Vera gazed at the bristling, fantastic monster. The giant robot had no head. She tried to imagine her Herbert sealed inside that giant, stamping coffin, that rock-shattering hulk.

She knew that Herbert would do it. Of course he would do it.

"This was just an old dream of his."

"That guy is no dreamer. That guy is a serial entrepreneur. We get it about guys like him. We know how to handle guys like him in California. It's no use logjamming him, or sabotaging him, or getting in his way, or 'verifying' him. No, all that kind of crap is counterproductive. The one effective way to deal with a guy like him is to double his ante. Just pony up the money and double his bet."

Montalban leaned back and shrugged. "Well, I can do that for him. I can do it, I promise. Because I've done that kind of thing before. My whole family does it. We've been doing it for years."

"What are you doing to Herbert?"

"I'm *financing* Herbert. The world *needs* Herbert. Herbert is a geek technofanatic who's also a serious player, and those are rare people. He's a great man. Really. It's just that, politically speaking, it's not great that he's here in Mljet. We don't really much want a guy like him, with a private army of brainwashed robot cultists, sited in a violently unstable region like the Balkans."

"This is my home," Vera murmured.

"Fine. It's not *his* home. If he ventures off to Antarctica, that's a different matter. If he fails there, well, that's one solution. If he tackles the Big Ice and he wins, well, then we *all* win. Because we've bought our world more time."

Montalban wiped his sweating upper lip. "Personally, I really hope that he can somehow pull that off. Sincerely, I hope that. I do. I know that big Aussie is crazy, but I'm with him all the way. Los Angeles just can't take many more refugee Australians."

"I would never do anything against Herbert and what Herbert wants to do."

"All right, good: now you're talking sense. So: Let's talk about you. Mljet and you: the public face of the New Mljet. The consortium needs an attractive young woman with skill and ambition who has some people smarts. We'll be facing a big transition here, a complete change in the infrastructure. That would be your role."

"So I'm the project manager."

"That's an Acquis title. Your title with us will be chief hospitality officer. That is not a figurehead post, by the way: don't get me wrong. You wouldn't be the workaday prime minister here: you'd be the queen of this place. I'm offering you a crucial post with a lot of situational perquisites. You will be allocating resources over every inch of this island. And I mean major resources, world-class, world-scale. Instead of that ragtag of refugees that you reeducated in the camps, you'll have a top-notch technical-support team! You'll have your own office of PR girls from the environmental design group at San Jose State . . . They're young people, young, like you and me. They're very forward-thinking."

"So it's me here, and it's not Herbert."

"Exactly. We need a much calmer, gentler hand with this place. You have a much more sensitive, more feeling approach to Mljet than your robot commissar there."

"Suppose that I say yes to you."

Montalban leaned down, plucked up his film, and crumpled it briskly. He pocketed it, and smiled at her. "Then it's simple. Our next step would be Vienna: a conference of the stakeholders. That's a summit of typical Acquis higher-circle drones, and some ranking Dispensation activists. Your boss will be there, too, of course. Your brother Djordje will be hosting that event in Vienna. I'll be there to present you to the money people. They're some very seasoned investors. They were the trust behind the reconstruction of Catalina Island, after the big fires. They can handle this sort of thing."

"Why are you doing all this, John?"

"Because I'm a white-knight investor, and I'm saving the world. And, through no coincidence, I'm also saving you." He gazed at her for a long moment. "You don't believe me. Well, you don't believe me *yet*. I've done it before, Vera. I've already done it *twice*. I can prove to you that I know what I'm doing, though it will take me a while. A merger-and-acquisition like this can keep a banker happy for years."

"You're asking me to betray my comrades here. They're the cadres who did all the work here."

"Well, the cult will face a strategic choice," said Montalban. "They can choose him, or they can choose you. The attention camps here will be shutting down—they're too controversial. If the cadres are zealots for their great man and his brain intrusions, then they can join him in Antarctica. If they stay here with you—and you're welcome to them— then they can enlist in our repatriation program for the natives of Mljet. We'll be restoring the people who properly belong here. We'll be reconsecrating Catholic churches, restoring the picturesque rural villages . . . The national and religious elements in the Balkans, they're stakeholders here too, you know."

"So this is quite a big, fancy plan you've brought here from your big, fancy city."

"It's the way of the big, fancy world."

Vera narrowed her eyes. "Suppose that I just say no to your way of the world."

Montalban nodded slowly. "You can say no to the world. People often say that here in the Balkans. But it never makes any sense to do that. Why? Why would you say no to peace, and wealth, and power, and security? This arrangement gives you everything that you wanted! It means that you win, it's your personal victory! You took a failed, criminal place that was an open sore, and you saved it, you healed it! You made your home island much better than it was in your whole lifetime, and you gave it back to the world! Things are finally as they should be. It's justice."

It took Vera three heartbeats to realize, with a pang of truth, that she wanted the island all to herself. She wanted Mljet to remain a quiet place outside the world. Its own place. An authentic place that was nobody's tool or pawn or property. A wild and natural place, blooming under the sun, beholden to nobody. It had never occurred to her that her homeland might be saved for other people.

"You don't believe in nature," she told him. "You don't believe what I believe. I even believe in reality."

"Well, I believe in ecotourism and the heritage industry. Because those are two major, wealth-creating industries."

Vera allowed him a nod.

"It won't be easy work, Vera. It's hard work. It'll take labor and investment to bring a heritage mediation online here. But I know that we can do that, together. I'm sure we can. I can promise you that. In ten years, right here where we're sitting, the troops of Augustus Caesar will be massing to invade the Balkans."

Vera's heart sank a little. "Ten years . . . What? What did you say?"

"That's right, ten years. That has to take ten years. Because the Roman Empire has only recently conquered this island. You could see how new and raw that little town of Palatium is. The Pannonian Wars on the mainland, they will be going hot and heavy right through the reign of Tiberius. That will be our major tourist draw here."

"I don't understand."

Montalban chuckled. "I suppose not. Well, just take it from me, then: the theme-park business can be a very steady, long-term earner, as long as it's got a solid heritage connection and a unique value proposition."

"I know that you must think that I'm stupid . . . Can't you talk to me like a normal person? Please?"

Montalban gazed around the island a long moment, as if seeking some kind of solace from the sunshine, the flowers, and the foaming shore at low tide. "Vera: In the Dispensation, the businesspeople *are* the normal people."

"It's not normal to talk about history as if history was a business."

"You are absolutely wrong there, Vera. History *is* a business. History is the *only* business. It's abnormal to do business without history as the absolute and final business bottom line. That's why industry wrecked this planet: because people ran the world like a fire sale. They never understood the past, the future, and the proper human relationship to space and time. The only way to think sustainably is to think synchronically!"

Realization dawned. "Wait, now, I do see what you're saying! You're a Synchronist. You're from a Dispensation cult! You're stealing my island from my cult just so you can sell my island to your own cult!"

Slowly, Montalban shook his head. He was feeling sorry for her. "Vera, I am not the extremist in this discussion."

"Yes you are. Synchronists are cultists. You're crazy."

"No, I'm Californian. And I came here on behalf of investors, real-estate people, developers—the global mainstream. So that they can co-opt this extreme, experimental situation into a much more conventional, rational, profitable situation. Is that distinction clear to you yet?"

"No! It's not clear. You're not explaining *anything* to me. You're just letting a lot of big, mystical words fall out of your mouth that make you look good and make me look bad."

Montalban thoughtfully examined the wavelets lapping. His hands twitched in his trouser pockets. "You know what they call this situation? This is a classic 'clash of paradigms.' "

Vera set her lips. "You know what they call people from California? They call them 'flakes.' "

"Acquis people can be pretty stubborn," Montalban mused. "I've met a lot of Acquis people in my business life. They can be really wonderful people, don't get me wrong there, but somehow it always boils down to a paradigmatic culture war. We have two sets of mental software, and two different operating systems."

"Maybe we're lucky that there's just two sets and not a thousand of them."

Montalban brushed sand from his walking shoes. "I suppose we are lucky, though we live in a world in disaster. Multiparty states never accomplish anything."

"You're still talking nonsense, though, John. You know that, don't you?"

"All right. Fine. I'm talking nonsense. I apologize. You explain something to me, then. Tell me why your friend there is playing with my daughter, while she's got her brain inside a kettle and she's wearing robot construction equipment that could break every single bone in my little girl's body."

Vera glanced up the beach at Karen. Karen and the little girl were getting along splendidly. Mary Montalban was scampering along the beach like a wound-up top, while Karen bounded over the child's head in boneware leaps that could have cleared the tops of trees.

"Have you ever had your brain scanned?" Vera asked him.

"I have regular medical checkups," said Montalban. "My brain is just fine. My brain is not a peripheral for heavy construction machinery."

"In other words, you believe we're monsters. You really hate us."

"I would never say that!" protested Montalban. "Look at me benignly tolerating all this! Am I denouncing you, or your crazy friend in the robot spacesuit there? Not a bit of it!"

"You hate what we do here. You're too American to understand us."

"Oh no, no no! Don't bring outdated nationalism into this, for heaven's sake! You've never even been to America! You don't understand how America works nowadays! Believe me, there are big patches of America that are extremely Acquis in their sentiments. Seattle is very Acquis. Raleigh; Madison, Wisconsin; Austin in Texas—they're all Acquis. San Francisco is Acquis! And Canada, too! Canada was Acquis before most of Europe was Acquis!"

"Do you think I'm a fanatic?"

"I never use pejorative terms like that, and I despise the evil demagogues who do! You're just—you're truly a woman of our age, that's what I think about you."

"Why are you here? What didn't you leave me alone here? I never wanted you here. I was happy here."

"Vera, I know that you think that you are evil. You have no esteem for yourself. But you are not evil. You were created through evil, but you are sweet and good. You're a very good person. You were born in an unhappy place at a time when that place was evil. That's the evil part. You—you've been part of everything that happened here to make things better. You raised this place from the rubble and you held the whole place up. You almost did it alone."

Vera burst into tears.

"Your colleagues here think the world of you," said Montalban. "They trust your judgment. They're proud of you. That's why you're the central figure here. If you move, the whole thing will move. You must sense that. You're intelligent, you must know that."

Vera choked on a sob. "I'm having an emotional fit."

"I've seen those fits," Montalban agreed. "Believe me, I know a lot about those."

"I'm just not all right without my helmet. I need a scan so I can know what I'm really feeling."

Montalban looked at her soberly. "You really look a lot prettier without that canteen on your head."

"Scanning helps me. It is a powerful tool."

"That," said Montalban, "is why that tool has been restricted to a very small group of users in an otherwise hopeless situation."

She could see that her tears were affecting him strongly. His face had grown much softer. He looked thoughtful and handsome, truly sympathetic. He looked at her as if he loved her more than anything in the world.

"If you never scan your own brain," said Vera, wiping at her cheeks, "how do you know what you feel about all this?"

Montalban looked at her slowly. "Vera, that is a truly weird question."

"I think you should put on a helmet," said Vera, sitting up. "You could put on Karen's helmet! You should put on her helmet, and then you and I should have a really good talk, heart to heart."

Montalban, instantly, went pale. "That's just not admissable," he told her. "That is just not a move that you and I should undertake."

"I was very scared of it too, at first," said Vera. "But I wear a scanner every day now. It's not bad for you. It's brilliant."

Montalban forced an uneasy smile. "I'll stay pretty dull, thanks! I know a thing or two about that practice! Shaving patches on my skull? No, we don't ruin an expensive haircut on impulse, do we?"

"You don't really need to shave any skin patches," said Vera. "Because you won't be running any boneware."

"I don't have the proper training for your helmets. You have to have your brain scrubbed first in those concentration camps."

"They're *attention* camps! How can you say such nasty things about us? You're a fool! You have no heart. You don't know anything real."

Montalban jumped to his feet and walked off down the beach. Vera caught up with him and seized his arm. "An attention camp saved my life," she said. "Can't you understand that?"

"That's for helpless refugees who are cornered and have no other choice," he said. "I'm not helpless and cornered. I don't care what you call that practice: that is an extreme form of sensory control."

"It's sensory *analysis*. See, you don't understand it, you're talking about it all wrong."

Montalban's opaque eyes, always rather shifty, began to dart from side to side. "You want to read my mind. You want to pry inside my own brain."

"John, don't hate me. I don't believe that you and I are enemies. We don't think alike, we can't, but . . . I know that I like you. I think we could have been good friends."

" 'Friends.' *Friends?* Hell, woman, I married you!" Montalban waved his hat at his reddening face. "I should never have come here. You don't know what it does to me to see you like this. To come here . . . and to bring the *child*, for God's sake . . . She's going to make me regret this."

"You mean Radmila. She didn't want you to do this."

"You said her name, not me! We don't have to discuss Radmila. Radmila Mihajlovic doesn't exist. My wife will never cross your path, ever. Because she hates your guts. For years, I could never understand why."

"Radmila hates me?"

"Like a passion. Like a curse. She's eaten up with it. Then I met Djordje. Djordje told me some things about what happened here. Terrible things. Then I met Sonja. And oh, my God. Now I *do* understand it, all of it, and that is much, much worse."

Vera put her head in her hands. She began to cry again, much harder.

"I can almost fix that damage," he told her. "I've come so close to fixing it, so many times. Djordje is almost all right—he's a tough businessman, but he's smart, he's no weakling. Sonja fights for what she thinks is right. Mila has done amazing things—she's truly gifted. And you— you're the *good* one. You're kind and sweet, you're the one with the best intentions."

Vera made a choice in her heart. "If I could believe you, John, I would do what you say."

"You would do what I say? You mean agree to the deal, go through with it?"

"Yes. But I have to know. I have to know it's the truth."

"All right, if that's what you want from me, then I guess we'll really talk. I guess we have no other choice. So: Fine, let's do it. Go get your lie-detector helmet. It doesn't scare me. I've seen worse. Just pull that crazy thing off your girlfriend's head before she tears my little girl into pieces."

They retreated up the trail and into the pine woods. They found a ragged clearing there. It took Vera half an hour to properly fit the scanner to Montalban's skull. His daughter sobbed in fear.

Karen had to take the child away. Karen hated leaving Vera in this moment of crisis, but when Vera ordered her to leave, Karen did as she was told. The emotional rejection cut Karen to the quick. Tears ran down Karen's face in streams. She and Mary Montalban clung to one another, sobbing as if they'd just seen someone die.

Montalban was entirely new to neural tech. His brain had not been properly calibrated over a long period of use. So, when Vera examined his neural output, his affect showed her nothing much. He had a kind of flatness. Almost an unnatural despair.

"Are you sick, John? You're not very spiky."

"Tranquilizers," he said.

"You take mood medication?"

"I have a very complex personal life," Montalban muttered. The bluff, cheery, American look had vanished from his face. With his head stuffed uncomfortably into Karen's dusty helmet, Montalban looked like a martyr in a crown of thorns.

"So," he demanded. "Do you see everything that I'm thinking now?"

"Well . . . no, of course not. I do see a lot of slow P300 recognition waves." That meant that Montalban recognized her. He knew her very well. He had been looking at her for years.

His brain lacked the sparkly affect of Acquis male cadres, who saw her, mostly, as a pretty woman. Men did that. At the bottom of any virile psyche, there was always some brisk neural reaction to a pretty woman.

There had never been any man on Mljet who looked at her with so much heartfelt confusion and grief. Montalban was looking at her as if the very sight of her were killing him.

"What do you see inside of me?" Montalban grated. "Do you think I'm crazy? Am I lying to you? Or is it all just as I told you?"

"John, this technology is not like you imagine it. Try to relax."

"These knobs *hurt*," he whined. "How can you let big rubber knobs squeeze your skull like that? Can't you crackpots build some more *sensitive* scanners? Build them into a nice little sun hat, a beret or something."

"That's a safety helmet. It's designed for construction work."

"There's another part I just don't get. Helmets and skeletons! Why don't you just *buy a bulldozer*? Bulldozers are cheap! Get a dragline, get an excavator!"

"We tried working that way," Vera told him. "But it *feels* wrong to us. It *means* more to our people when they can save the world with their own hands."

"You can't save the world on gusts of emotion!" he shouted. "That idea is for fanatics and losers!"

"You are so bitterly unhappy," Vera told him. "You're depressed! Your affect is very low and bad—that means you've lost heart in what you're doing. You know what? You're working much too hard at something that you don't like. You need a vacation."

Montalban's affect leaped violently. He began to laugh. He was at this quite awhile. "That was a really good joke," he said at last. "Thank you for telling me that one."

"She's made you so miserable," Vera said.

"No," said Montalban, "she was great to me. I knew what I was doing. I wanted to rescue Radmila. And I did that, I won. The Dispensation is a great force for good. I found a lost young girl and I turned her into a star. I transformed her. Although Mila was always bound for glory. We really know what glory is, in Hollywood."

"What *is* glory?"

"It's celebrity, of course! What else could it be? It only took Mila a few months to find her feet within that scene. After that, her knight in shining armor—meaning me—I was in her way. A little bit. She and I, we don't fight about that reality. No, we never fight. I facilitate. I don't make problems for her. I solve all her problems. Mila works hard for our Family-Firm. We've got the kid. We love our kid."

"She's bad for you. She made you unhappy."

"Sonja made me unhappy."

"What?"

"Djordje knows. He's the one who introduced us. When things were going very rough with Mila, he found Sonja for me. I helped Sonja, because I had to help Sonja. Sonja is saving the world. In a different way. Because you're all different women. *Very* different women. Yet *you're all the same entity*. You are caryatids."

Vera felt a rush of bile at the back of the throat. "John, let's take that helmet off now."

"You wanted the truth from me, didn't you? Here it is. You are the best of the lot. You are the best, because, of all of you, you're the one who needs me the least. Mila is a Hollywood girl, she's a star. Sonja is a knight in armor. If a man gets in Sonja's way she will chew him up like a matchstick. I haven't yet met Biserka, but we trade a lot of mail. Because Biserka's on the lam! The law wants her. She's into forgery, human trafficking, and *bank robbery*. You know how hard it is to rob a bank these days? Biserka, that woman, good God!"

"If you don't stop shouting, I'm going to scream."

"That's what you always tell me! Always, every last one of you! I talk to one of you about the other units, and you always break down and scream at me! Except for your *mother*. Your mother. A female warlord so paranoid she could only trust copies of herself . . . God help us. God help the whole world."

Vera put her hands over her ears.

"We're gonna talk your mother down from up there!" Montalban shouted, his face reddening. "That job is not *impossible*! We're going to talk her down from that hostage situation up there! Me and Djordje! We have some big plans, and we're recruiting a lot of help."

Vera stood up. She walked on wobbling legs. She took ten steps, fell into a thornbush, doubled over, and vomited.

She retched and then wailed in pain.

Karen found her quickly. "What did he say to you? What did he *do* to you?"

"Take me to Herbert," Vera said. She drooled vile acid, sneezed, and spat into the soil. "Just get me away from him! Get me away from here. Take me to my Herbert."

IT TOOK A LONG TIME to find Herbert. Stunningly, the sensorweb did not know where Herbert was. Such a thing had never happened before. He had always been locatable for her.

Herbert had escaped the sensorweb by boarding a boat. It was a primitive wooden yacht, old, simple, with patched sails and peeling white paint. Vera tottered from the dock and onto the dented, fish-smelling deck. A ragged crewman said something to her in Croatian.

She glanced once at the sailor. He meant nothing to her, he was even less than a newbie: some Balkan local in a sleeveless striped sailor's shirt, a floppy canvas hat. He wore sunglasses: not even spex. She saw her own face mirrored twice, on the shining lenses on his unshaven face.

"I came here to be with Herbert," she told the sailor.

The sailor smirked at her. Then he threw her a careless salute and set to work to cast off.

Once the sails were up and the sailor was busy at his tiller, Herbert emerged from belowdecks. Herbert wore swimsuit trunks and a borrowed shirt much too small for him. She had never seen Herbert out of his Acquis uniform before. There was a forest of hair all over his arms and chest.

With a flourish, Herbert unfolded a mildewed canvas deck chair. Vera sat in it. Then Herbert sat at her feet.

"How was your day?" he said.

"He wants me to defect," she told him. "He wants me to leave the Acquis and join his civil society. He said that I could have the whole island if I became Dispensation. That was his bribe for me."

Herbert didn't seem much surprised by this. "So, what did you say to the gentleman's ambitious proposal?"

"I didn't say much. But I couldn't do it. I can't."

"I *knew* that!" Herbert crowed. "I knew you'd never sell me out! I knew you'd turn that son of a bitch down!" He rolled to his bare feet and fetched a big hand-woven wicker basket. He flapped its wooden lid open and produced a bottle of prosecco. "All the gold in California can't buy Vera Mihajlovic! Damn it, this calls for a celebration."

Vera accepted the wineglass he offered her. He yanked the cork from his bottle with a pop like a gunshot.

The wineglass was elegant and pretty. It was Austrian crystal. It brimmed with a foaming crest of bubbles.

"You could have ordered me not to see that man," she said, teary-eyed. "You didn't have to test me like that."

"Vera, I can't do that to you. I can't order you to do anything. I would have had to beg you. I would have had to beg you, please, not to break my heart." She had never seen him so happy as he was at this moment.

"I always know what you're feeling, Vera. But I never know what you think. So, yes, I did test you. I have tested you with nine years' hard labor. Well, precious, I promise you: That was your last test from me. The last one. From now on, everything between us is different."

"You really thought that I would leave you?"

"I know that you love me, Vera. But I know you love this place, too. This island is a part of you. You *are* this beautiful place. Could I order you to leave this island with me—for a terrible island, the worst in the world—if you wanted to stay and be that rich man's 'Duchess of Mljet'? I couldn't do that."

He tipped his glass against hers, then sat back and drank. Vera sipped at the fizzing wine. She disliked alcohol. Drinking alcohol to alter one's emotions, that was such a strange thing to do.

Herbert refilled his glass and gestured with the bottle's neck, at the long silhouette of darkening Mljet. The wind of early evening was brisk, and their crewman was making good speed on the rippled waters.

"I spent nine years of exile on that little rock," Herbert said. "If not for you, I would never have gone there at all. I was an empty man when I first came there. My wife dead. Kids dead. Broken and defeated in my own homeland. Full of horror. The world was in turmoil: half upheaval, half collapse—and it still is! You see those cliffs, those hills? You know what that island was to me? That was a prototype. A test case. An experiment. And now look! We have won!"

She did not know what to tell him. The truth was so far beyond any words that he would understand.

She knew very well what had happened, why they had met. She'd been in an evacuation camp on the Croatian mainland, along with a battered host of other weeping, traumatized women from Mljet. Nobody had any food, or clothes, or medicine. They had nothing. They had nothing but mediation.

The social workers, the Acquis rescue people, were there to get people to talk. That was postdisaster counseling, they said, and they seemed to believe that talk, bearing witness to what they had suffered, was more important to people's survival than food. Likely it was.

So the women were indeed talking, exchanging their names and some private bits and pieces of their broken lives. And one humble woman said, in her meek yet hopeful little voice, that maybe the lost island of Mljet could be redeemed someday. Maybe (said another woman) by "sensorwebs."

"Sensorwebs" were a foreign idea these women knew practically nothing about, but they'd heard that word and knew that webs were supposed to be important and powerful. There, in the midst of their loss, hungry and wounded and drowning in woe, that was their straw of hope.

Vera knew better. Because she'd grown up in a seething, private bunker full of webs and sensors. Vera knew about event streams, burst rates, delta-change criteria, glitches, and collisions. Ubiquity had been installed in their bunker, as their nanny, and their spy, and their crèche, and their test bed for tomorrow's superwomen: a nest of clones, who, just like their mother, would hunger always to put the world to rights.

And, inside that wicked fairy tale, that black deception of false righteousness, they had grown up, believing that it was manifest destiny. While it was nothing of the kind. It was a snare, a delusion, a monstrosity.

So Vera had lost her senses.

She screamed at the startled women that it made no sense to cover the world with scanners and sensors, unless you also had scanners for the heads of the evil fools who had wrecked the world in the first place. Vera did not know why she had to scream that, except that she felt it, and it was the truth.

The truth, of course, caused a big, hateful commotion among all the women, who screamed back at her and scolded her for talking that way . . . but then something strange happened. Some Acquis person, most likely a woman, had been watching the proceedings on the web.

For some reason, maybe a deep, tender sympathy, maybe some bureaucratic quirk, this woman had web-searched ideas . . . busily exploring and linking tags and concepts, correlating things and events, "refugees," "reconstruction," "sensors," "brain scanners."

Somehow, from the tangled glassy depths of global webdom, up popped some Australians, busily losing their own fierce battle to save their island continent. These distant Australians, so painfully familiar with refugee camps, knew a lot about scanners, neural tech, and heavy machinery.

World-spanning, instant connectivity was the stuff of being for a global civil society. So, somewhere up in the Acquis administrative stratosphere, cogwheels turned, galactic and distant.

Six weeks later, Vera found herself meeting Herbert Fotheringay, an Australian geoengineer.

A small Acquis neural corps was formed to redeem Mljet. Vera thought that Herbert had done that, while Herbert had always said that she had inspired it.

Now, sitting years later in the sagging deck chair in an old boat with the island sinking into darkness, Vera knew that no single person had ever done that. Mljet was a web of emerging technologies, around which people accreted.

Nothing much had been "invented" on Mljet. The brain scanners, the attention tracking, the neural software, the social software inside the camps, the sensors, the everyware, the communal property, even the heavy-duty exoskeletons—they all had years of development behind them, somewhere else.

The one innovation was the way they'd been brought to life by people willing to believe in them, wanting to believe in them.

Herbert had always claimed that she, Vera, had "inspired" his efforts. Maybe. There was no way for any woman to deny that she had "inspired" a man. It was true that she had been a girl in distress, demanding rescue.

What if a man came to the rescue? What if an army came? What if the army launched a thousand ships? What if they won? What then?

"You're very lost in your own thoughts," he said tenderly.

"I am," she said.

"Well, you've certainly put a pretty spanner into their works today," Herbert said briskly. "That'll complicate matters upstairs. But I'm glad of it. I'm glad that snarky little real-estate hustler can't patch his deal together and use you as his bait and his billboard. To hell with him and all his Yankee funding. I had hell-all for funding when you and I first tackled that place"—Herbert waved off the starboard bow—"and as for tackling the Big Ice, that is work for grown-ups. Vera: You and I will walk the Earth like Titans. You and me. Wait and see."

"Big machines," she murmured.

"Darling: I'm past that now. It's behind me. That's what these years have finally taught me. Any fool with a big budget can assemble big machines. We're not mechanics, we are two engineers of human souls. We are. It's what we feel in our own bones—that's what matters in this world. The one mistake I made here was letting them set the limits on how we *felt*."

"Did you make any mistakes here, Herbert?"

"In one sense, yes, I was blind. The children! No society thrives without children! When I saw how deeply you felt about that child, that niece of yours—then I knew what I had failed to offer you. Yes. I failed you. That tore me up."

"I'm sorry you were hurt, Herbert."

"Yes, that did hurt me, but the pain has opened my eyes. I once had children. They died in Australia. That ended that part of my world, I never got over that grief. But if we beat the Big Ice, you and me, then it will *rain* in Australia."

" 'Australia Fair,' " said Vera. Herbert had talked about his own home island, sometimes. A place much bigger than Mljet. The biggest island in the world. He spoke of how he had loved his homeland.

"I may never set my foot in a renewed, revived, redeemed Australia. But our children will live there. Vera, our children will laugh and sing. They'll be free. They'll be happy."

There was a violent snap as the boat came about. The yachtsman tied off his mainsail, and tramped the little deck in his cheap rubber shoes. He spoke in Croatian. "*Srecno i mnogo! Muske dece!*"

Vera blinked.

"*Dobrodosao, zete!*" The sailor clapped Herbert across the back.

Then he reached out his glad hand to Vera, and she realized, with a shock of revulsion, that the sailor was Djordje.

"You have really screwed up," Djordje told her cheerfully, in his German-tinged English. "I told John Montgomery that you would never do it his way—the smart way. All the world for love! Well, you cost me a lot of good business, Vera. But I forgive you. Because I am so happy, very happy, to see you settled in this way."

"You should express some sympathy for your sister," Herbert told him. "On the Big Ice, I'll work her harder than ever."

"There is no pleasing you global politicals," said Djordje. He found himself another deck chair, one even shabbier and more mildewed than the one that Vera perched on. "You spent nine years on that god-forsaken island there? That evil hellhole? And you never took one vacation? Truly, you people kill me."

Vera grabbed hard for the shards of her sanity. "How have you been, Djordje? This is such a surprise for me."

"Call me 'George,' " he corrected. "My life is good. I have another baby on the way. That would be number three."

"Oh my."

Djordje helped himself to a fizzing glass of prosecco. "That's not what you say to wonderful news like mine, Vera. You say: '*Mnogo muske dece!*' 'Hope it's a son!' "

Vera had not seen Djordje face-to-face in ten years. He'd been a scrawny seventeen-year-old kid on the night he'd sabotaged the sensor-web, jumped the bunker wall, and fled their compound forever. The agony of having their little brother rebel, defect, and vanish was the first irrefutable sign that all was not well in caryatid fairyland.

The seven world-princesses, Vera, Biserka, Sonja, Bratislava, Svetlana, Kosara, and Radmila: they all had joined hands, eyes, and minds in their mystic circle, and sworn to eradicate every memory of their traitor-to-futurity. Yet he had left their ranks incomplete, and the tremendous energies that unified them were turning to chaos.

Toward chaos, hatred, and an explosion of violence, and yet here was Djordje, their traitor, not vanished, not eradicated, as he so deserved to be: no, he was prosperous, pleased with himself, and as big as life. Bigger. Because Djordje was all grown-up. Grown-up, Djordje was very big.

He was half a head taller than she was. His face was her face, but big and broad and male. Djordje had a bull's forehead, a bristling blond mustache, and a forest of blond bristles on his chin and cheeks and neck. His chest was flat and his gut was like a barrel and his big male legs were like tree trunks.

She was horribly afraid of him. He was here and smiling at her, yet he should not be. His existence was wrong.

"Your brother has lent us this boat," said Herbert. "So that we could be alone—just for once! Out of surveillance. So I could ask you to marry me."

"It was my honor to lend you my old boat," said Djordje nobly. "And I approve of your aims."

"Nine years under a sensorweb," mourned Herbert. "Nine years in attention camps where the system watches your eyeballs! My God, it was Acquis-officer this, boss-and-subordinate that; no wonder we both were so stifled! You know what the next step is—after we marry? We need to work together to widen the emotional register of the neural society! No more of that hothouse atmosphere: half barracks, half brothel . . . something grand, something decent!"

"How?" said Vera.

"In Antarctica! It's a huge frontier."

"There's grass in Antarctica," said Djordje. "There's grain growing there. They're brewing beer off the melting glaciers. Truly!"

Herbert burst into deep, rumbling laughter. "I love this guy. He is such a funny guy."

Vera sipped her bubbling wine.

"You'll do all right, Vera," said Djordje. "You never had a father figure. Life with an older man suits you."

"Oh my God," said Herbert, "please don't tell her that!"

"Herbert, you are a genius," Djordje told him. "Every one of those girls has got a genius on the hook, someplace! The caryatids pick men up like carpet tacks. They are like a magnetic field."

Djordje emptied his glass. "Do you know what makes me so happy, tonight? I have both of you here, on my old boat. At last, I am saving you. It's like I dug you two out of a coffin. No skull helmets on you, no skeleton bones on you! We're all free! I took you offshore! We are far outside the limits of the Mljet everyware!"

Djordje wildly waved his arms at the cloud-streaked twilight. "So: Go ahead! Access your mediation! Boot an augment! There's nothing out here! We're free and out at sea! I haven't been this happy since I stole this boat ten years ago."

"Can I have more of that wine?" said Vera. The two men clashed as they grabbed for the bottle. Herbert hastily topped up her glass.

"My children love this boat," said Djordje.

"I would imagine," said Herbert.

"They love life aboard here, nothing but wind and sea," said Djordje. "Because kids are kids! Kids are the ultimate check on reality! You can't have a posthuman, brain-mapped toddler."

"There's a lot to what this man says," Herbert offered. He found a wheel of soft cheese inside the picnic basket. "When I was a kid, my granddad had a sheep station. We didn't even have television out there. Life was life."

The sun was fading over distant Italy, and the evening breeze grew sharper. The little yacht held its course across the Adriatic, leaning, jumping the chop.

"I stole this boat because it is a simple boat," said Djordje. "I could have stolen a fancy boat. The harbor was so full of them. The boats of rich idiots. All hooked up to their maps and global satellites." He laughed. "I cut that chip out of my arm—they never found me. This boat was just wood and water. Nothing else! The web ran out of ways to spy."

Vera found her voice. It was raw, but it was her own. "Do you spy on me with your web, Djordje?"

"A little, Vera. I have to look after you a little. You're a danger to yourself and others."

"How is your wife, Djordje?"

"Call me George," he said. "My dear wife, Inke, is just fine."

"Inke doesn't get a little bored with you? With her church, and her kids, and her kitchen?"

"That's right, Your Highness," said Djordje, with a level stare. "My Inke is a boring woman. She is nothing like you. My Inke believes in God, she's a mother, she's a housewife. She's a real human being, and she's worth about a thousand of you."

Vera shrank back in her deck chair, hissing through her teeth.

"Don't hurt Vera's feelings," said Herbert.

Djordje shrugged. "As long as we have the facts confirmed."

"The fact is that Vera is a very fine Acquis officer."

Djordje wasn't having any of this. "Look, we're all family now, so spare me your politics. Me, the wife, the kids: We are not political people. We're the real people in the real world. Okay? You fanatics and politicals and geeks and crusading communists . . . You say you want to save the world? Well, we are the world you're trying to save. We're the *normal* people."

Herbert emptied his glass. "I can sympathize."

"I am normal, I live decently. I have shareholders and eighteen hundred employees in Vienna. I'm into import-export and arbitrage, logistics, shipping-and-packaging. Industrial everyware: That's me, George Zweig."

"I do understand that, George. Please calm down."

A ghastly moment passed. Djordje was not getting calmer. "I'm okay, Herbert. I'm fine with life, I'm fine with all of it. It's a family thing, you understand? It's not too easy for me to be with your little bride here. I'm the rational one among our group. Really."

"This world is so full of trouble," said Herbert.

"Just keep Vera out of jails and camps," said Djordje. "Vera is the sweet one. Sonja is a soldier. Sonja is killing people. They should arrest Sonja. They should arrest Biserka. They should try to arrest my mother."

"I hate you," said Vera. She spat over the side of the boat.

"Shut up," Djordje explained.

"I want you to die, Djordje. To hell with you and your precious children and your stinking little wife. If I had my boneware on, I'd break you into bloody pieces."

"Well, you can't break me, you little whore! You never could, you never can, and you never will."

She lashed out. "I'm not going to marry him!"

Djordje was stunned. "You love him. You *said* you would marry him."

"I never said yes to him. You didn't hear me say yes."

Djordje looked at Herbert. He offered a sickening smile. "Women."

"I'm not marrying anybody. Never."

"You're a virgin," said Djordje, like a curse. "You're not human. You're a robot. You're a walking corpse."

"Look, don't do this to each other," Herbert told them. "This is really bad."

"No, this is good," said Djordje. "I want to hear this little bitch spit out what she wants! You want to sell this guy out? You want to go for the big money! At the end of the day, our home belongs to *you*, doesn't it? It's all about you, Vera, you, you, *you!*"

Vera jumped to her feet. "I'm going to kill you now."

Djordje was out of his chair in an instant. With a roundhouse swing of his right hand, he knocked her to the deck. With a roar, Herbert rose. He threw his brawny arms around Djordje. His bear hug lifted Djordje from his feet.

"You little slut!" Djordje howled, kicking his legs in a frenzy. "I owe you a lot more than that!"

Vera watched the two men struggle. She touched her flaming, battered cheek, and lifted her gaze. Overhead, uncaring stars dotted the troubled skies.

She took one deep sobbing breath, and flung herself into the sea.

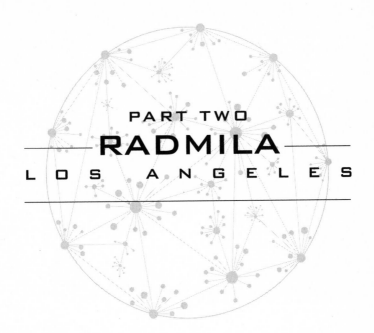

PART TWO

RADMILA

LOS ANGELES

RADMILA CLIMBED DOWN THE THROAT of the rehearsal pit. Her skirt floated around her kneecaps, a jeweled mass of air-tecture, brocade, and electric chiffon.

Glyn spoke up in her earpiece. "Mila, get back up here."

"I need one last run-through for my chair stunt. Just to test this costume."

"You are perfect," Glyn pronounced. "You were perfect when you left makeup."

"This is for Toddy. Tonight I've got to be *superperfect*."

"Roger that," said Glyn, a little sourly.

Radmila found her footing in the blackness. Sensing her presence, the rehearsal space woke around her. Wireframe exploded from the darkness. Prop sticks tumbled loose from their racks and flew like flung batons. The sticks clanged together, joining end-to-end.

The pit suddenly held the skeletal frame of a theater set: couches, a chair.

"Okay," Glyn told her, "you are a go."

Radmila dug her reactive slippers into the memory foam. "This pit is good. This place is so state-of-the-art. This is, totally, the hottest rehearsal pit that the Family-Firm has ever built."

"Just watch your hat," said Glyn patiently.

Golden footmarks glowed on the floor. Radmila braced herself for performance.

"Whoa," said Glyn, "I've got a bad stress readout from your left ankle."

"My ankle is fine now!"

"The everyware knows you better than you do," said Glyn.

Radmila rucked up the hem of her costume. The stage gear protested scrunchily. Kinetic textiles never liked departing from their script.

Radmila flexed her left knee and extended her foot. "Okay, so let me see it. Show me now."

Narrowly focused beams sprang from the walls and ceiling. They brilliantly painted her leg with projected data. Her bones and ligaments appeared, neatly coded and labeled: "Navicular." "Cuboid." "Anterior Talofibular." The working pieces of the human ankle. What ugly names they had.

Radmila bent at the waist, gripped her extended toes, and rotated the joint. The simulated meat and bones writhed in a lively fashion, very glossy and painterly. Yes, she felt one leftover pang deep in there. One ugly, ankle-sprain pang. "Damn."

"You've overdone it. Let's cancel your stunt tonight."

"I can't cancel my chair stunt!"

"You're booked for that big hotel opening Monday. They want your full set: your precision jumps, your vaults, all your backup dancers . . . If you wreck your ankle here tonight, your investors will kill me."

Radmila's temper, always sharp before she went on stage, sharpened further. "Am I supposed to publicly appear tonight in the Los Angeles County Furniture Showroom, and *deny the public* my signature stunting-with-furniture?"

"Oh, is the diva losing her composure?" mocked Glyn.

"We can tape my ankle. That won't take a minute."

"Look: Tonight should be simple. You catwalk over to Toddy. You sit on Toddy's fancy couch. Toddy lectures her public all about historical furniture, and you just listen nicely and be all ingenue about it."

"I hear your concept," said Radmila. "Your concept stinks."

"We're in a furniture museum! Toddy's fans are a million years old! They won't care if you don't fly around the room like a fairy princess!"

Radmila seethed silently. What a pain Glyn was. No one could pull the rug out from under you like a member of your own family. Glyn understood Montgomery-Montalban family values, nobody knew them better—but Glyn had never taken those values to heart. Because Glyn was a stage technician, not a star. Glyn had no magic.

"Toddy specifically asked me to stunt tonight. At dinner, Toddy asked me in front of everybody. I know that you heard Toddy ask me to stunt."

"If you're finally asking *me* about that idea, well, I think your cheap stunt upstages Toddy at her retirement show."

"That's *why Toddy wants me to stunt*," said Radmila. "She's *handing it over* to me in public tonight, don't you get that? Toddy is the old school. Toddy's retiring! Her public's very sentimental, they love an emo pitch like that!"

"The investors don't love emo pitches," Glyn said crisply.

"Think in the long term," said Radmila, and this was a very Family-Firm thing to say. So Glyn finally had to shut up.

Radmila struggled to compose herself. The last-minute backstage squabble had blown open the gates of her stage fright. Radmila's fears always attacked her before she went on. Always. She never breathed a word about her fears to anyone, which meant that she felt them more keenly.

What did she have to be so scared about, before a performance? Nothing—but everything. Her stage fright rose within her like a hurricane seeking a center. Her fear and trauma had to fixate on something.

Suddenly, it centered on Toddy.

Yes. She was so afraid of losing Toddy. Toddy was her diva, her coach, her mentor. Without Toddy, she was ugly and useless. She had no talent. She had no looks. She was just a lost girl who happened to have a strong rapport with ubiquitous systems.

Tonight the angry public would surely find her out. She was nobody's star at all, she was a fraud, a fake. Harsh, cold, staring eyes would drain all the blood from her body. The whole world would collapse. The shame would kill her.

Radmila stamped both her feet at the speed of her thudding heart. "Okay, launch me!"

"Roger that!"

Radmila sashayed through her glowing footsteps, head high, shoulders back. Perfect. She leaped two meters and landed like a bird on the back of the skeletal chair. Ten out of ten.

The simulated chair arced back on its two rear legs, FXing with supernatural ease. Radmila wheeled in place atop the chair. Light. Brilliant. Her slippers flexed, the chair teetered, the wire flexed. The FX
system adjusted its parameters several thousand times a second.

She was superhuman.

"Am I perfect?"

"You are so totally perfect," Glyn agreed.

"Am I *super*perfect?"

"Get off the damn chair," Glyn grumbled. "You're gonna nail it
tonight! You always nail it. Just watch the hat. Now get back up here."

Radmila vaulted off the mock-up chair and skipped, her thudding
heart gone easy in her chest. She flung out both arms and gestured at
the empty air, her fingers held just so. Invisible wire flexed around her
and flung her out of the rehearsal pit.

A folding canvas director's chair hopped over and flopped itself open for
her, amid a busy crowd of Montgomery-Montalban stagehands. Radmila
sat serenely, spreading her costume and grooming it. What a fuss these
stage clothes made about themselves: all that multilayer circuitry, the plastic threading, sensor pads, electric embroidery . . . Gleaming lights, con-
ductive snaps, antenna yarn, laser-cut dust-repellent golden foil: Stage
costumes looked terrific when they were turned on. When you sat still inside them, awaiting your cue, it was like wearing a hot-dog booth.

Radmila slipped on a pair of stage spex, groped at a midair menu, and
touched her earpiece. Toddy was gently lecturing her audience about
historical trends in Californian home decor. "Mission Style." "Arroyo
Culture." "Tuscan."

Every star had a métier, and Toddy Montgomery was a decades-long
sponsor of home-decor products. Californian furniture was of huge,
consuming interest to Toddy's core fan base.

The Family-Firm was a network: real estate, politics, finance, everyware, retail, water interests . . . and of course entertainment. A network
as strong as the LA freeways. A network whose edges were everywhere
and its center . . . well, if the Family-Firm had any center, it was
Theodora "Toddy" Montgomery.

Toddy's costume cascaded over her gorgeous chair: she wore her stiff
support bodice, lace collar, her signature monster hat, her dainty feet
just peeping out from under her big petticoats.

"Miss Mila Montalban will be joining us," said Toddy. There was a happy patter of applause.

Miss Mila Montalban was a trouper and a star. Miss Mila Montalban could do anything for her Family-Firm. She owed the Family her whole existence, and she was loyal and true. She would die for them. If a bullet came for any Montgomery-Montalban, Radmila Mihajlovic would swan-jump in front of that bullet with a deep, secret sense of relief.

Toddy paused for one long, strange moment. Then she caught up her lost thread and rambled on. Old people were so patient and garrulous. They never seemed to switch topics.

Glyn broke in. "Three minutes, Mila . . . Oh Jesus! Now what?"

Radmila stood on tiptoe. "Am I on?"

"We just got a tremor alert."

"What? That's the fifth tremor this week!"

"It's the seventh," Glyn corrected. Glyn was always like that.

"Well then," said Radmila, touching the mechanized crispness of a long blond curl, "the show must go on."

"Do you know what kind of hell we'd catch if there was a Big One and we didn't clear this building?"

"I sure know what kind of hell we'd catch if we shut down Toddy's retirement show."

"We can reschedule her retirement. Nobody reschedules an earthquake."

"Oh, just come off all that, Glyn."

"You come off it," said Glyn. "We built this place on a fault line! If this building topples over, it'll crush us all like bugs!"

This flat threat gave Radmila a serious pause. How could Glyn fail to trust the ubiquitous programming of the Los Angeles County Furniture Showroom?

"Put me on, Glyn. This building is totally modern."

"It is not 'modern,' " said Glyn, "it is 'state-of-the-art.' There's a big difference."

"What do you want from me? Toddy is on! Put me on, too!"

"Two minutes," Glyn agreed, but in the Showroom crawlspace, the normal chaos of tech support had a sudden hysterical edge.

The Family's security people always lurked backstage, wearing their masked black Kabuki costumes, and frankly doing nothing much, usu-

ally. Most of the Family's black-clad stage ninjas weren't even real Security. They were Family members whose faces were painfully famous,
so they were happily invisible in masks.

A ninja reached out his sinister black-gloved hand and gently patted
her costumed shoulder. "Break a leg," he murmured. The ninja was Lionel, her brother-in-law. Lionel was all of seventeen, and whenever his
big brother John was gone on business, Lionel was always making gallant little gestures of support for her. He was a sweet kid, Lionel.

Toddy was babbling, and the soundtrack noodled through a gentle
repertoire of medleys. Radmila listened keenly for her cue. Her cue was
overdue.

The reactive DJ system drew its repertoire from audience behavior,
and Toddy's core fans, her favorite shareholders, were getting anxious.
Through any of a thousand possible channels, the tremor alert had
jabbed them awake. These fine, dignified old people were not in a panic
just yet, but knew they might soon have a good excuse.

Their interactive music had the air of tragedy.

Radmila finally went on. Her hair was okay, the face was more than
okay, the costume would do, but her stage hat felt like a big live lobster.
As a tribute, she was wearing one of Toddy's signature stage hats, a huge-
brimmed feathered apparatus that framed a star's face like a saintly halo,
but the old-school hat hadn't synced completely to the costume, and the
awkward thing, appallingly, *felt heavy*. It should have wafted through
the stage-lit air like a parasail. It felt like a bag of wet cement.

Toddy rose from her couch, ignoring Mila's entrance. It was unheard-
of for Toddy Montgomery to miss a cue. Radmila was shocked. She managed the first half-dozen steps of her planned routine and then simply
walked over.

Toddy turned to her: beneath her huge hat was the tremulous face of
a scared old woman. "Thank you for joining us at this difficult time,
Mila."

This was not in the script. So, improvisational theater: Never, ever
look surprised. Keep the stage biz flowing; always say "YES, AND."

"Yes, of course I came here to be with you, Toddy," Radmila ad-libbed.
"Wherever else would I go?"

"We're evacuating all the children first."

"Yes, of course. The children come first. That's exactly how it should be."

"The seismic wave is in Catalina. This one is a Big One."

"Surf's up," Radmila quipped. There was one moment of anguished silence from the murmuring audience, then a roar of applause.

Radmila sat and smiled serenely. She crossed her legs beneath her gleaming skirt. "I suppose we women will be leaving, too—once they get around to us."

"I never like to leave a party," said Toddy. She fought with her badly confused costume, and managed to sit.

An antique sandalwood trolley rolled over with a delicate chime of brass bells.

"Tea?" said Toddy.

Alarm sirens howled. The sirens of Los Angeles were terrifying. A scared coyote the size of a ten-story building might have howled like LA's monster cybernetic sirens. The sirens had been planted all across the city, with intense geolocative care. There were networked packs of them.

Toddy turned her stiff, aged face to the sky. A twirling, linking set of geodesics, thin beams looking delicate as toothpicks, danced across the stars. Los Angeles was famous for the clarity of its skies. "It's been such a lovely night, too."

"You've never looked prettier," Radmila lied, and then the earthquake shock hit the building. The antique couch below them bounded straight into the air.

The entire studio audience went visibly airborne, their arms spontaneously flopping over their heads like victims in a broken elevator.

The museum floor dipped from rim to rim like a juggler's airborne plate. It rose up swiftly under the audience.

The floor gently caught them as they fell.

The silence was cut by startled screams.

Radmila scrambled across the couch and groped for Toddy. The old woman had swooned away, her mouth open, eyes blank. There seemed to be no flesh within her massive, glittering costume. Toddy was a pretty, beaded bag of bones.

A second shock hit the museum. This shock was much bigger than the first, an endless, churning, awesome, geological catastrophe. The museum reacted with a roller coaster's oily grace and speed, ducking and banking. They were suspended in limbo, an epoch of reeling and twisting, rubbery groans and shrieks for mercy.

Radmila found herself audibly counting the seconds.

The earthquake rushed past them, in its blind, dumb, obliterative fashion.

The sirens ceased to wail. People were gasping and shrieking. Radmila twisted in her stubborn costume to look at Toddy. Toddy was unconscious. Toddy Montgomery had a very famous face, an epic, iconic face, and that face had never looked so bad.

Radmila clambered to her feet. The panicked audience was struggling in semidarkness, while she had the stage lights. The audience badly needed her now, and a star on stage could outshout anybody.

Radmila tore the dented hat from her face. "Did you see what this building just did for us? That was *completely amazing!*"

Radmila dropped the hat and clapped her hands. The stunned audience caught on. They heartily applauded their own survival.

"The architect's name is Frank Osbourne," Radmila told them. "He lives and he works in Los Angeles!"

Those who could stand rose to applaud.

The museum floor beneath their feet was miraculously stable now. Their building was as firm as granite, as if earthquakes were some kind of myth.

Toddy was entirely still.

The sirens began again, different noises: fire alarms. The fire warnings had a gentler, less agitated sound design. Los Angeles fires were much commoner than earthquakes.

With tender respect, members of the audience began setting the prized furniture straight. They sat with conspicuous dignity, and simply gazed up at Radmila. They still wanted to be entertained.

A black-clad shadow vaulted from backstage, did a showy, spectacular front flip.

Lionel had made an entrance.

Lionel had thoughtfully brought her some scripting. The two of them hastily conferred. Lionel leaned his black-wrapped head against hers to whisper. "Grandma's had a power failure."

"I know that."

"I'll get her offstage, you manage this crowd."

Radmila commanded the audience. "Ladies and gentlemen, all the elevators in this structure are working beautifully. So we will have you out of here very quickly. Your limos are coming. We'll evacuate anyone who is injured. So people, please look to your neighbors now, send out reports, send a prompt . . . The city's comprehensive relief effort is already under way . . ."

The museum's lights flickered nastily. They came on again, raggedly, and in a dimmer, amber, emergency glow.

The sound system died on stage. Radmila's software failed, and the full weight of her costume fell on her, across her shoulders, back, thighs. It was like being wrapped in dead meat.

"Help me carry Grandma," said Lionel, tugging at the inert mass.

Slowly, Radmila fell to her knees. "Oh no. I can't move." Radmila was able to turn, to look into Toddy's face. The old woman's eyes were two rims of white. Her lips were blue. She wasn't breathing.

"My God, she died! Toddy is dead!"

"Well, she's not gonna stay dead," said Lionel. "She's a Montgomery."

QUAKE REPORTS WERE POURING IN from the urban sensor-web, popping out of the background noise as their relevance gained weight.

Things were grim in the aging slums of Brentwood, Century City, and Bel Air, with fires, smashed tenements, and rumors of looting.

All over the city, Dispensation flash gangs were throwing on their uniforms, grabbing rescue equipment, pouring into cars.

The LA skyline was lit by laser torches. Dispensation people never waited for orders during a civic emergency. They took their dispensations and they charged in headlong posses straight for the thickest of the action. They'd all seen enough hell to know that the sooner you stopped the hell, the less hell there was to pay later.

LA's freeways had ridden out the quake: of course. There were no constructions in the whole world so strong and ductile as the freeways of Los Angeles. LA's rugged urbanware was like a spiderweb from another planet. During any LA quake, almost by reflex, people would pour into their cars to seek the proven safety of their freeways.

Current traffic was bumper-to-bumper, but it was bumper-to-bumper at a comforting hundred and thirty kilometers per hour.

Radmila flicked off the news projection on the limo's windshield. A crisis this size would be best confronted from the Bivouac, the Family-Firm's secure fortress in glamorous Norwalk.

Lionel, gallantly, was escorting her home. He'd helped her to fight her way free from the grip of her costume. Hastily wrapped in a dusty equipment tarp, she'd fled down a Showroom elevator and into a waiting Family limo.

Lionel had found her some spare clothes in the limo's trunk: some unknown relative's flowery surfer shorts, a big smelly male undershirt, and a sand-caked pair of flip-flops. Radmila was wearing that under her spangled stage jacket, torn loose from its support circuits.

"You look so fantastic just now," said Lionel.

Radmila glanced up at the big rearview mirror. The Family's limo was unmanned, but it had all the fine old car traditions: a big knobby steering wheel, human foot controls on its floorboard, everything. "I look like some drunken beach floozy."

"No, no, you look *exactly the way girls were supposed to look in movie disasters*," Lionel marveled. "Sort of half naked, dirty, and ripped-up, but still intensely glamorous."

Freeway lights flashed rhythmically on Lionel's eager young face. Lionel was a Family star. He had a strong and growing pull in the male fifteen-to-twenty-two demographic.

Lionel still wore his black Kabuki stage gear, which had certainly come into its own in this dire situation. Lionel's knightly security gear was scorch-proof, rip-proof, well-nigh bulletproof, and full of handy pockets. Best of all, it was entirely independent of the net and it carried all its own software processing. Radmila felt safe with him.

Lionel generally dressed like a kick-ass, paramilitary LA street kid, but he was the kind of superbly eye-catching street kid that only a very rich kid could possibly be. Lionel was a child of advantage: he did hormonal bloodwork, ate a strict nutraceutical diet, trained in gymnastics, and had three martial-arts coaches.

Radmila suffered in the high-tech Family gym, but Lionel lived in that gym. Lionel could walk on his hands better than most teens could walk on their own feet.

Radmila handed him a tissue from the glove compartment. Lionel took the hint, and wiped his grandmother's stage makeup from his lips.

Lionel had puffed air into the old woman's dead lungs. He'd pounded her heart into action with his fists. Lionel was core Dispensation: he knew first aid.

"You did really good tonight, Lionel. You have saved your grandmother's life."

Lionel held his chin high. "You have to use your head when you're working security."

"That's exactly right."

"I made the right choice," he said artlessly. "See, that dead costume *killed Grandma*, right? It *smothered her*. I wanted to pull my knife and slice it off of her. But I didn't. I waited for her power to reboot."

"That was smart. You were thinking like a grown-up. Your brother will be proud."

"The system crashed—but only for a little while," Lionel said. "As soon as her underwear came back on, that got her breathing. We can't panic and wreck the system. Because we *are* the system." He nodded, pleased with his insight. "It takes three trained staffers to tuck her into that costume. So I'm sure glad I didn't improvise."

"When we get back home safe, I'll improvise you a nice roast-beef sandwich."

"Are you sure that I did the right thing tonight, Mila? I mean . . . Grandma was dead."

"You did just fine, Lionel. You're a wizard, you're a true star." Radmila propped her flip-flopped feet on the greenly blinking dashboard. "I sure wish John was home tonight. John would mix me a drink. Nobody mixes a nice Greenhouse Tequila like he can."

Lionel pulled something large and ugly from a Velcro slot on his chest.

"So what's that thing?" Radmila said.

"Hey, this is my cool street blade, sister!"

"Let me see it?"

He handed it over, hilt-first.

The knife's awkward handle was wrapped in length after length of multicolored electrical wire. Lionel's homemade knife was made entirely from junked computer parts. A dozen big silicon chips—all black and heat-discolored—had been set into a melted plastic handle. Those chips were like a jagged row of shark's teeth.

"This stage prop sure is weird," Radmila said. "It smells awful! Why does it stink so much?"

"Yeah, that's the blood they put on it!" said Lionel. "When you make a prison shiv, you get, like, every guy in your prison gang to drip some blood on your blade! That screws up the DNA evidence."

"California doesn't have any 'prison gangs.' California doesn't even have prisons."

"Yeah, so this is, like, a modern *electronic-parole* prison shiv!"

Radmila held the makeshift weapon with one thumb and two fingers. It was more than merely strange and awkward: it looked insane.

The more she looked at this desperate, far-fetched contrivance, the worse it made her feel. It was not a stage prop at all. Some stranger somewhere had put a fanatical, psychopathic effort into making this strange parody of a knife. Its very crudeness was scary. It radiated a determined, lethal, sacramental feeling. Evil was pouring off of it, like the peppery dust from a shattered mass of concrete.

Radmila looked into the guileless young eyes of her brother-in-law. "Can I keep this knife for you?"

"Keep it? What, keep it where? Are you gonna tuck it into your bra?"

She wasn't wearing a bra. "Well, you shouldn't carry a thing like this."

"You can keep my knife if you want it," Lionel said, putting a brave face on his wounded feelings. "You're the one who gave that to me."

"I never gave you *this* thing. This thing is not my style."

Now Lionel was was upset. "But you did! You came onto my action set and gave that to me. It was all wrapped up in pink butcher paper."

"Where would I get a prop like this? I haven't done an action role in ages! I hate violent action roles. I do ingenue roles and supportive-girlfriend."

"Okay," Lionel said, blinking, "Fine, I get it. That's all right." He tucked the knife back into the slash in his suit. "See! It's all gone! End of story, roll credits."

His face had paled with her unmeant insult. There was some profound misunderstanding going on here.

Radmila knew that it had to be her own fault somehow. Because it was always her own fault. In nine years of knowing them, in becoming one of them: Every time she'd ever put a foot wrong with the Montgomery-Montalbans, it had been her own fault.

She was always outthinking and outfeeling the Family-Firm. She was always failing to grasp how simple and clear they were.

The Montgomery-Montalbans were California aristocrats. They were rich and powerful and secretive and very civilized. Being aristocrats, they were naturally slightly stupid, and in their utter devotion to their Family values, there was something sunny, airheaded, starry-eyed, and cosmically lucid about them.

That was their charm. They had a lot of charm. Charm was their stock-in-trade.

It was unthinkable that sweet Lionel, who doted on her, would ever lie to her. So, maybe she really had brought him the ugly knife. That was remotely possible. She often carried packages for Lionel whenever he was on his sets. Just as she would faithfully bring snacks and toys to her own daughter, whenever Mary was on. To show up with a gesture of support, to be there physically, breathing the same air, eating lunch on set—that was a steadying, reassuring Family thing. Family stars did that for each other all the time. Just to show that—no matter how weird things might get in Los Angeles—you had someone who understood and cared about you.

Mary. Mary. Mary Montalban. Her baby was so far away from her now. The baby's father, too. John was so much like his brother Lionel. Except that Lionel was fine, or at least okay, while John was doomed to be her husband.

John was the smartest Montgomery-Montalban, the cleverest one. Nowadays, John understood a lot of things. He understood things much too well.

A pang of guilty love for her nearest and dearest rose within Radmila. Her fit of passion was strong enough to taste, like a taste of bloody iron. Her love for her family was a very blood-and-flesh kind of love. It was large and tragic and liquid and squishy.

Ever since the pain and terror of fleeing that nasty little island in the Adriatic, Radmila had known, with a heart-crushing clarity, that no human being could ever love a monster like herself. Still: The only thing of any value in life was to love and be loved. Knowing she would never find any love, she had despaired of love and tried hard to hide from love.

So love had arrived to find her, instead. The love of her Californian family was like a Californian tidal wave. It was large, and rich, and Pacific, and powerful, and muddy, oily, salty, and slightly polluted. It swept all before it and it surrounded everything it touched.

"This is such an awful night," she said aloud. "I hope your grandma isn't so totally dead now that . . . Oh, I can't even say it."

"You know what?" he said. "I need to cry."

"You can cry. I'm here for you. I'll listen."

A child of a disaster-stricken world, Lionel had to work his way up to his tears. He kept at the effort, though, and presently began to sob.

Taillights blossomed redly across the freeway. Radmila realized, through her own watering eyes, that this surge of brakes was the sign of another aftershock. The new little quake hadn't slowed the traffic much. Nature had convulsed beneath the highway pillars, and the freeways just soaked that right up.

What a beautiful city this was: this huge, dense, endless place. So many cities in the world had been wrecked by the climate crisis. "Extinction 6.0," the Californians called it. Californians were always making up new words that the rest of the world found themselves forced to use.

The Angelenos were thriving, although a city built like theirs, clearly, should never have survived.

Los Angeles was a crowded, polyglot mess of a place, trapped between a killer desert and a rising ocean. The city of Los Angeles had blown more climate-wrecking fumes out of its tailpipes than most nations. If there were any justice in the global mayhem of "Extinction 6.0," Los Angeles should have been the first place to die: the first city in the world to drown, convulse, starve, riot, black out, and burn right to the ground.

Yet there was no justice in the climate crisis. Not one bit of justice. The climate crisis was not concerned with justice: it was about poverty, stench, hunger, floods, fires, thirst, plague, and riot. So, although Los Angeles did burn in many places—Los Angeles had always burned, in many places—Los Angeles grew much faster than it burned.

If this tormented world had a world capital, this city was it. Sprawling Los Angeles was checkered across its bulk with "little" regions: Little Chinas, Little Indias, Little Thailands, Little Russias. Clusters of busy refugees from disordered places that were no longer nations.

Los Angeles was a refugee-harnessing machine. Modern refugees thrived in this city as in no other city on Earth. Some of them, like herself, even got rich.

The prospect of catastrophe had never cowed Angelenos. Because Angelenos had never believed in any myth of solid ground. Instead, they survived through selling dreams and illusions. The turmoil beneath their jostling hills had created Tinseltown.

Los Angeles existed to be almost chaotic and yet to survive chaos, to thrive on chaos. The endless weave and roll of LA's automated traffic. The pixelated windows in the scalloped walls of a thousand skyscrapers. The night sky was alive with mighty beams of light: police searchlights leaping down from helicopters, signal lasers up from dense knots of street trouble. This city had the fastest, most efficient emergency responses in the world.

When the earth heaved under your feet, you had to run so fast, just to stand firm.

Lionel's sobs faded quickly. Teens were like that. Teens were strange people, even stranger in some ways than the very old. In their delicacy and temporariness, teens had an ageless quality. Teens were kids, and yet teenage kids were fearless and brave: they didn't much mind dying. Teens were both Peter Pan and Dracula.

"Mila?"

"Qué pasa, hermano?"

"Are you a lucky little lady in the City of Light, or just another Lost Angel?"

"Lionel, classic poetry won't help us right now. We had a really bad night, but we're gonna plant our feet, get very steady, and hold all this up. All right? We can do that. I promise you. We'll dead-lift the whole world straight up over our heads. If guys like you and I don't do that, who will?"

"I had to breathe my own breath right into her dead old mouth," said Lionel.

"You did the right thing. Really."

"Am I too stupid to live?"

It meant a lot to her that Lionel would ask her such a thing. His neediness immediately made her strong. "Okay, so listen to me now. We could have all been killed tonight. The software in the whole building might have blown out, like your grandmother's costume. If everyone had died in there, and I had died, and you had died, and your grandmother, the support staff, her audience, everybody—that would have been, like, an amazing, perfect exit for the wonderful Toddy Montgomery. An amazing superstar exit from this world."

Radmila drew a deep breath. "Well, no diva gets a clean exit like that. Nobody. Not me, not you, not even your superstar grandma. So our situation right now is, like: We're completely screwed up. Our town is broken by a quake and parts of it are on fire. People are dying out there tonight. Toddy died. We're crying inside our limo. But the Family-Firm is going to deal." Radmila pushed hair back from her sweating forehead. "You get me? We shuffle all the cards and we deal. First thing tomorrow."

Lionel contemplated this fierce declaration. "You know what?" he said. "I understand why he married you."

Radmila's eyes gushed tears. "What a sweet thing to say."

"No, he's really a smart guy, my big brother. Smarter than me."

"I tried so hard to please him and this Family," Radmila sniffed. "That beautiful old woman . . . I went to political meetings. I even read Synchronist philosophy. Do you understand that stuff? I don't think anybody does."

"My brother does."

"You think John is truly a Synchronist? He doesn't talk that way just to sound cool?"

"What's small, dark, and knocking at the door?" quoted Lionel. "The future of humanity."

Radmila began to sob aloud.

"You should have another baby, Mila. The Family future needs that."

Radmila howled.

"I know you can't stand John around you anymore," said Lionel, "but in a world as messed up as this world, a guy like my big brother: he is a *force for good*. It's like he's a plastic surgeon . . . It's like . . . one tiny injection, that won't even hurt, and whoa, I can bench-press the whole world . . . I went for that pitch of his totally, and oh my God, one of these days I swear I'm gonna kill somebody!"

The car made its methodical way toward their home.

"Killing people is too easy a job for you, Lionel," Radmila told him.

"Killing people is for suckers. If we take good care of our own Family and we wait awhile, the bad people die all by themselves." She took a measured breath. " 'He was just seventeen, you know what I mean, but the way he looked . . .' "

"That was so beautiful," said Lionel, leaning back at last. "That's what's so great about the classics. They give you that terrific sense of roots."

TODDY MONTGOMERY HAD TAUGHT Radmila many useful things about life. Especially about life as an idol and star. Almost every single thing that Toddy taught about wealth and fame and glamour was grim and dull and dutiful. In the long run, those things always turned out to be the only things that worked.

"Never forget" was Toddy's usual preface: "Never forget that just because you get it doesn't mean you get to keep it." "Never forget that the world expects something from a somebody." "Never forget that Hollywood was built on the backs of us women."

There were dozens of these wise sayings of hers. To her shame, Radmila had forgotten most of them. "Never forget that behind every woman you ever heard of is a man who let her down," that one was memorable. "Never forget that charm and courtesy cost a woman nothing . . ."

Toddy herself had conspicuously forgotten one important thing. Radmila Mihajlovic was the cloned creation of a Balkan war criminal. That awful fact preyed on Radmila's mind every time that she saw her own face in a mirror, but Toddy never breathed a single word about the subject. She seemed to have simply forgotten it. Toddy was a major star, and Mila Montalban was her handpicked disciple, and that was how things were.

Like all Synchronists, Toddy was rigorously bodycentric. Her philosophy was obsessed about the flow of time through human flesh. It followed that Toddy's cure for every kind of crisis centered on the body: exercise, sleep, nutrition, and determined primping. "Never forget to go to the gym every morning," Toddy would say, "because that's the worst thing that will happen to you all day, and that's such a comfort to know."

It was particularly important to go to the gym whenever you were bewildered, feeble, lousy, grieving, and scared half to death. For a woman to go to the gym in such conditions was a show of steely mettle. It proved that you were serenely surpassing the limits of lesser, less committed, little people.

So Radmila rose early from her lonely bed of memory foam, threw on her dancing skeins, and crept silently downstairs to confront the Family's machines.

The Family gym was walled with display screens. Machines mapped and recorded the transformations within her flesh. Her organs, skin, blood, hair. The screens showed her the six hundred and fifty different muscles in her body. They mapped two hundred and six different bones.

It wasn't very hard to shape a muscle. Fed and properly stressed, a muscle would change shape in a week. A professional actress took more interest in the slow, limestone-like re-formation of the bones. If you watched the bones closely, mapping their glacial movements day by day, you could learn to feel the bones. Toddy claimed that she could act with her bones.

Pain was the sign of ugliness leaving the body.

Radmila had slept briefly and badly, but she kept at her rigorous labors till some Family kids thundered in: Drew, Rishi, Vinod, and Lionel, of course, who was their ringleader. Whooping, the Family teens literally bounded off the walls: kongs, cat jumps, dismounts, cartwheels, and shoulder rolls. It was thoughtless of them to stunt so much on such a dark day. Radmila aimed a grown-up scowl at them. That calmed them down.

Stupefied with exercise, she nestled into the gym's black support pod. Sleep hit her like a falling wall.

Inside the pod's velvety, mind-crushing darkness, an oneiric dream stole over Radmila. She dreamed of weightlessness: a dream of LilyPad. It was John who had taken her up to LilyPad, as a privilege for her, as a sign of his trust for her.

Some quality in weightlessness had soaked into her flesh forever. The body could never forget that experience: it would come back to her on her deathbed. She dreamed of the warm silence of orbit, of the accepting and impassive Earth so far below them, with tainted skies, its spreading deserts, and its long romantic plumes of burning forests.

In the orbital sanctum of LilyPad, for the first and last time in her life, Radmila Mihajlovic had forgotten herself. She had forgotten to police her inner being within her walls of trauma, fear, and self-contempt. Because she had escaped the world. There was no weight in orbit, no hateful burden for a caryatid to support there. Outside the boundaries of Earth, love was deep, viscous, fertile. Love was all-conquering.

Radmila woke, and she knew that it had been a good dream. To have a dream so sweet and promising, at a time of such grief and confusion: It meant that she was strong. She would power her way through this impossible time. She would do her duty, she would bear up. Today, tomorrow, yesterday—the "event heap," as Synchronists called it—the event heap would sort itself out.

Radmila was hungry. The body mattered. The Montgomery-Montalbans were early risers and convinced believers in a proper breakfast.

But there was nobody around to share her meal. There was one special sunlit breakfast nook overlooking the Family's gardens, where she made a point of breakfasting with John and Mary, but John had gone away, and he'd taken the child with him. The breakfast nook, all Perspex and cellulose, was one of the prettiest spots in a beautiful building, but now it felt like a reproach to her.

Whenever John was gone on his business, Radmila would eat a more formal breakfast with Toddy, but Toddy Montgomery would not be dining this morning. No.

So Radmila ventured downstairs to the kitchen to eat with the staff. The mansion's gleaming kitchen was weirdly deserted. The staffers were kind and good to her: they knew that the Family's stars were just the graphic front ends for the Firm's commercial interests, but the staff were big fans as well as Family employees, so it always meant a lot to them whenever Radmila dropped by.

The staffers had all left. They were all Dispensation people, so they'd swarmed out of the Bivouac to go fight the emergency.

Radmila sullenly turned on a countertop meatrix and printed out a light breakfast. She nourished herself in ominous silence. Then she went to her boudoir and costumed herself in a morning gown.

It was time to go and see about Toddy. Radmila had few illusions about what she would see there, but she knew it was the right Family thing to do.

Uncle Jack was in Toddy's master bedroom. Jack was overseeing the family's robots as they methodically pried Toddy's treasures from their quake-proof sticky-wax.

It seemed that Jack hadn't slept all night. Yet Jack still had his buoyant smile and he was beautifully dressed: the role of a Family star was to keep up appearances.

Radmila cued a soundtrack and made her entrance. "It's so good to see you."

"You, too," said Uncle Jack.

Toddy owned a host of pretty knickknacks: fabjects, hobjects, govjects, all her awards, of course; her art collectibles, mementos, and her Twentieth-Century Modern-Antiques, for those had always been her particular favorites.

Uncle Jack was methodically stripping the bedroom of every trace of Toddy and her possessions. Every stick of Toddy's famous furniture was already history.

Uncle Jack was in here, rather than out warring with the ongoing urban catastrophe, for Uncle Jack was old and sentimental. Even after retiring from his own stardom, he had devoted himself to running gentle simulation games for children. Jack preferred to rusticate in his play worlds rather than duke it out over politics and budgets.

Kindly Uncle Jack had been the first person in the Family-Firm to decide that she might be okay. "Our Johnny has found himself a pretty foreign girl," Jack had said, "an illegal alien, no prospects, no capital, bizarre education, unspeakable heritage"—and then Jack made himself her friend.

In the sunlit, louvered spot where Toddy's big, frilly bed had once stood, a bright-eyed entity was busy inside a medical bubble. The creature in that bubble was alive, but it was no longer Toddy Montgomery. The creature did not recognize Radmila. Random, empty expressions crossed its waxy face. It scratched at the black bruises on its long, skinny haunches, and it stared into a crystal ball.

"I almost thought that she knew me for a moment, when they rebooted her last night," said Jack. "But I was dreaming. I'd hoped that she might recognize you now. You were always the daughter in this Family that she loved best."

"They revived her body . . . ?"

"Yes, she's pretty much exactly as she looks. I'm really sorry."

The old woman had always been particularly obsessed with her biosphere hobjects. Those complicated pocket worlds, so safe and protected and serenely distant from reality, always consoled her somehow. The gleaming world in Toddy's distracted grip was comforting her even now.

"She's still interacting with that hobject there," Radmila said hopefully. "Surely that has to mean something . . . I mean, if she can still engage with it."

"She's become part of it," said Uncle Jack remorsefully, "and it is part of her."

"I never understood what people see in those things."

"I understand that matter quite perfectly," said Jack, "but that certainly doesn't make me like this situation any better."

"So—what do we do now, Jack?"

"We have to deal with the legal snarl." Uncle Jack shrugged. "She had her Living Will and all that business, so we plucked her loose from her life support . . . And here she is. Her simpler organs and tissues, those are all juiced-up and hyperactive, but her poor tired old pumpkin up here . . ." Jack patted the fine, silky hair on his own skull. "She can't speak anymore, she can't walk . . . She tore all her clothes off, she won't stay dressed . . . I think she might be able to feed herself. Someday. She's still got her appetite. Those monkey hands and eyes keep right on going, but she's way overdrawn at the brain bank."

Radmila stared through the tender skin of the antiseptic bubble. "I guess something like this has to come to all of us, sooner or later . . ."

"She was medically dead for fifty-seven seconds," Jack said. He turned away from the pod, pulled his wand, and brusquely shot a command at a robot.

Radmila had nothing to say to that. Being Hollywood stars with strong political interests, the Family-Firm had suffered many scandals, intrusions, voyeuristic interventions, vile rumors, sometimes even armed assaults . . . Yet this was the single worst, most heart-sickening calamity she had ever seen the Family suffer.

Jack spoke again. "When I was a kid your age . . . there was this curse called 'Alzheimer's disease.' Have you ever heard of that syndrome?"

"No."

"Well, it's gone now. That syndrome was even worse than this. In some ways."

"Oh wow." Radmila drew a breath. "So, let's take some action. What can I do to help right now, this minute?"

Jack was pleased by this, for it was a very with-it, Family-Firm thing to say. "Well," he said, "you can help me make the Family's Directors see some sense about the situation . . . Her investors will truly hate this development."

"Okay. I'll do that. What's our game plan?"

Uncle Jack pointed skyward with his elegant ivory wand.

Radmila was incredulous. "We launch her into outer space?"

"Plenty of room up in LilyPad." Uncle Jack nodded. "That's the Family's attic. At least it's way, way out of Californian legal jurisdiction. That was always the best thing about outer space, if you ask me."

Radmila had no counsel to offer about hiding a crazy old woman in orbit. Such events had certainly been known to happen. Jack knew about that, and she knew about that; adults didn't have to linger over the details. It was a dispensation. A way to duck the consequences of a tangled legal, ethical, social system that couldn't deal with catastrophe.

That was the true genius of the Dispensation. They weren't exactly revolutionaries, but they always had some brand-new way to shuffle from the bottom of the deck.

Radmila dodged a robot with a socketed tray of stray hobjects. "What will the investors make of her prognosis?"

"Stars don't die easy, but the woman did die."

"She doesn't look very dead this morning. The brain is just another organ, isn't it? There must be some kind of investment path for us there."

"Of course there's an investment path," said Uncle Jack. "We could waste an incredible amount of our Family capital trying to revive our oldest star . . . Or we could invest that same amount of money into you. Or into Lionel. Or best of all, into little Mary . . . What course of action has the best long-term return for our Family? You can do the math."

"I hate math," Radmila lied.

"We have to think in the long term. That is our core Family value. So we stick by our core values now, eh? We've got to cut and run on Toddy. She's become a sinkhole. We've got to get those knotheads to reroute her investment stream. As soon as we can."

"I would never ask the Family to do that for me."

"Well, it's time for you to ask for that. No, more than that. You're a big, grown-up girl now, Mila. It's time for you to bite off a chunk and just *tell* those sons of bitches who the star is. You have to do that for us. You're the Family's biggest star now. Nobody else will be able to ask for that, and make that stick with our investors."

"That sounds so selfish of me."

"It is not selfish. It's practical. Toddy always did practical things. Toddy did a hundred things like that, and worse things, harder things. Being beautiful, that is not a pretty business. You can see where that leads. Because: Look at her. That's your own future, girl. That is what you will be asking for. In the long term, inside there, that's you."

Inside the puckered plastic bubble, the naked creature sucked at her wizened fingers and glared madly into her fine glass toy. Radmila realized, fatally and finally, that she would never get another kind word from Toddy. Not another smile, not another knowing nod of approval. Grief rolled through her like thunder.

Radmila wanted to die. She'd never wanted to die in this keen way before. She'd never realized that dying could be such an aspiration.

She drew a breath. "No, that is *not* me! Not my future! Never! By the time I'm her age, this world will be *transformed*! That future world will be *nothing like* this world! The brilliancy, the lightness . . . we don't even *have words* for that world."

Her outburst surprised Uncle Jack. "Mila, I never realized you were quite so Synchronistic."

"My husband insists on all that."

"Are we entirely on the same page here?" asked Jack. "By Synchronistic standards, I rather let the Family down . . . God knows I tried to buy into that modern highbrow stuff, but, well, my heart was never in it."

Jack's embarrassment was painful. "Well," she said haltingly, "I do know, for sure, that Toddy would want me to remain a star . . . So I'll do that. For her. She gave us all that, because she had so much to give to her audience . . . She brought so much grace and elegance and beauty into people's lives . . . Toddy Montgomery never forgot her public! Toddy always wanted to give them beautiful dreams."

Jack's nose wrinkled a bit. "That's how you remember her?"

"I know I'm talking silly star-hype . . . but I can remember how she made me *work*. Discipline, personal transformation, and thorough rehearsals. Toddy made me what I am. I've lost so much . . ." Radmila waved vaguely at the peach-colored bedroom walls. "She built all of this, and all I can do is to try to hold it up."

"That won't be easy," Jack told her, "but she handpicked you. Everybody knows you've been groomed for that role. You're in a strong position, if you can stand the pressure."

"Jack, I can stand it. I can stand anything. Worse things have happened to me than this. You will help me, won't you?"

"You always called her 'Toddy,' " Jack said. " 'Theodora Montgomery.' Well, I remember another woman—Lila Jane Dickey from Hawkinsville, Georgia. That's who I remember when I see that thing in the bubble. You meet a creature like Lila Jane maybe once in a generation."

Jack chased a busy robot from the windowglass, which was already spotless. "You ever heard of a thing called 'AIDS'? AIDS was another plague."

"Of course I've heard of that one, Jack."

"Well, Toddy, or rather Lila Jane—she showed up in this town right after we first cured that illness. Curing AIDS was awesome. It was like somebody hit Hollywood with a promiscuity bomb. You could literally see the dust blow right off the sexual revolution."

Uncle Jack liked to talk in an old-fashioned way. There was something deeply touching and endearing about him. That nostalgic glow in Jack's fine old face was illuminating her dark mood. The future might be painful, even chaotic, but no one could rob the Montgomery-Montalbans of their heritage.

"Toddy was the bomb," said Uncle Jack. "Any star might choose to sleep with some big director, but Toddy liked to sleep with the *technicians.* The ugly, geeky, meta-media guys! Yeah, she cut through those nerds like the scythe of doom! She even *married* one of them—she married Montalban."

Jack tugged at his tasteful cuff links. "I told her, way back then: 'Lila, he's a nouveau riche Spanish-language digital media mogul! And we're proper Hollywood stars, so he's just not our kind of people!' But I was dead wrong, and Toddy knew better. It took a visionary to carry off her strategies. Toddy was so totally clued-in. The Next Web was sure to take over the world. The Next Web had everything, because the Next Web *was* everything! All it needed was some oomph! It needed some big sexy va-va-va-voom! And Toddy had that stuff by the megaton! All people could do was stare."

Jack stared into Toddy's medical bubble. "Not that I like to stare at her just now . . . but yeah, the people stared, all right. Even the *machines* stared. Forget TV, movies—the old entertainment vehicles. Toddy could scratch her ass on any public beach and pull down ten million web-hits from homemade spy videos. She walked through her life in a universal cloud of voyeurs."

Radmila blinked. "Toddy never told me much about those aspects of her profession."

"Oh, come on, come on! Your generation never thinks like that at all! That's all over for you. You young folks are an entirely different breed of star. You crazy superhuman kids, you don't even have four-letter words for sex! Birth rates, children: That's what you people fuss about. You think that sex is all engineering."

"Gender roles *are* engineering," said Radmila.

"Fine, sure, go ahead, be that way . . . Well . . . the Toddy you knew was a wise old woman. The girl I knew was young: a hungry, very determined pop idol with a body like a force of nature. And even though I'm as gay as a box of birds, I sure had the better deal out of that one."

RADMILA DID A COSTUME CHANGE, snapping herself into her formal Dispensation uniform. To dress in this way: so simple, stern, and functionally ergonomic—it always helped her morale. She was proud of her medals and the hotlinks racing down her lapels: they were the visible evidence of endless fund-raisers, hospital visits, ribbon cuttings, awards ceremonies. "Community leadership."

The Family's Situation Room was a legacy from old Sergio Montalban. It was the master geek's addition to the Bivouac, part of his dogged campaign to stabilize the family finances. When Sergio had been Family chairman, the Situation Room had been his dashboard for the Family's fortunes.

The Family's fortunes had prospered mightily, but the pioneer's hardware had been badly dated. Today the Family's investments were so interwoven with the urban fabric of Los Angeles that maps made more sense than spreadsheets.

So the Family used the plush, hushed Situation Room as an informal romper space. They watched old movies in there. Most modern Angelenos couldn't watch movies—because they couldn't sit still and quiet for two solid hours without taking prompts from the net. But the Montgomery-Montalbans were a disciplined, highly traditional folk.

The Family-Firm didn't exactly "watch" the old movies—not in the traditional sense—but they would crowd together bodily in the Situation Room, slouch on beanbags, cook and eat heaps of popcorn, and crack silly jokes while movies spooled on the walls. The Situation Room had been the scene of Radmila's happiest hours, when she was pregnant and gulping chocolate ice cream. John had been proud of her then, truly happy about her, and Family members always went out of their way to be kind to a pregnant girl. It was the first time in her life that Radmila had been part of a human family: accepted, relied upon, taken for granted, just plain there.

Radmila even rather liked to watch the old movies. Especially the very, very old silent movies, which seemed less bizarre and abrasive than the other kinds.

The Situation Room was crowded this morning, but the Family-Firm's games today were grim. The Directors had brusquely abandoned Sergio's screens. A modern autofocus projector painted the wall with a geolocative map.

This disaster map was busily agglomerating the damage reports from the net, which were flooding in by their millions. The map filtered this torrent of noise, so as to produce some actionable intelligence.

Southern California was measled all over with color-coded dots: scarlet, tangerine, golden, cerulean, and forest green. The map refreshed once each second, and as it did, all the colored dots denoting their small threats and ongoing horrors would do a little popcorn jump.

Politely, Radmila did a star entrance into the Situation Room. They could tell by her gloomy choice of soundtrack that her news was bad.

Glyn was manning the interactive table near the wall. Glyn had the most experience with the Family's big crisis map, so she was required to drive it. Glyn peered up from her hectic labor. "Mila, how is Toddy?"

Radmila killed her soundtrack and silently shook her head. The Family knew the truth instantly. They'd all feared the worst, but they'd dared to entertain some hope.

Radmila conjured up a chair and had it carry her to Glyn. Glyn groped at her touchscreen, jacked her target cursor around, and stared at the busy projected dots, but Glyn was taking this news harder than anyone. Glyn was twitching all over and on the verge of tears.

Toddy's heirs sat before the disaster map in their ragged, worried half circle, glumly clutching their control wands. Guillermo, Freddy, and Sofia Montalban were the Firm's driving forces these days. Buffy and Raph Montgomery had shown up to make a Family quorum.

Doug and Lily were Buffy's children, while Rishi and Elsie were Raph's. The Family grandchildren clustered in the back of the Situation Room. They were the younger folk, so it was their business to run out into the field and do sit-reps.

Radmila slid her fingers over Glyn's pale knuckles. "Let me drive this, Glyn."

"I can do it," Glyn said tautly.

"Glyn, take off. Some breakfast would do you good."

Nobody else seemed to realize this, but Glyn was coming out of her skin. Glyn was always the quiet, self-sacrificing one in the Family-Firm: the one who was always there for everybody else. Glyn was the normal one, the quiet one. Glyn was no star. She wasn't a Synchronist. Glyn took no interest in Dispensation politics. Glyn never made any big, starry public appearances. Glyn had the lowest public profile in the Family.

Because Glyn was Toddy's clone.

Glyn had been the biggest public scandal that the Family-Firm had ever suffered. Even the tragic assassination of their governor had caused them less turmoil. It had been an epic Hollywood calamity when the public learned that one of Toddy's wealthy geek lovers had cloned Toddy. The legal and political fight to get custody of that little girl— away from her so-called parents—had brought the Family years of heartache.

But Hollywood scandals faded, since there were always some hotter, fresher scandals. Thirty years had passed, and now Glyn was a sturdy fixture of the Family, just as loyal and just as welcome as any other adopted child.

But that was not how Glyn herself had felt about that situation. Glyn had never been at peace about that issue; no, not for one single day.

Glyn half collapsed in her command chair. Radmila had never seen such a strange, desolate, bewildered look. At least, she'd never seen that look on Glyn's face. She'd certainly seen that look on her own.

What was this strange, hot feeling that welled up within her? It felt like love, but it was so dense and heavy and there was so much pain in it. That powerful feeling overwhelming her now: It was pity. She felt so much pity for poor Glyn.

The Directors went about the Family's dire business, highlighting the stricken map with their wands and murmuring together. It struck Radmila, with a revelatory force, that Glyn had never been the clone of Theodora Montgomery. No, never. Glyn had always been the clone of a stranger: Lila Jane Dickey.

That was a sudden, boiling insight into her best friend's basic character. Suddenly, Radmila held the golden key to Glyn's role in the world. As an actress, she had captured Glyn's character; she held Glyn right in the palm of her hand. Radmila felt a little stunned.

"Glyn," she said tenderly, "I know that you'll be all right."

Glyn's lips trembled. Glyn was anxious that no one else in the Family should know this, but Glyn was secretly overjoyed by the loss of Toddy. Glyn was grieving, her eyes were wet with hot tears, but the destruction of Toddy Montgomery was the happiest day of her whole life.

How many people in the world were like this? Radmila wondered. How many people had to conceal the shame and horror of their secret lives?

All of them, maybe. Everybody in the stricken world.

Glyn was muttering aloud. "I think, maybe . . . yes, maybe I'll go lie down a little."

"Eat, Glyn," Radmila told her. "Sleep is good hygiene, too."

"You can run this map now. You can do all this for us."

"Sure I can, Glyn. You can depend on me."

Glyn pulled herself slouching from her chair and trudged from the Situation Room. Glyn never made any poised entrances and exits, like a star would do. The Family had tried to make Glyn a star, they had sunk some money into improving her, but the treatments had just never taken on Glyn. Nobody knew why.

Radmila settled herself into running the disaster map. The Directors were cautiously projecting little chips of the Family's resources into the ongoing swirl of relief. They did this interface work with long pointer wands. They looked soberly elegant yet slightly awkward, like socialites with badminton rackets.

Rishi chose to walk in front of the map, covering his suit with projected cityware. The map swiftly re-formed itself behind his body. Rishi was a younger member of the Family, so he lacked a Director's wand. Instead, he held a fat black plastic brick in his hand, a gooey interface all dented with his fingers. "What are the stakeholder specs on Grandma's celebrity endorsements?"

"They've still got her immersive-world endorsements," Guillermo said. "Those endorsements don't need any real Toddy."

"Her investors say they need a guideline concept right away," Rishi insisted.

"We tell them that my mother is 'stable,' " said Freddy.

"Meaning?"

"Our guideline concept is 'stable,' " said Freddy stoutly. " 'We are closely tracking developments as Toddy's condition evolves. Her benchmarks now are consistent with her benchmarks yesterday.' "

"That'll work." Guillermo nodded. "Go feed 'em that, Rishi."

Rishi stepped out of the projection, and clamped the gooey brick to his ear.

"Look at all that damage around the Showroom!" Freddy complained. "Why did we build that palace right on a fault line?"

"Because the land was cheap there," said Guillermo. "Zoom that zone, Glyn. I mean, Mila."

Radmila obediently zoomed.

"See, look there! Everything that *we* built there came through the quake like aces. That is so beautiful! Rishi, I want you to get through to that architect's people—Frank Osbourne. We need to congratulate him! As a Family courtesy."

"I'll do that," said Rishi.

"Let's check housing values," said Freddy.

Radmila stroked the touchscreen and peeled an onion of interpretative overlays. Real-estate values were the X-ray of the Angeleno soul. The real-estate map was already spattered with high-volume blobs of rapidly moving money.

As might be expected, a strong postquake surge of investment was already hitting the blue-ribbon districts of Watts, Crenshaw, La Mirada, Lakewood, and Paramount. And Norwalk, of course, that fortress of glamour and privilege where the Bivouac stood firm: there were some scattered blue and yellow trouble-dots in Norwalk, but nothing dreadful.

It was the poorer, dodgier neighborhoods that were always stricken hard in times of crisis: grim, crime-ridden Beverly Hills, the fire-tormented canyons of Mulholland, the stricken shores of Malibu . . . There the dots clustered into complicated, hopeless wads of bleak pastels.

The slums along the tortured Pacific shoreline were the worst parts of the city. Torrance, Hermosa Beach, Santa Monica . . . Racked by the rising seas, these had been the first real-estate zones to become uninsurable. Money was stuck there, nailed there. You could almost smell the money burning.

The cooling Pacific had retreated slightly during the past ten years of the climate crisis, but that good news, paradoxically, made real-estate matters much worse. The uninsured had been feuding over their shoreline slums for decades, in tooth-gritting, desperate, crusading, save-my-backyard urban politics. The prospect that salt water might leave their basements made them crazy.

"You know what we need here?" said Raph, lightly popping the tortured map with the saffron beam of his wand. "We need to stop swatting flies at this emergent level and get ourselves a big strategic overview."

Raph always talked like that. He was his father's son, a Montgomery, and frankly a little dim.

"We'll handle this quake the way we always handle a quake," growled Freddy Montalban. "The grown-ups circle the wagons, and we send out the kids to commiserate. Wind up the Family's charity machine . . . Big star turns to lift the morale in all the worst-hit regions . . . Let's make a quick list of those. Mila, find us that casualty map."

Mila struggled with the interface.

Raph was agreeable. "We could send little Mary up to Malibu. Mary is great in the derelict properties."

"Little Mary is in Cyprus," said Freddy.

"Mljet," Radmila broke in, forsaking the puck for the joystick. "Mary and John are touring Mljet."

"I can't even pronounce that," Raph lamented. "So, how soon can we ship Mary home for some quake duty? Little Mary is super with the tot demographic."

"The Adriatic is the other side of the world," said Guillermo. "That's about as far away from LA as it is possible to get. In fact, that's why we wanted to invest over there. Remember that big discussion?"

"Can't we *fly* Mary back in?" said Buffy, brightening where she sat. Buffy Montgomery loved to fly. Buffy had been the heart and soul of the Family's scheme to buy LilyPad. That was entirely typical of Buffy, because LilyPad, for all its spacey gloss, was a big white elephant.

"John would never fly," Radmila told them. "Jets were a major cause of the climate crisis."

They knew better than to say anything about John's principles. John's father, the Governor, was dead. So John might bow his knee to his grandmother Toddy on occasion, but otherwise, John did his Family duty as John himself construed that duty. Which was to say, John was almost impossible.

Troubled, Radmila had lost her way in the map's widgets. To improvise, she pulled an old trick that Toddy had once taught her.

"So what was *that?*" said Freddy at once.

It was an old trick, but often a good one. Most trend-spotters using the net looked for rising news items that were gaining public credibility. But you could learn useful things in a hurry if you searched for precisely the opposite. News that should have public credibility, but didn't.

Sometimes the public was told things that the public couldn't bear to know.

Radmila had discovered a different map of Los Angeles: Los Angeles seen from deep within the Earth.

"Get rid of that," said Raph.

"What is it?" said Sofia, who was sitting there dutifully, but using her two wands as a pair of knitting needles. Sofia had always been like that. Sofia was Family because she had three kids. By three different men, but that was Hollywood.

"That's a forecast for underground weather," said Raph. "So-called. Everybody knows that you can't predict earthquakes."

The map was a garish space of exotic flows. It was a scientific map: ugly, user-unfriendly, speckled all over with menu bars, to-do lists, threat meters, and behavioral prediction.

Those scratchy-looking color-blobs had to be lava, or magma, or strain tensors in the shifting continental plates. All very complicated. Radmila had never seen this map before, so she was at a loss.

Still, it was obvious at a glance that the heavier action was outside this part of the map. So Radmila scrolled the map sideways.

The map's edge led her to a nexus: a big maroon knot. It looked like a bloodstain.

Freddy flipped his wand around and painted a circle onto the projection. "That node there looks interesting."

Guillermo said, "So who is hosting this map?"

"Who made it?" said Freddy.

Radmila had been hastily accessing the tags, so she was a little ahead of the game. "Some kind of Acquis science group. They're based in Brussels."

"It's from Brussels?" scoffed Raph. "Get rid of it!"

"Better let me drive," Freddy decided. He rose from his seat and set his solid, suited bulk into Glyn's abandoned chair.

Freddy lacked any grace at net surfing. He simply found every tag that looked big and active and pounded it. He popped up his personal notepad and hauled cogent chunks of data onto it. Freddy was a seasoned Family businessman. He never bored easily.

"Okay," Freddy summarized, after seven tedious minutes. "We seem to have some kind of major movement of liquid rock . . . an *unprecedented* movement . . . deep under Yosemite Valley."

"They made all that up," said Raph. "That's some Acquis political ploy. Propaganda. They're always like that."

Guillermo popped loose the electric snaps of his uniform jacket. "You really think that Acquis scientists would lie about magma?"

"Maybe not 'lie,' exactly. But the Acquis are always big alarmists. That's all a simulation. It's not like they're actually down there looking at the real lava. You know that's impossible."

"But they're scientists! They don't know we're looking at this map of theirs! They've got nothing to gain by lying to us!"

"They're doing this to harm our cultural values," said Raph.

"Your thesis isn't quite clear to me, Raph. What are the scientists doing with this map, exactly? They're launching some huge culture-war conspiracy to fake the data, just to make us feel unhappy about our earthquakes?"

"Fine," said Raph, losing his temper, "what are *you* trying to say to us? That there's some kind of brand-new, giant weird volcano growing under California? What next, Guillermo? Are we supposed to act all happy about that idea? We don't have enough troubles this morning? Our hometown just got hit by a Richter Six!"

"That is the *point*," said Guillermo.

"*What's* the point?"

"That's *why* we're getting hit by so many earthquakes. This huge lava movement underground: That might be the root cause of that problem."

Raph shrugged. "That notion sounds pretty far-out to me."

"Raph, you're always saying that you want the big strategic picture. This is a big strategic picture. Boy, is it ever big."

"Yosemite is a park," said Raph, straining for politeness. "Yosemite Park doesn't make earthquakes."

"Let's look that up," Freddy counseled. "I'll tag our private correlation engine for 'Yosemite' and 'volcano.' "

This action took Freddy about fifteen seconds. The results arrived in a blistering deluge of search hits. The results were ugly.

They had hit on a subject that knowledgeable experts had been discussing for a hundred years.

The most heavily trafficked tag was the strange coinage "Supervolcano." Supervolcanoes had been a topic of mild intellectual interest for many years. Recently, people had talked much less about supervolcanoes, and with more pejoratives in their semantics.

Web-semantic traffic showed that people were actively shunning the subject of supervolcanoes. That scientific news seemed to be rubbing people the wrong way.

"So," said Guillermo at last, "according to our best sources here, there are some giant . . . and I mean *really* giant magma plumes rising up and chewing at the West Coast of North America. Do we have a Family consensus about that issue?"

Raph still wasn't buying it. "The other sources said that 'Yellowstone' was a supervolcano. Not 'Yosemite.' Yellowstone is way over in Montana."

"You do agree that supervolcanoes exist, though. They're a scientific fact of life on Earth. That's what I'm asking."

"They exist. If you insist. But the last supervolcano was seventy-four thousand years ago. Not during this business quarter. Not this year. Not even one thousand years. Seventy-four thousand years, Freddy."

Freddy looked down and slowly quoted from his notepad. " 'The massive eruption of a supervolcano would be a planetary catastrophe. It would create years of freezing temperatures as volcanic dust and ash obscured the warmth of the sun. The sky will darken, black rain will fall, and the Earth will be plunged into the equivalent of a nuclear winter.' "

Guillermo's face went sour. "Okay, that is total baloney. 'Nuclear winter,' that sounds extremely corny to me."

"That's because this source material is eighty years old. Geologists know a whole lot about supervolcanoes. Nobody else in the world wants to think about supervolcanoes."

Buffy was losing her temper. "But this is so totally unbelievable! The sky *already* darkened! The black rain *already* fell on us! We *already have* a climate crisis, we have one going on right now! Now we're supposed to have *another* crisis, out of nowhere, because California blows up from some supervolcano? What are the odds?"

"Well, that question's pretty easy," said Freddy. "A supervolcano under the Earth doesn't care what we humans did to the sky. If it blows up, then it just blows up! So the odds of a supervolcano are exactly the same as they always were."

Rishi, who was bright, had gotten all interested. "Well, what exactly *are* the odds of a supervolcano? How often do supervolcanoes erupt, and turn the sky black, completely wrecking the climate, and so forth?"

It took Freddy a good while to clumsily bang that one out. Maybe a minute and a half. "Sixty thousand years, on the average. That would mean we're already fourteen thousand years past our due date."

A contemplative gloom settled over the conclave.

"Look," said Raph at last, "I'm a Synchronist like the rest of you guys, but let's not get completely goofy here. We can't go making our investment decisions on a forty-thousand-year time frame. That's not due diligence and sustainable business planning. That's just plain weird."

"The pace of quakes in LA has been picking up," said Guillermo. "That trend is clear."

Raph had a ready answer. "Well, that comes from climate change. All those heavy rains lubricate the local fault lines. And we get rising groundwater, too."

"Raph, how come climate change can cause earthquakes, but super-volcanoes don't cause earthquakes?"

"Okay, so you got me there." Raph shrugged. "I never said I was a scientist."

Freddy contemplated the geological display map. "Mila, give us that current-situation map again."

Radmila did this. The Family studied the colorful popping disaster dots with a renewed sense of dread. They were clustered on certain lines. Those seismic lines.

"Do we have any Family game plan for the *complete destruction* of California?" said Freddy.

"John does," Radmila said.

Freddy lifted his brows. "Oh?"

"Yes. John once told me that if the planet Earth became completely unfit for life, there would be two places for our Family to go: up into orbit, or down under the Earth."

"I never heard John say that to me," Buffy complained.

"We were floating up in LilyPad when John told me that. On our honeymoon." They had been floating at a porthole and gazing at the distant Earth. There were certain angles of orbit, in the host of whizzing sunsets, when the sweet old planet had looked thin and meager: like some small, distant town on the skids.

"John's such a romantic," said Freddy, who had never liked John much.

"Our Family would *do that!*" Radmila shouted. "We would do it, we would cut a deal with that reality! We'd be floating up in the sky, in some kind of bubble. Or under the ground, in some other kind of bubble. Of course we would do it! What else *could* we do? This Family thinks in the long term, because the Family has to survive!"

Rishi came forward. "I have Frank Osbourne waiting for you."

Freddy was glad for the change of subject. "Let's have a word with the gentleman."

The starchitect's avatar appeared in a corner of the Family's situation map.

"So, Frank," said Freddy, "you're in a simulation at the moment?"

"Gotta be in a simulation," grumbled the architect. "All the big construction business happens inside simulations."

"You didn't notice the most recent big earthquake?"

"Was there a tremor?" Osbourne said. "I'm logging in from Vancouver."

"No? Then let us be the first to tell you that your new showroom museum came through a major seismic event with flying colors! Congratulations."

"No kidding?" said Osbourne. "Swell!"

"Except for a power outage," Guillermo put in sourly.

"I told you to let me handle the power!" the starchitect shouted. "I told you I needed full command over the grid! I told you that! I told you all that from day one!"

"We did our best for you on the very difficult power issue, Frank," said Freddy cordially. "Actual architecture differs from virtual architecture. We can't just reconfigure everything on the fly."

"Didn't you read my white paper? You can't make those obsolete distinctions anymore! Bits and atoms: Bits are *bits of atoms*! The sensorweb is Reality 2.0! So it's all exactly the same! Debate over!"

"It's great to see you're the same old Frank Osbourne," said Freddy. "We've really missed working with you. That was always so stimulating."

"Yeah?" said the avatar, its host of tiny polygons brightening a little. "So, how'd your mossy old mansion come through the latest quake? When are you guys gonna do your major facelift on that place?"

"Do you have something specific in mind for us, Frank?"

"For you? For the Montgomery-Montalbans? Absolutely I do! You know those mobile geodesics in the LACFS?" The architect called his posh structure "Lack-Fuss," an irony that hadn't been lost on Radmila.

"Spontaneous construction!" the avatar declared. "The potential there hasn't *begun* to be tapped! We could do *amazing* things with that technique. *Incredible* things. And *fast.* I could do that tomorrow! If it weren't for those Neanderthals in the seismic code departments!"

The avatar's face wasn't moving much, but they could hear Osbourne furiously hissing through his teeth. "That's all political crap! It's got nothing to do with public safety! It's all about the trades and the subcontractors. They're a lousy bunch of featherbedders! They're a vast conspiracy!"

"We've heard that before," said Freddy.

"Yeah, but *you people* could handle a thing like that. Easy! That little zoning war in La Mirada, you people were wizards at that."

"That's very kind of you, Frank. We appreciate your confidence in us as clients."

"You people are such a class act," the architect said. "It was sweet of you to tell me about my latest triumph in reactive engineering. We might try to get the word out about that, a little. Spread that around on the net some."

"We're doing that right now, Frank," Freddy lied calmly. "The eyewitnesses certainly won't soon forget it."

"That is just great. That's tremendous. That is out of this world. You sweet people call me any time you want, all right? Don't mind my secretary."

"We'll do that, Frank. You stay busy."

The avatar vanished.

Radmila seized her chance to bolster the Family's mood. "You always handle him so well, Freddy."

"He's just another brilliant, irreplaceable creative genius." Freddy shrugged. "They're all the same."

"I want to say something now, please," Radmila said, standing and triggering a soundtrack. "I felt something so deep in my heart today . . . This terrible loss our Family suffered . . . and this nightmare about this volcano . . . I know that bad things can happen in this world. We've suffered a very great loss. And yes, things are getting worse: so that a great disaster seems likely to happen. But that *doesn't scare me.* No. That's what I want to tell you — right now. I'm not afraid. Because I believe in us."

They were all staring at her. Machines couldn't have stared half as hard.

"So, please listen. The Sixth Great Extinction has happened already. Because the human race has *ruined the world.* We have a severe climate crisis, and it's terrible. Whenever we look up at the sky, we see danger and ugliness, and we know that's our fault."

She drew a breath, squared her shoulders. "But just suppose . . . That no matter how bad we human beings thought we were, there was something even *worse* waiting for us. Suppose that *the world* ruined the *human race.* Suppose that a giant volcano burst up out of the Earth, and it just *wrecked everything.* For no reason! It turned the sky black. The innocent died in millions, even billions . . . and everything that we loved about the beauty of this world was turned into ashes, right in front of our eyes . . . and we had to survive in the darkness and the ugliness, and life would be that way *for centuries . . .*"

Their mouths hung open.

"I can tell you exactly what that would be like. Because I *already know.* I know that we would *fight that like hell*! We would fight! We would never, never despair! We would help one another. We would teach our children how good things had been. We would save every precious memory from our heritage. And when we fixed the Earth, and we *would* fix it— we would make it *better* . . . We would make the new Earth a *lot* better."

Radmila stepped into a pool of sunlight from an overhead window. "So: You see what I want to say? If there's a world catastrophe caused by a supervolcano, then it means that our human disaster, our own big crime against the sky, was just too small to count. Maybe we did our worst as human beings, but we were too small to matter. So we can just *forget about that.* We can *forgive ourselves that*! Because the world would have been ruined anyway. We don't have to obsess anymore, or feel so proud about our own evil! All we have to do is survive and plan to prevail! We survive the next catastrophe and we rebuild our world. We can do things like that in this Family. I know that we can do it. We're doing it right now."

The silence was broken by Lily, who hadn't said a word until now. "That was totally the coolest extended set-speech that I ever heard Mila perform. That was just totally wow."

"Me too," said Doug. "That's exactly how I feel, too. Except I couldn't put that into an extemporaneous monologue."

"I was just dying over here!" Elsie complained, jumping from her chair. "I never know why I show up for these stupid Family business meetings! But now I do know. Mila's got all the brains in this Family. So stop wasting your time with that arguing, and let's do what she says."

THE BIGGEST URBAN FIRES in Los Angeles were crushed within twenty-four hours. That left the delicate political task of destroying the worst-damaged buildings.

For political work in the climate crisis, this kind of triage was the ultimate urban-management challenge.

The intractable problems of LA's seaside urban slums had taught the Family that lesson long ago. The Family had learned that damaged buildings had to be demolished, and that demolition had to be done at breakneck speed, while the original pain of the disaster was still fresh. Otherwise, the cost of prolonged litigation would soar unbearably. Completely new buildings could be built for much less money and effort.

The classic Dispensation gambit was to charge in and discreetly smash the damaged buildings while also rescuing their inhabitants. Naturally the legal system had caught on to this sneak-attack technique and put a stop to it. The next refinement was to smash the damaged buildings while leaving the façades apparently intact. The interiors were rebuilt in modern fashion with quick-setting fabricated plastics, so that the old-fashioned building still appeared to stand there, observing all the legal proprieties. Unfortunately this fraud was also too obvious; plus, there was something cheap and vulgar about it.

The latest refinement, one pioneered by the modern Los Angeles star system, was to smash the damaged buildings quickly, but in as loud and public and glamorous a way as possible. The buildings would still end up demolished, but they'd be killed in front of huge street crowds, who would watch the effort and heartily approve it as an act of mass entertainment.

The huge street crowds certainly weren't hard to find; they were composed of the refugees and the destitute, packed like sardines in their bunks and cots across a huge expanse of Southern California. Having briefly been a refugee herself, Radmila knew their lives: Angeleno bread and circuses. Crackers, soup, foam mattresses, and immersive illusions.

The city grid of Los Angeles doubled as a giant game board for immersive game players: one would see these game adventurers, mostly young, angry, and unemployed, on foot, on bicycles, clambering walls, jumping fences, bent on their desperate virtual errands. And since the Montgomery-Montalbans, as media aristocrats, owned the means of game production, they could guide those crowds of gamers wherever they liked.

An engineered urban mob had its purposes: to demolish buildings, for instance. This daring act required a planned coalition of LA's poorest and wealthiest: the poorest, who owned no real property but had the numbers and the overwhelming street presence, and the richest real-estate developers, who could supply cover with the police and who stood to profit handsomely by the eventual reconstruction.

Wrecking the damaged fabric of LA had become a massive, daylong popular festival, complete with parades, original music, gorgeous costumes, mass dancing, and the flung distribution of favors and bribes to the roiling crowds of the poor. In the world capital of the entertainment business, this was the fastest and cheapest method yet found to rezone the city.

This practice had never been legalized, but as a classic Dispensation work-around, it was pretty close to an all-around win-win-win. Many learned academic papers had been written about LA's innovative deconstructive rezoning. The practice was spreading rapidly to other cities.

Radmila did a celebrity signing, for a crowd-drawing star turn by a local idol was strictly required. She briefly graced an assembly of forty local top game players, who were being feted and petted. These gaming champs were mostly scrawny, scampering male teens: leapers, stunters, backflippers, window climbers . . . They looked and dressed very much like Lionel Montalban, their beloved pop idol.

Radmila signed commemorative books, handed out prizes, allowed them a lingering touch of her star-spangled feudal robe. Stars were the linchpin of this effort. No everyday landlord would dare to sue a major star. The costs in bad publicity and lost public goodwill were much bigger costs than simply accepting the fate of dead buildings.

The Montgomery-Montalbans had always been very big on new construction: Toddy had been genially ribbon-cutting for years. The violent smashing of defunct buildings was, by contrast, one of Radmila's personal specialties.

Toddy was no longer there to advise with show production, and her steadying, classic hand was sorely missed. Radmila's carnival would briskly smash three damaged buildings in a mere hour and a half: a ten-story former insurance building in Central City, a twelve-story hotel on Figueroa, and an adjoining mall.

The Family had piled on the effects with a lavish hand, but not a sure one.

It was late August, and in the dog-day Greenhouse heat, Radmila's dance costume showed a lot of her skin. "Never forget," Toddy would have said, "that in show business, we women have to show." Radmila did not mind showing her body to her public—that was what she built her body for—but to cut big flesh-baring holes in electronic costuming seriously damaged the integrity of the performance garment.

Radmila's signature stagecraft involved split-second performance stunts, a superhuman proof-of-concept best held in upscale venues like Sacramento's California State Legislature. The Family-Firm had gained enormous political capital through being publicly superhuman.

Still, the collapsing buildings were the real stars of an effort like this. Collapsing buildings overwhelmed any stunt any mere actress could do. The overblown demolition machinery that smashed the buildings supplied the coup de grâce of urban spectacle. Of course they were not mere dynamite or wrecking balls, they had to be obligatory monstrous stage props. The latest mechanism of destruction had been designed for the Family-Firm by Frank Osbourne. Osbourne, like many Angeleno architects, was enamored of set design and sincerely hated all premodern buildings. He loved to see real-estate leveled.

Osbourne's writhing and rambling urban destroyer had been first designed within an immersive world as a popular hallucination. Still, the toy physics in a modern sealed immersive play world were almost identical to the genuine stress dynamics of real-world architecture. So Osbourne's game contraption worked: it stepped seamlessly out of the immersive play world, into the real-world streets of Los Angeles, and it smashed things.

Osbourne's walking anti-city burned ethanol and ran on three wiggling accordion legs of crystal-steel rebar and nanocarbon cable. Since he'd built only one of these monster devices, it naturally looked like nothing else on Earth. The gamer crowds were delighted to see Osbourne's monster in action. They were used to playing with monsters. They no longer drew distinctions between immersive games and the city streets. Advances in modern entertainment had erased those notions.

The air still stank of the newly doused urban fires when Radmila's twenty backup dancers filed onto their metal stage—a stage bracketed on top of Osbourne's walking monster. The dancers had slightly puppetlike dance steps, for they were following immersive cues.

The cue arrived for her obligatory labors. Radmila bounded onto the stage, with the urban-scale version of her signature entry track. The racket was audible for blocks around.

A flurry of aerial stage lights followed her as she shimmied through her paces. The city wrecker rose beneath her feet like a thrill ride. Its snaky legs slithered, buckled, wriggled. It clomped the cracked side-walks with the tread of doom.

With its complex, gripping feet and its unstable tentacle legs, Os-bourne's city wrecker could walk straight up the sides of buildings. When it did this, the tripod's stage tipped and dropped like a falling el-evator. That fluttered the floating veils of the backup dancers.

Of course all this dramatic stunting was entirely safe, since it had been simulated a million times within immersive worlds. Still, a city-crushing metal monster looked very remarkable in daylight, especially if one was ten years old.

As the city breaker cakewalked through the chosen streets, it fired dust-glittering beams into the doomed buildings—lasers of some kind, she'd been told. The lasers were entirely for show, for the buildings had been booby-trapped by busy Dispensation operatives. It was a pleasure to see such professional work. The useless old buildings literally curt-sied to the public as they fell. The precisely wrecked structures fell with a soft mock intelligence, as if they were truly tired of standing there and genuinely glad to make way for the Shock of the New.

Radmila dutifully mimed her awed rapture at these catastrophic goings-on. The demolition was conforming to schedule, but her pride was rather hurt. Radmila knew there was something kitschy and cheesy and intensely Californian about surfing over the city on a dance stage. This overbaked and overpriced public spectacle revealed a kind of childishness in the culture. To simply destroy a badly damaged build-ing should not require any dancing bimbos. The Dispensation was a military-entertainment complex, it always had to throw its marked cards into the magician's hat, its disappearing rabbits, its custard pies . . . As an artist, she felt that this was demeaning to her.

And yet, it always pleased Radmila to have a popular hit. Show busi-ness did have its native satisfactions for her: shoulders back, chin up, big smile, deep breath, just go . . . Do it: *perform*, be there in public, *be pub-lic*. In certain timeless, gratifying zones of raw sensation, Radmila ab-sorbed showbiz right through her own skin.

Performance was a spiritual act. The unfolding ensemble: that happy roar from the crowds, the rank smell of the smoke, the dust and her own sweat, the physical effort of her dancing, the pervasive rhythms . . . Los Angeles was a mystical city by nature. It required its sacraments.

Radmila felt herself vanish into the ambient substance of the spectacle. She could feel herself just . . . holding it all up. And then letting it fall: with one almighty, dust-hurling thump.

With a final bone-blasting flourish of her soundtrack, Radmila wirewalked off the top of the rollicking tripod, capered straight up the side of a building, and "vanished into thin air."

Ascending into the heavens was something of a Family cliché. Still, when it came to live street art, the best tricks were the oldest ones.

Safely out of the public eye—if one didn't count the flying spycams of the amateur fans, those pests, those nuisances—Radmila fled to her portable trailer.

There she powered down her spangled demolition costume, disembarked from it, dumped the wig, and sat before the darkened makeup mirror, half naked, panting for breath and chugging ice water.

She sponged off her makeup, wrapped herself in anonymous black security gear, and ventured over to Glyn's trailer.

Glyn was still running the event's dying spasms of street choreography, flicking her puck across an urban weave of placemarks and camera angles. "You were really on today," Glyn told her.

"Yeah, the good people of La-La Land, they sure love those bigbudget effects."

Glyn casually peeled up a screen, deployed some police muscle, and smoothed it back again. "No, Mila. Those street crowds love *you*. I checked their skin responses, their pulse rates, everything. They always love to watch some big weird machine kick some ass, but without you in their picture to give them something to care about, nothing much matters to them."

"Oh, that was just my slutty costume talking. Hot and sexy never really suits me."

Glyn sighed. "I am waiting so hard for the day when you stop doing that."

"Stop what?"

"When you stop *putting yourself down*! You were terrific out there!

You were close to perfect! Why can't you be happy about that for one minute? Stop selling yourself short all the time! I swear to God that drives me crazy."

"I'm not perfect. Toddy would have been superperfect."

"That is not the issue. Theodora is history. And anyway, Toddy was *never as good as you think she was.* Yes, she was a big popular star—so what? She was like any pop idol—she was a scared, hungry woman who needed the public to love her. And the public did love Toddy, because Toddy loved her public. She was the love-slave of those unwashed morons. She loved them more than she loved you, me, or herself."

"I should aspire to that level of artistry."

"Have you completely lost your mind? That is not 'artistry'! And you could give a damn about the public, Mila. You wouldn't care if the public all got killed! And they *still* connect with you. That's the amazing part."

Glyn scratched at her control screen. "You will never be a great actress, but you've got some true rapport, you're a true pop star. You're like the Gothic Bride of Shiva. The people here love it whenever you strut out and shake your ass and smash up our city. They know you're very dark inside. Because you are. You're *very* dark. And so are they."

"*You're* dark inside."

"Yes, I am dark inside. So sue me."

"All right, so what's eating you today, Glyn? Why are you being like this? I guess it wasn't my performance." Radmila laughed. "You know why I aced all that? Because she wasn't watching me. Just for once. She's really gone! I never felt so free!"

Glyn sent a half-riotous crowd of fans stumbling down the street in a cavalcade of glowing dots. "I finally figured out what to do with myself."

"You got any gin in here?"

"I will never marry," Glyn told her somberly. "I will never have a child. Because I am a monster. I cannot bear to have Toddy's children with Toddy's spare body."

"You got any performance drinks? Maybe a little taurine, some vitamin B?"

"No. No, and hell no. And also, hell no, shut up and listen to me."

Radmila sat down to listen. She put her cheek in her hand.

"Given that fact," said Glyn, "that I will never marry and I will never leave the Family . . . and given the fact that you married into the Family and you can't leave it, either . . . well, we have to do something big. She built this huge tradition, and now she's gone. We are her heirs. That means it's all up to us."

"I'm listening to you," Radmila said.

"It's too bad that you can't stand your husband anymore. That's a big drawback."

"I can stand John," Radmila protested. "John is the smartest guy in the Family. He's smarter than you."

"Yes, John is smart," Glyn said, "but John's always in the Adriatic, or he's in orbit, or he's doing a charity tour of refugee camps, or he's working late hours at the bank, or he's in bed with one of your sisters. John is never going to be there for us. Anyway, John is not a star. John can't do the things you can do."

"John's a knight in shining armor. John is gallant to the ladies."

"John is a poor little rich boy who wants to rule the world. He's a mess inside."

"That is not true," Radmila said stoutly. "There were two years—well, twenty months—when I was delirious about him. I don't care if I live for two hundred years, I'll never love like that again. If I'd been burned into ashes and thrown out the airlock and scattered into orbit, it would have been worth it to me. I was so completely happy. It was worth my whole life, every heartbeat, just to learn that love was possible."

Glyn silently rolled her eyes.

"Of course," said Radmila, "then John did figure out some things about me."

"Men do that," said Glyn.

Radmila was suddenly blanking with raw fatigue. She had just spent two hours rehearsing and dancing. Her bones were numb.

"You got a new boyfriend?" Radmila said clumsily. "You never act this strange without a new boyfriend."

"My mother just died," Glyn said patiently. "That's what's new for me. Toddy's worse than dead, and she's not even my mother . . . I'm not Toddy, I was never Toddy. I do have one quality, though, where Toddy and I are just the same. I have ambition."

"Uh-oh."

"So, we take over," said Glyn. "You and me. That's what I want, that's my big plan. That's what I'm telling you. You play the major Family star, and I am your tech support. It's very traditional. I make you our dynasty's Queen of Los Angeles. All the older people: they're our investors and backers. They still matter, because they have the capital—but you and me, we're the executive directors. We are the directorial team: because you're the only one who understands me, and I'm the only one who understands you. That's right, isn't it?"

"Of course that's right, Glyn." Radmila loved everyone in her Family, but Glyn was the one she loved best. Except for Mary.

"We both know how to work," said Glyn. "Because she trained us. So, from now on, we do *all* the work."

"That makes you happy, Glyn? I want you to be happy."

"Shut up! This isn't a theme song, so stop talking like some blitzed-out drama queen! This is not about our being happy, that's not the way to frame this. We are the *players*. We take power because we *belong* in power. You're the graphic front end, and I am the back operation. The Family-Firm is our bank. Are you cool with all of that? I get tired of repeating myself."

"Can we really get away with doing that?"

"Yeah, we can," said Glyn. "I will tell you how. They will give it to us if we ask for it in the right way. Every night, we go in for the Family dinner. We put all the toys and machines aside, there's no calls, no prompts, no nothing. It's just us. People. We all sit there together and we eat. And at the head of the table—there was Toddy. But there's nobody sitting there now. There's a ghost there."

"Yes. That's very true."

"Well, either somebody sits in that chair at the head of the table . . . and the others let her sit there—or else we stop meeting for dinner. In which case, the Family *dies*. Because, although we're a huge corporation, we're also a human family. We need a warm body with a heartbeat to cluster around. Or else we all scatter. You understand what that means, right? If we scatter?"

"Of course I understand that!" Radmila said. "I'm Family! It's breaking my heart."

"Who belongs at the head of the table?"

"John's dad should sit there. The Governor. But somebody shot him."

"*You* belong there."

Radmila bit her lip.

"You know that you belong there, Mila. You. So, don't waste any more time. The mourning period is over. We're sick of mourning anyway. You end the mourning for us. You just tweak your soundtrack, you dress to kill in total star-style, you prance to the head of the Family table and you just sit down. You don't ask anybody's permission. You just belong there, and you pass us the mashed potatoes. You can do that. You have to do that. Because I can't do it. Nobody else is willing or able."

Radmila pulled at a sweaty lock of hair. "I'm the head of the Family?"

"No. You're the *heart* of the Family. *I'm* the head. The head doesn't matter all that much—because I've been doing all the thinking lately anyway, and nobody ever notices."

Glyn was her best friend. Radmila had to let her down easily. "If that would work, I'd do it. But Toddy's kids won't let me do it. They're older than us, and they've got priority."

"That's the key," said Glyn. "Because you're *not* an older woman. You're a young woman, so you can give the Family children. The next generation. Futurity. That's what you announce to them tonight."

"I gave them a child already."

"No," said Glyn soberly, "you say you plan a major Family expansion. The patter of dynastic little feet. You want to have *lots* of children. Seven children. You promise them that. And you mean that when you say it."

"*Seven* children? Who, me?"

"Toddy had seven children. If you count me. A matriarch needs motherhood. That's why they will let you do this. It's because you're the mom, that's why. That's a pretty weird kind of power, but it's the kind that brooks no dissent."

"You've really thought a lot about this."

"I'm rich, but I'm not stupid."

"I'm way too busy to expand the Family by having seven kids. I have my star obligations. We have other women in the Family. Let them have more kids."

"They're all too busy, too. No woman ever has the spare time to get pregnant. Especially a rich woman. No rich and famous woman wants to lie on a couch burping ice cream while her belly button turns inside out. Bearing kids is demeaning, hard work: it's work for the poor. But do you want to run the Family? Those are your dues. You give them children and a dynastic future, and they will bow the knee to you. I promise you they will. They have to."

Radmila understood why this mad scheme had sprung into her best friend's head. Neither of them had ever been in a conventional family: with a father, with a mother . . . They were two women who had both come into the world by other means entirely. This coup would finally put them at the center of things.

"You're proposing that I bear *six more* of John Montalban's children? John would like some say about that."

"John will do whatever you tell John to do. I know that John has been with Vera, and John is with Sonja, too. That's very bad. He's a head case about you and the others. But you're the one who married him."

"You know that what John did to me is unforgivable. The fact that those women exist is appalling to me. I hate them. I hate him for loving them."

"Yes, Radmila, I know all that. That fact is burningly, blazingly obvious to me. I know that better than anybody. I'm exactly like you: so I know all about that. You're the only one in the world who can't stand it."

Radmila's heart was pounding in her ears.

"Listen," said Glyn, her face rigid. "I cried a lot these last few days. I cried a whole lot about my own big drama-trauma, and I have made up my mind. I grew up. My mother's dead and I grew up. I have new grief, so I got over my old grief. I want you to do the same for me. Just grow up. Get over your past. Get over being Radmila Mihajlovic. Get over her, she's as dead as Toddy Montgomery. From now on, you have to be different. Because you're not the little lost clone girl with no real mommy and daddy. You are the star. And you will become a megastar. I promise."

"Why are you saying all that to me? You know that will make me crazy."

"I can say it because you're *not* crazy, Mila. If you were crazy, I might forgive you for the crazy way you behave. I know that you're sane: but sometimes, you are just *too damn stubborn to live.* I know all about you, the three sisters, your brother Djordje . . ." Glyn stopped. She smiled in sweet reminiscence at the thought of handsome Djordje. That was never a pleasant thing to see.

"I know about the three *dead* girls, and the horrible ways that they died. I know about your *mother*. My so-called mother was a piece of work . . . but *your* so-called mother doesn't even walk this Earth!"

Glyn looked her straight in the eye and drew a determined breath. "So: I know all that, I still love you, Mila. I do love you. You know that I do. So: Just stop shaking all over like a banana leaf. You don't pull that stupid crap on me anymore. Not on me. I'm tired of seeing you do that, that is all done, it should be long over. You and me: We may have no blood relation, but we are closer than any two sisters. So listen to me: I learned all this from *you*, Radmila. I learned it from what you said to the Family. Sometimes, a huge crime just *doesn't matter*. You were completely right about that."

"No, my crime always matters."

"Get over yourself. Become a different woman. This is not some little secret island in the Balkans twenty-seven years ago where they happened to clone some people. This is *Los Angeles*, stupid! This is the big time, in a big town! In the years to come, we'll move Toddy's investments into *you*. There are *no technical limits* there. When you swan around this city, all brilliancy, speed, lightness, and glamour, you will be so huge, so gorgeous, so totally vested in stardom they won't even *have words* for you. The past will be *done*. Finished. Sealed inside a plastic bubble dribbling on itself."

Radmila was sweating. "But I never asked for that. I don't want it. I can't believe you're telling me to have seven children!"

"Radmila, we've never been part of the human race. This is how we buy into all of that."

"I *did* buy into it. There's Mary."

"Your children will all be fine children. Seven is not too many. You are making up for the rest of us decadent aristocrats. You will be proud of your children. I know Mary. I love Mary. Mary is my favorite niece. I know her better than you do. Mary is not one of you-and-yours. Mary Montalban is definitely one of us-and-ours."

Radmila smiled and wiped her eyes. "Well, thank God for that, at least."

"Mila, you are really close to achieving a huge, lasting, major, public success. Just wise up a little. You are the perfect person to revive this Family and lead it into futurity. You are a lovable person. Toddy loved you. John loves you. Jack loves you. I love you very much. The other Family people, they all respect you, they've decided you're all right for us. But that kid of yours: *Everybody* loves little Mary. *Everybody*. She is adorable and she is destined to be huge. This is your golden chance to turn yourself into the source of unity in our sad, strange little clan. If you turn down that chance because you'd rather be so hurt and proud and emotionally remote from us, you will never get another. Because you won't deserve it. So do you hold it up, or do you kick it down? That is your choice."

"Okay," said Radmila, "I just heard your big, passionate set-speech. That one was pretty good. You obviously rehearsed that thoroughly, so it was great. So: I choose to hold it up."

Glyn brightened. "Really?"

"Yeah. You have just talked me into it, Glyn. Because you talked me into it with my own advice. I can't be such a hypocrite as to deny what I said to my own Family. Yes. You are right about putting the past behind us. We absolutely have to do that, we *both* have to do it. We must. We will get over ourselves, we will turn our faces straight to whatever comes next. I love your big bold plan. Your plan makes perfect sense to me. I will make up with my estranged husband. Fine. I will step into the ruby slippers of the dead superstar. Great. Somebody has to do all that: of course I'll do it."

Radmila leaned in. "And you, Glyn Montgomery: You think you're pretty smart, but you'd better work like you've never worked before. Because the Firm's gotten fat and lazy. We need skill and discipline. You think you know what pain and trouble is all about? You are the fair-haired child of fortune, girl! You don't know half of what it means to suffer in this world. Well, I do know that: and you *will* know it. So you just get ready."

Glyn stared at her in astonishment. Glyn was genuinely frightened. But Glyn was frightened in a new and different and much more constructive way.

This was going to work. This had to work. Radmila would make it work.

RADMILA'S FAMILY COUP D'ÉTAT went according to Glyn's careful plan. If the new Montgomery-Montalban system was not yet a regime, it was at least a provisional government. It was a huge emotional relief to the Family-Firm that someone—anyone—had stepped into the aching gap left by Toddy Montgomery.

So that first bold act would carry Radmila a little ways, but to cement her position, she would need a Dispensation-style juggernaut of rapid and effective action.

So: a major household remodeling project. The Bivouac was well overdue for a remake and remodel, and it was one arena where Radmila would not be challenged.

Toddy Montgomery had placed the gymnasium in the basement of the mansion, for a lady did not show her public that she had to sweat. Obviously, in the modern Los Angeles star system, where stars were physically dominant, swaggering street presences, the gym had to become the lady's power base.

So: Radmila moved the gymnasium into the former Situation Room. Radmila hired—not Frank Osbourne, he was too much the seasoned establishment starchitect—but one of Osbourne's best disciples, a younger woman freshly gone into her own practice. This young architect was ambitious, modish, and contemporary, and she badly needed a leg-up.

Grateful for her big break, the new decorator didn't dawdle. Radmila's new gym was transformed. It was no longer a dusty place of clanking iron and steroidal machismo. No, it was the "Transformation Spa," a gleaming balletic wonderland of Zen river pebbles embedded in clear Perspex, reactive areogel yoga mats, sunlight-friendly, semitranslucent, ultra-high-strength oxide ceramic roof panels, with a one-way treatment that repelled passing spyplanes . . .

Furthermore—lest the Family-Firm feel neglected—the newly emptied basement was swiftly transmuted into the new Situation Room, or rather, the Montgomery-Montalban Situation Bunker.

If California was facing a looming supervolcano, then the revived and vigorous Family-Firm would not wring their hands about that challenge. Their new Situation Bunker was entirely mounted on tremor-proof springs, and fully sealable against volcanic, seismic, atomic, biological, and chemical mishaps.

The Situation Bunker was soberly traditional in its design philosophy— American Superpower traditional. It was a bunker fit for the Joint Chiefs of Staff Planning for D-Day: pragmatic, sleek, no-nonsense, efficient, incorruptible, and continental in scale. Very Bell System, very Westinghouse, very General Motors.

There was some mild grumbling about Radmila's ambitious reforms, but Glyn held up her end, Uncle Jack was with her all the way, Lionel was infallibly enthusiastic, and there were no Family arguments at all about the new nursery.

Furthermore, no one could deny that a young matriarch was much more fun than an elderly matriarch. For all Toddy's wisdom and street smarts, Toddy's last years had had a Hapsburg Empire feeling, an overwrought, enfeebled system tottering toward its grave on a baroquely gilt walker. With Radmila in charge, the Family-Firm had a spring in its step again. There was a clear dynamic visible. There was forward motion.

Since the house was not finished, the Family could not die.

Radmila moved more of the star budget into the coming generation: Lionel and Mary. Let it not be said of her that she was personally hogging the limelight and eating the Family's seed corn. No: she aspired to be steady, dutiful, fully professional, an engine of production.

Radmila still went to her gym, but not with the fanatical intensity of a front-line diva. A woman planning for motherhood needed some body fat. Even if Radmila didn't bear the biblical horde of kids that Glyn demanded, there would have to be one. One or two. Three. There would have to be children, no matter how one felt about one's husband: any Queen of England knew that. That was a dynast's reality.

Early October arrived. Soon John would return from his meanderings in the Adriatic. The Family-Firm would be watching that reunion with care; it was a crucial performance for Radmila. She was determined to ace it.

Radmila performed her gym routine—"the worst thing that would happen all day"—and retired into her new oneiric pod for beauty sleep. This brand-new gym pod—oblate, speckled, seamed, it looked like a giant hemp seed—was said to feature all kinds of exotic benefits to neural well-being. It was like a Zen spa with a hinge.

As far as Radmila could tell, there was little more to this pricey dream machine than Californian hype. The pleasant flashing lights, the droning swoony ambient noises, and the so-called aroma "therapy" had done nothing much for her, or to her. Still, given that she was one of the product's sponsors and it was quite a handsome little earner, she saw no harm in using it.

Radmila climbed into the pod and clicked it shut. This time, as she fell into a pleasant doze, something about the pod's routine touched her brain—not with the harshness of an Acquis neural intrusion, but in a civilized, consumer-friendly fashion.

Radmila tumbled into a lucid, prophetic dream.

She dreamed that John had come home. John was not the gloomy, burdened, and apologetic philanderer whose company she dreaded. No, he was the younger John, the daring swain who had discovered her. In Los Angeles, Radmila had tried so hard to be a skulking stateless nameless thing, and yet John had located her, and John knew who she was and where she came from. He even cared about her and what happened to her.

She had little more to offer this prince than sweet surrender, but this seemed to be what the prince most desired from a woman in his life. Her abject emotional and sexual dependence on him steadied his self-image. He was no longer a rich young parlor radical with some rather sinister interests in emergent technologies. John Montgomery Montalban was made powerful by his marriage to her. She was his proof to himself that he had the power to transform himself and others.

Here he was back again, smiling and full of good cheer, the young John, the tech magician, and he had brought her mysterious gifts, as he always liked so much to do: two of his black hobby-objects. One hobject was a fizzing black shoe box, and the other one was even more mysterious, high-technical, and powerful, and it was . . . in stern dream logic . . . another fizzing black shoe box . . .

"Eureka!" cried the young John in his ecstasy: charismatic and sexy. "I have saved the world!"

What could it be? John was so busy with his colored wires and tubes . . . Never a moment for her, not a smile, not a kiss or hug . . . The first black shoe box was nothing much, the even more sinister shoe box was nothing much either, but to *connect* the two shoe boxes . . . Of course! Networking! A network would change everything!

Now the brilliant John, with all the passionate conviction that had first won her heart, was declaiming something solemn and arcane and yet fantastically convincing about his amazing black boxes . . . The first was sonoluminescent cold fusion, a host of screaming tiny bubbles hotter than the surface of the sun . . .

Banging on the shoe box, yes, John cried, sonoluminescence, a true miracle technology that had never quite worked yet.

The second fizzing black box was chemosynthetic black bubbling slime straight from the Freudian bottom of the ocean . . . It was a true biological miracle, it made life from darkness and nothing, it could live on pure volcano goo . . . John was pulling the black volcano goo out of his black box as he ranted about it to no one in particular, it was stinking of primeval sulfur, it was oily, drippy, satanic, it was all over his hands, it was running down his perfect sleeves like black blood . . .

Bubbling wildly as it dribbled, spewing oxygen in fizzing sheets, it was the stuff of breath and life, this stinky chemo goo bubbling merrily like California champagne . . .

The radiation from the fusion bubbles was *wildly stimulating* the black slime bubbles, somehow it was exactly what the germs needed to do their magic. The radiation was a tonic to the magic germs, it made their metabolism a hundred times more efficient, no, a thousand times, a million times . . .

Her husband's black boxes were slurping poison out of the air, just vacuuming carbon dioxide, fizzing like reverse geysers now, all yeasty and industrial . . .

She wanted to laugh wildly in her dread and ecstasy, for the two black bubbling boxes were sucking centuries of industrial poison out of the sky, just gobbling pollution and turning it back into coal and crude oil, literally *tearing the filth right out of the firmament!* The unhealthy sky under which she had passed her whole life was peeling back before her dreaming eyes like a wrinkled skin on badly scalded milk . . . and behind that skein of horror and decline and utter hopelessness, the revitalized sky was blue, blue, bluer-than-bluebird blue . . .

Radmila's eyes shocked open. She tore herself from the gentle grip of the hallucination. She pried herself from the oneiric pod . . . She lay breathing shallowly on the color-coded elastic floor of the new gym . . . Her head was reeling. What on Earth had that machine done to her? It had torn something loose within her, something dark and ugly and yet integral to her being . . . It had oiled and loosened up some ancient trauma within her . . . It had popped off of her like a rust flake.

She had lost something dark and complicated deep within herself. She was a different person now. Freer, much easier at heart. She felt footloose. Mellowed. Agile and even giggly. Full of honest joy.

She stared at a fluffy morning cloud through the tinted panels of the roof. "Oh my God," she told the cloud, "I've finally become a Californian."

RADMILA AND TODDY HAD ALWAYS ATTENDED the same hairdressing lab. This salon lab was an intensely private place, likely the best such lab in the world. Staffed by committed cosmeceutical professionals, it was chilly, hushed, and cheerless. That state-of-the-art establishment was much frequented by the political elite. Generally Toddy and Radmila went there together, arriving in a Family limo with darkly tinted windows, then departing under deep cover.

Sometimes there were clouds of hobject spyplanes whizzing over the place, all run by paparazzi idiots with websites. These toys never got anywhere and never saw a thing, for the hairdressing lab was the single most secure locale that Radmila knew.

Radmila had spent a great deal of the Family's money at the hair designers'—for the Family partly owned the lab. This fact didn't make the local hair designers treat Radmila any better. On the contrary.

Presented with a fresh surge of Family capital, they had simply and brusquely ripped out all of her hair. The new implants, their roots soaked in fresh stem cells, were state-of-the-art: radiant blond filaments that were genuine human hair, but with a much-enhanced ability to behave.

Radmila's damaged scalp was soaked with hot, wet, antiseptic foam. Her head was locked by a stainless fume hood where robot surgical arms whirred on tracks, took unerring aim, and deftly pierced her scalp. Implanting fresh hair took forever, like being tattooed. And, of course, it hurt a great deal.

Any session at the hair lab was always boring and painful. Today it was extravagantly painful, but it was no longer boring.

Because her brother Djordje had demanded an audience with her. And, so as to show Glyn that she had fully renounced all her troubles—she had agreed to meet Djordje in person.

With a final vindictive burst of needling at the nape of her neck, the hairdressing robot finished stitching her scalp. A somber, white-suited technician arrived, removed the metal hood, rinsed her deftly, and wrapped her head in a hot medicated turban.

The fresh implants twitched in her violated scalp, itching like lice. Few women in modern Los Angeles knew what lice were like, but Radmila was one of them. Toddy Montgomery had known what lice were like, too. Lila Jane Dickey—the larval, teenage form of Toddy Montgomery—she had known about lice, and she had known much worse things.

"So—you really don't hate me anymore?" Djordje said, rocking on his heels and watching her as she suffered. It was terrible to have Djordje standing so close to her. He was literally consuming her air.

Djordje—or "George Zweig"—was a tall, hefty, somewhat out-of-shape Viennese businessman in a tasteless European suit. He looked like he was wearing the clothes that his silly wife was buying him. He sported a thick, bristling mustache, and Radmila could swear he was carelessly losing his hair. Why didn't he take care of all that?

"Djordje, you are one of my husband's business associates. I don't enjoy seeing you. But I'll see you for political reasons, because I know that global politics has to trump my merely personal concerns."

"That is great news," said Djordje. "Your cordial attitude is very cheering. You talk much more sense than the other girls do. I am proud of you, Radmila, truly I am. Because you have become 'Mila Montalban'! Your career is amazing! You're the only one of us to truly *succeed* . . . you're an American superstar!"

Djordje pinched the bridge of his beefy nose between his thumb and forefinger. "Events went badly in Mljet. I don't know what John has told you about that. Vera is hostile and ignorant. She is mentally unstable. She has fled into some disaster area in the mainland Balkans and she will not speak to anybody."

"I don't care. Do not mention her name to me. Please."

"Right. Sure! Fine!"

There was a horrid silence between them.

"I have two children," Djordje told her. "May I show you their pictures? They're normal children."

"Shut up."

"Fine," said Djordje. "Let me tell you why I flew here, all the way to Los Angeles." He licked his mustached lip. "Your friend . . . your *husband*, Mr. John Montgomery Montalban, has met with a small business setback, as I said to you. A lot of Acquis capital was invested in reviving Mljet, and there was broad hope for a general consensus that—"

"I'm glad that part's over, at least," said Radmila.

"What?"

"Those atrocities that the Acquis were committing on that filthy little island. Those attention camps. The brainwashing. My head hurts all over just thinking about that. John may not own that island yet—that scheme was a stretch, even for John—but I'm sure that John has put a swift end to that business."

"Mr. Montalban still hopes and plans to turn the island into an entertainment destination . . . I did my best to help him there, but . . ."

"I don't want you to talk to John any longer. Or to Glyn, either. Leave Glyn alone. You have no place within my Family-Firm. Do you understand that? You're an intruder and your presence isn't welcome."

Djordje's face changed. It became much harder. "I do understand that," he told her, "but I must point out that it was John Montgomery Montalban who came looking for *me*. I don't have the vast wealth that you have slyly married into—because I made my own way in this world. I mind my own business. My logistics business. Primarily, interface logistics between the Acquis and the Dispensation. Your husband has meddled in an Acquis project while enlisting my help. He has compromised my relationship with the Acquis."

"Take your problems up with John."

"You just told me *not* to take my problems up with John. I can cut my relations with your John—he's a very charming fellow, but he's not entirely faithful to his word. Still, I want to be made whole with the Acquis. I want a return to my status quo ante before your husband interfered with my business affairs. That's only proper, isn't it?"

"Suppose that I solve your problems. Do you promise you'll stay far away from Los Angeles, Djordje? You won't contact me, or anyone in my Family, anymore?"

"I might agree to those terms, Radmila. If Dr. Feininger also agrees to your terms. Dr. Feininger also flew with me here to Los Angeles. He wants to redress this unfortunate Mljet situation. Dr. Feininger is upset. He has good reasons for that. If you can mollify him, then I will do as you ask. Otherwise, you and I have a quarrel."

"You're threatening me."

"I'm glad that you noticed," Djordje said cheerily. "If you don't want my threats, then don't offend me. Let's just be reasonable . . . no, let's be pretty! You are so pretty, Radmila! What on Earth did they do to you, all those movie-star people?"

"We're not *movie* stars, for God's sake. We're just 'stars.'"

"In Vienna, we still love the old cinema. We love many fine, civilized things, in Vienna. It would be pleasant if you Americans would stop degrading them."

Radmila ached to leap to her feet and slap the smirk off Djordje's face. It was a luminous, creeping, burning urge.

Toddy would never strike a man in the face. What would Toddy do?

Radmila smiled sweetly and touched one finger to her cheek.

Djordje's eyes widened.

"Djordje dear, your friend has come a long way to Los Angeles, under some trying circumstances. I apologize to you for your present difficulties. I promise that I did not intend those troubles. Why don't you check out of this clinic, retrieve your possessions from security, and send your Dr. Feininger in here to see me? I have an offer to make to your Acquis friend and I think he will be pleased to hear it."

"You mean all that?"

"Yes, I do, and I don't lack for resources. I plan to put things right, and I'll trust to your sense of decency not to trouble my Family further."

"That strange tone of voice, that way you move your lips," Djordje marveled. "That is *amazing*. You've truly changed, Radmila. You're gorgeous, you're famous, you're rich . . . You're a complete alien! I hope you're happy."

"I'm happy when the people I love are happy."

"What a wonderful, inspiring thing to say. Those words give me such hope. I watch all your performances! You truly have talent! Don't believe those bad reviews. You're improving steadily!"

Radmila said nothing. She assembled a smile.

"Radmila, you are so much closer to escaping our curse than the rest of us. Maybe that has been fated to happen. As children . . . we were created and raised as an evil plan for this world. But in a world as truly evil as our world truly is—maybe we can act for good. When I look at you, I can almost believe that."

"I'm glad that we had this heart-to-heart talk, George. It has cleared the air. Let's not keep your important friend waiting."

Djordje shuffled from polished foot to foot on the antiseptic clinic floor. He seemed genuinely moved. "Listen, Radmila: Please be careful with him. Dr. Feininger is my friend. That doesn't make him *your* friend. He should have taken his issues up with your husband. For him to come here to confront you, instead: That's not good news for you."

"Oh, I may be only a humble star, but I am from a political family. I've met Acquis pundits before."

Muttering, dithering, intolerable, Djordje finally left her alone. At last, Radmila was able to draw one clean, untainted breath. Her heartbeat slowed. That had been very bad.

But it was not so entirely bad as she had feared. She'd managed to play her way through that ordeal. She'd simply acted her way through it without ever breaking character. Stardom was full of suffering.

Radmila even felt a little bit guilty about refusing to glance at the pictures of Djordje's children. Maybe someday she'd be able to meet Djordje's children and establish some kind of relationship with them. After Djordje was dead, of course. That was a pleasant thought: especially the part about Djordje dying.

Once, and once only since leaving Mljet, Radmila had met one of her sisters: Sonja. They had simply blundered into each other: of all the people in the unlucky world. The horror had occurred on a peaceful tourist overlook above the glassy ruins of New York.

Radmila had glimpsed a pretty woman in a Chinese military uniform, brandishing a pair of elaborate binoculars, leaning at the railing of the overlook, and carefully studying the blast pattern.

Then that woman, sensing danger somehow, had turned and looked back, and that woman was Sonja.

Before Radmila could decide on anything, to scream or to run, Sonja had stalked straight over, silently, fluidly, and kicked Radmila in the stomach. Sonja's black-booted foot came blasting forward with blinding, immediate, practiced speed and slammed all the wind out of Radmila. That devastating kick had knocked her cold.

Other tourists had helped her after Sonja had stomped away. When John arrived, deeply worried, Radmila had lied to him. She had claimed that she had fainted, overcome by the shocking sight of the famous ruins of New York. John, who had loved her very much at the time, had known at once that she was lying to him. All kinds of trouble had followed from that.

The trauma of that event had been much worse than confronting Djordje, here in her home stronghold of Los Angeles. Being a man, and the last and the youngest, Djordje was less painful than the others. Djordje had always been different in that way.

At least she knew that Djordje would go away. Djordje was a traitor: he had always excelled at running away.

Now Dr. Feininger entered the hairdressing clinic. The Acquis diplomat seemed discomposed. The hairdressers' security people were even more ruthless to visitors than they were to the clientele.

"How do you do, Dr. Feininger? Let me persuade the staff to fetch you a chair."

"Oh no no, please, I don't want to speak with those people." Dr. Feininger had an overly perfect, German-accented English. She could hear him carefully machining his verb tenses. "So: Miss Mila Montalban, at last we meet. In person, so much smaller you seem than in your simulations!"

· Radmila offered him a tender smile. "You flew here from Europe just to meet me? How exceptional!"

"Yes, I have what they used to call 'jet lag'!" Feininger pretended to yawn into his manicured hand.

"Please tell me all about your fascinating trip!"

"I logged every minute on my pundit site," said Feininger, shifting on his feet. "Round and round we spin inside that ring of magnets, many gravities . . . We were fired into suborbital arc . . . Free-fall, truly weightless . . . ! You could see all of it! Though I don't compare my mediation with yours."

"I'm sure that your pundit site is very popular with your viewers." Feininger's enthusiasm for his toys reminded her of John. She had

Feininger tagged by now: he was what they called an Acquis "thought leader."

As a postgovernmental organization, the Acquis was peppered all over with radical, crazy extremists, but pompous, netcentric blowhards like this guy were the organization's meat and bread.

Nothing ever made pious, politically correct Acquis geeks happier than some dully public "frank exchange of views." Radmila had met so many of them, at so many tiresome, life-draining political events, that she could literally smell Acquis thought leaders. Dr. Feininger smelled of cologne.

"What city is your own home base, Dr. Feininger?"

"My base is Cologne."

Radmila laughed musically. "Such a beautiful city!"

"I never expected to meet an American star so simply and modestly dressed," said Feininger, eyeing her cleavage in her terry-cloth gown. "One expects an American star to . . . well . . . billow, if that's the right word."

"Oh, we stars do billow. But this is my private life, and I chose to meet you here very privately."

"I understand that important distinction," said Feininger. "In political life, one also treads a fine line between public credibility and personal authenticity."

"It was brave of you to personally fly to Los Angeles," said Radmila. "I'm so proud that spaceflight is finally returning to vogue! Aerospace once meant a lot to California. We're so sentimental about our heritage . . . New attitudes from Europe, that's encouraging. We have some new American launch methods—those giant slingshots, I forget what you men call those . . ."

"Those are called 'tensile accelerators.' "

"Yes, that was it." Radmila nodded respectfully. "Dr. Feininger, do you suppose, someday, those two methods might be combined? Then we could settle outer space—mankind's dream come true!"

"I happen to know rather a lot about this topic," said Feininger unsurprisingly. "Sadly I must inform you that no, the Acquis spaceflight methods, which are very extensively tested and constructed on the strictest precautionary principles, are by no means the same techniques as the aberrant efforts of certain American zealots who fling giant nanocarbon slingshots up the slopes of the Rocky Mountains."

"Have you ever seen that kind of space launch performed, Dr. Feininger?"

"What, me? No, certainly not."

"Would you *like* to see that done? My Family-Firm has a private launchpad."

"I see. I wasn't aware of that."

"Yes, we need that private launchpad in order to reach our private space station."

"I did know that the Montgomery-Montalbans had built a space station."

"Well, we didn't exactly *build* that. The Government of India built LilyPad. We simply took over management when India suffered their difficulties."

"Terrible business about India."

"Very terrible. We have so much to learn from Indian spiritual values."

Feininger wasn't happy about his lack of a chair or the way he'd been treated by the local staff, but he was clearly pleased to meet a Hollywood star so willing to talk his kind of utter crap.

"I like to think," said Feininger slowly, "that I have rather good instincts about people. You are not at all like your public image. I can sense that the private Mila Montalban is a rather fresh, direct, and unpretentious woman."

"I hope you won't tell anybody that," Radmila twinkled. "My public-relations people get all upset with me when I fail to allure and mystify."

"May I ask you something, Miss Montalban? Not a personal question, but a public political issue? Why do you own a giant war machine that destroys the homes of helpless refugees with heat rays?"

"What, you mean in an immersive-world simulation? I can't remember my roles in immersive worlds—there are just too many."

"No, I meant last August," said Feininger politely. "In the streets of Los Angeles. You were lasciviously dancing on the top of a giant walking tripod that fired laser weapons into people's homes."

"Oh that!" said Radmila. "You mean our urban-renewal festival."

"That behavior truly baffles us in the Acquis," said Feininger.

"Please try not to worry," said Radmila, wide-eyed. "I'm just an actress. It's all for show."

"Leaving aside the social-justice aspects of preferentially wrecking the neighborhoods of the poor," said Feininger, "are you aware of what happens, technically speaking, within the legs of those tripods?"

"Should I be?"

"I know the sinister genius who constructed that device," said Feininger. "His name is Frank Osbourne, and he *repeatedly* seeks out radical construction methods that are judged unsafe by Acquis central committee. Then Osbourne *deploys* those methods! Not in harmless simulations—in *real life*! He builds structures with dangerous crystalline iron and unproven nanocarbon piezo-cables, and then he uses those hazardous devices to *demolish historical buildings*. A deliberate provocation!"

"Frank is a very theoretical architect," said Radmila. "I think you're reading too much into his acts of whimsy."

Toddy's tea trolley rolled into the room. Toddy had gone to repeated effort to have tea served as she recovered from her hair-design interventions. Toddy would sit, sip tea, and stare into her hobject globes . . .

Toddy was no longer here, yet her infrastructure had survived her. Fresh tea had just arrived for the insane husk of a woman who'd been quietly fired into orbit.

"Oh, the tea is here!" Radmila chirped. "I do hope you like Indian tea, Dr. Feininger."

"It's Indian tea?"

"Yes of course! They're restoring plantations in Assam!"

With surprising spryness and multicultural fluidity, Feininger sat cross-legged on the floor.

Radmila joined him, arranged the cups, and poured. Their ritual took a leisurely six minutes. They scarcely spoke. When they were done, the two of them had reached a certain level of rapport.

Radmila fully understood why the Acquis pundit had attacked Frank Osbourne. Osbourne was a Dispensation architect. So naturally Osbourne would push the limits of whatever the Acquis considered acceptable practice. Feininger was not truly upset about Osbourne. Feininger was angry because of Mljet.

Feininger wasn't wearing a neural helmet or attention-camp blinders—Feininger was a professional, he wasn't some crazy Acquis engineer of human souls—but Feininger knew that John had gone to Mljet to interfere with that effort.

The Acquis cadres in Mljet were cranks, radicals, and zealots. Of course some Dispensation agent had arrived there for containment and push-back. John had ventured to Mljet as a Dispensation activist.

John would lure the cranks aside with a tasty carrot if he could; if that effort failed, he would slide a stick straight through their spinning wheels.

Because John seemed so polite and refined, people underestimated him. His quietest attacks, always carried out in a low, scholarly voice while wearing a business suit, were brutally effective.

Feininger understood modern global realpolitik. His bluster about the architect was his counterploy. Feininger was radiating the obvious: she could sense that in the poised way he held his teacup.

Acquis interests had been threatened on a certain part of the global game board. Feininger could try to defend that dodgy Adriatic territory—those weirdos with helmets and skeletons—or he could boldly and swiftly fly over to counterattack within Los Angeles. That was what Feininger had come here to demonstrate.

All in all, his choice of a target—the Family's favorite Los Angeles architect—that was a civilized gambit. Feininger had to know about Vera in Mljet. He could have been nastier with her.

Feininger would not get nasty, because Feininger was almost exactly like John. Dr. Feininger was an Acquis counter-John. Dr. Feininger, having learned what John could do, was planning to out-John John. Dropping by to put a scare into Mrs. John—there must be Acquis strategists chuckling over that tactic, behind a network screen someplace.

"Dr. Feininger, I'm only a pop star. While you are a moralist. A thought leader. You're a global techno-social philosopher."

Feininger laughed. "If it's any help, we go through vogues just like you do."

"I know about the Acquis. We Americans have a lot of Acquis people. In Boston, San Francisco, Seattle . . . Still, they can't compare to the truly global Acquis thought leaders. The American Acquis don't think as creatively as you do."

"I didn't expect to hear this from you," Feininger allowed. "This might be significant."

"I'm thinking: we need to try something unexpected. Fresh. Contemporary. Of the moment. Something unexpectable."

"This should be interesting."

"Mind you, this is just my own personal proposal. I'm in no position to dictate terms to my Family-Firm—I hope you understand that."

"I know who Mila Montalban is," said Feininger, smiling at her. "So do half the people in the world."

"Well, I'm thinking: a public event. Nothing too 'global.' Because that word sounds so old-fashioned now. I'm thinking *postglobal*. Superglobal. A quiet, elite kind of political summit. Held in orbit."

"A political summit held in orbit?"

"Yes, up in LilyPad. You wouldn't exactly call LilyPad 'the space frontier' . . . because sweet LilyPad is not a primitive place, exactly . . . but it's certainly *remote*. And, Dr. Feininger: We don't want any *boring*, *tedious* people at our theory summit held in outer space. We should be inviting: the very exceptional, very high-level thinkers . . . visionary, nonpartisan people, the people far outside the global box . . . Not even one hundred people. The truly significant postglobal civil society thinkers. Maybe fifty of you."

Feininger considered this suggestion. He was flattered to be one of the world's fifty most important thinkers. Then it dawned on him that he was being asked to pick and validate the other forty-nine.

This was much more important to him than any small Adriatic island.

"Seventy people?" he said.

"Sixty, at the very most? We'd be stretching the launch services."

"If you could launch fifty, the magnetic pad in Eastern Germany could launch twenty-five."

"We could *house* seventy people. We could feed them and give them nice fresh air."

"You could do that? You're sure?"

"Not me personally as a society hostess, but the Montgomery-Montalban Family-Firm . . . Our guests rarely complain about our hospitality."

A slow smile appeared on Feininger's lips. "And would your space event have cachet, Miss Montalban?"

"Europe does cachet, sir. Here in California, we do glamour. And we do glamour by the metric ton."

Feininger set his teacup down with a tender clink. "Glory, lightness, speed, and brilliancy."

RADMILA WALKED THE ARTIFICIAL BEACH, vamped before the floating cameras, and gazed into the sun-glittering Pacific. Six lunatics were surfing out there. For the life of her, Radmila could not understand surfers in Los Angeles. Obviously riding on a wave was a nice stunt performance, but *inside the ocean?* There were whole chunks and shoals of broken China bobbing around out there, all glass, nails, slime, and toxic jellyfish.

The scanty fabric of Radmila's swimsuit belonged to a sponsor. So did the hairstyle, the watch, the sunglasses, and the hat. This privatized beach, like all modern tourist beaches, was a fake, as elaborate as an immersive world.

Radmila was looking sexy today, as contractually required. Looking sexy was a basic theatrical craft. The critical problem came when the severe labor of looking sexy made one forget to actually be sexy. Radmila did not feel at all sexy, in this swimsuit, on this beach. She felt dread.

Certain men direly wanted to have sexy sex with professionally beautiful women: sex with the stars. Those men were delusionary. Sex with a star was an awful idea, like having sex with a rosebush. You were not supposed to get into bed with a rosebush. You were supposed to give it horse manure and sell the blossoms.

Radmila knew that her most loyal fans, her truest devotees, were not men gloating over her gym-toned body and her tawny, sunlit skin: her biggest fans were all women. They were humbled, jittery, self-critical women with an underlying streak of resentful violence. Her fans were women very much like herself, except less lucky and more stupid.

She, Radmila Mihajlovic, had become Miss Mila Montalban. She had done that because she had, almost by miracle, found the technical and financial capacity. There was just no way—no way at all, no way in hell—that the similar fantasies of her fans could ever be fulfilled.

The fans could never become like the stars. This body that flaunted its perfect female curves before the camera: she had created this body through an exhausting, comprehensive ordeal. Having seven children was easier, for that was the sort of thing untrained women had once done without anesthetic.

So she wasn't walking on a beach, being pretty. She was tormenting her fans with her star glamour. In some strange way, this unity in frustrated suffering was the true relationship of stars and fans.

That was why her fans loved to see her suffer. Fans knew that she deployed her charm and beauty as a weapon to tantalize, and they were spiteful about that torment and they wished her the worst. Their hatred and envy of celebrities could be lethal.

It was especially awful to "confide" to one's fans, artlessly discussing one's starry hotness, through some low-life aggregator of planetary eyeballs . . . Pretending to reveal her personal secrets to the fans was the worst and vilest toil in the industry.

"Exclusive star interviews." They were ancient rituals. They always made her long for death.

Yet the fans had to be fed. For the fans were forever hungry.

"Yes, my John brings truth and justice to some of the most desperate people in the world . . . I miss John every day. I want John to fly home to me. He promised he would break his own rules and he'll fly here in a rocket. Yes, those rumors are true. No, not that we're breaking up. That'll never happen! The rumors are true that the fire is back in our relationship! John and I had our rough spots, we had our trouble and grief, but you just can't keep us down! Just you wait and see, you're going to see some very good, very happy news from both of us . . ."

When the interview at last expired in its puddle of flaccid lies, she fled in a Family limo, then went to join Lionel. Lionel was kind to her, because Lionel understood these things.

Lionel was having a late lunch at a posh restaurant. The restaurant was noted for its excellent seafood, because it marched on gleaming centipede legs deep into the restive ocean and it grew all its seafood by itself. The "swordfish," for instance . . . that gleaming white flesh on Lionel's platter was very far from a wild, sea-native swordfish, but a DNA scan would never tell.

Lionel had matured a great deal since Toddy had (as the Family privately phrased it) "passed up." His personal upgrades had cost much more than Radmila's makeover, and since Lionel was so young and ductile, the effects on him were drastic.

Lionel had put on kilos of male muscle in his back, legs, and shoulders. His eyebrows were thicker, and blue stubble haunted his lips and chin.

Most critically, Lionel had changed his signature look. The new personal dresser had swiftly ditched his Peter Pan delinquent street-kid costumes, and made Lionel sexier, more transgressive. He looked like a bad boy in power now. He looked slicker, like the upscale version of an undercover cop.

Radmila arrived at the table, hidden in stage-ninja gear. None of the diners took much notice of her: Lionel always had his bodyguards in this restaurant. Lately he'd had a whole posse of them. The Angeleno street gangs loved Lionel. They were his biggest fans.

Glyn silently passed her a menu and a half-empty shaker of tequila. Radmila poured and drank. Alcohol was blue ruin, but she wouldn't have to look so painfully sexy again for quite a while. She was going to put on weight. John was going to get her pregnant. That was all arranged.

The older Family folks—Guillermo, Freddy, Buffy, Raph—they'd been surprisingly calm and accepting about the new Family order. In the sudden power vacuum of Toddy's absence, it was Lionel, Toddy's grandchild, who was proving the hardest to handle.

Lionel was starting to have adult ideas. His generation's take on reality was unique.

"What does that mean, 'grasp the nettle'?" Lionel demanded.

"A nettle is a weed," Glyn told him. "It stings you when you touch it."

"But why would people let plants sting them? Plants don't even have brains."

"Our Family budget is like a nettle," Glyn told him patiently. "When you stick to that budget, that hurts, but you just have to accept that."

"We're rich."

"We're not infinitely rich, and a Family star is supposed to spend his star allowance on enhancing his star potential."

"That's what I did," said Lionel. "I know that I spent money, but I'm almost eighteen."

"Lionel: You bought weapons."

"Glyn: Just listen to me for once, okay? I'm not Little Mary Montalban, the world's most adorable child star! I'm a tough guy! I'm a ghetto, barrio, Los Angeles dirty-pop, kick-your-ass, street-credibility star! We do agree on that, don't we? I'm the Family's gangster star."

"You're Dispensation. You're a spontaneous-reaction, volunteer grassroots star of our street militias. Those people aren't 'gangsters.' "

Lionel sighed and looked to Radmila. "Mila, just tell her. Please."

"Lionel does have a certain point," Radmila said. "His core demographic is rebellious male teens. Especially, lower-income."

"That is where the Family placed me as an idol," Lionel said. "I am playing the role I was given. I'm playing straight to my fan base."

"*Weapons*, Lionel?"

"Sure, technically, shoulder-launched rockets are 'weapons.' But practically speaking, they're rapid urban-demolition equipment. You wouldn't know this, being a girl—but *very few people* ever get killed by shoulder-launched rockets. It's the *buildings* that get killed by shoulder-launched rockets. It's all about 'warchitecture.' "

Lionel pointed his leather-gloved finger outside the gorgeously lit restaurant window and at the gray, lightless, derelict structures lining the shore of the Pacific. That endless mummified seaside slum was a sight to daunt the bravest real-estate developer: armored in chain-link fencing, wrapped in razor wire, with ancient vidcams and hand-lettered death-threat signs. Many of the buildings were swathed in tattered plastic shrink-wrap against the rising damp.

"Ever since I was born," said Lionel, "I've had to look at that mess. That giant monument to human stupidity. I want that all gone. And no, I don't mean some nice legal settlement. I don't mean forty more years of insurance cheats and litigation. These are abandoned, uninhabitable ruins, ruined by the climate crisis. They belong to morons who don't even live there now and will *never* live there again. While *my* people, my viewers, my core audience, the poor people, Glyn, the street kids without shirts and shoes—they are living heaped up in their Little Foreign Ghetto villages. They are piled on top of each other like used tires."

Lionel clenched his gloved fists dramatically. "So we have two basic moral choices here. Either we do nothing about that, and the poor people eventually riot and set fire to their own slums. That would be the tra-

ditional Los Angeles method. Or else we provide some inspired civic
leadership. My people charge out here and they just *set fire to all that.*
Yes. My people just smash it. They blow it to pieces, and burn it to the
ground. It's all abandoned anyway—so that takes my fans maybe a
week."

Glyn was nervously fiddling with the restaurant's gorgeous silverware. The silverware was tagged and interactive and came with a dazzling panoply of oyster forks, butter knives, and two-tined olive piercers.
"You're really serious about this."

"Think it through, Glyn. Two years later, we've got a bunch of
flood-friendly projects built on high pilings. We get a major construction boom in LA. Sure, we get some legal trouble first—of course we
get that—but the casualties, *very low,* and suddenly we are right into a
brand-new era. Low-income housing—during a climate crisis—that's
got to be within the shoreline areas. That's got to happen. It's the only
urban policy that makes any sense. And if we had any guts, we'd just
do it."

Glyn glared at Radmila. "Your political scripter wrote that for him.
Lionel never used to talk like this. Never."

"No, no," Radmila said. "My scripter's not that good! I never heard
that kind of talk before."

"Who's writing your set-speeches, Lionel? Who have you been linking to?"

"Admit it," said Lionel smugly, "my set-speech just now was fantastic.
You don't have, like, one single good word to say against my awesome
new set-speech."

"Your gangster fans are gonna shoot each other with rockets! It'll be a
total bloodbath."

"Like you care about that!" scoffed Lionel. "All you want to do is
write games that send them running the streets like bowling pins. You've
got them where they can't tell immersive games from the LA street
grid."

Glyn shook her head. "I know that we can get away with some demolition work right after an earthquake. You're talking about smashing
the oldest, biggest real-estate mess in all of California. We'd be held responsible."

"Not you, Glyn: *me. I'm* the responsible party—and I am an underage juvenile. That's why my plan works. We just give them a very classic set pitch: He's the troubled rebel star kid burning out on drugs! That's a hundred-year-old Hollywood story, everybody knows it by heart. Sure, my fans become arsonists. My fans are juvenile delinquents, so they got in over their heads. So what? My fan base has got a lot to be arsonists about!"

Glyn was very troubled. "You actually *love* your fans, Lionel?"

"What else is a star for? Without them, we're nothing! Why else do I go through all this? I personify the blighted aspirations of my viewership, that's why I do it! That's why my fans pay to watch me work! If I give them an awesome carnival like this—hey, I'd become the Voice of a Generation."

Radmila leaned in over the table. "That was a very good monologue, Lionel. I feel proud of you. But that's extremely radical, and you're really pushing it. You can't just abrogate the legal process and set fire to large urban areas! Acquis pundits would show up and they'd hit us over the nose with a broomstick. That's just not how our Family-Firm does business in this town."

"Yes, I know that I'd be a scandal—but think in the long term. I'd just go into a dry-out clinic. That's all that would happen to me. Because I'm a kid! So I take a year off . . . over in . . . what the hell's that stupid island . . . in Mljet! Mljet would be perfect for the story. It's, like, wall-to-wall Acquis rehabilitation geeks over there. So: I go put on their neural helmet, their exoskeleton, their whole nine meters . . . That doesn't scare me! That's all very newsworthy. We just feed the people my ongoing personal scandal, we blow that spectacle up as big as it needs to get. They get obsessed with me—me, the star—and they just *forget* about the massive urban fires and the rocket explosions. I personally overshadow all of that. And my adventure costs our Family, what? The fare for my cruise ship? My reputation as a sweet-tempered kid? It costs us *nothing*! And in return—we'd liberate a huge, booming acreage of real estate in the world's most dynamic city!"

"Mila, you talk some sense into him."

"Glyn, he *is* talking sense. Pure Dispensation sense. That could really be made to pay."

"He wants to provoke a huge urban riot! He's going to burn down the slums in Los Angeles with an armed mob!"

"He's even smarter than his big brother. I didn't know that. Our Family-Firm has some true depth-of-talent."

Glyn was furious. "You're taking his side to annoy me! You know that isn't a reasonable policy! You're giving me all kinds of grief just because I'm not a star like you and him!"

Lionel smirked at her. "Glyn, you're always claiming that you want to produce, and not be a star. Okay, great, fine: Take my proposal to the Family-Firm. Go on, I dare you to put my plan onto their agenda! Those old-school folks have got some guts! You're a geek and a bean counter."

Defeated, Glyn turned angrily on Radmila. "You don't have any more sense than he does! I thought at least I could trust *you* to stay within your budget."

Radmila blinked. "What do you mean—you mean my space summit? 'The Theodora Montgomery Memorial Forum'? I know that's not some easy weekend in Bohemian Grove, but that'll pay off for us ten times over in the long run. Didn't you see how happy Buffy got when I tasked her to plan that? Buffy always wanted to be a political hostess."

Glyn scowled. "No, Mila, I didn't mean your Family duties. I meant your extravagances."

"My what? What extravagances? My hair? My skin? My mitochondrial upgrades? I'm totally pacing myself! You're making me have a baby."

"I mean your shopping sprees, Mila!"

Lionel was immediately interested. "What stuff did you buy? Was it nice?"

"I don't even know what Glyn's talking about."

"I've never interfered in your private purchases," Glyn said primly, "but the budget flagged me when you started going crazy . . . and with *what*? A hundred pairs of couture shoes, perfumes, lingerie, whole crates of bad Napa Valley champagne?"

Radmila was appalled. "When did that ever happen?"

"Two weeks. Three weeks. Since you took over the Family. You lost control: what happened to you?"

Lionel was agog. "Wow! John likes perfumes and lingerie?"

"What, is your brother crazy? John's a political activist, he likes girls who are weird refugees! Look: I don't have any time to shop for myself! I'm always in the gym or on the set! If I have one spare minute, I sleep!"

"Mila, if you didn't buy those things, who did?"

"It wasn't me. The last thing I personally bought was . . . I think I bought cousin Rishi some garden tools for a birthday present."

Glyn was intelligent, so it didn't take her long to defeat her false assumptions. "I was really stupid. I should have known that some idiot embezzled all that stuff. Someone is pretending to be Mila Montalban."

"Wow, that's identity theft!" said Lionel. "I thought that was impossible! I mean, they've got all kinds of secure biometrics and stuff."

Glyn and Radmila said nothing.

Lionel bulled on. "You know, I mean biometric security for your credit purchases—like, they measure your body so they know it can only be you."

Radmila put her fork aside and rubbed at her aching eyes.

"Okay, now I get it," said Lionel. "There is someone here who is just like you. There's a clone loose here in Los Angeles."

Glyn and Radmila glared at him silently.

"I mean, another clone besides both of you two gals. A clone who's like an evil-twin identity."

The two of them exchanged glances.

"Wow!" said Lionel. "That is dynamite! This is a hot entertainment property, all of a sudden! Because we're living in a real-life crime! How many suspects are there? Wait a minute, wait a minute—I already know that! There's Sonja . . . There's Vera from Mljet . . . Hey wait, there's your mom!"

Glyn leaned forward and slapped him.

A HOLE IN A SENSORWEB was called a "blackspot." The laws of physics decreed that there were always blackspots in the world. Computer science could assume perfectly smooth connections, but the Earth had hills and valleys and earthquakes and giant volcanoes. The sky had lightning storms, and even the sun had sunspots. Wireless connections were not magic fogs. Real-world wireless connections were waves, particles, bits: real things in real places.

So: If you didn't want to be seen, or heard, or known in a world of ubiquitous sensorwebs, there were options. You could find a blackspot. Or create a blackspot. Some blackspots were made by organized crime or official corruption. Other blackspots just grew in their natural blackness. Maybe there was nobody home to plug things in, or to reboot systems. Enterprises went broke, buildings fell down or went derelict.

The unsustainable could not be sustained. There were climate-crisis disaster areas—China, Australia, India, central Asia—where the blackspots were colossal.

When the seas rose, when hurricanes blew through, Earth tremors shook the land. Plague, famine, and pestilence . . . Stuff just got lost. Even in the modern world. Even in Los Angeles. There were always places in any major city where crime was visible, and yet tolerated. Red-light districts, narcotic shooting galleries, corporate boardrooms, city halls . . . There were thousands of tiny blackspots. Steel elevators. Brick basements. Narrow alleyways between two metal barns.

Or the black, stuffy, terrifying innards of a car trunk.

Sometimes people had mental blackspots hidden inside themselves. People forgot that they lived in a dangerous world. They prospered for a while, they got used to being privileged, they got fatally complacent. People forgot to see straight, they overlooked things, they stubbornly ignored the obvious.

You could try to obscure that human limitation, deputize it to surveillance systems, conceal all the seams, try to make the system perfect, perfect, superperfect, secure, secure, supersecure . . . but any simple breakdown in sanitation was enough to chase people away. Any place with no running water and no toilets was halfway to a blackspot already.

And you might end up in a place like that. Tied up. Abducted. Alone. Hungry. Thirsty. Humiliated. Reeking of your own urine.

Derelict buildings, dreadful places, worse even than the car trunk from which you had just been dragged . . . Even a little kid could set fire to a wrecked building. How many kids were you willing to wound, or injure, or kill with an automatic antitheft "armed response"? After all, the kids were just kids . . . kids were always trying to look around . . . explore . . . do some graffiti . . . throw some bricks through the glass windows . . . steal some furniture . . . vandalize the building and burn everything to the ground.

Teenagers were energetic and had poor impulse control. Teenage kids were stigmergic, they learned and acted like termites—they had no grand master plan, but they learned fast and easily from their peers, whatever they saw other kids doing.

So many places like that in Los Angeles . . . in every big town really . . . where security cameras had stored months of perfectly shot and focused video of a steadily gathering mayhem. The mere fact that a machine "saw" things happening didn't mean that a machine could apprehend the crime, prosecute it, convict it, put an end to it . . .

What if the surveillance itself was the victim of the crime? They called that "sousveillance"—when angry people countersurveilled the surveillance. Some bold souls made it their business to spy out all the surveillance spies, map them, track them, spot them, shoot them, steal them, hack them, tap them, hold the machines to ransom . . .

Radmila rolled around on the grimy, derelict, unlit floor, testing the plastic wires that bound her arms. Her wrists were cinched, her arms were trapped behind her back, her ankle was snagged to a piece of furniture. Wire had no knots. She couldn't break wire or pick wire or chew wire.

Nobody would ever find her in here. Not in this blackspot. She was as good as dead. That fast, that simple.

Radmila was strong and her body was flexible. Given a week, she might have shrugged and wriggled her way out of the wires. But whenever she worked hard to escape her bindings, she needed some air, and the duct tape over her mouth was there to deny her that air.

It was extremely dangerous to have her mouth duct-taped shut in this way. She could die easily from that, because she might begin to weep in here, from her fear and despair and shame, and then her nose would clog from the weeping, and she would black out, and smother to death in her own snot.

That simple, that quick, that dead.

She had vanished from her world in twenty seconds. She had left the set, carrying the heavy hem of her costume, and naturally followed a friendly, beckoning ninja security staffer, then suddenly, instantly, with no warning, *wham*, her elaborate costume went stone-dead all around her. Then she was body-blocked straight into the open trunk of a car.

In seconds, off rolled the car, one mobile blackspot with Mila Montalban hidden inside of it. Who would ever see that? Who would ever guess that? Who would know?

Frantic with herself, Radmila had managed to squirm free of her destroyed costume, inside the cramped black confines of the car trunk.

That was an impressive physical feat, something few women could have done, but the air was thick and stuffy in the black car trunk, and when she was done she was half stunned.

Then the trunk popped open. Before Radmila could think, act, or even shriek, she was struck by something that shot through her like lightning. Her hands were lassoed, her mouth gagged with tape.

When her kidnapper ran out of wire and tape—that took a while— she was hauled, ankles-first, up a set of barnacled stairs and through the yawning, graffiti-bombed door of a derelict Malibu beach house.

This blackspot lair featured drooling patches of mold on every wall, warped wooden flooring, strange arching cantilevered walls of old cement . . . custom-designed and full of architectural genius. This must have been a gorgeous Malibu beach getaway, once, back when the sky was stable and the sea behaved itself. Some nice place for a rich family.

The airy living room, its sea-viewing windows sprayed opaque, was full of loot.

Someone had been on some dainty feminine crime spree. Cosmetics, mostly. Sweet, tempting little beauty kits that a thieving woman could easily hide in her hands. And other loot, more ambitious: handbags, women's boots and shoes . . . stockings, perfumes, jewelry exploding from small discarded plush boxes . . . pink-cased electronics, sexy vicuña scarves, sunglasses in crushproof cases, cashmere throw rugs, thirsty towels, thirsty hand towels, thirsty face towels . . . Thirsty tampons, thirsty condoms . . . And crates and crates of thirsty booze.

Dying of thirst from the shock of her abduction, unable to move her bound, numbed arms, Radmila stared in anguish at a wooden rack of California chardonnays.

After dark fell, Biserka returned from her busy wanderings. Biserka was still wearing the Family-Firm ninja costume she'd used when she had kidnapped Radmila, only now this fake, phony costume of hers—it was amazing how shoddy it looked now, it was a cheap, halfhearted effort like some kid's Hollywood souvenir—it was ominously covered with freshly dug dirt.

Biserka plucked her black ninja hood off and ran her black-gloved fingers through her sweaty, smashed, blond hairdo. Biserka had six fancy emerald studs in her ears and green weepy eyeliner streaming down both cheeks. She'd been sweating like a pig inside that cheap costume.

"Time for Miss Montalban to go walkies," Biserka remarked.

Radmila lashed out and kicked Biserka in the shin. Biserka stepped back, with a sour, tired expression. She then came around, leaned down, and pinched Radmila's nose shut with her thumb and finger.

In moments Radmila had a scarlet agony in her lungs and fatal darkness roaring in her ears.

"You don't do that again," Biserka explained. She left, stooped behind the couch, opened a beautiful shoplifted Italian leather satchel. She removed a bloodstained parole breaker's knife. It had the blackened chips, the melted plastic, and the stink.

She then seized a hank of Radmila's hair and sawed loose a fistful of it.

She threw the hair into Radmila's watering eyes. "Do you want to walk for me now, or will there be more attitude?"

Radmila gusted air through her nose and shook her head.

Biserka stuck her fingers through the network of cinched wires around Radmila's chest. She hauled her upright, with an effort. Tired, she changed her mind and shoved Radmila onto an abandoned couch, which exploded with dust.

"I have a feeling we won't see this locale again," Biserka said, gazing around the mold-spotted walls and the damp-collapsed ceiling. "That is such a pity, but, you know, you get a sixth sense about a blackspot. I'm a girl who has a very negative rapport with ubiquitous systems."

Biserka's English had an odd foreign accent. It might have been French, or Chinese, or maybe both French and Chinese.

"I travel light," said Biserka, "so we have to leave my toys here as a nice surprise for sneaky kids. Kids these days! They love to steal, because they have so little . . . But professional theft is over! All the smart players traffic in revenge! Vendetta. Venganza. Rache. That's the universal language. It's hard to steal from people—but to steal *the people* . . . Goods are trackable, but people are *stalkable*."

Biserka gazed around her derelict hideout and sighed. "All my pretty toys! Should I burn the house down? You think?"

Biserka rummaged in a handcrafted box that might once have contained some fine hobject. "I do want my pearls. They're my favorites. I'll let you carry my pearls." Biserka sank her clawed fingers into a mass of strung pearls and pulled them out like cold spaghetti.

"I was being funny, you know, because 'Biserka' means 'Pearl.' So I tell the jewelers: 'I'm Mila Montalban, show me all your pearls.' And they are like: 'Oh yes certainly Miss Montalban! Such a pleasure to see you here in person! Would you like to see the wild pearls from the years before the seacoasts rose, or would you like to see the modern cultured pearls?' And I reply: 'Why not see both?' "

Biserka thrust the dripping mass of pearls into Radmila's face. "So: They bring out all these for me! Little lumpy bastards—the wild pearls from the old days! And then—they bring out these *really huge gleaming superperfect ones*!" Biserka draped strands of pearls, one by one, over Radmila's head.

"And I say to them, 'What's the damage?' and they reply . . . what a fraud! These little stinking mean dirty ones cost a cut-off arm and one leg! And all these big white perfect round ones, pearls which didn't even grow from mother oysters . . . they are so cheap!"

Biserka cinched the thick rope of pearls around Radmila's neck. She hauled Radmila to her feet.

Then Biserka hauled her forward, tugging at the leash of jewels. "Where's the *justice*? I hated them for that! I mean: People did that to the *whole world*, didn't they? Such a pearl of a world, they had once! And now look at it!"

Biserka dragged her outside and down the stairs of the derelict building. There was a big black hearse parked in a seaweed-strewn gravel driveway. That hearse hadn't been there before, when Biserka had first abducted her.

Radmila tried to look around, feeling jewelry bite into her throat. Tall brown palms towered over the mansion, all of them killed by rising seawater.

Biserka meant to force her into the black hearse. Radmila moaned.

"Pretty evening for a drive," said Biserka.

Radmila snorted through her nose.

"You're planning to kick me again and then try to run away," Biserka diagnosed. She placed one flat hand against Radmila's collarbone and pushed her. Radmila, her arms trapped behind her, reeled helplessly, stumbled, and fell.

Biserka pulled Radmila's shoes off. She filled each shoe with a handful of sharp gravel. Then she daintily tied the shoes on. "So now— happy dancing girl—let's see you run, hey?"

Radmila had to take four steps to reach the hearse. Those steps were like walking on sharp nails. Tears came to her eyes.

Biserka heaved her through the door of the hearse, then joined her on a velvet pew in the back. They sat together next to a huge, dirt-stained coffin.

"I could rip that tape off your lipstick," said Biserka, studying her, "but you'd give me all kinds of lip for that. If you're mean to me, I might lose my temper!"

The black hearse rolled silently into motion. The machine left the shoreline, humped and bumped over a broken patch of flattened woven-wire fencing.

In a matter of moments, they were in the indestructible LA freeway system, quietly cruising under the flashing lights.

"I know you're wondering about this big dirty coffin here," said Biserka, languidly kicking it with rhythmic, bongolike thuds. "Well, there's some good news for you. The coffin is not for you. The casket has an occupant already."

Some time passed. Biserka enjoyed a chilly sip from a cocktail thermos. "You're not alert anymore," she said. "Are you *ignoring* me?"

Radmila turned toward her, eyes burning.

"That's better. Good. Okay, now I'm explaining tonight's events to you. You can't understand all this, because you are this rich-chick blond actress and you're kind of stupid. Never mind. Because *I* had a long time to think about this. It's been one of those asymmetric terror things where the enemy is very rich and has all her skyscrapers, but I always have the initiative. So: You become my hostage now. Only, Radmila: I don't want *you* as my hostage, because, wow! Wow, wow! I can't stand the sight of you!"

Biserka kicked the side of the coffin harder, with her cheap black rubber ninja boot. "*This* man is my hostage. This dead gentleman in his coffin. I dug him up out of a graveyard today. What an exciting day full of action for Biserka Mihajlovic!"

Radmila looked longingly at the thermos.

"You are thirsty, but you don't want to drink this," Biserka told her, yawning. "It would put you out flat on your ass!" Biserka rolled her neck on her shoulders, and massaged the back of her own skull.

"So, as I told you: the graveyards. I know that sounds weird to you: my dear lively sister Biserka, in the graveyards? But graveyards are

blackspots! People don't wire the graveyards, because there are no paying customers in there, and they don't imagine that the locals would get
up and leave. So there's an *imagination gap* in a graveyard."

Biserka giggled, and enjoyed another sip from her thermos. "Because
I can work fine in graveyards! They never scare me! I love them! Because they're a huge blind spot for everybody stupider than me. For people like you. Huh? So, you know, who else is in there in graveyards?
Besides me. Well, *your people* are in there, that's who. Every famous old
family has famous dead people. Like Svetlana, Bratislava, Kosara! Half
of *us* are dead already and we don't even have real graves!"

Biserka wiped her mouth on her black ninja sleeve. She had a tattoo
on her right wrist, a homemade tattoo, the kind of artwork people did in
jail cells while afflicted by long lengths of time. "So, me and my friend
the funny backhoe are working in this blackspot, and up comes this gentleman here: the former governor of California. Your husband's dad."

Biserka waited a patient moment. "All right: don't get so excited. I
wasn't the one who shot him. He won't get any deader now. When we're
done with our family business, I'll leave him somewhere—with a
beeper on him. You can come fetch him and bury him back into the
ground. You can hush it all up. The Montgomery-Montalban Family
hushes up so many matters and hides so many troubles already."

Biserka rubbed her nose. Someone had broken it, years ago. "So: I
don't hold you for ransom. I mean, yes, I stole some things by pretending to be you, but that was just to be funny. That was so easy, yes, it's boring me. No: I don't want you as my hostage. I want your people to help
me with my project! My very personal project that I have! My project is
about a crazy woman in orbit. And not your crazy woman in orbit, stupid! Not your old fat actress! No, our mother. Yelisaveta Mihajlovic.
The warlord's black widow, guns and narcotics and software . . . Mother
abandoned us, but she did some things well!"

Biserka stared out the hearse window at a passing high-rise; it had a
giant ape climbing on it, but that was only a projection. "But: two crazy
women up in orbit? How could you do that, Radmila? *Two?* That's too
much. It's annoying me! It's disgusting me! It's just not right! That's *too
many* women who are trying to fit into the same outer space! It reminds
me that Yelisaveta is still up there, flying over our heads every day, and
I don't like the way that makes me feel!"

Biserka scraped mud from the edge of her rubber boot. "I knew that you married big money. Fine, I married some money once. A bedful of money is nice! But you married people with *orbital launch capacity*! Wow! That means we can *reach our mother*, Radmila! We can put one bucket of sand, or some bolts and nuts, into Mama's orbit. Bang! Boom! One moment, no warning, Mama's dead in her flying coffin! And when that happens, then I *give you this coffin back*."

Biserka looked out the window of the hearse at the towers along Figueroa, then back at Radmila again. "You're not happy with my brilliant, genius plan?"

Radmila shook her head. Her heart was crushed within her. She had never felt such shame.

"You're not happy? But imagine how much better we both feel when that old woman falls from heaven in small burning pieces! I know some people in China who have space rockets. They could help us."

Biserka snuffled as lights flashed over her face. "Look at you, feeling so sorry for yourself . . . A billion people died in Asia from the climate crisis. A *billion*. And I helped them to die. While you never looked. Because everyone was supposed to look at *you*, Radmila! Black skies and starving mobs and empty rivers, and the world is supposed to watch you. And worship you! Because you might take your clothes off! Or something. You're a dress-up doll made from plastic."

Biserka shook her head in wonderment, then shrugged. "So you deserve to die, Radmila, but . . . first things first! First I drop you in a bar in Norwalk—tied up like this, in your underwear. You hop right in there, you call home, tell them you got drunk. You had a bad casting-couch date with your big-shot producer, whatever, I don't care. You handle that. But if you screw me over—and I know that you want to, because, wow wow wow! I'd certainly do that to you—well, I'm going to kill. Not you. Someone else. Not you—because you're too necessary to my plans. And not the governor here, because he got shot already."

Biserka paused to laugh. "But I will kill Glyn, you know, that downmarket fat-assed clone of the superstar! That Glyn thing really annoys me. Really. Just thinking about that Glyn makes me crazy! We Mihajlovic girls, we don't have enough trouble that you have to find *her*? Glyn, another clone, who loves you? She adores you? That stinks, that's the worst!

"So I will kill your Glyn, because Glyn has no big bodyguards. So that's easy. Your Glyn will be out for a buttered bagel in her black turtleneck and her tummy-flattening girdle, and she will walk by some junker car and one instant, no warning, Glyn is Glynereens. She's Glyndust." Biserka chortled. "A smart car bomb in a world of sensorwebs! That's one afternoon's work!"

Biserka straightened in the hearse's pew. "So. You can do as I tell you, Radmila, which is easy and good. Or you can try to screw me out of what I want, and I will make you die of grief. You heard that, right? You remember my great plan, right? I don't have to beat it into you."

Radmila moaned violently and shook her head.

"It seems that you have something important to say about my plans for our future."

Radmila nodded.

"It must be really important, with you fussing like that so much."

Radmila nodded harder.

"Okay, I tell you what. You turn around, give me your hands. Then I cut off the tip of your left little finger. Just the tip, not all of it! Then I take that tape off your mouth and you tell me about your objections. Your crucial input is at least that important, right?"

Radmila shook her head.

"Oh, so it's not so important! I thought so. So: Now I tape your eyes shut. Before I kick you out of this car. Duct tape! It's wonderful! It holds the whole universe together."

Biserka undid the brass buckles on a splendid travel bag. She pawed inside it. Her bag held flat black rubber sandals, a sports bra, cotton pants, athletic socks, panties, an arsenal of fancy toiletries, sunglasses, tampons, chewing gum, a host of pills, and a long black rubber shotgun.

Biserka shook the bag upside down and mourned. "Oh, I left my duct tape back at my blackspot. Because I used it there. What a shame."

There was a loud thump on the roof of the rolling hearse.

"Okay, I didn't like that. Something hit the car. That was bad."

Radmila rolled her eyes upward, then crinkled her brows and hunched her shoulders in silent laughter.

"All right, what?" Biserka shouted. "What?" She tucked her nailed fingers into Radmila's cheek and ripped the tape from her face. "Tell me now."

Radmila worked her sore jaws.

"All right, what? What hit the car? Tell me."

"That was nothing. It was a bird."

"That was a lie! You lied to me."

"I'm not afraid of you, Biserka. You don't scare me. You have killed me with the shame of what you've done, I will never face my Family again, I will never work in this town again . . . But you are small and weak. You have no business here. I never did anything to you."

"You EXISTED!" Biserka shrieked. "Everybody who isn't on a desert island knows I look like 'Mila Montalban'!" She slapped the wrinkled tape back onto Radmila's lips. Being rumpled, the duct tape failed to stick well.

Biserka opened the window of the hearse. Snakelike, she jammed her skinny torso through it, then made a desperate lunge.

She came back with a toy gripped in her hand: a flying toy made of foamed propellers and plastic blocks and nakedly exposed circuits.

"I know what this is. I used to see a lot of these."

Radmila kept her face still. She'd never seen a flying spyplane of quite this type before, but she certainly knew what it was. Some fan had built that.

There were networks of those fans out there, happy little voyeur perverts who would swap their recipes for making spy toys and then share their spy photographs. The fans were scum. But there were always some of them around. Like mice: If you saw one, it meant a hundred.

"This one doesn't even have a gun," Biserka scoffed. "All it's got is stupid pirate media and big googly eyes!" She opened the hearse, stuck the toy airplane out, and smashed it in the slamming door. Cheap plastic parts flew everywhere. A broken wad of them landed in Radmila's lap. They were commodity pieces that had cost a few cents in a hardware store, and they'd been stuck together with hot-glue. A sloppy job. Some kid. Some fan kid with a kit-part and a bunch of other fans to egg him on.

One blurry picture, one snapshot . . . of a major star tied in bondage in her underwear. With a coffin, in the back of a hearse . . . Some fan spy must have seen that image, for at least a few seconds, a few hundred frames of stolen video.

An image like that would spread from fan to fan like ink on a towel.

So all this would be over. Not yet, but everything had to end. Those little pirate kids on networks—they'd even destroyed the movies.

Radmila stared out the window.

"Okay, princess, just for that, we go back to the safe house! No freedom for you! I wanted you free to carry my message, but now I keep you!"

Twenty minutes passed, in which Radmila said nothing. She had already lost everything.

Biserka had no safe house anymore. Her blackspot safe house was on fire. Rocket flares were flying. The glare of flames lit the dark interior of the hearse. The flames backlit capering figures, running, dancing.

"Oh Lionel, Lionel, that gangster bad boy . . . that tasty morsel, Lionel," mourned Biserka. "I had such plans and hopes for him. Now he's found my hideout and I want to kill myself. I think I will. Right now! I will ignite this hearse and I will blow both of us into little pieces and there won't be anything left here but a cloud of your own DNA."

Radmila rolled her eyes in contempt.

Biserka crawled into the front of the hearse, to mess at length with its interface. Distant sirens were howling, but the fabled rapid-response corps of Los Angeles were slow to fight these fires. Maybe because the fastest and most agile gangs on the street were the arsonists.

"Lionel and his friends are getting out of hand, Radmila! That's a whole lot of pretty fire! I've seen towns on fire in China that were burning less than your town is burning tonight."

Biserka was frightened suddenly. "All right, you're always claiming you love them so much. Go stop them from rioting. Go on, I'll untie you. Go be superhuman. You can do that. You're superperfect." She pulled the wadded tape from Radmila's lips.

"Kill us both," Radmila said. "It's easier."

"You stink," Biserka decided. "I think I'll go help them, instead. I'll say that I'm you, and I'll tell them to burn everything. I'll burn everything you ever built here! Because I look like you. I look more like you than you do."

Flames lit the horizon. A dense, oily wave of smoke rolled over them. Biserka kicked open the door, left the hearse, slammed it behind her.

Radmila hated her life.

The hearse suddenly started again. It rolled, slow as a minute hand

and just as inexorable, into the Pacific surf. Like every form of networked machinery, the car showed a supreme contempt for its own survival.

The hearse wobbled. Pacific surf rolled rhythmically over the windows. Seawater seeped under the doors.

Radmila managed to wriggle sideways in her bondage. She got her knees up, her legs up.

The foaming tide would not drown her until it reached the coffin.

The tide rose steadily. The coffin began to float.

PART THREE
SONJA
THE GOBI DESERT

HE WAS BOWLEGGED, he had lice, internal parasites, and tubercular lesions, and he was nineteen years old. His life was one long epic poem about heat, cold, thirst, hunger, filth, disasters, and bloodshed. His fellow tribesmen called him "the Badaulet," which meant "Lucky."

Sonja tuned her clinic lights to a mellow glow and turned up the infrasound. Lucky's tough, tireless, scrawny body went as translucent as glass. His sturdy heart jetted blood through the newly cleansed nets of his lungs.

Sonja had killed off Lucky's parasites, filtered his blood, changed his skin flora, flushed out his dusty lungs and the squalid contents of his guts . . . She had cut his hair, trimmed his nails . . . He was a desert warlord, and every pore, duct, and joint in him required civilizing.

"Lucky dear," she said, "what would you like more than anything in this whole world?"

"Death in battle," said Lucky, heavy-lidded with pleasure. Lucky always said things like that.

"How about a trip to Mars?"

Lucky stoutly replied—according to their machine translation: "Yes, the warrior souls are bound for Heaven! But men must be honest with Heaven and rise from the front line of battle! For if we want to go to the garden of Heaven, yet we have not followed in the caravan of jihad, then we are like the boat that wants to sail on the dry desert!"

"Mars is a planet, not Heaven. It's a planet like Earth."

"Even a pagan woman with your pitiful ignorance can follow the path of jihad!" said Lucky, grunting a little as her oiled fingers readjusted the bones in his neck. "Women can equip a man for righteous battle with their gold and jewelry!"

"I have no gold or jewelry."

Lucky reached out deftly and seized a thick hank of her hair. "Then cut and sell these golden tresses! Your beauty will buy me guns to punish all of Heaven's enemies!"

"What a sweet thing to say."

There was no use her denying it, especially to herself: she had fallen for him. He was a dismal, bloodstained creature from what was surely one of the worst areas on Earth, yet he radiated confidence and a sure sense of manly grace.

This was not another impulsive fling, though Sonja had never lacked for those. This time was one of those serious times.

Maybe she had fallen, somehow, for their quirky machine translation, for Lucky's native tongue was an obscure pidgin of Chinese, Turkic, and Mongolian dialect, a desert lingo created by the roaming few who still survived in the world's biggest dust bowl. It was the trouble of reaching him, of touching him, that made their pang of communion so precious to her. Talking to Lucky was like shouting through an ancient crack in the Great Wall of China.

She felt a powerful, deeply spiritual rapport with him, for once she had been so much like him: young, bewildered, foreign, aggressive, and heavily armed. In China, yet not quite of China. For this young war hero to become an honored guest of the Chinese state—he must have waded here through a tide of gore.

Sonja disentangled his callused fingers from her curls. "Lucky, you feel some pain here, don't you?" She patted him intimately.

"Yes, that is a pain in my ass."

"I will fix that for you." He'd fallen—from a horse, most likely—and his cracked fourth lumbar vertebra had a growth on it, a tender, frilly, ligamentous benign tumor like some Chinese wood-ear mushroom. People's interior organs—and Sonja had spent years studying them—they were subaquatic organisms, basically. They grew in bloody seawater.

"Stop fixing me, Sonja. You fix me too much."

"Dear Badaulet, that big pain you feel down your leg comes from one small broken bone on your back. It is right . . . here. Do you feel that? Here it is: that is your pain. Because there is a network of nerves there. The network is pinched, the network has a fault. See how I can touch that network fault? My fingers can feel that."

"No, no! Stop that! My back is strong! It's my stupid ass that has the pain." Lucky twisted his neatly trimmed head, showed her his newly polished teeth and smiled. "Rub me all over, slowly, as you did before. That part is good."

"Lucky: You are strong and beautiful, but I know your body better than you. I know what you feel."

"Stop dreaming! You can't tell me what I feel, woman! Only Heaven knows the secrets hidden in the breasts of men!"

"Oh, I know enough of your secrets to heal you as a man." She lowered her eyes. "That will hurt at first."

"Oh woman, why do you always talk so much? I know what you want from that bold, rude way you look at my face! You can't hurt me! You and your sweet little hands . . ." Lucky grabbed snakelike at her fingers, and missed them as she instantly snatched them back.

He really didn't think that she could hurt him. Of the many outlandish things that Lucky had said to her, this one was the most absurd.

The Badaulet was an outcast, although he was entirely sure he was a prince. She had once thought she was a princess, and become an outcast . . . "Badaulet, this evening I will bathe you, and dress you in your fine new uniform. You will meet the greatest heroes in the whole world." Grappling his arm, she coaxed him over onto his belly, so that his spine was exposed.

"Who is that, what did you say to me?" Lucky touched his translation earpiece and frowned.

"Your banquet hosts in Jiuquan tonight are the taikonauts! The astronauts! The cosmonauts! The *taikong ren*. The *yuhangyuan*. The *hangtianyuan*. Do you understand that? I mean the Chinese heroes who flew to Mars and returned to Earth."

"Oh yes, the famous Great Pilgrims to Heaven. I understand. They mean to honor the Badaulet for my valor in combat."

"To meet these heroes brings great good fortune. They are the future!"

"Did your men of valor fight on Mars?"

"No. They collected rocks there."

"Though they have returned from Heaven, if they failed to fight the jihad they have earned no merit."

Sonja planted the point of her elbow into Lucky's spine, and with one decisive lunge she ripped the tumor loose.

The Badaulet gasped in agony and writhed like a hooked fish.

"You felt that pang all down your leg, didn't you?"

He was angry. "You hurt me now! You cut my hair! You washed my guts! You stole my clothes! You burned me with hot wax! And I'm no better, Sonja! I hurt! You promised you would fix me and I hurt."

Sonja rolled him over onto his back. For the first time since she had met him, Lucky had gone gratifyingly limp. Normally he was as nervous and tensile as a bundle of barbed wire. His torn spine was bleeding a little, inside of him. Not too much. She had done it precisely right.

What amazing skin this boy had. There were hen-scratched scars all over him, pits, pocks, frostbite, dimples . . . "Lie quiet now . . . Rest and heal . . . Shall I sing to you while I make you feel better? I'll sing you a little song. I know many old and beautiful songs. I will sing you 'The Ballad of the Savage Tiger.' "

As she sang, Sonja suited actions to his needs. The springy, salty vitality of the masculine body, how endearing that was. The body was irrepressible, it wanted to live despite everything. The sexual body, with resources for new life.

Sonja had come to treasure poetry, during the long marches between flaming cities. On the deadly, broken roads of a China in chaos, in the teeming refugee camps, she had come to understand that a memorized poem was true wealth—it was a precious work of art, a possession that could not be burned or stolen.

Sonja crooned:

> "No one attacks her with the long lance,
> No one shoots her with the strong bow.
> Suckling her progeny, rearing her cubs,
> She trains them in her own savagery.
> Her reared head becomes the great wall
> Her waving tail becomes the war banner.

The greatest pirates from the eastern sea
Would dread to meet her after dark,
The savage tiger, met on the western road,
Would terrify the greatest bandits.
What good is any sword against her?
When she growls like thunder, hang it on the wall!
From the secret foothills of Tai mountain
Comes the sound of women weeping,
But government regulations forbid
Any official to dare to listen."

Lucky was blissfully quiet now. He had wisely chosen not to argue with her anymore. A host of ducts and long hydraulic chambers and strange stiffening flows of blood . . . And yet, human beings emerged from these oblong glands and their conduits, men and women were sired by all this gadgetry—well, not herself, of course, but most people had a father . . . People emerged as single-celled genetic packets out of this complex, densely innervated, profoundly temperamental fluid-delivery system.

The secret of humanity. Here it was, in her hands.

No matter how many human bodies Sonja encountered, and how well she grasped them and their intimate functions, there was always some new magic in a new one.

Sonja switched filters and gazed straight into Lucky's brain. His arousal was ferociously devouring a host of tagged radioactive sugars. Sex was like a bonfire in his basement.

Women often knowingly told other women that "men only wanted one thing," but it took a sensorweb to catalogue and reveal that. To see it was to believe it. To know all was to forgive all. A man wanted that one thing he wanted because there *wasn't room in his head* for anything else.

A bonfire of gratified lust was roaring around in Lucky's skull. Hormones washed through him in visible tides. With surgical delicacy, she rubbed him with three oiled fingertips. Instantly, an aurora of utter bliss boiled through him. He teetered on the brink of unconsciousness.

This was the world's most human "humane intervention." It was the one consoling act that, during its few sweet minutes, could obliterate loneliness. Obscure horror. Dismantle grief.

The famed rewards of Heaven for the warrior-martyr were seventy-two heavenly maidens doing just this.

THE AIRLOCK INTO THE FABLED MARS DOME was very likely the single most paranoid security space in all of China. The Martian dome was under the strictest official state quarantine, so the disinfected visitors went in there wearing single-seamed, quilted space gowns, soft little foamy space boots, and nothing else whatsoever. Visitors were allowed no tools, no possessions, no equipment of any kind. Not a fleck. Not a speck. Their bare humanity.

Sonja always had trouble with this airlock, for there were old bits of shrapnel inside her: pieces of another human being. A suicide bomber. Lucky and Sonja tenderly held hands on their waffled and comfortless plastic bench while the security scanners whirred overhead. There was nothing much to do except to gaze out the windows.

The Martian airlock featured two oblong portholes. Their shape mimicked the two world-famous portholes in the Martian landing capsule. These portholes helped some with the monotony of security scans, for the portholes offered boastful views of downtown Jiuquan.

Certain knowledgeable pundits called Jiuquan "the planet's most advanced urban habitat," although, as a supposed "city," Jiuquan had its drawbacks. Jiuquan, which had sprung up around China's largest space-launch center, resembled no previous "city" on Earth.

Jiuquan bore some atavistic traces of a normal Chinese city: mostly morale-boosting "big-character" banner ads—but it had no streets and no apparent ground level. Jiuquan consisted mostly of froth, foam, and film. It looked as if a fireworks factory had burst and been smothered with liquid plastic. Solar-sheeted domes more garish than Christmas ornaments, linked with pneumatic halls and rhizomelike inflated freeways. Piston elevators, garish capsules, ducts and dimples and depressions, decontamination chambers. Hundreds of state laboratories.

Jiuquan was thirty-eight square kilometers of zero-footprint, a young desert metropolis recycling its air and all its water. Jiuquan was an artificial Xanadu where fiercely dedicated national technocrats lived on their bioplastic carpets with bioplastic furniture, interacting with bioplastic screens, under skeletal watchtowers and ancient rocket launch-pads.

Oil-slick paddies of bacterial greenhouses, deftly fed by plug-in sewers, created fuel, food, and building materials, all of it manufactured straight from the dust of the Gobi Desert. A city built of dust.

A radical yet highly successful experiment in sustainability, Jiuquan was booming—it was the fastest-growing "city" in China. It was sited in the Gobi Desert with nothing to stop its urban expansion but the dust. And Jiuquan was made of dust. Dust was what the city ate.

Sonja was finally allowed to clear the steely skeins of the Martian airlock. Dr. Mishin, who had been waiting for her, rose to his feet and hastily jammed his dust-grimed laptop into his dust-grimed bag.

Leonid Mishin was a Russian space technician who had wandered the world like Marco Polo and finally moored here in Jiuquan. Mishin dwelt inside the Mars simulator, as one of its few permanent residents.

Everyone else in Jiuquan also resided in an airtight bubble of some kind, but Mishin's bubble, the Martian simulator, was officially considered the most advanced bubble of them all. This made up somewhat for the fact that Dr. Mishin was never allowed to leave.

Dr. Mishin labored in his confinement as a "senior technical consultant," which was to say, he led a career rather similar to her own as a "senior public health consultant." They were both émigré servants of the Chinese state, multipurpose human tools used to fill cracks in the walls of Chinese governance, or to putty over a rip in its seams. The Chinese state had thousands of such foreign agents. The state impartially rewarded any human functionary that it found to be skilled and convenient.

Lucky was still battling with the airlock's fabric. The interfaces there had baffled better men than him.

"You slept with that barbarian," Mishin concluded at once.

Sonja rolled her eyes and ran her fingers through her hair.

"Yes, you did that, you did!" Dr. Mishin mourned. "What is wrong with you? *Him*, of all people? A creature like *him*? Have you finally lost all self-respect?"

"Leonid, do you think our age difference matters? I'm only twenty-seven."

"They cut off people's heads out there! They do it on video!"

"The Badaulet is very loyal to the state.·He believes that the Chinese state is divinely sanctioned by the Mandate of Heaven. You should take him seriously, he's an important political development."

"He's a tribal lunatic! There's no reason for you to involve yourself with him! What do you expect to gain from him? There's nothing left but sand and land mines between here and Kazakhstan!"

Why was Mishin so bitterly jealous? His sexual politics were his worst flaw. Yes, true, she had a penchant for taking lovers, but this was China. For every hundred women in China there were a hundred and thirty men. What else should the world expect?

And Jiuquan, a deeply technical city, had an even more destabilizing male-female imbalance. Mishin was from Russia, where the men died young and the women were lonely. He was being a fool.

Lucky kicked through the airlock, snarling and slapping at his earpiece. "What is wrong with that stupid tent, that ugly prison? It trapped me in there and it tried to kill me!"

"Badaulet, this is the wise scientist that I told you about: Dr. Leonid Mishin. No man in this world knows more about the future potential of Mars. Dr. Mishin will be our official state guide today."

Lucky, still angry, stared in raw disbelief at the chilly pink sun crawling the seamless, alien, purplish sky. The Martian extraterrarium, logically, ran on Martian time—it featured 24.6-hour days and 687-day years. The wine-dark plastic firmament displayed accurately Martian stellar constellations, including two racing, tumbling blobs of light that mimicked Phobos and Deimos.

Mishin was usually a polished Martian tour guide, but he was upset with her. Yet he'd been so kind and eager about it when she'd said she was coming to visit him. What a shame.

Lucky rubbed his nose. "Why does Mars stink?"

"The breathable air within this model Martian biosphere," Mishin recited grudgingly, "was created, and is maintained; entirely by our extraterrestrialized organisms. Through the ubiquitous oversight of the state and the heroic efforts of the dedicated scientific workers of the glorious Jiuquan Space Launch Center—" Mishin drew a breath. "—this project has become the model, not of Mars today, but of the *future* Mars! Your translation understands all that, sir? Yes? That's very good!"

Mishin wheeled in his insulated worker boots, waving his uniformed arms at the glowing Martian sunset and the spare, frozen scrub that dotted the rusty soil. "At this moment you are privileged to step within the Mars of Tomorrow! Here, spread all around you, is the living, air-breathing harbinger of Humanity's Second Home World! The development of Mars is China's most ambitious megaproject—and this dome, which is merely a model of that future effort, ranks with the Great Wall of China as the most ambitious construction on the surface of planet Earth!"

It was a pity that they'd lost valuable time while trapped within that balky airlock. With the setting of the pink sun in its tear-proofed plastic sky, the Martian bubble was getting bitterly cold.

The three of them crunched briskly across the rust-red cinders, staring at the Chinese and Latin botanical labels stuck in the tough, humble scrub: harsh tufts of spiky needlegrass (*Stipa gobica*). Indestructible, colorless saltwort (*Salsola passerina*). Bone-colored Mongolian sagebrush (*Artemisia xerophytic*).

Mishin rambled on, but Sonja had heard his lectures. She could not help but remember what John Montgomery Montalban had quipped while he was walking in here. She and Montalban had been lovers at the time, and, to her stunned amazement, Montalban had somehow managed to smuggle a fancy glass ball into the Martian dome. It was a tiny, liquid city that he confidently tossed from hand to hand.

Montalban had whispered to her, endearments mostly, but sometimes he would slyly subvert the official discourse with classic poetry from his distant California . . . The Dispensation, the Acquis, they always tried to mock or ignore Chinese national accomplishments. The global civil societies were afraid of nation-states. Especially the Chinese state, the largest and most powerful state left on Earth.

One hundred years in the past, Mao Zedong, the Great Helmsman, had chosen the province of Gansu, the city-prefecture of Jiuquan, the Gobi Desert at the edge of Mongolia, as a locus of Communist futurity. This was where China's spacecraft would conquer the sky. Little did Mao know that the sky of the Gobi Desert was the true future of China . . .

China, its sky reddening with endless smokestack spew, China as its own Red Planet . . . The world had never seen a technological advance so headlong, so relentless, so ambitious in scope and so careless of Earthly consequence as China's bid to dominate the global economy . . .

That was how John Montgomery Montalban perceived things around here . . . As a lover, she missed Montalban keenly, all the more so in that she had sworn never to meet him again. No one had ever been kinder, sweeter, more considerate, more nearly understanding of her troubles and pains . . . Of the five men that she had truly loved in her life, John Montalban was the only one who wasn't yet dead.

A jerboa bounded between her booted feet like a fur-covered tennis ball. Then they scared up a big captive flock of tiny finches, each thumb-sized desert bird with its own unique ID and onboard health-tracking instruments.

One greasy, bean-laden bush had thoroughly mastered Martian survival. It was bursting through the alkaline soil on an eager net of roots and runners. The way it flung itself out like that, all runners, green pods, and rooty crisscrossings . . . it was rather like a little city of Jiuquan, when you looked at it.

Lucky dodged the orating scientist, slipping around to place her body between himself and the other man.

This Martian extraterrarium, the most ambitious biosphere in the world, had cost as much to build as the damming of a major Chinese river. It surely deserved a much greater world fame—but the topsy-turvy life trapped within here was so frail, so advanced, and so imperiled that the state rarely allowed any human beings inside this place. The Martian biosphere was gardened by sterilized robots, Earthly twins to the state-controlled devices remotely exploring Mars.

Quite likely the state had wisely sensed that human beings had already wrecked one biosphere and would be cruelly thrilled to smash this new one.

The life struggling here had been carefully redesigned for extraterrestrial conditions. Some cloned organisms proved themselves in practice, while most mutants perished young. The extraterrarium was an entire experimental ecology of genetic mutants . . .

All creatures very much like herself, all of these. All those little birds, those hopping, shivering, tunneling rodents, the half-dozen runty central Asian ponies whose sixty-six chromosomes firmly distinguished them from domesticated horses . . . They were all her Martian siblings under the skin.

Every creature in here had been cloned—especially the bacteria. The Martian soil—that unpromising mélange of windy silt, crunchy bits of meteoric glass, volcanic ash, and salty pebbles—it was damp and alive.

Most of the microbes here were clones of native Martian microbes. The Chinese taikonauts had found microbial life on Mars: with deep drilling, in the subterranean ice. They had found and retrieved six different Martian species of sleepy but persistent microorganisms.

Those Martian bacteria were relatives of certain extremophile microbes also found on Earth. Very likely they were primeval rock-eating bugs—blasted off the fertile Earth in some huge volcanic upheaval, then blown across the solar system in some violent gust of solar spew. Giant volcanoes, huge solar flares . . . they didn't happen often. But they certainly happened.

Microbes cared nothing if they lived on Earth or Mars. Men had found alien Martian life and brought it back alive to the Earth. That was all the same to the microbes.

Maybe—as Montalban had once told her—there was something innately Chinese about exploring Mars. Every other nation-state with a major space program had collapsed. Nation-states always collapsed from their attempts to explore outer space. Nazi Germany, the Soviet Union, the United States—even the Republic of India, China's biggest space rival—they had all ceased to exist politically. Montalban claimed that the reason was obvious. Nation-states were about the land and its strict boundaries, while space was about the cosmos and the globe. So the national urge to annex outer space brought a nation-killing curse.

That curse had not felled the Chinese. No. No curse could fell the Chinese. The Chinese had prevailed over three millennia of river floods, droughts, pestilences, mass starvations . . . and barbarian invasions, civil wars, plagues, uprisings, revolutions . . . China suffered, yes—collapsed, never.

When the taikonauts had returned from Mars to land safely in the Gobi Desert, the Chinese nation, what was left of it, had exploded with joy. Hollow-eyed Chinese eating human flesh in the shrouded ruins of their automobile plants had been proud about Mars.

The Chinese were still very proud of their taikonauts, though the aging taikonauts, whom Sonja knew very personally, seemed a little shaken by their ambiguous role in history. The space heroes had left a glittering China in a headlong economic boom; they had returned from their multiyear Mars adventure to a choking, thirsting China whose sky consisted of dust.

Six kinds of dust:

The black dust from the Gobi Desert.

The red loess dust of central China.

The industrially toxic yellow dust that came from the dried riverbeds and the emptied basins of the giant parched dams.

The brown smoking dust of China's burning fields and blazing forests.

The dense, gray, toxic dust of China's combusting cities.

And, last but most globally important, the awesome, sky-tinting, Earth-cooling, stratospheric, radioactive dust from dozens of Chinese hydrogen bombs, digging massive reservoirs for fresh ice in the Himalayas.

Sonja had worked on the ground in China during the last of those years. Foreign soldiers had flown into China from every corner of the planet, always hoping to reassert order there. China could not be allowed to fail, because China was the workshop of the entire world, the world's forge, the world's irreplaceable factory.

The Chinese people had died in a cataclysm beyond numeration, while the Chinese state had prevailed. The bloody mayhem that had once gripped the Celestial Empire was methodically pushed beyond its borders. Pushed onto people like Lucky.

"I know this grass!" cried Lucky, plucking a cruelly barbed seed from the flesh of his ankle. "Camels can eat this!"

"All of these plants are native plants from China's deserts," said Mishin. This was a major techno-nationalist selling point. "When, in the future, mankind brings Mars to life, Mars will be Asian tundra and steppes."

"Who will live there?" Lucky demanded. "People like you?"

"Oh no," Sonja told him. "They will be people like you."

Lucky scowled. Lucky knew that he was not in Heaven. He was in an alien world, and he already lived in an alien world. "You told me about the horses? Show me some horses!"

"We do have horses here," Mishin assured him. "Central Asia's Prze-walski's horses. Genetically, these are the oldest horses on Earth." Mishin scratched his close-cropped head. "You, sir—you may have seen these wild mustangs in the new wilds of central Asia, eh? Maybe a few Przewalski's horses? There are large herds thriving around Chernobyl."

"Those little horses are too small to ride." Lucky shrugged. "I can eat them. I can drink their blood."

Either the state's translation had failed him, or Mishin simply ig-nored what Lucky had just said. "We plan to remove the horses soon for the sake of our new young star . . . See, here are her tracks! Right here! And this is her dung, as well!"

Broadly spaced pugmarks dented the chilly Martian soil.

"That is no camel," Lucky concluded. "That is no horse."

"She is our 'mammoth,' " said Mishin proudly.

Lucky patted his earpiece. "I never heard that word, 'mammoth.' "

"Do you know what an 'elephant' is?"

Lucky coughed on the cold, dusty air. "No."

"Well, both elephants and mammoths are extinct today. However: with the climate crisis, many mammoths thawed from the permafrost . . . In a genetically revivable condition! Sometimes people don't marvel properly at our fabulous Martian microbes . . . but our mammoth! Oh yes! A hairy mammoth revived fresh from the Ice Age . . . and she's been redesigned for Mars! Everyone adores our Chinese Martian mammoth . . . She's still our young girl of course . . ." Mishin held his pale hand out, at shoulder height. "So she's still quite small, but what splendid fur, such a nose and ears! Who can't love a beautiful cloned Martian mammoth?"

"I don't love a mammoth," Lucky said firmly. "Let us leave this place now."

"No, no, let's hurry! Our mammoth will sleep soon. She sleeps each day at regular Martian hours."

"Lucky," Sonja told him, "the state wants to send me to Mars. I vol-unteered to go. I'm in taikonaut training in Jiuquan Space Launch Center."

Lucky looked her up and down. "Yes, that trip would be good for you."

"Why do you say that?"

Lucky lifted one finger. "Your mother. She's already up there?"

Sonja glared at him in instant, head-splitting rage.

"Sonja, don't!" Mishin yelped. "Don't do that! Remember what happened with Montalban?"

Sonja's head was spinning. The thin Martian air did some nasty things to people. "Our guest wants to leave this place, Leonid. We seem to have tired him."

Mishin hastily escorted them back toward the balky airlock. Mishin himself never left the Martian simulator. There were microbes within him not yet cleared for public distribution.

"Sonja, you don't love your dear mother?" taunted Lucky, as they suffered the tedious hissing and clicking of the airlock's insane security. "Your demon mother, she who dwells in Heaven? You talk so much, Sonja, yet you never talk about her!"

"My mother is a state secret. So: Don't talk about my mother. Especially with this state machine translation."

Lucky was unimpressed. The prospect of the state surveilling him bothered him no more than the omniscience of God. "I, too, never talk about my mother."

Sonja lifted her sour, aching head. "What about your mother, Lucky? Why don't you talk about your mother?"

"My mother sold oil! She committed many crimes against the sky. In Tajikistan, in Kyrgyzstan. Other places. Many pipelines across central Asia. She was rich. Very rich."

"A princess, then?"

"Yes, all my mother's people were rich and beautiful. They had no tribes, they had schools. They had cars and jets and skyscrapers. All of them dead now. All. Dead, and nonpersons. No one speaks of them anymore."

Sonja shifted closer to him on the waffled plastic bench. She was sorry that she had lost her temper with him. He was only probing her, to see what she was made of. He had some right to do that. She did it herself all the time.

When she had been nineteen, twenty, twenty-one—young like him—she had had no discretion, no emotional skin at all. Especially about the always-tender subject of her "mother" and her "sisters."

Those violent passions were distant to her now, relics of the bitter days when she had become "Red Sonja." Nobody called her "Red Sonja" anymore. Not now, not when she was a certified war heroine with a cozy state post here in futuristic Jiuquan. At least, nobody called her "Red Sonja" when she could overhear them and take reprisals.

Sonja stared at the thin pox of Martian dust on her white plastic boots. The airlock was methodically blasting the last traces of life from that dust—a sterilization process that humans would never perceive, but a holocaust for bacteria.

"Badaulet, I should spend more time getting properly briefed about the guests that I escort here, but your suave manners, your smooth talk, they overwhelmed my girlish modesty so quickly."

"That was a joke," Lucky guessed.

"Yes, that was a joke."

"Stop making jokes." He patted his ear. "This machine never understands jokes."

The airlock fell silent. The hissing, incoming air, which had been pressing hard at Sonja's tender eardrums, went deathly still.

"This airlock does not want to cooperate with us today."

"This machine wants to kill me," Lucky said firmly. "It knows that I don't belong here. I belong on the steppes, under the sky."

"Maybe it wants to kill *me*. After all, I'm the fool who escorts so many visitors here."

"Why would it want to harm you, Sonja? You are the Angel of Harbin."

"The 'Angel of Harbin.' " Sonja sat up straighter. "I hate that stupid nickname! Yes, I'm a war heroine. Yes, I'm a pillar of the state and I am proud of my service! But 'Angel of Harbin'—I never chose that nom de guerre! Harbin was nothing so much."

Lucky was puzzled by this. He spoke rapidly, seriously and at some length, and the translator spat up one sentence. "They say that Harbin was the very worst of the very bad."

"Harbin was only typical. We had a good rescue plan in Harbin. We knew what we wanted to do and we knew how to win there. Now, Shenyang—*that* was bad. And Yinchuan, where they completely lost electrical power? Dead networks, no water, no sewer? For eighteen weeks? There was no body count there—because they *ate* the bodies.

When we marched out there to dig in—I sent out my surveillance cams—I *destroyed all that data*. Everybody in that rescue team was on trauma drugs after Yinchuan. Nobody remembers Yinchuan. Nobody *wants* to remember *that* place. It is lost, it's nonhistory. Even the state conceals Yinchuan, and no human being will ever ask."

"You were fighting that gloriously?"

"We didn't *think* we were fighting at all! We were medical teams, we were there to save innocent lives! But: When there's no water in a city? Then there's no innocence: it's all gone. With no water, there is no city—there's a horde. 'Every cop is a criminal and all the sinners saints.' "

That was John Montalban again. Montalban always loved to quote old American poetry.

The Badaulet turned his level gaze upon her. It was his keen black eyes, his abstract, fearless, predatory look, that had first attracted and aroused her. He looked so different from other bandits, and now that she knew about his globe-trotting, jet-setting mother, she understood. Lucky was a native of the Disorder.

Sonja knew what Han Chinese people looked like, and also Tibetans, Manchus, Mongols. To any practiced eye they were easily as physically distinct as French, Germans, Italians, and Danes. Yet Lucky was none of those: he was a global guerrilla, a true modern barbarian. Her lover was one of the new kind.

"Sonja, I have to know: Are there seven of you? Seven sisters?"

"There were seven once—three are dead." Bratislava, Kosara, Svetlana: They had been the first people she had ever seen killed. They'd been killed by a pack of young soldiers, panicked kids really, drunken kids half stumbling over their cheap carbines, kids the age of the Badaulet.

That distant episode on that distant Adriatic island: How empty that seemed to her now. Her twisted world of childhood had exploded in a sudden bloody horror, but, in comparison with the vast bloody grandeur of China, it was such a small world and such a minor horror.

In Mljet, though: that was the first time Sonja herself had killed someone. One could never forget the first time.

"Please don't talk to me about my dead," she told him, "don't talk to me about the past, for I can't bear it. Just talk to me about the future, for I can bear as much of that as anyone . . ."

Lucky was deeply moved. "Here with you, in this locked bubble, the wind and sky are not free . . . Everything stinks in here . . . The future should not stink . . . Do you love me, Sonja?"

"Yes."

"Why do you love me?"

"I don't need reasons. Love just happens to me. I love you the way that any woman loves any man."

Lucky folded his sinewy arms in a brisk decision. "Then we should marry. Because marriage is proper and holy. A temporary Muslim marriage can be performed in necessity in pagan lands and times of war. So I will marry you, Sonja. Now, here."

Sonja laughed. "You haven't known me long."

"I don't want to know you better," Lucky said. "You have given me your woman's body: the utmost gift a woman gives a man, except for sons. So: I don't want to go to Hell for doing that. It is my warrior calling to serve Heaven, die for Heaven, and go to Heaven. So: You must certainly agree to marry me. Otherwise, you are oppressing me."

"Can we discuss this matter after we leave this airlock?"

Lucky sat cross-legged on the rubbery white tiles of the sterilized floor. "We cannot leave! We are prisoners in here! So let us make our pact now and marry at once. I cannot ask your father to give me you, for you never had a father."

"You know a lot about me, don't you?"

"On the steppes, far outside China, I meet the Provincial Reconstruction Teams, from the Acquis and the Dispensation. They seek me out for my advice on how to survive, for they die there quickly. They know much about the Angel of Harbin. They know things about you that the state does not say. They say that Red Sonja killed five great generals."

"That is *not true*! That's a lie! I have never killed any uniformed Chinese military personnel! I swear that, I never did that—not even if they were laying down barrage-fire on my positions."

Sonja puffed on the thin, stale air. "My head hurts so badly. Something's gone wrong. We're supposed to dress for that big state banquet.

The Martian taikonauts are there, and they'll want us to drink! Lots of toasts with maotai . . . Five years, those three flyboys were stuck, without a woman, in their tiny capsule—good God, no wonder they're like that . . . Do you drink alcohol, Lucky?"

"I can drink kumiss!"

"You drink kumiss horse milk? Really? That's so cute."

"I will introduce you to these heroes as my wife!"

"I'm a soldier's woman," Sonja told him, pressing the heels of her hands to her throbbing temples. "That's what I'm good for. So: fine. Since you need marriage so much, for the sake of your soul and whatever: fine, I'll do that for you. I will be your concubine. I can do that."

"Truly?"

"Shut up! Because—I will only be your *Earthly* wife. Outside of this place—out in your desert—where the green grass grows sometimes, and the sky is sometimes blue, and there are horses and tents and land mines and sniper rifles—sure, out there I am your wife and I accept you as my husband. I do. However! Inside this space center, or in orbit, or on Mars, or inside that biosphere, or inside this airlock, any other area that is not of this Earth, then I am *not* your wife, Lucky. Instead, I own you. You are my slave."

"On the Earth, I am your husband, that's what you just declared to me?"

"*Only* on the Earth. Everywhere else, to be with Sonja is to be in trouble. I never lie to my men—no matter how much that hurts them."

"You think that you are getting a smart horse-trading bargain from me, woman, but you are wrong! So: Yes, I am happy now. We are married now, you are my bride. Congratulations." The Badaulet rose and pressed his nose to the finely scratched plastic of the porthole. "Now, wife of mine: Tell me about that light unmanned aircraft at ten o'clock, which is vectoring our way."

"What? Where?"

Lucky tapped at the porthole with his newly trimmed, newly cleaned fingernails. He had just spotted one single, tiny, black, distant speck, wafting high above the clotted and polychrome city. It could have been one speck of black Gobi dust on their porthole. He had better eyes than an eagle.

"I think that's a space probe," she said. "You generally hear a big thump from the coil gun whenever they launch a probe, but they make them so light these days—they're like space chickens."

"That is not a chicken or a satellite, because I eat chickens and I know satellites. That is an unmanned light aircraft. It is a precision anti-personnel bomb." Lucky turned to face her. "It was God who blessed me to marry you just now, for that aircraft is flying here to kill me."

Sonja blinked. "Are you entirely sure about that?"

"Yes I am sure. They have trapped me in here without my weapons. I know these aircraft, for I use them to kill. The Badaulet has many enemies. Soon I will die. And you, the bride of the Badaulet, you will die at my side. Heaven ordains all of this."

"Okay, maybe Heaven does ordain it. Or maybe *you* will die at *my* side, Lucky. Because I am Red Sonja, I am the Angel of Harbin, and I have more enemies than you do. My enemies are more advanced and more cunning enemies than your enemies."

"No, your enemies are only soft and womanly political enemies who live indoors. You don't have my fierce, warlike enemies of the steppes."

"Oh, don't flatter yourself, my husband! Once a teenage girl came to see me, she said to me, 'Are you Sonja Mihajlovic?' and I said, 'Yes I am, where does it hurt?' and she *exploded*. That girl blew herself up with a belt bomb! Pieces of her body flew into my body. She almost killed me! Just because of some stupid little nowhere village massacre that happened many years ago! And I didn't even burn those villages—my mother did all that! But I was inside a triage facility, so they slapped me right back together—wonderful work for a field hospital!"

The Badaulet hadn't understood a single word of this blurted confession, but his black eyes were wet with tender marital sympathy. "Are you afraid to die, my bride?"

"Oh no. Not really. Not anymore." Sonja had once felt tremendous fear about dying, but all that nonsense had left her years ago.

The airborne bomb took on visible dimensions. It might have been a child's kite, or a dried leaf, or a bedraggled crow. It was none of these things, for it was death on the wing. It was a small, sneaking, radar-transparent aircraft, so it flew rather clumsily.

"My comrades will avenge me for this," declared the Badaulet, "because I have faithfully avenged so many friends who perished in similar ways. Also, I have consummated my marriage before my wedding, which seemed a wicked thing to me—but now I *know* that part was *surely* divinely ordained. So I die happily!"

Sonja stood and spread her arms. She began to sing verse in Chinese.

> *"When will the full moon appear? I ask the sky with my wine*
> * cup in my hand,*
> *Wondering: What year might it be now, up in the lunar*
> * palace?*
> *I meant to be riding high up there, but I feared I could not*
> * bear the cold of that beautiful sanctuary.*
> *Accompanied with my shadow I dance; don't you agree that*
> * I am in heaven now?*
> *Moonlight sweeps my red pavilion, moonlight floods my*
> * decorated windows and shines on my sleepless soul.*
> *Oh Moon, without mortal sentiment: Why reveal your full*
> * face only when lovers part?*
> *Happy unions and sad departures are as common as your*
> * changing phases.*
> *May my lover and I both be safe and well, and may we share*
> * the Moon, although we are parted by a thousand miles."*

"That was poetry," said the Badaulet.

"Yes, that was my favorite poem in the whole world. It was written in the T'ang dynasty, when China ruled the world."

"This system understands your sad poetry much better than it understands your funny jokes."

The flying bomb slammed into the fabric surface of the airlock, and it bounded off. It flopped and yawed and wobbled and caught itself in midair, and gained height for a second effort.

"I always wanted to die while making love or speaking poetry," Sonja explained.

"If this air smelled better, I would oblige you."

The bomb returned for its second pass. Sonja threw herself to the airlock floor, curled into a fetal position, and clamped her hands over her ears.

Another sullen thump followed and the bomb bounded off again, harmlessly.

"Oh, get up, woman," the Badaulet scolded. "Meet your death on your feet, for your girlish cowardice is so undignified."

"Get down here and hit the deck, stupid! This increases our odds of survival!"

"There are no 'odds for survival'! There is only what Heaven ordains!"

Having endured many bombs in her past, Sonja ignored him, and doubled up tightly on the spotless airlock floor. "For God's sake, why are they trying to hit me instead of that huge Mars dome over there? That is China's greatest prestige construction, it's got to be a much fatter target than I am!"

"Sonja, my dear wife Sonja: Let us swear to Heaven that if we survive this cowardly attack, we will track down these evildoers and personally kill them ourselves."

"I love you so much for saying that! That is the greatest thing you have ever said to me! I swear I'll do it, if you will do it with me."

The plane smashed into the airlock and shattered. Brittle pieces of airplane plummeted out of their sight.

"Built by amateurs," Sonja said, craning her neck to stare.

"I am glad that it broke to pieces," said the Badaulet, still on his feet but panting harder, "but now we will smother to death in this sealed, trapped room."

Sonja didn't much mind meeting her own death. Still, to lose *him*, another husband, right before her eyes . . .

Sonja never heard the bomb explode.

SONJA'S SUPPORT TENT was scarlet and the moon shone through it.

Any narrow escape from death always made Sonja keenly sentimental. Escaping death had taught her that life had many tags and rags, loose ends, unmet potentials. Sonja rather prided herself on her serene fatalism, but there were always issues she felt unhappy to leave unsettled.

Escape from death put her in a generous, easygoing, affirmative mood. Because, now, all the days ahead of her were a free gift. Like icing on a pretty cake hit by a grenade.

"That drone bomb blew both my eardrums out," she told her brother, George. "The overpressure broke both of them. So the state built me brand-new ears. I have new and advanced Chinese cyborg astronaut ears. My ears are officially fantastic."

George blinked from distant Europe, on his video screen. "Sonja, how many attempts does this make on your life?"

Sonja blinked back. "Do you mean me personally?"

"Of course I mean you personally! Stop acting crazy."

"Why would I keep count of that? After I went to New York and I saw that New York City had been nuked . . . Why does anyone ever *bother* to count the dead? I'm just one person! If you don't count Radmila. Radmila was also there in New York City."

"Are you talking to me openly about Radmila now?" George was amazed. "Are you on drugs, Sonja?"

"This is Jiuquan, we don't trifle with stupid narcotics!" Sonja had a raging exfection. An "exfection" was very much like an infection. Except, instead of causing human flesh to waste away rapidly in a noisome mass of pus, an exfection was a kindly state-designed microbe that caused damaged human flesh to heal at more-than-human speed.

There were yellow, crusty, suppurating masses of exfection thriving all over Sonja's bomb-scorched shins and forearms. The crude bomb had shocked her and burned her, but since the airlock was made almost entirely of fabric, there had been no killing shrapnel.

The Badaulet had faced his own death boldly standing, so the bomb had broken both his feet. Her lucky husband was in a distant safe house hidden in the inflated bowels of the city, undergoing some much-embarrassed Chinese medical hospitality.

"Sonja," George told her, "if your brand-new ears are really working, then just for once, I want you to listen to me. I have an important proposal for you. I want you to accept it."

"Do you ever talk to Radmila, George?"

"Do I 'talk' to Radmila? I have *met* Radmila! We were *in the same room together* in Los Angeles, just last month! Radmila was *kind* to me!" George was sincerely thrilled.

"Then, Djordje, would you please tell Radmila—that I'm sorry I kicked her ass, that time in New York? That was wrong of me. I'm sorry that I snap-kicked her in the guts and I knocked her senseless. I was so jealous about her boyfriend, I was out of my head about Montalban. I should never have gone to New York no matter how much Montalban coaxed me. Never again, I'm through with him now: I promise."

"That may be more than Radmila wants to know. Radmila isn't very well right now. Things went badly in Los Angeles . . . there were riots. And huge fires."

"You do talk to Vera, though, don't you, Djordje?"

"I do sometimes talk to Vera, when Vera lets me—and stop calling me 'Djordje.' "

"So Djordje: Would you please tell Vera, just for me . . ." Sonja stopped, at a loss for words. She had no idea what to say to Vera. She hadn't said a word to Vera in nine years.

"Vera is not at her best lately either," said George, and his worried tone rang in her head like a bronze bell. "No one knows where Vera is— she's alive, but she's hiding in the woods somewhere in some death zone. Sonja, give up whatever you think you're doing there. Come stay with me in Vienna."

"What? Why on Earth would I do that?"

"Because you'll survive, woman! Like I'm surviving! I'm not like you, and Vera, and Radmila! I don't want to save the world! I'm just a fixer, I'm a logistics man! But listen: The world is changing. The world is not collapsing—or, at least, not as fast as it was doing before. The world is turning into something we never imagined. My shipping business is great! Global business is heading for a big, long, global boom!"

"I can't visit you there in Vienna, George. I just got married."

"You did *what*? What, again? You married someone? Are you serious?"

"My husbands are always serious."

"Montalban doesn't know anything about this new marriage of yours," said George thoughtfully. "That's going to be big news to John Montalban."

"You tell John Montalban that I am his black angel. Tell John I'm your big, long, global boom. Tell John I'm his giant supervolcano."

"Oh Sonja, poor Sonja. Now I know you're not yourself. Come on: giant supervolcanoes? We don't believe in giant volcanoes, do we? That's talking nonsense."

"Here in Jiuquan, all the people believe in that nonsense. The Chinese are convinced that a volcano will explode in America and wreck the world's climate."

"Why, because the Chinese wrecked the climate the first time?"

"Yes they did. With American help. And because here in Jiuquan, tomorrow's second climate crisis *won't even slow them down*. Not anymore. Not in the glorious future!"

"Sonja, it is definitely time for you to leave those cult compounds in China and rejoin the real world," said George solemnly. "No volcano will do anything that matters for ten thousand aeons. Exotic Chinese superstitions from inside some weird space bubble, that's what you're talking about. You've had enough of that. That won't work out for you. Trust me."

"Weather scientists were right when they said that the Earth's climate would crash. Why should geologists be wrong when they're predicting the same thing? Science is the truth. Science is science. Science is the future."

"Oh, what astronaut crap you're talking now! How many rich and famous scientists do you know? Did you ever see one lousy scientist get his own way in the real world? They're all hopeless eggheads full of make-believe theories!"

George drew a breath—she could hear him puffing in the busy cores of her new eardrums. "Sonja, please. When you were out there in the field—crusading to save civilization, or whatever—I cared about that, I helped you! You remember how may times I helped you go save your favorite Chinese civilization? But now they're trying to kill you right there in their own spaceport! What kind of 'civilization' is that to save?"

"This is China. Their system works differently."

"Look, I manage global logistics, so I learn something new every day," George boasted. "I can traffic in people like you! I'll *export* you from China. I'll export you right here to Vienna! When Inke heard that you were hurt again, she cried!"

Finally, Sonja was touched. Inke Zweig. Good old Inke. She had once spent a family Christmas together with Inke, when George, thankfully, wasn't around.

First, Inke took her to Mass, insisting that she kneel and pray. Then Inke took her home, and Inke got very drunk on dainty, reeking, German herbal liqueurs. Then Inke, sobbingly, told Sonja all about her life. Inke vomited up her soul right at her kitchen table.

It was a boozy, sisterly, holiday heart-to-heart, all about Inke's house, and her kitchen, and her kids, and her favorite cabbage and sausage recipes, and the will of God, and her husband, and Inke's grinding, life-blighting fear of her hostile and terrible world.

Inke was intelligent—she was perceptive enough to know that the world was in lethal danger—but Inke was too timid to do anything useful.

So, Inke had married, instead. Inke had forfeited every aspect of human agency to the man in her life. Inke had hidden herself in her thick fog of housework and piety, where she could cook, pray, and have babies.

And this strategy even *made sense* for the woman, this self-abnegation was Inke's version of a heroic act. Inke Zweig was a sweet and tender and vulnerable creature. Inke loved her kids dearly. Inke's kids were even great kids, because they didn't know one single useful thing about reality. They thought their mom and dad were terrific and all-knowing and proud and prosperous.

Her kids even loved their aunt Sonja, for no particular reason that Sonja understood. They gave their aunt Sonja fancy Christmas presents from prestigious Viennese stores.

"Sonja, you are family: Inke always says that. Inke would love to look after you," George promised. "You wouldn't have to see me at all! I'm on the road most days. You could have your own private wing of the mansion! Or—if my global business keeps booming—you can have your own apartment building!"

"Vienna is pretty," she told him. "I think you made a good choice, working there."

"Sonja, you won't survive. To get killed—like our others were killed?—that was tragic. But to *want* to be killed, like *you* so obviously want to be killed? That is sheer foolishness!"

"Djordje, suppose that I go to Europe, and I lose my temper there, and I kill *you?*"

"Oh, you would never do that!" George lied. "Any more than I would ever kill *you.*"

Sonja thought about his proposal for all of fifteen seconds. No, his sad, meager, bourgeois little notions wouldn't do.

"George," she told him sweetly, "I want you to help me leave Ji-uquan."

"Great, great! Excellent news! Now you're talking sense! You name the date!"

"I want you to find some Provincial Reconstruction Team—Acquis, Dispensation, whoever—located in central Asia. Well outside the borders of China, out in the desert, where the wild people are. Get them to put in a formal request for my aid and expertise. It's always much easier for me to travel outside China when the state has the formal documents."

"All right, fine, one small moment here," said George, "let me use my correlation engine! With this amazing new business tool, I can change your life from right here in my chair! My new network engine is Californian! In ten years the whole Earth will have a new economy!"

Sonja's keen ears heard George busily tapping at keys. " 'Scythia'?" George said, almost at once. "Would 'Scythia' do for you? Scythia is a poststate disaster region in the middle of Asia. You could go anywhere in Asia and claim you were going to 'Scythia.' "

"I know about Scythia. I also need special travel gear, George. Some private-militia, hunter-killer, Scorpion-tag-team, covert-penetration gear." Sonja paused. "That's not for me. It's a wedding gift."

This demand made George unhappy. "You know that I stopped facilitating that market. Those years were the bad old years. Those years are behind both of us now."

"I'm sure you didn't forget how to globally traffic in arms."

"Sonja, don't say that sort of thing about me. That hurts my feelings. I am paying to do this for you, and I will not pay to see you get killed in a desert. I want you to *not* get killed, that is my program. Forget rushing into the wild desert with many big guns. That is not practical."

"I have to leave here. I'm attracting trouble. So I have two choices: space, or the desert. We have no manned launches scheduled in Jiuquan. Oh, there is one third choice: if I'm willing to go to Antarctica. The ice desert. In Antarctica, I would be wearing a giant nuclear-powered robot suit and building glaciers with my fists."

George was interested. "Is it so bad for you in Jiuquan that the state would send you into exile in Antarctica? That's the sister project to that giant Chinese project in the Himalayas."

"How did you know all that?"

"Never mind."

"Antarctica is very like Mars. The Chinese state would reassign me to build fresh ice at the South Pole. There I would be out of reach of any flying bombs. Except for the state's own flying bombs."

"That's a strange tangle," George said thoughtfully. "Your state's plan for preserving your welfare is very ingenious and very not-human. An autonomous bureaucracy makes peculiar, lateral moves."

"The Chinese state loves me," Sonja told him. "I've always had a special rapport for ubiquitous systems."

"You don't want to go to Antarctica?"

"No," she shouted, "I don't want to hide from the bandits in a nuclear robot suit! That useless strategy is for *cowards*! You find the bastards, you triangulate their position, and you *fry* them! Then you seize their computers and phones and arrest everyone that they know. That's my war."

"Are you *required* to say that sort of thing, Sonja?"

"I don't 'say' that. I *do* that."

"Let me do another search on my beloved new engine," said George. "It never fails to hit on correlations of major interest."

George tapped away. He was such a soft European idiot. George had no grasp of harsh reality; he was useful but weak. The state needed strong people, like herself and the Badaulet. It needed human agents willing to venture beyond its limits.

Being a nation, the Chinese state had many national limits. It held power: because it commanded the rivers and the national canals. The state commanded anything to do with the nation's precious water resources: the distilleries, dams, the reservoirs, the plumbing, the sewers, the water-treatment recyclers . . . the streets, the traffic . . . the national power grid, the urban video system, the telecoms, the archives and every Chinese satellite, of course . . .

George was postnational, global . . . but his beloved "global business" had been selling human flesh in public, when, during China's worst crisis, the Chinese state never grieved and it never faltered and it never gave up restoring and extending control.

The state controlled public health. The state destroyed disease. The Chinese state destroyed disease with the ruthless and dispassionate efficiency of a computer defeating human grandmasters at chess. Sonja hated and feared disease more than any other horror she had witnessed. Any enemy of disease was Sonja's friend. She was grateful for what the state had done.

"Scythian ice princess," George announced.

"What did you just call me?"

"This is a beautiful correlation here. Only a very speedy and glorious network could have linked these phenomena. Listen to this: I am looking at a Scythian ice princess. She's not pretty, because she is a dead Bronze Age woman. She was buried in central Asia in a tomb of permafrost. But: That permafrost was melting quickly. So the Chinese used their Martian ice probes to search for frozen tombs in the Asian desert . . . and the Chinese found this Scythian princess, this tattooed mummy that I am seeing at this moment, and they dug her up with a secret strike-and-retrieval team. That ancient corpse is under scientific study—there in Jiuquan, in the same hospital, with you! She is not one hundred meters away from you! Top *that*, eh?"

George chuckled gleefully. "She is two floors away from you, locked inside a medical refrigerator! Correlation engines are *amazing technology*, aren't they? I have used business-to-business networks all my life, but this is *supernatural*. Can you imagine how much data the net has sorted, to find that out so quickly? And I possess that speed and power, on my desk, here in Vienna! The world will be transformed!"

Sonja ran her fingers gently over the seething, blistering, restorative exfection on her forearms. "George, why should I care about your 'Scythian ice princess'?"

"You don't care—and I don't care that you don't care, because *I care*. This dead Scythian woman has *human gut flora that dates back before antibiotic pollution*. She has her original human commensal microorganisms! Does that sound familiar to you?"

Sonja was in Jiuquan, so of course microbes sounded familiar to her. "George, no one wants any *ancient, wild* microbes. Those microbes are *backward* and *feudal*. Those microbes are of academic interest only. You want Jiuquan's *fully advanced* internal gut microbes, created in the state's genetic-recombinatorial labs. Those microbes are state secrets, and very valuable."

"Oh no, I want those *good old-fashioned all-natural* microbes," George said firmly. "Just—don't scrape any nasty goo out of some Asian corpse. I want the genetic sequences of the microbes. Just the pure data. Could you supply that microbe data to me? Could you do that, Sonja?"

"Probably. I am a public health officer here. Yes, I could do that."

"Excellent!"

"If I get you those Scythian microbes—will you ship me what I need for my military operations, with no more trifling?"

"Yes."

SONJA METHODICALLY READIED HERSELF for vengeance: to find out who to kill, why, and how. Vengeance was a rather more thorough, thoughtful, and comprehensive effort than it had once been for Sonja.

When Sonja had first arrived in China—fresh off the boat at the age of nineteen—she had known that she was heading for a cataclysm. She had desired that fate, she had sought that out: the bold desperado, without a homeland, joining a foreign legion.

She'd instantly fallen in with much bolder desperadoes. All the men Sonja had loved were keen-eyed, domineering, headstrong, fearless men. They were men at home in hell. However, their courage, while always necessary and always in short supply, was not what was needed to make a cataclysm *stop*.

On the contrary: Raw courage was superb at *provoking* cataclysms. Any gutsy teenager, boldly careless of his life, could empty his gun into some archduke and create colossal chaos. Stopping cataclysms required imposing order.

Sonja had come to understand the order as the hard part of the work. To end a war meant either restoring an old order, or invoking a new order. Neither work was easy. Order, unlike war, required unglamorous skills such as political savvy, business sense, and rugged logistics.

Restoring order required a crisp, succinct articulation of the big picture and why one's efforts mattered in that regard. It required a tremendous knowledge of details. It needed the patience to build a long-lasting, big-scale enterprise that would not collapse instantly from guerrilla attacks. And it needed a cold-blooded ability to make firm choices among disgusting alternatives.

George was a merchant and a fixer, never the kind of man she liked. Yet George, for all his countless demerits, had a definite rapport for ubiquitous systems. George had a positive genius for handling border delays, security compliances, fuel costs, detours on the planet's weather-shattered roads and bridges, documentation hurdles, no-fly zones and confiscatory carbon-footprint taxes, port congestion, cargo security, regulations both in-state and offshore, liaisons with manufacturers, outsized and overweight shipping modules . . . Boring things, dull things. Yet George could ship things to her, and that mattered.

Bravery mattered much less. A brave woman could be "very brave" in a field hospital. She might hold the hand of a dying child while it coughed up blood. That moral act required a courage that left dents all over one's soul, while, in the meantime, any tedious holdup in the flow of medical supplies could kill off *entire populations*, not tender children killed tragically in their ones and twos, but masses killed statistically in their hundreds and thousands.

Privates and sergeants bragged about courage: digging foxholes and kicking in doors. Colonels and generals talked soberly about supply trains and indirect fire. Barbarism, disorder, chaos, and murder were the ground state of mankind, so foxholes and ambushes were in infinite supply. Public order was about leveraging the things that were in short supply: with sturdy supply trains and superior firepower.

It had taken Sonja quite some time to comprehend all this, because, as a nineteen-year-old adventuress, she had been far too busy learning Chinese, sopping up a patchy medical training, and establishing her personality cult. But she had finally learned such things, well enough. She'd had teachers.

The fortunes of war favored the bold, if the bold survived. Sonja was nothing if not bold. Eventually, an important apparatchik had descended from the murky heavens of Beijing's inner circles to manifest a personal interest in her glorious career.

This gentleman was Mr. Zeng, a thoughtful, open-eyed chief of the "Scientific Research Bureau." Which was to say, Mr. Zeng was a Chinese secret policeman.

Having been publicly befriended by the important Mr. Zeng, Sonja had become a de facto member of Zeng's "clique," or "power center," or "faction," or "guan-xi network," as those terms were generally phrased by offshore Beijingologists. The twelve weeks Sonja had spent in high-society Beijing as Zeng's "protégée," or "client," or "escort," or, not to put too fine a point on it, as one of his mistresses, was the closest Sonja had ever come to achieving true power within the Chinese power structure.

Mr. Zeng was a top domestic spy in an authoritarian, cybernetically hyperorganized, ultrawealthy nation-state in a calamitous public emergency. So Mr. Zeng had extreme and scary and even lunatic amounts of power. This power did not make Zeng happy. He faced many serious problems.

His beloved country was measled all over with Manhattan Project–style technofixes for his nation's desperate distress. As state secrets, these bold, wild projects were so opaque that nobody could number them. Furthermore, Beijing's cliques were so corrupted that they might well have sold these projects to somebody. The Acquis and Dispensation doted on buying China's crazy projects, and, mostly, shutting them down.

Mr. Zeng clearly derived some benefit from his personal liaison with Sonja. As a woman, Sonja lightened a few of his many cares of office. Sonja would not have called their activity a "love affair," as she didn't much care for him personally. Still, for her, it was definitely a transformative encounter.

Mr. Zeng was not merely a top spy, but also a Stanford-educated biochemist who spoke four languages. Zeng was a searingly intelligent workaholic. The only trace of whimsy in Zeng's character was the guilty pleasure he took in the garish and decadent entertainment vehicles of Mila Montalban. Everyone in Zeng's sophisticated social circle doted on gaudy American pop entertainment. Hollywood was so entirely alien to their deadly crises that it seemed to refresh their spirits as nothing else could.

Mr. Zeng was an icily rational gentleman. It showed in the methodically sacrificial way that he played board games with his cronies.

In their pillow conversations, Zeng gently explained to Sonja that "saving civilization" (her professed goal in life) had very little to do with her brashly tackling emergencies with her own two hands. No, if any civilization was going to be "saved" at all—said Mr. Zeng—the planet's civilization was in so much trouble that it could only be saved by something new, huge, unexpected, extreme, and indeed almost indescribable.

The planet's current power structure: the sudden rise of the Acquis and the Dispensation, and the abject collapse of nation-states generally, with the large exception of China—that power structure was predicated on arranging just such a situation. The planet was dotted all over with radically extreme experiments intended to "save civilization."

The problem was that most of these innovations did not work. They could never work, because they were too far-fetched. It cost a lot to try such experiments. Worse yet, it was much harder to shut down failed experiments that it was to invent brand-new ones.

The largest such intervention in the world was, of course, Chinese. It was the Chinese effort to geologically engineer the Himalayas so that China's rivers would once again flow. China had performed this feat with the twentieth century's single most radical world-changing technology: massive hydrogen bombs.

Mr. Zeng had been among the people planning and executing that national effort. Chinese geoengineering had not been an easy plan to explain to concerned foreigners. China had gotten its way in the matter by offering to drop hydrogen bombs on anyone who objected.

Glumly recognizing China's implacable need to survive, the planet's other power players had bowed to the Chinese ultimatum. There was a gentleman's agreement to let the Chinese get on with it, and to not dwell too painfully and too publicly on their insane explosions digging monster ice lakes in the Himalayas. Instead, the Acquis and Dispensation turned up their quiet diplomatic pressure, while enjoying the benefits of some ancillary planetary cooling.

That was how the serious players worked while literally saving the modern world.

So—Zeng continued gently, playing with her curls—if Sonja truly wanted to "save civilization," she should not continue to do that by taking small-arms fire in her medical tents at the edges of thirst-crazed cities. Serious-minded statesmen did not bother with such activities, since soldiery was one of the vilest of callings and best reserved for angry and ignorant young men. Instead of behaving in that backward way, Sonja should consider volunteering for duty at the highly prestigious Jiuquan Space Launch Center, where there were extremely advanced and unexpected medical experiments under way. These antiplague measures involved combining microbes and medical scanners, and the implications of their success were extreme, even more extreme than blasting many large new holes in an Asian mountain range.

Sonja did not, at first, respond to Mr. Zeng's recruitment proposal. She knew for a fact that Zeng was a secret policeman, and she knew in her heart that he was a mass murderer.

Mr. Zeng was not a small-scale, face-to-face killer in the bold way of the warriors that she knew and loved best. Mr. Zeng was the kind of killer who deployed a nuclear warhead the way he might set a black go-stone on a game board.

So, instead of going to Jiuquan, Sonja boldly volunteered to take some of those newfangled scanners and microbes and test them out in practice in the field. Mr. Zeng remarked that this was characteristic of her. He said that it was endearing, and that he had expected her to say that. He praised her bravery, patted her bottom wistfully, gave her a number of valuable parting gifts, and told her to stay in touch.

So Sonja swiftly fled from Zeng's embraces and took his spotless state-secret equipment to the filthy mayhem in Harbin, where that equipment more or less worked. It worked against all sane expectations and it worked radically and it sometimes even worked beautifully.

Mostly, it worked because no one in her barefoot-medical team, including Sonja herself, had ever quite understood what they were supposed to do with cheap lightbulbs that made flesh as clear as glass, or black-box devices that combated infections by "fatally confusing" germs. In Harbin, everyone had made a lot of valuable fresh mistakes.

Before the Harbin episode, Red Sonja had been notorious within paramilitary circles, but after Harbin, Sonja had become an official national heroine. Which was to say, she was a kind of sleekly feminine hood ornament for the state's least-imaginable enterprises.

To refuse such a role was unthinkable. To accept it was unimaginable. Passionately embracing the unimaginable—that always moved the world more effectively than horribly embracing the unthinkable.

This was the course of action which had directly brought Sonja to her present predicament. And she had had methods by which to deal with such problems. Zeng's finest gift to her was a word: a simple, quiet word. That word was the password to a clandestine web service, run by Zeng's intelligence apparatus. Like Zeng himself, this service was in the state, and of the state, and for the state, and yet it was somehow not quite of the state.

Zeng's gift was best described as a Chinese power-clique I Ching, a political fortune-reader. It read the tangled, subtle Chinese nation as one might read a sacred text.

The Chinese nation consisted of the vast, ubiquitous, state-owned computational infrastructure, plus the fallible human beings supposedly controlling that.

The state machine was frankly beyond any human comprehension. While the human beings were human: they were a densely webbed social network of mandarins, moguls, spies, financiers, taipans, ideologues, pundits, backstage fixers, social climbers, hostesses, mistresses, cops, generals, clan elders, and gray eminences; not to mention the mid-twenty-first-century equivalents of triad brotherhoods, price-fixing rings, crooked cops, yoga-fanatic martial-arts cults, and other subterranean social tribes of intense interest to the likes of Mr. Zeng.

Sonja did not fully trust Zeng's I Ching because, just five months after entrusting the password to her, Mr. Zeng himself had been killed. Along with thirty-seven high-ranking members of his exalted clique—many people even more senior than Mr. Zeng himself—Mr. Zeng had smothered inside an airtight government basement in a Beijing emergency shelter.

This terrorist assassination, or mass suicide, or political liquidation—it might have even been a simple tragic accident during a heavy dust storm—had come with no visible warning. If Zeng's gift were truly useful, then, presumably, Zeng should have used it to avoid his own death.

So: Maybe Zeng's ambivalent gift was nothing more than a superstition, a pseudo-scientific magic charm against the pervasive fear so common to people in any authoritarian society. Maybe this service was a manly gesture that Zeng offered to all his women—not because it was helpful, but because it made his women feel better. There were times when Sonja despised herself, and felt sure that this was true.

Still, Sonja used it, because—as Zeng had pointed out—she herself was featured in it.

In Zeng's weird network of slowly pulsing simulated blobs, she, Sonja Mihajlovic, was a small, fluffy blue cloud.

She was a little fluffy cloud, and, since her role was to legitimate the medical activities inside the Jiuquan Space Launch Center, she was a cloud of political obfuscation. Her purpose was to be the Angel of

Harbin, and thereby to allow the Chinese state to quietly inject ID tags into every Chinese citizen, to quietly compile massive DNA databases of every individual, and to thoroughly scan the Chinese body of every Chinese individual, head-to-toe, at a cellular level.

To the extent that her reputation for bravery and integrity would stretch to cover this, Sonja was further to ensure the global credibility of the national blood samples, the microbial stool samples, the lymph samples and brain scans, the exotic probiotic gut organisms of possibly Martian descent . . . Everything and anything that China did to survive.

Totalitarianism was blatant, old-fashioned, and stupid: it stamped the face of the public with the sole of a boot, for as long as it could do that. A ubiquitarian state was different. Because it flung one, or ten, or a thousand, or a million boots every nanosecond, when no human being could possibly see or feel what a "nanosecond" was.

Sonja understood her role. She knew its consequences and she felt that she knew what she was doing. She chose to do these things, not for her own sake, but for the cause of public health.

Sonja had come to realize, through her own experience, that public health had little to do with any individual conscience. If a million people were dying, you didn't heal them by crying over one of them. The issue was not the pain and grief to be found in any one sickroom, or one house, one street, one neighborhood, city, province—it was all about massive scaling powers, exponential powers-of-ten.

Did people die, or did you save people? People died with statistical regularity, until you found and used some power large and strong enough to avert their woe.

When that power reached a certain level of invasive ubiquity, the power of computation would directly confront and crush the power of disease. Because they were two rival powers. Diseases were everywhere, while surveillance was everyware. Everyware crushed diseases, subtly, comprehensively, remorselessly.

The sensorweb could scan the actions of bacteria invading a human body, and, like a Chinese army general, it could defeat that invading horde in real time.

Even an invading bacterium had a certain military logic: any germ had to observe its environment within the human body, orient itself, "decide" on a course of action, and then execute that strategy.

The state was far better at grasping such strategies than any bacterium could be. Once it had a human body firmly staked out in its scanners, it would wage a computational war-in-detail against internal disorders, baffling, frustrating, starving, arresting, and poisoning bacteria.

Wherever the bionational complex spread its pervasion, diseases gasped their last. Diseases simply could not compete. What the state's nationware could do within the individual human body, it could also do at the level of streets, cities, provinces—everywhere within the Great Firewall of China.

This great feat was real, for she herself had seen it, and had done it in Harbin. It would take the world a while to understand what that accomplishment meant. It always took the world a while to comprehend such things. But it meant that infectious diseases were doomed. Diseases had been technically outclassed, they would not survive. That was a far greater medical breakthrough than older feats like sanitation, or vaccines, or antibiotics.

Bacteria would surely fight back—they always did. But this time, they were done. They could mutate against mere antibiotics, but they could never hide from the scanners. Being single-celled creatures, bacteria could never get any smarter. So epidemics, without exception, were going to be tracked down, outflanked, outperformed, and exterminated.

That was not the end of the grand story, either: that was only its beginning. One day soon there would be no hunger in China. People outside Jiuquan—outside China—they lacked basic understanding of the potential of a human gut with fully advanced, reengineered bacteria. But: Those newly farmed microbes made old-fashioned digestion, that catch-as-catch-can spew of wild internal microbes, seem as backward and primitive as hunting-and-gathering.

The new Chinese microbes turned people's insides into booming internal factories of energy and protein: so tomorrow there would be no famine. The Chinese state was going to re-line the nation's guts with the same seeming ease that the Chinese had once covered the planet's feet with cheap shoes.

Never any more starving children, no more human bodies reduced to sticks of limbs and racks of protruding ribs. Obsolete. Defunct. Over. Nothing left of that vast tragedy. Not one microbial trace.

So: Two mighty Horsemen of the Apocalypse, Famine and Pestilence—

they had already been shot dead in China. They were titans in scale, so it would take them maybe forty years to fall from their thundering black horses and hit the dust for good. But they were over, doomed. And she, Sonja, Angel of Harbin, ranked among the victors.

Plague and Starvation would be history. Their apocalyptic depredations would be forgotten as if such things had never occurred. In the future, they would have to be explained to people.

That still left Sonja's two other Apocalyptic enemies, War and Death, still very much in the planetary saddle, but nevertheless, in Jiuquan—in Jiuquan!—she'd just been scorched by an antipersonnel bomb and yet she was going to be on her feet, healthy, unmarked, clear-eyed, and partially bionic, in a week. In ten days, at the most.

Developments of this scale, the most grandiose scale possible: These were the schemes that kept Sonja standing firm at her duties. Forged in the heat of combat, she was an iron pillar of the state.

Except on Mr. Zeng's analytical screens, where the Angel of Harbin was not an iron pillar but a vulnerable fluffy blue cloud.

With her bioplastic notebook uneasily poised on her exfected knees in her watery hospital bed, Sonja saw, with a sinking, seasick sensation, that her blue cloud looked distinctly stormy. In Zeng's world, this was the hexagram sigil and omen signifying that one was (in a colloquial translation) "getting too big for one's boots," that "the heat was on," that "tomorrow's prospects were dim."

As she studied these cryptic hints, Sonja realized for the first time that Mr. Zeng's service had a name in English: it was a "correlation engine." She had been using a correlation engine all this time, in another language and another context. Apparently these radical techniques had escaped Chinese state secrecy, and become so common lately that even Western businesspeople like George saw fit to use them.

Sonja certainly was not in "business." Sonja was a state heroine. Profits were not her concern—but purges were. As a state operative, if you didn't already know for sure who the chosen victim was and why, then that victim was probably you.

This established, Sonja had to discover who had tried to kill her. There were three basic varieties of killers in China: the people supporting the state, the traitors against the state, and, worse yet, the people like herself and Mr. Zeng, the people definitely with the state yet not eminently of the state, people who were plausibly deniable and eminently disposable.

After some deft string pulling, the local police saw fit to share the results of their investigations with Sonja.

The attack plane had been vaporized by its payload of explosive. However, one of its wings and parts of its landing gear had cracked and fallen off. Those fragments were rich with criminal evidence.

For the Jiuquan police, any grain of stray pollen was a clue that blazed like an asteroid. The police knew the range of the plane, from its wing shape and its fuel capacity. They knew, roughly, what landscapes it must have overflown, because of the pollen lodged in its crude seams. They further knew that the plane had been hand-built, recently, in the desert, from snap-together panels of straw plywood.

It was a toy airplane made in a secret bandit camp—made from pressed Mongolian hay. The plane's lightweight panels were so carelessly glued that they might have been assembled by a ten-year-old child.

As a further deliberate insult, the plane had somehow been salted with DNA from several high-ranking officials who had once been major figures of the Chinese state. Fake DNA evidence was no surprise to the local police, of course—even the cheapest street gangs knew how to muddy a DNA trail, these days. Still, given that the police in Jiuquan were absolutely sure to study DNA evidence, this was a nose-thumbing taunt, a knowing terrorist provocation. It showed a mean-spirited cunning that could only be the work of true subversives.

So, Sonja had the profile of her enemies: they were not of the Chinese state. They were ragtag political diehards, pretending to state connections, skulking outside the state's borders, and trying to liquidate her. They were anti-state bandits who wanted revenge.

It had never been Sonja's intention to provoke revenge attacks. Sonja had never wanted to kill anyone. Her first jaunt into China had been as a teenage camp follower in a medical relief column. Its poorly armored trucks were piled to bulging with rations, water barrels, tents, cots, bandages, antibiotics . . . Not thirty kilometers from port they'd been ambushed with rockets and small arms, their convoy shot to pieces and everything of value stolen by feral, screeching, dust-caked, rag-clad bandits who had scrambled back into the barricaded rubble that had once been their town.

That was Sonja's introduction to the true situation on the ground, and what followed had been unspeakably worse. As Sonja's first husband had put it: "It is necessary to incinerate the towns in order to save the cities," and he had incinerated many such before he met the death he'd always courted.

Ernesto had been a brave man from a distant corner of the Earth who had come to offer his hands and his heart and his medical knowledge and his strong, shapely, noble back to a stricken people—and, as many did, Ernesto had swiftly found it necessary to shoot many of them. Specifically, Ernesto had to shoot the gangs of malcontents who interfered with his redemption of the masses.

Nobody called Ernesto the "Angel" of anything, because when he sent his convoys tearing through the Chinese landscape he moved like a bloody hacksaw through a broken leg.

Sonja had been his wife, a caress and a whisper of comfort to Ernesto in his darkest hours, yet China didn't lack for bitter people who remembered things they had done. Along with many similar things Red Sonja herself had done since, in the same cause.

So: This latest episode of attempted revenge was part of her older story. It was simply a smaller and more personal story, because the scale of the havoc had dwindled. Bandits had once skulked in screaming thousands in the ruins of China's major cities. Bandits were now skulking in crazy dozens in the dusty wilderness far outside the state's armed boundaries. They were still bandits.

Bandit warlords came in a thousand factions, but they were all the same. Most were already gone, and the rest had to go.

AN UNMANNED POLICE VEHICLE deposited Sonja and her new husband at the ancient slopes of the Great Wall. Then it turned and fled with an unseemly haste back toward Jiuquan, leaving the two of them abandoned under the dazzling blue tent of central Asian sky.

If they were lucky in their lethal venture, they would never be seen by anyone. Sonja and the Badaulet were now a two-person "Scorpion team." Their task was to venture across the wilderness, spy out the camp of their enemies, call in a covert strike, and have the bandits annihilated.

They had both done such work before, so the chance to do it in tandem was a blessing to them as a couple.

The Great Wall of China was a sullenly eroded, ridge-backed dragon on the Earth. The color of dirt—for it was mostly handmade of dirt—it wriggled over an astounding expanse of central Asia. In the state's recent hours of need, technicians had brusquely drilled fresh holes and topped the Wall with the state's surveillance wands, transforming an ancient barrier into a modern surveillance network.

The new Wall consisted of the old Wall, plus tall, thin, gently swaying observation towers. Each needlelike tower was blankly topped with a mystical black head, a sphere devouring every trace of light that touched its opaque surface.

No merely human being could outguess what the state watched with these towering wands, for, potentially, the state surveilled everything within the Wall's huge line of sight. Not just passively absorbing light from the landscape, but sorting that light as data, sifting through it, searching it, collimating and triangulating and extrapolating from it . . . comparing each new nanosecond, pixel by pixel, to the ever-growing records of its previous observations.

The state's impassive visual ubiquity rambled on for thousands and thousands of closely linked kilometers, rooted in the ancient bricks and dirt of the longest, heaviest human structure ever created, its black towers like a fruiting bread mold in the immemorial substance of the planet's greatest fortress. There was not a single human guard along the new Wall. Like astronauts on the Martian surface, people were politically glorious yet practically unnecessary.

Hand in hand, Sonja and the Badaulet skulked past the monster ruins of a once-thriving tourist town. A life spent on horseback had made the Badaulet bowlegged, yet now he had an odd, spry, hop-along shuffle, for the Jiuquan clinic had done extraordinary things to the broken bones of his feet.

The medical operatives had also tactfully replaced Lucky's bomb-blown ears, so that the two of them no longer needed any earplug translation units. Their new language translators were sophisticated onboard devices the size of flecks of steel, and they ran on blood sugar.

These sensory devices in her head—alien impositions—joined the chips of bone shrapnel lodged deep in Sonja's body. For seven years, she'd been part of a zealot's personal graveyard. Tiny chips of the dead woman's bones were melting away in her flesh, year by year. Sonja was metabolizing them.

Sonja was sure she would get used to her ears. As for the presence of another woman's bones in her own flesh: those had expanded her options. Vera, Radmila, Biserka: they were merely identical clones, while Sonja had become a hybrid chimera. Life always had fresh options for survivors.

This desert town in Gansu Province had once catered to wealthy tourists, gallivanting from around the world to tramp the Great Wall. Like all globalized tourist towns, the place had once been sophisticated. The town was now deader than Nineveh, for an urban water war had broken out here.

Water wars had a classic look all over China. They were small wars, or large deadly riots, fought with small arms: with automatic rifles, shoulder rockets, and improvised bombs.

The weapons were wielded by people who had once been cheerfully peaceable neighbors, but were crazed with hunger, thirst, and despair. It was dreadfully simple for China's host of workshops and forges to manufacture rifles. Cheap, simple rifles were much easier to make than, for instance, little homemade robot airplanes. Their computerized sights were brutally accurate. They were rifles reborn as digital cameras: point, click, and kill.

Some part of the civilian population here had hurriedly surrounded the last water wells. They had hastily piled up barricades to survive the stinging sniper fire from the excluded.

Thereafter, the besieged held the water, but those outside the walls could run around to make more guns and bombs. The dead city was a visible history of wild sorties, doomed assaults, random acts of arson, mining and countermining.

The stricken town, which had once sold placid postcard views of its Great Wall, was a crazy mass of tiny walls. These small walls had been piled up, in thirst and heat and darkness, by thousands of human hands, using hand tools.

The walled divisions tore through former neighborhoods. They were probably ethnic divisions: between the local Han Chinese, the Hui Chinese, Uighurs and Kazakhs and Kyrgiz, as well as a few hundred trapped foreign tourists and businesspeople, unable to believe how suddenly their pleasantly exotic life had gone to the extremely bad.

With every human soul covered head to foot in windy torrents of black Gobi dust, with the air thick with miasma from merciless urban fires, no previous social distinction would have made much difference on the ground. A water war wasn't a mere civil war but a hell on Earth, where you either seized water or you died.

Breathing through cloth, bricking up the windows, heaving their possessions from their homes and stores to form impromptu barricades, struggling to climb through burnt-out high-rises to dominate the free-fire zones . . . in a matter of weeks, with hand tools and their own backs, they had churned their urban fabric into this vast, scumbled-up, fatal labyrinth: a graveyard of sandbags, cruel palisades, sharpened stakes of iron reinforcing rod, high-piled, bullet-riddled washing machines, the twisted hulks of bomb-seared cars.

Eventually, the survivors had been led on an organized long march, the weakest of them dropping like flies, to some new locale where the state guaranteed them some water. The people of their city had never come back to their death trap. If they ever returned, they would never again live in this doomed, unsustainable way. They would be living in Jiuquan-style bubbles where every drop of the water was micromanaged by state machines.

The rains had been good this year. The ruined town was rankly overgrown with tall, weedy, sulfur-yellow flowers.

It took them four hours to march outside the line of sight of the Great Wall, with its mystically swaying and Taoistically impartial wands. This effort achieved, they stripped themselves and buried every traceable relic of China in a cairn of anonymous rocks.

Sonja then made a special point of plucking the state's radio ID tags from the flesh of their arms. That was a simple matter when you knew what you were doing, and, when done correctly, it was only slightly bloody.

They then climbed, barefoot, wincing, cautious, and entirely naked, over the crest of a long hill to the predetermined spot where George had hidden his bounty.

An unmanned cargo helicopter sat there. It was a kind entirely new to Sonja, though she considered herself a connoisseur of helicopters.

Crazily lightweight and transparent, all veins and segments, it looked like a sleeping dragonfly.

It bore Indian markings, and if it had really fluttered in from whatever was left of India, it must have traveled a fantastic distance.

The cargo helicopter was lying precisely where its global positioning system had placed it, inside a rugged little declivity, with poor lines of sight but a decent amount of sunshine for its exhausted batteries.

Sonja had a hard-won philosophy when it came to long marches through harsh territory. Sonja believed in traveling light. Her cargo consisted mostly of fabrics.

Everything else within the helicopter, she had ordered as a wedding gift for the Badaulet. The Badaulet had no such minimalist philosophy about his own goods. On the contrary: He had a gorgeously barbarian "more is more" aesthetic.

The Badaulet's gifts were a sniper rifle, a plastic pistol, binoculars, a gleaming titanium multitool, self-heating meals for those of an Islamic persuasion, a canteen, chemical lightsticks, paracord, a radio, a razor-keen ceramic dagger, a global positioning system, ammunition, and a veritable host of horrible little marble-sized land mines.

The Badaulet was painfully shy about his nudity, so he quickly tunneled into his desert camouflage. He swiftly disappeared. His new uniform was spotted with colored chromatophores, like the hide of a squid. It had a similar bush hat, with a face net.

Sonja's signature garment was her blindingly white robe. It was a simple baggy mess of dust-repellent fabric. Any fabric that was "dust-repellent" was also somewhat skin-repellent, so it was a stiff and unforgiving thing.

Sonja lashed the fabric to her wrists and waist and ankles with her signature magic charms, which George had included in the shipment. Long, crisscrossed black cords, with hexagrams, yin-yangs, lucky ideograms, crucifixes, Stars of David, tiny Muslim moon-and-crescents.

Ernesto had once told her that only a madwoman would dress in such fashion. She had made herself a big white target for snipers.

But Sonja, who unlike Ernesto was still alive, had sensed in some occult fashion, she had *known*, that the war surrounding them was not about their supposed enemies: the real war was about the dust. It was about the black dust, gray dust, red dust, yellow dust, that catastrophic omnipresent filth that penetrated every aspect of human existence. Peace would come—it would *only* come—when brought by cleanliness. Cleanliness brought by something—an angel, a saint, a prophet, a machine, a system, an entity, anyone, anything capable—that was *in* the dust but never *of* the dust.

Time and again Sonja had walked into the hellholes where they stored the sick and dying—the dead factories, the empty schoolyards— where, at the first sight of her, *a medic without any dust,* the moaning, sobbing crowds fell silent . . .

In the midst of the filthiest inferno, there were people and things and actions and thoughts that were not of that inferno. They were beyond the grip of hell.

The people could never leave hell with bullets. They needed a figure shining and white and clean who would hold out her two compassionate hands and pour fresh cleaning water on their split and aching faces. Despair was killing them faster than any physical threat.

It was they, not she, who had begun hanging magic charms on her— the knickknacks they'd been clutching in their desperate hope of redemption. She looked different, she *was* different, and they were hanging meaning on her.

They needed to hope in order to live, and for a dying public, a public image brought hope. A radiance that might come to them, bearing a handheld lamp: radiance to the bedside of the sufferer at the midnight of the human soul. There to wash the filth from their suffering feet.

Hope would cure when all other methods failed, when other treatments weren't even noticed. True anguish, the killing kind of despair, could *only* be relieved by ritual . . . If the sky turned black and the air was brown, an armed general could reason and bluster and bribe and threaten—not a soul would stir, even to save their own lives. An emotionally damaged teenage girl could drift by, in spotless white, dangling superstitions and jabbering lines of poetry, and they would rise as one and they would follow.

At this point in her life, Sonja found it hard to believe that she had done those things. But she *had* done them. Repeatedly. Spontaneously, tirelessly, in inspired trances, drawing strength from the light she saw in others. Extreme times pulled strange qualities from people. There were times when it helped a great deal to know that one was not entirely human.

Some men called her crazy—her second husband, and her third, in particular—but they were merely putting their own madness into better order by piling accusations on her. Because if Red Sonja was the crazy one, *why were they all dead?*

The Angel of Harbin had the gift of giving. Those who took it in the proper spirit, lived. The others . . . men, mostly . . .

From time immemorial, when a soldier left a battlefield, his body racked, his nerves shattered, for "rest and relaxation" . . . "Rest and relaxation" were the last things on any man's mind: any soldier fresh from battle immediately sought out a woman. If she merely opened her legs for him—if she said and she did nothing else whatsoever, if she asked him no questions, if she didn't even speak his language—all the better for him . . .

The Badaulet still had no horse. Sonja knew this as a failing on her part. There should have been a horse in George's shipment. But George, who was no poet, did not care to ship live animals in a helicopter, so Sonja could supply only a rough equivalent: a clumsy and graceless off-road pack robot.

She examined the robot with sorrow. When the crumbling Great Wall had been a vivid, living Chinese enterprise—for in its dynastic heyday, the Great Wall of China was no passive barrier, it had also been a highway, an imperial mail route, and the world's fastest visual telegraph—any Chinese bride would have endowed her warlord with a horse.

A world-famous "blood-sweating horse." Sonja had seen gorgeous T'ang dynasty pottery of those horses, and Chinese bronzes as well, with stallions as the emblems of Chinese state power at its most confident, serene, and globally minded. Superior Chinese war ponies, earth-pounding, indomitable, fit to run straight to Persia with wind-streaming manes and dainty hooves like swallows, surely the most beautiful horses that civilization had ever offered to barbarism.

Instead, she had this lousy robot. Hauled from its plastic mounts on the copter wall, the ungainly device mulishly escaped control and scampered straight up the harsh slopes of a nearby hillside. Sonja hated the robot instantly. She knew that it was bound to be a grievance.

The pack robot was as ugly as a dented bucket. It featured four eerily independent legs. Each leg swiveled from a corner of its cheap and brutally durable chassis.

Since it was not a beautiful male animal like a Chinese T'ang dynasty stallion, the robot did not trot with any dark animal grace. Instead, it moved by detailed computer analysis—as if it were playing high-speed chess with the surface of the Earth.

This meant that, on a cracked, eroded, thirty-degree slope of bitterly eroded Gobi Desert rock, a slope that would break the hairy legs of the toughest Mongol ponies and require rope and pitons from any human being, the robot scuttled along like a cockroach. Ever untiring, unknowing of anything like pain, the robot flicked out its horrid, metallically springy, devilishly hoofed legs, and it flung itself hither and yon, leaping from the minutest little purchases—tiny pebbles, invisible niches in boulders. It shot up and down treacherous hillsides like a thunderbolt.

The Badaulet was the picture of satisfaction. "I love you very much."

"You don't mind my very ugly, very stupid robot?"

"No," the Badaulet insisted, "I truly love you now. No man I know has such a clever wife as you. I had expected us to die quickly riding the Silk Road, for the planes drop many land mines there, and the mines have eyes and ears and they are clever. But with this mount, we will cross the desert on a magic carpet. We will surround ourselves with our own land mines to kill anyone who dares to bothers us. Each night I will sleep beneath the stars in your warm and tender arms!"

The scampering pack robot knew no difference between day or night; it could "see" by starlight as well as it "saw" anything at all. Its greatest single drawback, among many, was that it blindly trusted the latest data downloaded into it about the conditions on the ground. This meant that, despite its nasty genius at knuckle-walking the uneven landscape, it had a distressing tendency to pitch into unseen arroyos and ramble off unmapped cliffs.

Worse yet, unlike horses or camels, the robot had no natural rhythm in its gait. So that, when they crouched within the thing's bucketlike cargo hold, its hurrying tread felt like one endless, sickening set of panic stumbles.

To endure the numbing hours of travel, Sonja wrapped herself in a riding cloak. The heavy cloak grew steadily heavier with the passing hours, for it was an air distillery. Its fibers were sewn through with crystalline salts, which chemically sucked humidity from the desert breezes.

When the Badaulet scolded her for guzzling at his canteen, she stripped off her dark cloak, gave it one expert caressing twist, and clean water gushed down both her wrists in torrents.

A curdled look of astonishment and disbelief and even rage crossed her husband's face. The Badaulet had always suffered badly for his water. Water had been the cause of bitter discipline to him. The loss of water meant certain death . . . Yet here in this simple stupid rug, this plain womanly thing from off her back—she had only to twist it, and all his suffering was elided, erased, made senseless and irrelevant.

"My cloak is yours," she told him quickly.

He grumpily threw her magic cloak across his own back, but he hated her for that.

"You must wear this," he said at length, "for it grows heavy."

"No, dear husband, it's for you. It is sturdy, it will last for years."

"You wear this," he commanded. "In those foolish white robes you could easily be shot."

She obeyed him and put on the cloak, for she knew she had given offense. They were entering hills, unkindly hills like ragged black boulder piles, but the hills caught falling water and where there was water there was grass.

Sonja stopped, gathered some grass, stuffed it into a fabric rumen bag.

Sonja did not worry much about human bandits lurking in the Gobi—bandits were unlikely to survive in any place this barren. Death in the desert came mostly from autonomous machines.

The killer machines of the great Asian dust bowl came in three great families: autonomous rifles, autonomous land mines, and autonomous aircraft. They were all deadly: a few cents' worth of silicon empowered them to rain death from above, or to punch an unerring hole through a human torso, or to wait for silent years in a puddle of machine surveillance and then tear off a human leg.

The aircraft and the sniper devices were harder to manufacture and maintain, for they were frequently blinded or clogged with clouds of dust. So the land mines were the worst and most numerous of the three. The land mines had all kinds of arcane names and behaviors.

Most land mines were scattered where human victims might logically go: roads, trails, highways, bridges, and water holes, any place of any former economic value. The great comfort of a robot pack mule was that it didn't bother to follow trails. Also, land mines were unlikely to recognize its uneven, highly unnatural tread as a proper trigger to explode.

Knowing this, the Badaulet was eager to exploit their tactical advantage and to catch up with their enemies. Lucky was convinced that their would-be assassins had released the killer plane at the limit of its striking range, and then beaten a swift retreat back into the deeper desert. The Badaulet thought in this way, because this was the tactic he himself would have chosen.

His pack robot was tireless. He was also proud of the fact that it could run in pitch darkness. He would have blindly trusted it to carry him off the edge of the Earth.

Being a new bride, Sonja gently persuaded him to stop awhile, despite his ambitions. They located a nameless hollow, a shallow foxhole in the wind-etched, dun-colored desert. Utterly barren, their honeymoon hole had all the anonymity of a crater scooped from the surface of Mars.

As the Badaulet scoured the horizon for nonexistent enemies, Sonja climbed stiffly from the robot's bucketlike chassis, folded the robot flat, kicked dirt over it to disguise it, and opened her blister tent.

This tent had a single mast in the center, a lightweight wand that clicked together like jointed bamboo and socketed into a ring. The power within the wand brought the fabric to life. In moments, the tent was as moist and pale inside as the skin of a newly peeled banana.

They would sleep together here.

Against all odds, in the few moments in which she had gathered up grass, a large, evil desert tick had latched on to Sonja. It had inched straight up her dusty legs to her constricting waistband, sunk its fangs into the tender skin near her navel, and died. The first taste of her toxic blood had killed that tick as dead as a brown Gobi pebble. How gratifying that was.

Sonja checked the sloshing rumen bag, where fermentation proceeded. She tapped foamy water from the bag, damply inflated a paper-dry foam sponge, and set to work on the Badaulet. Lucky had many babylike patches of hairless new flesh, healed by a rapid exfection. His

nerve cells would be slowest to regrow there: he would have some numb
spots. It would help him if his bride dutifully made his spots less numb.

Warm air drafted cozily up the domed walls, but her husband
seemed unpleased. "This is improper."

"We are married! Anything must be all right if it pleases you."

He slapped at the woolly skin of the tent. "I can't see the stars!"

"Yes . . . but aircraft can't see *us*." Sonja liked the stars well enough.
She liked stars best when they were poised inside a planetarium,
mapped, and color-coded.

The real stars of the modern Earth, speckling the fantastic dome of
central Asia, these were less emotionally manageable. The high desert,
untouched by the glare of cities, was as black as fossil pitch, and the stars
wheeled above it in fierce, demented desert hordes. Those stars twinkled in the Earth's dirtied atmosphere—and their tints were all wrong,
owing to the fouling, stratospheric haze of all the Himalayan bombs.

The Milky Way had a bloody tinge in its sky-splitting milk . . . how
could anyone like to see that, knowing what that meant?

Was she getting older, to fear the stars? Sonja had often seen that
older people were afraid of the sky. Older people could never say precisely what disturbed them about the modern sky's current nature and
character, but they knew that it was wrong. The sky of climate crisis was
alien to their being—it scratched at the soul of humanity in the same
unconscious, itchy way that an oncoming earthquake would unnerve
cats, and panic goats, obscurely motivate serpents to rise from their
slumbers . . .

Redoubling her wifely caresses, she managed to distract the Badaulet,
and to soothe herself a little. On the air-inflated mat he turned eager,
then energetic, then tender. She felt raw when he was done, but she was
also open and emotionally centered and sexually awake.

Sleep claimed him as she thoughtfully licked the scabs on his arms—
those seven puckered little wounds, where she had plucked seven different state IDs from his flesh. Infection wanted a foothold in those salty
little wounds, but the microbes died under her tongue.

She slithered under his slumbering body like a prayer mat of flesh.

Heavenly voices woke Sonja. The voices broke like a revelation into
her interior nightmare landscape of thirst, dust, bombs, pain, black
suns, cities burning . . .

Her eyes shocked open. For long, tumbling moments she had no idea who she was or where she was—for she was no one, and she was everywhere.

A torrent of sound was falling through the walls of the tent, sound tumbling out of the sky. Deep, Wagnerian wails from a host of Valkyries . . . Those were starry voices, tremendous, operatic, obliterating, thunderous, haunting the core of her head.

Legs shaking, Sonja unsealed the tent and crept out naked and barefoot.

The cold zenith overhead was alive with burning ribbons. Clouds of booming, blooming celestial fire. Cosmic curtains of singing flame, sheets of emerald and amethyst. They were pouring out of the sky in cataracts.

Sonja jammed both hands to the sides of her skull. The celestial singing pierced the flesh of her hands.

This had to be some act of nature, she knew that . . . For it was simply too *big* for anything that mankind might have done. It was cosmic, too huge for mankind to even *imagine*. She was seeing a vast heavenly negation of all the worst or best mankind could think or do. It was singing at her, singing to her, singing *through* her—singing as an entity, singing as a divinity that bore the scale to her that she did to some anxious microbe.

The majesty of it emptied her of all illusions. It relieved an anguish that she had never known she had.

How easily she might have died, and never seen this, never heard this, never lived this moment. She had always prided herself on her easy contempt about her own death, but now she knew that she had been a fool. Life was so much larger in scope than the simple existence that she had dismissed so arrogantly. Existence was colossal.

The Baudaulet emerged from their tent. He saw the tilt of her chin and he gazed upward.

"The Mandate of Heaven!" he shouted, and his translated voice suddenly killed the warbling songs inside her head. All that cosmic music vanished instantly.

The heavenly curtains writhed and plummeted up there, but they did that in an eerie, abstract silence.

She stared at him. It was clear from his stance that the Badaulet heard nothing. Nothing but the wind. There was a wind out here, the wind of the Gobi.

She was shuddering.

"That is the aurora," she told him, "that is space weather. I have never seen the aurora in my life, but that must be it. I heard it in my head with my new ears!"

"Heaven foretells great changes on Earth," he told her.

"The aurora comes from the Sun. It is the energy of solar particles. They fall in sheets through a hole in the Earth's magnetic field. Then they tear into the outer limits of the air, and the air must glow. That is what we see tonight. And I *heard* it!"

"This is important," he told her, "so you must stop talking that nonsense." He pulled the belt from his uniform. Then, without another word, he began to beat her with his belt: not angrily, just rhythmically and thoroughly.

Having been beaten by lovers before, Sonja knew how to react. With a howl of dismay, she fell to the earth, hugging his ankles and begging forgiveness in a gabble of sobs and shrieks.

When she clutched at his knees, his balance was poor, so he couldn't use the belt effectively. He stopped his attempts to beat her. She continued to shriek, beg, and grovel. This was the core of the performance.

It was never about how hard men beat you, or how many strokes, or what they hit you with. It was always about their need to break your will and impose their own.

After savoring her shrieks and sobs for a while, the Badaulet grew reluctant. Finally, he belted his pants and pulled her off his legs. "Woman, why do you always carry on so? Put on your clothes! What is wrong with you? I didn't hit you so hard! It's just—when Heaven is manifesting miracles, you can't talk nonsense! We could both go to Hell!"

He was a hundred times more frightened than herself. The basis of his universe had been kicked out like a hole though a bucket. "Forgive my stupid chatter, dear husband! Thank you for punishing me!"

This submission stymied him. Of course the Badaulet had no idea on Earth what to do about this tumult in the heavens. Otherwise he would not have beaten her in the first place.

The sky was writhing violently with silent electrical phantoms. The wind died. In the absence of her vanished screams there was a vast and awful silence with not so much as a cricket.

"There is a great danger to my soul tonight . . ." he muttered. "I know that much, I know that is certain truth . . ."

"Let's watch the sky together! Is that all right?"

"It's cold. You are shivering, your teeth are chattering."

"I'll bring the mat! This might be a splendid omen, and not an evil omen! Look how beautiful it is! Maybe heaven is blessing our love, and our lives are changing for the better!" Sonja scurried into the tent and brought out a wadded double armful. "Lie down! I will hide my eyes and hold you tightly. Because I'm afraid."

She made a nest for them. Grudgingly—for now he felt ashamed of himself—he climbed on the puffy mattress.

He was shivering with cold and fear, so she warmed him. Mollified, he relaxed a little.

Time passed. The Badaulet watched the heavens writhing in silent display. Ghostly colors were leaching out of the sky . . . with the planet's nightly twirling and the sun's axial tilt, some confluence of distant fields was fading. The tongues of fire were in retreat.

At last he spoke up. "Woman, I believe that Heaven has blessed me. The world is changing, and a life as hard as mine must surely change for the better. I cannot *always* suffer."

She said nothing. She loved him only slightly less than before he had beaten her. He was a man: angry, vulnerable.

With one pinch she could rip the inner workings of his throat. He would drown in his own blood. Her legs were still smarting, so the temptation was there. She could leave him here, dead as mutton. Who would ever find him in a godforsaken place like this, who would ever know?

But why should he die at this one moment among all other potential moments to die? Wouldn't he die soon enough no matter what she did, or what he did? Her tears would dry on their own.

She turned her face to the flickering, guttering cosmos. He was already asleep.

HE WOKE HER in the chilly predawn, fully dressed and insisting that she start the robot from its bed of dust. The aurora was long gone, vanished as the Earth wheeled on its axis.

She advised him that the robot would run better if they unrolled its solar panels in daylight and let it crack some grass for fuel. The Badaulet stiffly rejected this counsel. He didn't much like her for giving it.

The Badaulet had tired of the magic distorting his life. He sensed, correctly, that it was somehow her own fault.

So, at his imperious demand, they set off reeling in the predawn cold and dark. She was hungry and thirsty, so she tried to drink from the rumen bag, knowing it wasn't ready yet. There was protein cracked from the cellulose there, and the taste seemed all right.

The robot conveyed them, in a crazed dance step, up ragged slopes, down black canyons, and across declivities. It ran across ground that would break a human leg like a dry stick. Queasy and low in spirits, Sonja felt unable to speak, and when dawn redly stung the rim of the world, the Badaulet suddenly began to confess to her. He was making up to her: not because he had beaten her during the night, for he considered that act entirely proper; but to revive her morale. So he spoke about the subject that always engrossed him most: his enemies.

The Badaulet was an agent of Chinese order in the midst of the central Asian disorder. He was always outnumbered, if never outgunned. His allegiance to the distant Chinese state was vague, and superstitious, and deeply confused, and lethally passionate. It was like a Cossack's love for Russia.

His faith, to the extent that he could describe it to her, was a cargo-cult patchwork of militia training, radical Islam, herbal lore, hunting and herding, and the shattered, scrambled, pitiful remains of Asia's traditional nomadic life. The Badaulet was not from any historic Asian tribe: he had no ethnic group. He was a native of globalized chaos.

The Badaulet's brief stay in Jiuquan had unsettled his young mind yet further. They had shown their pet barbarian Jiuquan's proudest cultural achievements: chamber music, calligraphy, various sports that one could perform while sealed in a plastic bubble . . . The Badaulet had found these accomplishments contemptible.

Then his Chinese handlers had shown him something closer to his heart: something unknown to Sonja. He boasted to her about it, obliquely: he claimed that it was far greater than any gift that she had given him.

So it had to be some propaganda enterprise from a local laboratory. Some stereotypical "amazing secret weapon" meant to stiffen the spines of China's barbarian allies. The Badaulet called it the "Assassin's Mace." He didn't say precisely what this weapon was—clearly, that was not for her to know—but the technicians had promised him he could try the Assassin's Mace someday, and wield it against his enemies. If he were loyal and true, that day would come soon.

The Assassin's Mace—there were a host of oddities in the taut suburbs of Jiuquan, where the cream of Chinese techno-intelligentsia labored on their secret productions. Secret weapons labs—Sonja had seen a few, she never liked them or their blinkered inhabitants. Secret weapons labs were obscure and torpid and heavy and loathsome.

The Acquis and the Dispensation hated China's state secrecy, for they were obsessed with rogue technologies spinning out of control. Internal combustion: a rogue technology spun out of control. Electric light: a rogue technology spun out of control. Fossil fuel: the flesh of the necromantic dead, risen from its grave, had wrecked the planet.

Global regulation, transparency, verification . . . that was the supposed solution of the Acquis and Dispensation, and China despised such things. China had walls and barriers. The good old ways, the trusted ways. The old ways to hide all the new ways.

The robot rambled, reeling, off the broken landscape and into a flatter steppe. This landscape was somewhat easier on Sonja's nerves. Big domelike tussocks of grass appeared. Some storm track had overpassed this area, slopping rain like the spatter from an overloaded paintbrush, and the desert was suddenly beautiful. In some ways the modern desert was better off than any other biome on Earth, for the desert never expected any kindness from the sky.

Here and there were brightly colored bits of human litter, plucked up by violent windstorms, flung from dead towns . . . plastic bags. Plastic shopping bags were the one artifact in the Gobi more omnipresent than land mines. Plastic bags had been cheap, present in uncounted millions in the daily life of cities. The bags were easily airborne, and although they tore, they never decayed. Over the decades, plastic bags could blow like tumbleweeds over half a continent.

Sheep tracks appeared. The Badaulet grew concerned. He dismounted the robot to study the tracks and to number the sheep, and, if possible, to reveal some trace of the shepherd.

After a quarter hour he returned from his tracking studies and solemnly handed her half a handful of sheep dung. Black manure like a pile of pebbles. It felt dry and light.

"This is the dung of a sheep," she said.

He nodded, and made a smashing motion with his fingers.

She broke one lump of the dung and it instantly turned to the finest black ash, a bacterial charcoal. This sheep had baked every calorie of nutrition out of the grass it was eating. The guts of that sheep were a microbe factory.

Sonja sniffed unhappily at her fingers. " 'Why does Mars stink?' "

Lucky brightened to see her making a joke, as if he hadn't given her a beating. "Today I wish I had seen that mammoth, and not just its stinking dung."

"There will be other mammoths to walk the Earth. Something always breaks the walls and stampedes out of the bubbles . . . I don't like this. The state does not allow this. This should not be happening. This is bad."

"A big herd of sheep, eighty, ninety," he told her, "with a boy on a pony, and the guts of his horse were the same way." Lucky shifted his sniper rifle from one camouflaged shoulder to another. "We ride with greater care now, and we watch the skies always."

It was a comfort to closely follow the sheep tracks. The busy feet of a flock that size would clear the earth of land mines.

Horse tracks appeared, the unshod hooves of Mongolian ponies, and then the signs of tents. These had been big round tents, Mongolian "ger" tents, which were portable yurts of crisscrossed sticks and woolly felt.

There were dead fires in the abandoned camp, with a host of human footprints.

This was not some minor group of fanatics skittering across the desert to launch one bomb their way. These were clear signs of families of people, a clan, with women, many children . . . Gathering grass. These Disorder nomads seemed to have an industrial obsession with grass. They had been cutting tufts of grass with hand sickles, and mincing that grass up into a kind of crude silage, and baking water out of the grass somehow, maybe with solar distilleries.

The whole village was methodically grazing on the grass. They even left behind an industrial grass dung, dry, fermented wads of the stuff mashed up like dirty oatmeal or dry beer lees.

"I'm surprised that we lack intelligence about these people," she said, "for it's clear they've heard of us and what *we* are doing."

"These people made the airplanes that attacked us. I thought there would be maybe two men, three bad men, a raiding team, my enemies," said the Badaulet thoughtfully. "Yet I don't know these people. They are many and well organized. We will have trouble, you and I alone, killing so many."

"No we won't. Not really. No."

"You didn't even bring a gun, woman."

"Give me a clear line of sight at them. I will put Red Sonja's evil eye on these bandit cult sons of bitches, and I have no care for their numbers.

"They swore to sweep the foe away with no care for their own lives;
Five thousand rode out in their sables and brocades.
Their piteous bones litter the banks of dry ravines,
Five thousand ghosts dreamt of in ladies' bedchambers."

The Badaulet mulled this recitation over. "They gave you the Assassin's Mace."

"Yes. No. Not that. Something else like that. There are many things like that in China."

"So you truly killed the 'five great generals,' Sonja? And you killed all their troops as well?"

"It never works the way it gets told in those stories."

The people of the tent village had no vehicles. They seemed to have knocked their camp down, thrown it on horseback, and instantly thundered off in all directions.

Yet their scattered swarm must surely have regrouped somewhere, somehow . . . With radios, telephones . . . or maybe with nothing more technical than drums, bugles, and tall flags on sticks. Genghis Khan had never gotten lost, and he'd ridden over the biggest empire on Earth.

The Badaulet removed his face net, pulled his visored cap over his eyes, and stared at the barren soil. He scowled.

"I can see a track," she offered.

"That thing is not a track, woman. That is a hole in the ground."

"Well, I saw another hole much like it. Back there."

The strange holes were violent gouges in the desert soil, spaced ten meters, eleven meters apart. Pierced holes, like the jabbing of javelins.

Some two-legged thing was running across the steppe, bounding with tremendous strides. And not just one of them, either. Suddenly there were many more such holes. A herd of the violent jumping things, a rambling horde of them.

"These are not the grass people of the camp," he told her, "these are running machines."

Sonja gazed around the abandoned vacuity of the desert. One single tiny bird chirped, breaking the silence like a brick through glass. "It's getting crowded out here."

They followed the jumping machine tracks, for this group had some clear purpose and their tracks were easy to spot.

These new marauders were like giant Gobi jerboas. They bounced their way for kilometers.

Eventually, the javelin-footed things clustered into a gang and scampered together up a steep, flat-topped hill.

Closely guiding the pack robot, the Badaulet circled the hill with great caution.

"Do we climb up there?" she asked him at last.

"They might be waiting there in ambush," he said. "They ran up there, each on his own two legs, and they did not come back down."

"It's getting late. I wouldn't want to meet these things in the dark."

"We go up," he decided.

The top of the hill, barren, chilly, nameless, was scabbed all over with the milling pockmarks, and there were helicopter skids.

"They all flew off," said Sonja. "It's some covert insertion team. Not Chinese. These people have robots that jump on two legs."

As if in sympathy, their own pack robot emitted a loud metallic grunt. Sonja stared at its crude prow, a blunt shelf like an ugly bumper. There was a fresh, new, round hole pierced in the bare metal there.

There was a second mournful bang and a second hole appeared, a palm's width away from the first.

"Don't move," said the Badaulet, standing, "it is trying to shoot us in the head," and he shouldered his rifle and fired. "I hit it," he reported, "but I should have sighted-in this target system properly," and he fired again, again, again, three discreet sniper gunshots not much louder than three clapping hands.

A thing in the twilit sky like a distant child's kite went tumbling into straw pieces.

"That plane was much bigger than the flying bomb they sent to kill us," he said. "It had a gun on board, and not a very good gun."

Sonja looked at the two neat holes piercing the robot's prow. The aircraft had an excellent gun; it just had poor programming. It didn't know what to do with their unusual target silhouette.

"I can see others now," he said, pointing, "over there, that is a cloud of them."

Her eyes could not match his. "I think I see some black dots in the sky. Are they flying in circles? They look like birds to me."

"No," he said, "those are not vultures eating the dead. Someone is standing there and fighting those planes. Someone brave, or stupid. Or else they may have armor."

"We have to leave this hilltop right away. We're exposed."

"My rifle here on the ground has a better control of trajectory than an airborne rifle," he said crisply. "I will extend my bipod, taking advantage of my clear line of sight, and pick off a few of those planes. The enemy of these evil planes should be our friend. Also, I admire his gallantry."

"That is gallant. It is also a good way to get killed."

Lucky stared at her and shrugged. "That is true. So: Get out of this robot. Put on your woman's black cloak. Run down this hill, find a hole in the ground, get inside it, hide. When I am done here, I will find you."

That was a speech Sonja had heard from men before. Not in Lucky's own words, but with the same tone and intent. Men who talked that way died.

Sonja put on the black water cloak, she left the robot, she scrambled down the hill, and she looked for a place to survive.

Given that the sky was full of airborne death, there were only a few hiding places near the hill that made any sense. One miserable little gully here, over there a rugged, stony half overhang . . . The hanging rocks were a better bet for survival, for she might pile up some loose rubble to build a wall.

Sonja picked her way to that wretched excuse for a shelter, and there was a dead man in it.

He had died inside the device that allowed him to run like the wind. It was a humanoid exoskeleton with long, gazelle-like stilts extending from his shins. The skeletal machine hugged his flesh so intimately that it looked grafted onto him. His skull was socketed into its big white helmet like the filling in a pitted olive.

Apparently the rest of his party had fled safely to their rendezvous, while Skeleton Man had suffered some malfunction, shown up too late . . . Likely it was the weight of all the loot he was carrying, for he had a frame pack that latched and snapped with obscene design precision into his exposed skeleton ribs. The pack was bulging like he'd stolen the family silverware. His loot was heavy and jumbled and awkward . . .

His treasure stank. It smelled to high heaven, a burned-plastic smell. Like a factory fire.

At first she'd imagined that the stench must be coming from his flesh or his peculiar hardware, but no. He was freshly dead, and he had been a professional . . . Not a soldier exactly, not her kind of soldier, but some global tech-support cadre. He wore charcoal-black civilian utility gear and no shoes at all—for he seemed to live entirely in the skeleton—and he didn't have one speck of ID on him, not a badge, not a pip, not a shoulder patch.

With that black mustache, with those skin tones, he might have been from the wreckage of India, or the wreckage of Pakistan maybe—but he was Acquis. He was definitely Acquis, for he was exactly the kind of young gung-ho global fool that some Acquis net committee could hustle up in fifteen minutes. Speed and lightness, the Acquis. They were always good at speed and lightness.

The pursuing harpy had shot at him repeatedly, because its small-caliber rounds kept bouncing off his exoskeletal ribs, but its efforts had finally put a dispassionately calculated entry hole through the left side of his torso and he'd died almost instantly.

It was hard to hate the machines, with that neat way that they killed. They had no more moral judgment than bear traps.

His exoskeleton was still functional. The robot suit was trying to do something about its human occupant, putting jolts through his dead flesh as if trying to wake him up. It was searching for his departed soul like a lost Martian probe contacting a distant antenna.

Sonja heard faint repeated gunshots. Then the Badaulet appeared, empty-handed. He looked from her, to the dead Acquis cyborg, and back again. "Many more planes are coming."

"Where's the pack robot? Where's your rifle?"

"I gave the rifle to the robot. That robot is a weapons platform. The rifle knows its targets now. It will kill those planes till it runs out of ammunition. More planes are coming, many more." He flicked his fingers repeatedly. "I think they have hundreds."

"And you're still alive? You *are* lucky."

Lucky began piling loose cobbles and boulders into a crude barricade. "The planes will see our body heat. We must hide behind rocks."

"Our dead friend here brought treasure with him. He just gave his life for that."

The Badaulet whipped out his long knife with instant fluid ease and slashed the backpack free from the dead man. Then, with a burst of wiry strength, he hauled the dead cyborg away from the rocky overhang.

Lucky propped the mechanized corpse into plain sight of the sky, half leaning it against a broken boulder.

The corpse was standing there, and it had a human silhouette. That was clever. Maybe luck was mostly a matter of experience.

Sonja hastily emptied the dead man's pack, hoping to find something useful for a last-ditch defense. The raider was carrying circuitry. A glued-together, broken mess of boards and cards. All of it old technology, maybe twenty years old. All of it burned, warped, smoke-blackened. This trash had been torn loose from some larger network installation, precisely slotted electronic hardware hastily knocked loose from its matrix, maybe with the looter's skeletal fists.

That was what he had come for, that was his mission: stealing garbage. There was nothing else in his backpack, not a ration, not a bandage, not a paper clip. He'd died for this worthless junk.

She threw the empty pack frame onto the barricade and helped the Badaulet pile rocks.

Sadly, not many rocks were handy. The nearest heap of useful rocks required a dash across open ground. Their crudely piled wall was the length and height of a coffin.

There was a sudden wet thwack as a passing plane shot the dead man.

Sonja threw herself on her belly. The Badaulet sprawled beside her, behind the piled rubble.

Sonja told herself that she wanted to live. With his warm, breathing body beside her, the smell of his male flesh, she wanted life, she desired it. If she wanted life enough to get clever about surviving, she would live through this.

There was hope in this situation. There had to be hope. The machines were uncannily accurate, but they lacked even one single spark of human common sense. Their rocky barricade was so low and so hasty that there had to be parts of their bodies exposed to enemy fire. But the stupid planes were strictly programmed to make uniformly fatal shots to the head or the chest. So they would aim at the head or chest every time, and if their bullets hit a rock, they suffered no regret and they learned nothing. That was hope.

They were weak little toy planes made of straw. They had single-shot guns. They couldn't hover in place. With each shot they would lose altitude, and with their humble little motors they would struggle to regain that height.

The planes had limited amounts of fuel or ammunition. They were real-world machines, they were not magical flying demons. Machines could be outsmarted. They could be outwaited. There would have to be some algorithm, some tick-off switch, some error-correction loop that would tell them: Try again later. The prospects are cloudy.

"I could have been in Vienna," she muttered.

"What?"

"I just wanted to tell you: My darling, I am so proud of you! It is an honor to be your wife. We are going to win this battle!"

"Yes!" shouted the Badaulet. "Heaven is on our side." He suddenly rose, scrambled over their miserable heap of rocks, and hastily shifted the skeletal limbs of the dead man.

Attracted by this motion, the machines began firing at the corpse again. Every bullet struck true; she could hear them banging neatly into the dead man's chest and helmet.

"I have his canteen," said the Badaulet.

She squeezed water from the cloak and dribbled it into the container.

"You are such a good wife to me," said the Badaulet. "Can you cook? I have never seen you cook."

"Do you like Chinese food?"

"It is my duty to like Chinese food."

Bullets panged into the rock barricade. Once again, something was wrong with her cyborg ears. Her ears were not hurting properly from the violent noises of ricochet. Their volume controls were problematic.

Lying prone, the Badaulet squirmed his way inside the black water cloak. Humped over, lumpy, featureless, he scrambled over the barricade and vanished.

When he returned, after an eventful ten minutes of aircraft fire, he had an armful of rocks.

"These rocks are difficult to carry," he announced, stacking them into place. "Also there are two bullet holes in this cloak and they are leaking cold water."

"Are you wet now? That's a shame."

"A human enemy would ricochet his shots off the rock wall behind us, and kill us. These machines will not think of that tactic."

"No. Machines never think."

Lucky sucked a splinter wound on his left hand. "It may be the will of Heaven to kill us."

"I know that. Do you think you might—carefully—turn your body without getting shot, and give me a kiss?"

This done, it occurred to her that to die while making love, delicious though that sounded, was impractical. Or, rather, it depended on the mode of death involved. Sniper fire from small aircraft was not one of the better modes.

"There is a thing that I can do," she told him. "It likely won't affect these aircraft that are shooting at us. But it will avenge us, if they have any human controllers nearby."

"What is that fine vengeance, my bride?"

"If I do this thing, anyone near us will die. Men, women, children. Also the larger animals with longer life spans: the horses, the cattle. They will die in a year and a half. From a great many apparent causes. Cancer, mostly."

"That is your weapon?"

"I thought I might have to use it. If you didn't simply shoot them dead. It is my best weapon."

"Where is this weapon? Give it to me."

"It is in orbit." She paused. "I mean to say, it is in Heaven, so you can't have it."

"I know what a satellite is, woman," he told her patiently. "A sharp-eyed man in the desert can see many satellites. Give me the trigger to your satellite weapon, and I will call down the fire. Then you can flee, and you might live."

"The trigger is inside me," she told him. "I swallowed it."

"You *swallowed* your weapon of vengeance?"

More bullets panged into the rock, for a fresh squadron of airplanes had appeared. Apparently these new planes had failed to share their data with the earlier assailants, for the dead cyborg in his skeleton was riddled with fresh bullets.

"It would be wrong to deploy a massive weapon such as you carry," he said thoughtfully, "for it would kill those gallant men fighting these air-craft along with us. I saw their truck through the scope of my rifle. I think they are Chinese. Chinese rapid-response, paramilitary. Brave men, hard men. I know such men well."

"Well," Sonja said, "then there will be some Dispensation coming here. Because there are Chinese military here . . . and the Acquis raiders like our skeleton friend, who is dead over there . . . the grass people in the tents . . . There has to be Dispensation. If they're not here al-ready, Dispensation will be coming here."

The Badaulet mulled this over. He agreed with her. "How many Dis-pensation, do you think?"

"I can't tell you that, but they will probably be Americans, they won't speak Chinese, and they will be trying to make some money from this trouble. That's the Dispensation, that happens every time."

"You forgot some important warriors also present here in this great battle, my bride."

"Who?"

"Us! You and me, my precious one!"

Three broken aircraft plummeted out of the sky. They tumbled like leaves and fell out of sight.

"I see that my rifle is properly grouping its shots," said the Badaulet, pleased. He then stood up and walked—not ran, he *walked*, sauntered almost—to the nearest source of handy rubble and brought back a heaping armful of new rocks.

"That's a good rifle, built by German professionals," he announced, dumping the rocks at her feet. Then he strolled off for more.

"Walk *faster!*" she yelled at him.

"You stack them," he said over his shoulder. He lugged back a boulder. "It's a pity my fine rifle has so little ammunition."

One more such fearless venture—Lucky clawed out a few more rocks somewhere, his fingers were bleeding . . . then he grabbed the dead Acquis cyborg, doubled him over with some casual kicks at his humming robot bones, and embedded the body into the wall.

Then he squatted, breathing hard with his labors.

Suddenly—instead of the bare cliff that would have suited a firing squad—they had created a little fort for themselves. They had built a wall. Bullets simply could not reach them. They could even stretch their legs out a little, raise their heads, think.

"Now we are besieged!" he announced cheerfully. "We can stay safe and secluded until we starve here!"

A useless bullet screamed off the dead man's ceramic bones. "We won't starve while he's lying here," she said. She regretted saying that—referring to cannibalism wasn't a wifely, romantic, supportive thing to say, and a cruel reward for Lucky's saving their lives . . . but the remark didn't bother him.

They rewarded themselves with lavish sips from the dead man's canteen.

Eventually, night fell. The besieging aircraft were not bothered by darkness, since they were firing at human heat. The machines fell into a parsimonious cycle, programmed to save their fuel.

The rifle on the pack robot had run out of ammunition. This failure made the aircraft bolder. They swooped repeatedly by the rocky fortress, silently, scanning for any clear shot. When they failed to find one, their little motors would catch with an audible click and hum, and they would struggle for altitude again.

Then the machines returned, again and again, flying out of darkness and seeking human warmth, like mosquitoes with guns. Her new ears could hear them with an insufferable keenness.

The Earth spun on its axis. The stars emerged and strengthened. The Milky Way shone its celestial battle banner, so bright that she could see the dogged silhouette of killer aircraft flit across the bloody host of stars.

Then Sonja heard a low, symphonic rumble. It might have been a classical bass cello: a string and a bow. Taut strings of magnetic fire.

She shook him. "Do you hear that?"

The Badaulet woke from his cozy doze. "Hear what?"

"That voice from the sky. That huge electrical noise. Electronic."

"Is it a helicopter?"

"No."

"Is it a bigger plane coming here to kill us with a bomb?"

"No! No, oh my God, the sound is *really loud* now . . ." Suddenly her husband's voice vanished, she could no longer hear him. She heard nothing but those voices of fire. Those colossal sounds were not touching the air. They were touching the circuits in her head.

There was no escaping them. She had no way to turn them off.

Celestial voices were sheeting through her skull. The voices were beyond good and evil, out of all human scale. She felt as if they were ripping though her, straight through the rocky core of Asia and out of the planet's other side.

The aurora emerged in the heavens, and the glorious sight of it gave no pleasure, for it was enraged. Its fiery sheets were knotted and angry tonight, visibly breaking into gnarls and whorls and branches and furious particles. The tongues of flame were spitting and frothing, with foams and blobs and disks and rabid whirlpools. Sheets of convulsive energy plunged across the sky, tearing and ripping. An annihilation.

"This isn't supposed to happen!" she shouted, and she could not hear her own voice. "This is wrong, Badaulet . . . there's something wrong with the sky! This could be the end of everything! This could be the end of the world!"

Lucky patted her thigh in a proprietory fashion, and gave her a little elbow jab in the ribs. His head was tilted back and she realized that he was laughing aloud. His black eyes were sparkling as he watched the blazing sky. He was enjoying himself.

A flooding gush of stellar energy hit the atmosphere, hard rain from outer space. The sky was frosted with bloody red sparks, as bits of man-made filth at the limits of the atmosphere lit up and fried.

Sonja's dry mouth hung open. Her head roared like an express train. Some orgasmic solar gush soaked the Earth's magnetic field, and utterly absurd things were pouring out of the sky now: rippling lozenges like children's toy balloons, fun-house snakes of accordion paper, roiling smoke rings and flaming jellied doughnuts . . . They had no business on Earth, they were not from the Earth at all. She could *hear* them, shrieking.

Sonja writhed in a desperate panic attack. The Badaulet reached out, grabbed her, pulled her to him, crushed her in his arms. He squeezed the screaming breath from her lungs. In her terror she sank her teeth into his bare shoulder . . .

He didn't mind. He was telling her something warm and kindly, over and over. She could feel his voice vibrating in his chest.

The convulsing aurora was so bright that it left shadows on the rock. Sonja clamped her eyes shut.

Suddenly, in trauma, she was speaking in the language of childhood. The first song, the first poetry, she had memorized. That little song she loved to sing with Vera and Svetlana and Kosara and Radmila and Biserka and Bratislava, and even pouting little Djordje, standing in a circle, arms out and palm to palm, with the machines watching their brains and eyes and their bridged and knotted fingers, to see that they were standing perfectly strong, all the same.

Sonja could hear her own voice. Her ears were trying to translate what she was saying to herself. The translation program blocked the noise pouring from the sky.

Sonja sang her song again and again, whimpering.

> "We are the young pioneers
> Children of the real world
> We grow like trees to the sky
> We stand and support tomorrow
> For our strength belongs to the future
> And the future is our strength."

THE SOUND OF WIND woke Sonja. Her ears were working again. She heard the faint sound of sullen dripping from the bullet-pierced water cloak.

Dawn had come, and Lucky was sleeping. He had been holding her tightly, so that she did not raise her vulnerable head above the parapet during her nightmares.

Sonja sensed that the planes were gone. There was no way to know this as a fact, however. Not without testing that theory.

Tired of having Lucky assuming all the risks, Sonja untied her dust-proof tarpaulin gown, held it high over herself with her arms outspread to blur her target silhouette, and stepped, naked and deliberate, over the rocky wall.

She was not shot, she did not die, there were no sounds of planes.

Yawning and grainy-eyed, Sonja clambered to the top of the hill. The dutiful pack robot was standing there, its empty rifle methodically scanning the empty skies. The pack robot had been shot an amazing number of times, almost all of the rounds hitting its front prow, which looked like metal cheesecloth. A few holes adorned the thing's rear bumper, presumably the results of targeting error.

Yet the robot was functional. Its pistoning, crooked, crazy legs were in fine condition. Sonja felt an affection for it now, the unwilling love one felt for a battlefield comrade. Poor thing, it was so dumb and ugly, but it was doing the best it could.

Sonja tore the rifle from its gun-mount and used its target scope to scan the landscape. What of their friends, allies, strangers—the ones pursued by a wheeling column of aircraft? No sign of them. Wait. Yes. A blackened spot on the ground, a ragged asterisk.

Heavy weaponry had hit something there, a truck, a tank, a half-track, whatever that had once been. Heavy weapons had knocked it not just to pieces, but to pieces of pieces. A falling meteor couldn't have crushed it more thoroughly: it was obliterated.

Sonja reviewed her tactical options. Retreat back to the den, pile up more rocks? Make a break for it, across country, back toward Jiuquan? Leave this hilltop, seek out a better overview? This hilltop's overview was excellent; the Acquis raiders had clearly chosen it on purpose.

Maintain the hardware. That action always made sense. Sonja searched through the baggage, found a clip, and reloaded the rifle. Then Sonja spread out the solar panels for the pack robot, tissue-thin sheets that stretched an astonishing distance down the hill.

This work done, she sipped some greenish yogurt from the rumen bag, which hung there, whole and unpierced. The ferment tasted all right now; during all the mayhem it had brewed up fine.

With nutrition her head cleared. She had survived and another day was at hand. Sonja took the rifle and carefully scanned the horizon.

Two riders were approaching.

They rode from the north, on two rugged Mongol ponies, ragged, burrolike beasts whose short legs almost seemed to scurry. These riders were men, and armed with rifles slung across their backs. The man in front wore furs—thick, bearlike furs—and a fur hat, and apparently some kind of furry face mask. The rider who followed him—incredibly—wore an American cowboy hat, blue jeans, boots, a checkered shirt, and a vest.

The quick temptation to pick them off with the rifle—for she did have the drop on them, and the rifle was loaded—evaporated. Who on Earth would ride out here, dressed in that fashion? It was almost worth dying to know.

The cowboy rode up to his friend, stopped him, and handed over his rifle. The cowboy dug into a saddlebag, and took out a white flag— apparently an undershirt. The cowboy then rode straight toward her hill, slowly and with care, waving his snowy white shirt over his head as he stood in his stirrups.

This man was surely one of the worst horseback riders Sonja had ever seen. She walked to the edge of the hilltop and waved back at him with her white sleeves.

Then she climbed downhill.

The cowboy was a young American, a teenager. He was strikingly handsome, and, seen closely, his clothes were vivid and gorgeous. His costume only mimicked the rugged proletarian gear of the American West. He was a cowboy prince: theatrical and dramatic.

He pulled up his snarl-maned, yellow-fanged mare—it appeared he had never ridden a horse in his life, for he drove the beast like a car— and he half tumbled out of his saddle. His cheeks were windburned. He was short of breath.

"Are you Biserka?" he said.

He spoke English, which did not surprise her. "No," she said.

"You sure do look like Biserka. I had to make sure. To meet you here, that's kind of uncanny. You are Sonja, though. You're Sonja Mihaj-lovic."

"Yes."

"What is that strange gown you're wearing? You've got, like, a white tablecloth with all kinds of yin-yangs and rosary beads."

Sonja stared at him silently. This man was certainly Dispensation. He had to be. No one else would behave like this.

"You look great in that getup, don't get me wrong," the cowboy said hastily, "that look is really you! I am Lionel Montalban. John Montgomery Montalban—you know him, I'm sure—he's my brother. You and me, we're family."

"John Montalban is here? Where is John?"

"John's in a camp with some of the locals. John sent me here to fetch you. I'm glad I was able to find you. You're all right?"

"If airplanes don't shoot at me, yes, I am all right."

Lionel Montalban nodded over his shoulder at his riding companion, who sat on his pony like a furred centaur. "The airplanes come from his people. So no, they won't be shooting you. Not when you are with us. Why are you on foot, Sonja? Where is George's robot?"

So: George had told John Montalban about the robot. Of course George would do that. George adored John Montalban. George was the man's factotum. His fixer. His butler. His slave.

Lionel was busy apologizing to her. "We lost track of your robot's position when those solar flares hit. That solar noise was sudden. Really sudden. And bad. Did you see the sun rise this morning? I saw it!" Lionel yawned. "There were *visible sun spots* on the sun's surface. I could *see those spots with my naked eyes*."

"Lionel Montalban," she said.

"Yes, what?"

"What are you doing here, Lionel Montalban?"

Lionel looked surprised. "You mean, what am I doing here, *officially*? Oh. Officially, I'm on an 'Asian wilderness vacation.' I'm giving up my 'juvenile delinquent drug habits.' I'm in rehab. My brother's gonna clean me all out in the fresh air with some bracing backwoods hikes."

Lionel turned on the charm: he grinned and winked. "What are *you* doing here, 'officially'? May I ask you that?"

Sonja said nothing.

"Never mind, Sonja! Whatever it is, it's okay by me! After that solar eruption—snarled communications all over the planet!—why sweat the small stuff? After a catastrophe like this one, nobody's gonna remember what *I* did, back in Los Angeles. Some riots, some burned-out neighborhoods, no problem! It's all part of the legend of Hollywood."

Lionel waved his arms gleefully, which spooked his horse. The beast jerked the reins and almost knocked Lionel from his feet.

Lionel recovered his booted footing with a gymnast's half skip. "*You* don't care about some derelict neighborhoods burned down in Los Angeles, do you? You don't care one bit, right? See, I'm almost home free!"

"What is John's assignment here?"

"Oh, this is John's usual work. We are shutting down an out-of-control tech operation. John never took me along for his work before, but, well, I learn fast." Lionel smiled. "Because I *have* to learn fast! Brilliancy, speed, lightness, and glory!"

It was a sinister business that the Acquis and Dispensation used the same slogan. Why had no one condemned them for that?

"Let me quickly brief you about my friend here," said Lionel. "The rider in the hairy wolf mask. He calls himself 'Vice Premier Li Rongji.' He is very serious about his name and his official Chinese title. He's a fanatic. So please don't tease him."

"Li Rongji was a great Chinese statesman."

"This man *is* the great Chinese statesman Li Rongji. He's a clone of a powerful Chinese official from twenty years ago. He's a clone, like you are. That's what John has discovered here. We found out that the Chinese state backed up its entire human regime. It cloned thirty-five key human politicians—I mean the *real* people inside the state, the crucial power brokers—and it hid them in a hole in the desert. The state even backed up *itself*. *All* of itself. It built itself a giant secret clone farm, and a giant secret library, and it hid that business underground in the Gobi, really deep underground, like nuclear-bomb-proof, in a kind of First Emperor of China airtight underground tomb."

Sonja scowled. "Why wasn't I informed about this matter?"

"Because you were five years old at the time. Sonja, you *are* this matter. You are informed, because I just informed you. I informed you because you are family." Lionel waved his arms again, and his horse, even angrier, almost succeeded in escaping him. When Lionel recovered— he was ominously strong, an athlete, an acrobat—his face was flushed.

"It took the Dispensation a long time to map and track down this rogue project," he said. "John has found *fifteen* different cloning projects that were all going on at the time you were born. The Balkans, that little island in the Adriatic: That was just the test bed for bigger projects elsewhere. Your project was small. This Chinese clone project was colossal. This one was the megaproject. And we're trying to *buy* it now. We're trying to buy whatever is left of it."

"There were *sixteen* cloning projects? *Sixteen* like me?"

"Most of those schemes never left the lab. Not one of those projects ever worked out as planned. Yours was a debacle for sure—and this Chinese one was the biggest debacle of them all. We're still dealing with the repercussions of it, right here and now. We got thirty-five extremely talented cloned people, running loose and walking the Earth, who were trained in an underground bunker to take over the world. They escaped from that bunker and they're *still* planning to take over the world. They were supposed to emerge after a world apocalypse and restore Chinese civilization. And they *still* want to take over the world, and they want it *on their own terms.* You see my friend there, riding the horse, the one with the tattoos and the necklace of human teeth? He's one of them."

This was appalling news. Sonja sensed that it should have stunned her, it should have been beyond her comprehension. But it wasn't. Sonja was used to appalling news. Every juncture in her life that had ever mattered had been appalling.

She gazed at the rogue, apocalypse cultist, as he sat on his Mongol horse. He was young and fully dressed to terrify.

"Your brother should mind his own business, Lionel. Someday John will get hurt."

"This *is* John's business, sugarplum! I have two secret clones in my own family! One is my niece's mother, and the other is my favorite set director." Lionel shook his handsome head. "My brother makes it his life's work to shut down crazy projects before they get out of hand. You should be grateful for what John's done for this world! John wants to see you, Sonja. He can brief you about this much better than I can."

"I will not meet John Montalban. Not again, never. I promised that I would never meet him again, or touch him, or look at him."

Lionel sighed heavily. "Is that your big personal story? You are so much like Radmila! That is exactly the sort of thing Radmila would say, except not with your weird Sino-Slavic accent. I love Mila very dearly, but *would you get over yourself*? Just for once? Because my brother is changing the whole Earth out here! It's not always about you, you, you, and all your clones!"

Sonja regretted that she had not killed Lionel, but there was no help for this. John Montalban was a power player. If Montalban was here, meddling, and in better command of the situation than herself, then she had no choice but to negotiate with him. She had involved herself with Montalban before, and though she had bitter cause to regret it, at least she understood what that entailed. "All right. Take me to see John."

"At last you're talking sense. It'll take us a while to reach him, it's a good distance."

"I have a man with me here. My husband."

Lionel blinked. "That's news."

Slowly and conspicuously, Sonja led Lionel—along with his silent bodyguard, escort, or assassin—around the hill. Mongolian horses were some of the world's toughest ponies, but the horses had a hard time of it—on ground the pack robot would have skimmed in moments.

Sonja returned to the site of the nightlong siege. A sturdier rock wall had appeared there. The dead Acquis cyborg had been hidden behind the wall. There was no sign of the busy and cunning Badaulet.

"You wait," she told Montalban, and she climbed laboriously back to the top of the hill. As she had expected, the Badaulet was lurking in wait on the slope with his rifle trained on the horsemen below.

"That loud fool with the strange hat is Dispensation," Lucky observed, for he was wise beyond his years. "I can kill them both easily."

"Don't kill them. The fool is Dispensation. The other is from the grass people, that tribe that tried to kill us. I am going with them to negotiate a solution. That is a flaw I have: I negotiate peace too often. Will you please come with me to help me? Our alternative is to shoot them both and run away. But that strategy won't work. If we kill these two scouts, there will be more airplanes sent after us."

The Badaulet shouldered his rifle. "You are my wife. We stay together."

"Then we must parley. Don't kill anyone unless I say. If you see me kill someone, or if I am killed—then kill them. Avenge me without pity."

The Badaulet nodded. "Let us go and learn more about our enemies. To learn about enemies makes them easier to kill."

They rode their bullet-riddled pack robot to the base of the hill. Lionel Montalban looked pale and shaken. "There's some dead Acquis guy wearing neural boneware in this little homemade fort."

"Is that so?" said Sonja.

"Yes, and that's bad. The Acquis is supposed to restrict their neural boneware to Antarctica. John made a formal settlement about that. There shouldn't be any Acquis spies with nerve gear walking the Earth in the middle of Asia."

Sonja felt keenly irritated, but she spoke politely. "Does your brother John want this dead Acquis body? John always wants dead bodies."

"That's all right, I geotagged it. We can fetch it later. I took a lot of video."

The little party then rode cross-country. Sonja made a deliberate point of scurrying ahead inside the superior pack robot, so that the primitive horse riders had to catch up.

"You are angry, my bride."

"Badaulet, did you ever have someone in your life who haunted you, and stole your existence, and was always in your dreams, and never let you be alone, no matter what you did, or how hard you tried to forget them?"

"No, my bride. I kill such people, and my enemies stay dead."

"Well, I have such people. I had seven such people. And soon, very soon—I will see someone who is even worse. Because I will meet the man who *married us*. First he found one of us, then he found all of us. He *investigated* us. Because he considers himself a wise scholar, this sage, this prince, this technician. He learned more about us than we ever knew about ourselves. That is how he mastered us. And he *did* master us. He bent us to his will. We cannot rid ourselves of him, although each of us has tried. He is our sultan, and we are his harem."

"Why did this prince come to this place? To take you away from me?"

"No. He doesn't need me. Not anymore. He has had plenty of me, because he possessed me. He came here to fulfill his own jihad."

"I see that my great rival is indeed a wise man."

Time passed; earnestly waving his cowboy hat, Lionel made a point of galloping up to catch them. "Lunch break!" he crowed.

Lionel was the only one among them hungry. Sonja and the Badaulet had altered guts, and were drinking fermented grass from their rumen bag. Much the same seemed to be true of the young marauder who called himself "Vice Premier Li Rongji," and whose scarred, shabby horse calmly dropped an ashy black dung.

Sonja had yet to see this tribal bandit dismount from his horse. A superb rider, he and his ugly animal might have shared the same bloodstream.

With a showy gesture, Lionel offered them the roasted flesh of a marmot. Marmots existed in great profusion in the region, since they had lost most of their natural predators. Lionel gnawed this chewy groundhog's flesh with a deft pretense of enthusiasm.

Then Lionel introduced himself to the Badaulet, though the two had no language in common. Nothing daunted, Lionel pulled out a handheld translation unit. He managed to spout a few cordial words at the warrior.

The Badaulet's black eyeballs were rigid with hate. He despised Lionel. Lionel, sensing this, redoubled his efforts to charm.

Though every human instinct warned her against it, Sonja decided to speak to Vice Premier Li Rongji. She walked empty-handed to the flank of the clone's horse and looked up into his masked face. He had stiff, taxidermy wolf ears and two mummified eye holes.

He was carrying, besides his long sniper rifle, a blunt combat shotgun that launched 40-millimeter grenades. Those searing, metal-splattering grenades hit almost as hard as artillery shells. One single man with one single such gun could briskly destroy a quarter of a city. He had a city-breaking machine on the rump of his ugly horse.

And his deadly grenade gun was made mostly of straw.

"Sir," she said, "I have heard that your esteemed name is Li Rongji."

"I am Vice Premier Li Rongji." His Chinese was excellent, clearly his first language. He even had the posh Beijing accent of high Chinese state officials.

"I have also heard, sir—although it was before my time—that Vice Premier Li Rongji was the premier architect for relief efforts during the great Xiaolangdi dam catastrophe."

"Yes, Xiaolangdi was one of my many important burdens of office before my unfortunate demise."

"Do you know who *I* am, sir?"

"I know that you are the mistress of this man's elder brother. You must have a powerful hold on that soft man's soft heart, for him to take such trouble for you, a mere girl, in the midst of his negotiations with us."

"I am Sonja, the Angel of Harbin."

He instantly wanted to kill her. His callused hands tightened on the horse's reins. He was hungering to kill her.

Yet he was intelligent, and hardship had schooled him not to act on impulse. Furthermore, he was keenly afraid of Lucky. He tugged the muzzle of his wolf mask. "Since you are Red Sonja, then this man who accompanies you must be the world-famous Badaulet."

It had not occurred to Sonja that the Badaulet was "world-famous." But if this vast steppe and desert was "the world" to this man, then, yes, Lucky was much more famous than herself. "That indeed is he."

"Please be so kind as to introduce me to this great man and gallant warrior."

There was nothing for it but for everyone to trade places. Lionel jumped into the bucketlike robot with her, while the Badaulet mounted Lionel's balky, snarling horse. With a few brutal whacks and sharp kicks, Lucky showed the horse that he meant business. The horse obeyed him humbly.

The Badaulet and Vice Premier Li Rongji were soon deep in conversation.

"How many are they?" said Sonja. "How many members of his cult?"

"Well," said Lionel, lounging at his ease—for the robot's reeling dance steps didn't bother him at all—"there were originally thirty-five clones, down in their indoctrination bunker. After the clones blew that place up and escaped, each one of them started his own tribal global-guerrilla cell. They were pretty naive and sheltered people at first—basically, they were cave dwellers—but they're clever. They were trained extensively on guerrilla tactics and statecraft. Their state was training them to emerge from their bunker after the Apocalypse and take over the world."

A chill shot through Sonja. "That's what *we* were trained for. We were also taught that we would take over the world. We would support the world with ubiquitous computing."

Lionel was unsurprised by this story; it was certainly old news to him. "Every survivalist project has its own vogue. Survival projects are always faddish and fanatical. To 'take over the world'? That must be the natural killer application for a secret clone army . . . All those clone projects were survivalist projects. They all failed, all of them. Because they lacked transparency."

Lionel lifted his elegant brows and spoke with great conviction. "Radical projects need *widespread distributed oversight,* with peer review and a loyal opposition to test them. They have to be open and testable. Otherwise, you've just got this desperate little closed bubble. And of course that tends to sour very fast."

"Your brother is preparing you for politics?"

"I'm an actor." Lionel shrugged. "An actor from California. So, yes, of course I'm preparing for politics." Lionel shifted himself in the robot's bucket, so he could study the Badaulet more closely. "Did you really marry that guy, Sonja?"

"Yes."

"I can sure see why! He's a *fantastic character,* isn't he? Look at the way he moves his elbows when he rides. Look at his *feet.*" Lionel narrowed his eyes, shifted himself, muttered under his breath. He was mimicking the Badaulet. Copying his movements and mannerisms. There was something truly horrible about that.

It was well after noon when they arrived at the nomad camp of the grass people, a place much as she had first imagined it. There was nothing to mark this camp as a menacing terrorist base, although this was what it was. To the naked eye, the terror camp was a few shabby felt tents and a modest group of livestock.

From the desert silence came a steady babble of happy voices, for the people gathered within this camp rarely met one another.

The largest tent in the camp was full of rambunctious children. The children were shrieking with glee. They were supposed to be attending a school of some kind, but the excitement of their clan reunion was proving too much for them. Their teachers—young women—were unable to get the children to concentrate on the classroom work at hand, which was building toy airplanes. Many toy airplanes. The kind of toy airplanes that could be glued together by a ten-year-old child.

Sonja's pack robot excited alarm in the camp. People rushed to see it, guns in hand. The locals looked like any group of central Asian refugees, except that they had many more children and they looked much better fed. Their parents had probably been urbanites a generation ago: people who went to Ulaanbaatar to see the beauty contests and drink the Coca-Cola.

The marauders stared at her, for camp people always stared at the Angel of Harbin. Some touched her white robes with wondering fingers.

In the hubbub, the Badaulet vanished.

John Montgomery Montalban appeared from the patchworked flap of a tent. Much like his brother, John also had a masked escort . . . his bodyguard, interpreter, tour guide—or the armed spy who was holding him hostage. Another of the clones.

So far, she had seen two clones among thirty-five. Sonja had vague hopes of killing all of the clones, but thirty-five? Thirty-five highly trained zealots, walking the Earth, scattered far across a desert? That was enough to found a civilization.

"I'm glad to see you, Sonja. Welcome."

Sonja climbed out of the robot and ignored his offered hand.

John Montalban pursued her, his dignified face the picture of loving concern. He still loved her. Sonja knew that he still loved her. He really did love her: that was the darkest weapon in his arsenal, and it brought on her a bondage like no other. "Sonja, I have some bad news for you. Please brace yourself for this."

"What now?"

"Your mother is dead."

Sonja looked him in the eye. John Montalban was telling her the truth. He never lied to her.

"She died in orbit two days ago," Montalban told her. "Everyone in the Shanghai Cooperative Orbiting Platform was killed by a solar flare. In my family's space station, my own grandmother was killed. It was a natural disaster."

"I am sorry about your grandmother," Sonja told him, and then her voice rose to a shriek. "This is *the happiest day of my life*! What *luck*! God loves me! She's dead, John? She's truly dead? She's *dead*, dead, dead?"

"Yes. Your mother is dead."

"You're *sure* she's dead? You saw her body? It's not another trick?"

"I saw a video of the body. A few systems on that space station are still operational. Most of it was stripped by that solar blast. That was a world disaster, Sonja. Communications are scrambled across the Earth . . . power outages, blackouts on every continent—that was the worst solar storm in recorded history. It was bad and it came out of nowhere. So this is not your happy day, Sonja. This has been a very grim and ominous couple of days for the human race."

"The human race? Ha ha ha, that counts me out!" said Sonja, and she was unable to restrain the bubble of pure, euphoric joy that rose within her. Happiness lit the core of her being. She began to dance in place. She wanted to scream the glorious news until the sky rang.

Realizing that nobody would stop her, Sonja tilted her head back, threw out both her arms, and howled. She howled with a heartfelt passion.

When Sonja opened her eyes, wetly streaming tears of joy, she could see from the looks on the grimy faces of the nomads that she still had her old magic. They were awestruck. Ten minutes alone with her as an inspired healer, and they would have done anything that she said.

"You don't really feel that way," John told her mildly. That was the worst thing about knowing John Montalban: that he was always telling her about her own true feelings. Worse yet, he was generally right.

"Djordje told the others about your mother's death," he said. "They're all in shock."

"I'm not shocked! I feel fantastic! I'm so happy. I want to dance!"

"Stop convulsing, Sonja. That first emotional reaction doesn't last," he told her. He put his arm on her protectively, and ushered her inside the tent.

The inside of the woolly ger tent was brisk and garish: there were scattered carpets, plastic ammunition crates, gleaming aluminum stewpots, and grass-chopping equipment. The place reeked of new-mown hay.

"I felt that I was just getting to know your mother," said John. "Her twisted motivations were the key to the whole Mihajlovic enterprise, but . . . no extent of her paranoia could protect her from a fate like *that*. There wasn't a cop, spy, general, or lawyer on Earth who could dig Yelisaveta out of her flying bolt-hole—and yet she was dead in ten minutes. Killed by space weather. I'd call that cosmic retribution, if not for the forty other international crewmen up there. Those poor bastards had maybe six minutes' warning of that catastrophe, and not one damn thing they could do to save themselves. Not one damn thing except to watch the wave roll in and fry them. I hate to think about a death scene like that."

Sonja remembered her taikonaut training. "Everyone is dead in the space station? All of them? They had a radiation shelter."

John shook his head. "For a blast of *that size*? That flare was ten times bigger than planet Earth!"

"The sun blew up? Truly?" That was a difficult matter to grasp.

"The sun is a star, Sonja. Stars are unstable by nature. Some stars are violently unstable."

Lionel entered the tent and noticed his brother's mournful look. His face fell in instant sympathy. "My grandmother was a very fine lady," Lionel offered, voice low. "She was the kind of great lady that a woman can become, when she's been poor, and hungry, and homeless, and a nobody."

John beamed at his younger brother. He was proud to see his fellow aristocrat commiserating with the little people.

Now the fuller extent of the strategic situation dawned on Sonja. The event that had happened changed everything. "You say that the Chinese space station is *empty*? Nothing in it but corpses?"

"Corpses," John agreed. "The Chinese station is one more large, failed, overextended technical megaproject. Although I had nothing to do with stopping this one myself."

Lionel smirked. "I think you're selling yourself a little short there, John."

Montalban shot his brother a warning glance.

"What?" Sonja shouted. "What is it this time, what have you done? What are you doing, John? What, what?"

"Not so loudly, please," said Montalban.

A busy nomad council of war was convening inside the ger. Outriders from a distant cell had arrived. The terrorists were briefing each other, issuing orders and making contingency plans. They were doing it all with paper. Little slips of grass parchment. Charcoal ink brushes.

"They never use electricity," said Montalban, "because it makes them too easy to track. That fact is making me, and my big correlation engine here, into the largest electronic-warfare target in a hundred kilometers. There are Chinese hunter-killer teams wandering out there, with who knows what kinds of weaponry. They use the local civilian populations for target practice."

For the first time, Montalban's bodyguard spoke. He spoke in a stiffly proper Beijing Chinese, and he spoke to Sonja. "This man said, in English, 'hunter-killer teams.' "

"Yes, he did say that, sir," Sonja told him.

"Red Sonja, you should tell your friends in Jiuquan not to send any more 'hunter-killer teams' into these steppes. Because we hunt them and we kill them."

"May I ask your name, sir?"

"I am Major General Cao Xilong, director of the army's General Political Department."

"You were a very able ideologist and military political thinker. You were a legend in your field."

"That," said Cao Xilong, "is why they have assigned me to oversee these fat Californian subversives in their ridiculous hats."

Montalban looked on, smiling benignly. Foreign languages had never been an American strong suit.

Sonja smiled politely at Cao Xilong. "May I inquire why your colleagues found it necessary to attempt to liquidate me with a flying bomb?"

"Yes. That matter is simple. We cannot allow the doomed Chinese regime to unilaterally impose their first-strike capacity against us. Political violence and war must be reinscribed into the geographies and architectures of cities in ways that—while superficially similar to feudal Chinese walls against roaming Mongols—inevitably reflect contemporary political conditions. Important here are these distinctions."

Major General Cao Xilong paused heavily, mentally searching for something he had memorized from a screen.

"•First, the demonstrated ability of the Jiuquan Space Launch Center to rival us in flourishing under postapocalyptic conditions."

The general was actually speaking aloud in bullet points. Sonja had never heard such a thing done before. It was deeply alarming.

"•Second, the seamless, ubiquitous merging between security, corrections, surveillance, military, and entertainment industries within China, making conventional urban-guerrilla warfare useless.

"•Third, the proliferating range of postglobalist private, public, and private-public bodies legitimized to act against nation-states, among whom we of the World Provisional Survival Empire must number ourselves."

The general stopped counting his fingers. "Contemporary cities are particularly vulnerable to focused disruption or appropriation, not merely of the technical systems on which urban life relies, but also to the liquidation of key human nodal figures who serve as the system's human capital."

The general then raised a fingertip. "The worst threats among those state running dogs are provocative figures who foment new relationships emerging from the long-standing interplay of social and urban control experiments practiced by the state elites against the colonized posturban peoples. Through continually linking sensors, databases, defensive and security architectures, and through the scanning of bodies, these running dogs export the state's architectures of control."

Sonja nodded. "I see. That's all very clear."

The general blinked, once. "You can follow our reasoning?"

"Yes I do. I know what you were doing when you tried to kill me, and the Badaulet. You wanted to kill our love."

Cao Xilong said nothing.

"You didn't need to kill me personally. I'm a former holy terror, but I've done nothing to you. You didn't need to kill him, either. He's just another cannon-fodder hero. But you did need to kill *the pair of us*, at the same blow, because we are together. You wanted to *kill our love for each other*, to keep us separate and polarized, because our love is dangerous to your plans. That's why we had to die."

"Bourgeois sentiment of this sort does not clarify the strategic situation."

"Maybe it's a woman's way to put it, hero, but *you knew that we were together*. You knew. How did you find that out? You've got spies, informants in Jiuquan? Oh: I know. You've got a correlation engine!"

"Of course we exploit the best intelligence methods available, although those must remain confidential."

"Listen—young genius—I've been working around the military for years. You don't scare me with your homemade grassroots rebellion. I know we're both clones, you and me—but to Red Sonja, you're just another tribal bandit who climbed out of a hole in the ground. You want to kill the men who love Red Sonja? Why don't you kill *him*?"

Sonja shot a sideways glance at John Montalban, who was standing and watching them debate, with his arms politely folded, and a look of intense pretended interest on his face. "*He* loves me fanatically, and while the Badaulet and I were in peaceful Jiuquan sharing a water bed, he was *already here in the midst of your camp* and he is *buying* you. You think you're a tactical genius? You are finished already! You are done."

"That would all be true," said Major General Cao Xilong, "except for one important factor which you have failed to grasp."

"And what 'factor' is that? Please do tell me."

"The Earth is doomed. The sun is proving unstable. And a giant volcano is on the point of eruption. The carrying capacity of this planet's biosphere under those conditions will fall by ninety-five percent. That means that, in fifty years or fewer, there will be only two kinds of society possible on Earth. The first is nomadic like ours, and runs lightly on the surface of the Earth. That society will survive.

"The second kind lives sealed inside technical bubbles, and they will go insane. Because that kind of life is a traumatic horror and it is an evil lie. So: This choice is not your choice, your weak and sentimental choice between your former lover and your current lover. Tomorrow's choice is between us and Jiuquan."

"You believe you can defeat Jiuquan? They are much more advanced than you are."

"I do not claim that we will defeat them immediately. At this moment, we could merely use our thousands of light aircraft to mine their roads, blow up the single points of failure in the electrical and water systems, and terrorize their population with mass slaughter of random civilians. They do already pay us tribute—to be frank, yes, they pay— but now you must imagine us attacking them from every point of the compass, around the clock, while the sky is black with volcanic ash. Of course we will win *that* battle. Because the world of tomorrow is hideous and we will own it. We will own the smoking ruins of the world. No one else. *Us, and those we force to become like us.* That is our great purpose."

John Montalban spoke up. "He just said 'world of tomorrow'! I don't know much Chinese, but I heard that. I'm very glad to see you and Major General Cao Xilong debating matters so cordially. That sounded like a fruitful exchange of views."

"Yes."

"I'm not surprised you would empathize so strongly with these strange and unfortunate people, Sonja. After all, their life experience—their sheltered upbringing, that traumatic exposure to the outer world—you can understand all that. You're a healer. I've seen you grasp the distress inside people, and change them for the better."

His fatuous words brought her nothing but pure dread. For all his tireless global meddling, he was from California, a place where people believed that the future was golden. While she was from the Balkans . . . a broken place, the cockpit of empires where the lost chickens pecked each other's eyes out . . .

The world to come was so much worse, so much more direly threatened than she had ever let herself believe . . .

But at least her mother was dead. No matter the city-killing look in the eyes of that nomad general—at least she had that transcendent joy to fully treasure. It was all she could do not to laugh in his masked, carnivorous face.

She suddenly broke from the general and strode into the middle of the tent, her ribs heaving.

Montalban followed her, touched her shoulder. "These people here . . . they're not beyond hope! They're just another runaway experiment." John rubbed his temples, suddenly weary. "I have so many colleagues working on 'Relinquishment' issues—colleagues in both the Dispensation *and* the Acquis . . . 'Relinquishment,' that's what we call it when we cram those techno-genies back into their bottles . . . 'Relinquishment' is difficult-to-impossible, and this *next* stunt I hope to pull—it's beyond me. It does not walk the Earth, it is literally out of this world."

Lionel spoke up. "I could make a good case that you're the best Relinquishment activist of all time, John. You have no peer in that work."

"Oh, come now."

"It's the truth! How many is this? Seven big projects defeated? Eight? You're doing the seventh and the eighth Relinquishment at the very same time!"

"Oh, it can't possibly be eight. I'm only thirty years old."

Lionel was cheering his older brother through his moment of doubt. "There were the hypervelocity engines. That was the first project you killed off."

"That wasn't 'Relinquishment.' Those were commercial competitors to our family's launch sites."

"There were those German tissue-culture labs."

"I was only tangentially involved in that scandal. Besides, there's tissue-culture practice all over the Acquis nowadays, so I sure wouldn't call that a victory."

"You knocked a huge hole in the genetics industry with that intellectual-property battle over DNA as an interactive network instead of patentable codons."

"That was all science paperwork! That was just about hiring smart lawyers and printing some letterhead. I didn't lift a finger."

"They lost billions, though. In terms of damage to hostile technologies — that was your best spanner thrown in the works, ever."

John Montalban was rallying. "Well, maybe. Maybe you're right about that one."

"Last summer you chased those neural fanatics out of the Balkans practically single-handed."

"They'll be back. Those boneware people are like mice. You chase 'em out of one spot, they pop up in a hundred other places . . . How many wild stunts does this make out of me? You're tiring me."

"There's our hosts here. They'll sure need some taming."

" 'Constructive engagement.' Simple diplomacy. They just need to be brought around to the world system, taught what side their bread is buttered on. Anyone could do that."

"But you spotted their hidden tomb, John. Tons and tons of burned machinery. The backup records of the Chinese state. That's gonna be the biggest archaeological discovery since the First Emperor of China burned all the books."

"No it won't. Bandits have been raiding that tomb for years now. There's probably some idiot raiding it right now. I had my informants, I had researchers, I even had inside help . . . and, hell, Lionel, the chances are really great that some lethal Chinese Scorpion team walks up to the two of us, now, out of nowhere, and we end up dead. Dead today. I'm gambling our lives, and the Earth's future, on something crazy that happened forty-eight hours ago. I'm gambling that the Acquis and the Dispensation have faster reflexes, after a catastrophe, than any nation-state. And they might dither. Or quarrel. And forget all about their necessity for speed. And brilliancy. And lightness and glory, and then we are both dead. And then we're not two rich idiots from California who are provisionally dead. We'll be the ashes of history."

Lionel pointed at Sonja. "There is her. You know that means hope."

"What, you mean Sonja? What about Sonja?"

"I mean all of them. I mean the Mihajlovic Project. That was your ultimate feat. That one was your greatest triumph, that was the most humane one, the most decent and loving Relinquishment of all."

Seeing the look on her face—Montalban always did that—Montalban was quick to apologize to her. "You have to forgive him, Sonja. Lionel's just a kid."

"Oh no," said Sonja through gritted teeth, "I love to hear him talk about us."

Lionel was stricken. "I didn't mean to hurt your feelings, Sonja. You are family—just like I said. You know that."

"What are you doing here, John? What is your great new purpose? You must tell me. I might be able to save you."

"Well," Montalban said, "at first, I came out here to the desert to dig up the buried brains of the state. Maybe it's a useless twenty-year-old backup, but even if its human cloned apparatus rebelled against it and set fire to it, there has to be a great deal of historical evidence buried down there. And I wanted that evidence, of course. We Synchronists always want history. Because history is the ultimate commercial resource. Someday the human race will have to come to terms with the vast genocide in China, and what the state did to the human beings within its grasp. Of course the state itself is never going to reveal that historical truth. So it is up to us, the outside scholars, the researchers, to steal whatever evidence we can."

"Evidence of *what*? The state saved Chinese civilization."

"Well . . . 'genocide' is such an emotionally loaded term . . . But it's entirely obvious from consumer demographic studies that the people who hindered the state—the burdens to its technical functions—were eliminated. There were over a billion Chinese people twenty years ago, now there are just under half a billion. No elderly, to speak of. No mentally ill. The handicapped are entirely gone. Criminals, liquidated. Even the people in the security apparatus, who were performing the liquidations, were themselves mostly purged . . . Even the male-female gender disparity was honed way back. The current China is very safe and peaceful. It's a hyperefficient machine."

"The strong survived. The weak died in the troubles. That's what happened."

"No, Sonja, that is just the party line. The state killed the weak and unfit. It controlled so many aspects of daily life that it had a million different methods to cull its herd."

"That is a slander and a lie."

"I know it's not politically correct of me to say that, but demographics never lie." Montalban shrugged irritably. "Look . . . I've gotten so used to combating the unthinkable, that I forget how the unthinkable can shock people. Yes, there was a genocide in China, during China's climate crisis. You look into the walled bubble from outside the walled bubble, and the dirty murk in there is very obvious. I'm not angry about it. I'm not condemnatory. I don't even want to discuss it right now. We in California could have accepted a hundred million refugee Chinese. We didn't do that. Nobody let them out. So of course they had to die. The real genius of the solution was programming *machines* to do the dirty work so that politicians could keep their hands clean."

John Montalban was rubbing one hand against the other. "My theory is that the architects of the regime's Final Solution were about thirty-five Chinese statesmen. I surmise that they were the very same thirty-five guys who were cloned, and then trained for war in a godforsaken bomb shelter buried in the middle of nowhere. They did that terrible thing because they were patriots. Then they marched out to die like heroes along with their own victims, leaving one last ace in the hole. They died in their own genocide and they left their clones. That's my big hypothesis. I haven't proved that idea yet. I don't know if I'll ever get around to proving it. But it's the sort of thing I have to know for my own satisfaction— so that I know that I'm making real-world decisions."

"If you libel the state in that fashion, the state will take reprisals against you."

Montalban sighed. "I am not 'libeling' the state. The Chinese state is the world's most remarkable case study in ubiquitous computing. It's 'ubiquity with Chinese national characteristics.' I don't consider that machine my enemy. It is not any moral actor, it's a machine. I don't condemn it. If the Chinese state committed 'genocide,' then the human

race has committed 'geocide.' The 'Fossil Fuel Project,' that was infinitely worse. That was the worst and most comprehensive blunder that
our species ever committed. Every human being had some share of guilt
in that monstrous crime. Am I 'libeling' us when I point out that the
human race got what it asked for? We blew it with the world's biggest
gamble, and the minor stunt I happen to be pulling right now, that is
just another return to the same table with much smaller stakes."

Lionel offered his brother a canteen. "John's been running at pretty
much full steam for three days straight. I don't think he's slept for three
hours. If he sounds a little overwrought, you need to cut him some
slack."

Montalban sat down on a patterned carpet; his burst of oratory had
drained him. The nomad tent had suddenly grown crowded. While
John had passionately ranted, busy tribesmen had carried the pots and
kettles from the place and cleared a small arena. A crowd had gathered,
sitting cross-legged, chattering and munching snacks. Fried meat of
some kind. It smelled like fried rats.

"Hey wow! Entertainment!" said Lionel. At the prospect, he brightened so much that he almost seemed to glow.

An overpowering melody came from nowhere, a sourceless wave of
powerful, thudding music. A woman strode into the tent, carrying the
soundtrack with her.

She wore a spangled golden headdress, a veil, a sequined bra, a spangled vest, and two thin skirts of overlapping chiffon. Bells chimed around
her ankles and golden bangles jingled on both her arms. Her eyes were
caked in kohl and her palms were stained red with henna.

She glided into the center of the tent, barefoot on the carpets, bathing
in the crowd's eager, yelping applause.

Her music faded to a steamy, rhythmic clicking. She stamped her
slippered feet in time so that her silver anklets jingled, and banged her
red palms so that the bracelets clashed.

Then she gazed seductively around her crowd, and saw Sonja. She
stopped at once.

"Now we're in for it," Lionel groaned.

"I thought I told you to keep Biserka under wraps," said Montalban.
"Where did she get that crazy costume?"

"Downtown Hollywood maybe? She's so tricky!"

Shivering with rage, the veiled dancer stalked over to confront John Montalban. "You have just *completely ruined* my best scene."

"We didn't know you were having a scene," said Lionel.

"I especially didn't know you were stealing Mila Montalban's best theme music," said John.

Biserka yanked the veil from her painted lips. "How did *she* get in here?" Biserka demanded. "You said she'd been killed by airplanes and robots and something."

"Last night that seemed pretty likely," John said, "but Sonja's a trooper."

Biserka turned to glare at Sonja. She spoke Chinese. "Well: Look around you. I win."

"Are you speaking to me?"

"What are you, bitch, five years old? I'm telling you that *I win*! You *know* that I win. You tried to chase me out of China: well, these are *my people* here. These are my very special people, the people who love me, the people who are all my good friends."

"Where did this ragtag find the money to hire you?"

"I did it for *love*," Biserka shrieked. "*You're* the one that's the mercenary! You whore, just look at them, look at their faces, see how much they love me! I taught them everything! I taught them what the real world is really like! Before me, they were like lost children."

Lionel intervened. "What's the name of your big victory dance, Biserka? Tell me about your cool new routine."

Biserka shot him a grateful look. "It's all about victory! And what happened in outer space! And my mother's death! And it's my interpretative dance performance about the world's bravest, noblest people—*my* people! They are going to *overthrow all the systems*, and cover the Earth in free blackspots, and break the walls of surveillance and haul the oppressors out of there . . . and pile their heads up in pyramids!"

Hands on her hips, Biserka drew a breath. "I choreographed it all by myself! I call it 'The Seven-Veiled Dance of Shiva, the Goddess of Destruction.'"

"Shiva is a male god," said Lionel.

"Really?"

"Yeah, Shiva is a male dancer, like I am."

"Never mind that, Lionel," said Montalban calmly. "Let Biserka dance. She has an eager public waiting here."

Biserka pouted. "You've gone and spoiled it all. How could you let *her* come in here? I was really, really happy today, for the first time in my whole life! I was happy for maybe one hour! I can dance! You know I can dance. I learned some hot new moves in Los Angeles, and you were going to love those! Now my timing's all messed up and it's all ruined."

"No problem," said Lionel, beaming supportively. "Just get ready to run your theme again. When I throw out my hand like this"—he gestured—"that's your cue."

Without warning, music blasted from Lionel's flesh: brassy, insistent, heart-thudding. Lionel strode confidently into the empty performance space, drew himself up with a winning smile, and did three backflips with a half gainer. Then he threw out his hand.

The stunned audience, who had never seen such behavior from any human being, howled in awed delight.

Biserka came to with a sudden start. She began to dance.

It was not that Biserka danced shamelessly. It was much worse than that. Biserka knew what shame was, and she was using their shame as a weapon to titillate them. Biserka danced corruptively. One wanted to hide the eyes of children from the spectacle. Though the children were quite enjoying it.

Sonja knew that it was her duty to put a swift end to this. She would kill Biserka. Killing Biserka would be the crown of her lifetime.

Sonja was stopped short by a hand on her elbow. It was the Badaulet.

Lucky put his lips next to her ear, so that she could hear him over the howls and the sticky, slinky music. "Our hosts have been telling me about the Chinese state," he said.

"They're lying to you."

"Well, you are my wife, and I want you to tell me the truth."

Sonja wrenched her arm free from his grip. "I always tell the truth to my men." No matter how much it hurt them.

"Are these young men really the Chinese state? They're the former leaders of the Chinese state, only living in the wilderness?"

"Yes. That is true."

"But they are bold men like me, and brave like me, and they ride and fight like me. And they do not hide behind Chinese walls because they aim to conquer the world."

"They won't succeed." She pointed. "*He* is going to conquer the world. He's already conquering the world. He's doing it right now while he's watching that slut dancing for him."

The expression on Montalban's face could have been canned and poured over cereal. He was transfixed by Biserka's dancing. He was fascinated.

Biserka sensed this and was playing to him. Biserka knew that she had him. She had found some aching hole in him, found a stained chink in the white knight's armor. It wasn't, after all, that hard to find. That part of him that belonged to her. She was reeling him in.

The Badaulet watched Biserka's flurried writhing with unfeigned disgust. "Your lord and master there is a decadent weakling."

"I'm sure he would tell you that he is 'healthily in touch with his darker side.' "

"I could kill him. He's not so much of a man. His younger brother, the one who dances like a woman, he's strong, but he has long hair. They are only two men, they're not two gods. In the eyes of the one God, I'm as good as them. Only, I have pride and cleanliness, and decency, and aspirations to please my Creator. If I put my body next to his body, I can put my knife through him."

"Don't do that. To kill a guest is dishonorable. Also, he's so rich that he might not stay dead."

"You love him," he told her. "That's why you urge me not to kill him. I want you to tell me, as my wife, that you love me better than him. That you will leave him and his life, and live my life."

"I know that you deserve that from me," she told him, "but I already swore once by everything I held sacred that I'd never see him, or hear him, or touch him again, and, here he is." Sonja began to cry. "I swear I can't help it."

"Any woman among these noble people would be a better wife to me than you are," he said. "They all admire me very much, they need my warrior skills. If I join them, I will be high in rank, they will give me *twenty* women like you. *Better* women than you."

"I don't doubt it," Sonja said between her sobs. "The only thing I ever

wanted was to be dutiful and good. I'm just so tired and sick of everything. I can't go on."

"Look at the way that slave dances for him," he said. He was revolted.
"She's like a *worm*. She's an *unclean reptile*. I can't take part in this dis-
gusting orgy, this is *wrong*. Our marriage is over, Sonja. I Divorce You. I
Divorce You. I Divorce You!"

Sonja howled in pain and grabbed for him. "Oh please don't divorce
me, please don't!" He tore himself from her grip and stalked away.

Sonja was trembling from head to foot. She was cracking inside.
There was an abyss inside her. She had lived for years in that abyss once.
It was a red abyss.

Carried by blazing impulse, Sonja stalked into the middle of the dance
floor. She raised both her arms overhead, but this incantatory gesture did
nothing. Biserka had seized everyone's attention. Biserka had stripped off
three of her veils and was beaming with malicious delight. She capered
around Sonja, waving her chiffon headdress, delicately wriggling.

The crowd rose and surged forward. They formed a tight circle. They
were dying to see a fight.

A hand in her back shoved her forward.

For the first time, Biserka was afraid. The taunting look left her face.
Biserka looked pretty when she was afraid. She had always been the
frightened one, always. When the soldiers had come to kill all of them,
Biserka had thrown herself on the ground to lick their feet.

Sonja spat into her face, then turned and walked away.

A deadly insult and a feigned retreat. It was the oldest and simplest
and most effective of stratagems. In the roar of voices, Sonja counted
heartbeats and then lashed out backward.

A rear heel kick was the strongest blow that a woman's body could de-
liver. It hit Biserka straight in the chest as she rushed forward in her rage
and hate and panic, and it struck her so hard that she flew backward and
stumbled into the arms of two spectators and knocked both of the men
down.

Biserka did not move again.

Sonja dusted off her hands. She glared at the men in the tent, who
had grown silent and respectful and ashamed. She jerked her head at
the open door.

The crowd got up in a body and left the tent.

Montalban and his brother were busy on the carpet.

"Poor Biserka," mourned Lionel.

"She's alive," said Montalban.

Sonja was regretful. "That's because I missed her heart."

"Well, you broke three of her ribs and you've put her into shock. Oh, for God's sake stop standing there gloating, Sonja. You're a woman, you're not a killer robot. You've got medical training, come and help me with her."

THE SUDDEN END OF THE FESTIVITIES put a damper on the clan's convocations. Without any apparent orders being taken or given, they were breaking their tents, rolling their carpets, chasing sheep, splitting up, atomizing into the steppes.

Her ex-husband was already long gone. The angry Badaulet had thundered off over the bloody horizon somewhere. She wondered if she would ever hear any news of his death.

Eventually, there were only four of them left. The nomads had evaporated, leaving four people in a well-trampled and utterly anonymous patch of half desert, half steppe. Herself, the two Montalban brothers, and the unconscious Biserka, lying in a robot full of bullet holes, with her heels propped up and her head set low.

"Hey look!" said Lionel, alertly gazing into the darkening sky. "See that little glint up there? That little spark of moving light? That's it! That's the dead Chinese space station. We can actually see it from down here with the naked eye!"

"The satellites must keep spinning," said Montalban. "Every power player agrees on that. Because without satellites there is no geolocation. Without geolocation, we would be truly lost and abandoned in this desolate place, instead of merely standing around here in the functional equivalent of Hollywood and Vine."

"Are we going to get away with stealing a Chinese space station, John? I've seen you do big real-estate deals before. But that's a *space station*."

"We do not plan to 'steal' the dead space station, Lionel. That is a derelict property. We are rescuing it. We are redeeming it in the general public interest of planet Earth. It is a fixer-upper. It is a turn-around property. And that station isn't much bigger than LilyPad when we took that over from the Indians. We are the natural party to take over a lost piece of orbital real estate."

"You will not get away with that," Sonja told him. "You will not be allowed to do that."

"Probably not, Sonja dear, but it certainly seems worth a try."

"It is a direct threat to Chinese national interests if you board that facility. The state will not stand for that foreign intrusion."

"I can certainly understand that nationalist point of view," said Montalban. "I'm sure that the Chinese are scrambling for new launch capacity in Jiuquan right now. However, China is not the whole Earth. My family and my various political allies, to our great good luck, happen to be planning an international, orbital summit of Acquis and Dispensation political pundits. In fact, we had to postpone that summit when we heard there was bad solar weather. Our private space station, LilyPad — which does not have any mysterious weapons of mass extermination aboard it — happens to be in a rather remote orbit. Whereas the Chinese station — which has long been rumored to carry horrific weapons of mass destruction that can scramble the DNA of people on the ground through God only knows what horrible mechanism — that abandoned hulk, full of corpses and former war criminals, it orbits so close to the Earth that, if we don't put a new crew aboard it immediately, it's going to tumble out of orbit and possibly land on a major city."

"That is completely untrue. That is a pack of lies. There is no danger of that happening. You made all that up. It's all a snare and a political diversion. You are a pirate, you are stealing it."

"Ah, but you forget that huge solar flare, Sonja. Solar flares heat the Earth's outer atmosphere. That has increased the orbital drag on the space station. So of course the space station is a public hazard and it must be rescued at once. We are not pirates, but the responsible parties. The whole world will agree with us."

"That's a lie, too."

"It's not a lie. It's the 'precautionary principle.' We can't be *sure* that isn't really happening. Maybe there's a strange interaction with the solar magnetism and the particles of Chinese hydrogen bombs in our upper atmosphere. Maybe that's what caused all these blackouts and the mayhem around the world. Do you think the world has any *time to waste* while the Chinese bureaucracy pulls its firecrackers out of mothballs to fly up there and do its sorry cover-up?"

Lionel was laughing wildly. "Just listen to *that*! Listen to him go! When he gets all wound up, there's just nobody who can touch him! Wow! He's had *less than forty-eight hours* to advance this political line! And he didn't do it with his friends and his servants handy, either! He did it *in the middle of a savage desert*. Call me a fanboy, but . . . well, the stupid cute ones run for public office, and the smart ones manage the campaigns."

"We're shooting the works here, Lionel. We have to give it our best," said Montalban.

Lionel nodded. "Absolutely, brother!"

After Montalban's raging burst of oratory, nothing whatever happened. There was nothing around them. They were nowhere and in noware. Night was falling. There was utter emptiness.

"I'm thirsty," Biserka moaned.

Lionel tipped water into her mouth. She sipped it and passed out.

"How will you know if your scheme has worked?" said Sonja.

"I can tell you," Montalban confessed, "that I haven't the least idea. There simply wasn't any time to arrange for that. I threw the gears into motion—in network nodes all over this planet—I don't even know who is first onto the space station. They're not exactly two-fisted astronaut hero types, these Relinquishment intellectuals. Plus, there's some likelihood that *another* solar flare will erupt and they all get fried up there. But—*some* global pundit is absolutely sure to invade that facility, even if it's just to float around in free fall making snarky comments about the bad industrial design."

"I would go up there," said Lionel. "I love orbit."

"Oh, I'm definitely going up there, if we somehow survive down here. I'm going to retrieve the body of my dear correspondent, Yelisaveta Mihajlovic. I wouldn't dream of having that lady jettisoned into outer space . . . I don't care how much space junk there is up there already; I swear she won't become part of it."

Sonja sat heavily on the comfortless floor of the desert. It had never occurred to Sonja that anyone would go to fetch her mother's body down to Earth. That concept had not crossed her mind for one instant.

She had been blind to that idea. She had always been blind to so many ideas. She was a rigid, staring, damaged creature. There were so many spaces within her own stony heart, places where she could not look.

"Don't cry," said Montalban.

"I'm not crying."

"You're about to cry," Montalban predicted, with accuracy. "You're about to crack up because you can't bear your burden. Your lifelong burden is finally overwhelming you. It's too heavy and it's just too much for you. We know about that, Lionel and I. So we are removing your burden preemptively. Just for once. As a mercy. Your war is all over, Sonja. We are pulling you out of the cold. You are never going back to that place in the world, because you are ours now. We *own* you. Just let them *try* to take you back from us."

"Look there," said Lionel, pointing.

"What do you see?"

"It's a contrail, some kind of arch across the sky. Not a satellite. Moving way too slow for that. Some kind of suborbital thing."

"I do see it! Right! That could be a Chinese ground-to-ground warhead," said Montalban cheerily.

"That is the west," said Lionel patiently. "That way over there, that's the east. China is east."

"Is *that* the east?" said Montalban, puzzled. "Really? I should have stepped outside of that tent more often."

"Sonja, do you have binoculars? A rifle? Anything with a telescope on it?"

Sonja muttered at them from the chilly ground. "All I own is this badly damaged robot, which my ex-husband left to me as an act of contempt."

But they were ignoring her words, for something had suddenly bloomed overhead in the darkening Asian sky. "Holy cow," said Lionel, "what the heck is that thing? I've never seen a thing like that in my life!"

"What is that, a comet? I hate to say this, but that looks like a flying squid."

"It's like some zeppelin bullet that opens up just like an umbrella! Who would *build* a thing like that?" Lionel paused. "Why haven't they sold *us* one of those?"

"The world is full of skunk labs, Lionel. We can't know every tech project in the world. I'd be guessing—well, I'd bet that these were just the first guys to hit the Return key. They must have scrambled whatever they had on the ground."

The exotic aircraft drew nearer to them. It was floating to Earth rather elegantly, silently, and emission-free. It was like a giant dandelion seed.

"Okay," said John authoritatively, "I think maybe I've heard of these after all. That's some kind of fibrous suborbital pod. It's Acquis. It's European and it's Acquis."

Lionel was unimpressed. "Of course it's Acquis, John. Anybody can tell from the design that it's Acquis. I think it's Italian."

"I think you're right."

"That craft is going to land precisely on our stated coordinates. Like, within a five-meter range. I think we'd better move before it lands and crushes us."

Arm in arm, the brothers took several measured steps away across the desert. The flying device drew nearer. It was stellar and radiant and huge. It was like a flying tinsel chandelier.

"No, it's going to land nearby us," Montalban decided, and the two of them strode back to the robot to await their airborne delivery.

"Los Angeles is the capital of the world," Montalban pronounced. "Say what you will about the Chinese—and I love them dearly, we do business every day—there are a hell of a lot more Chinese in Los Angeles than there will ever be Angelenos in Beijing."

"You sure got that right!"

Montalban drew a triumphant breath. "As we stand here in the gathering dusk of old Asia, it's the brilliant dawn of a new West Coast New Age! It's time to break out the Napa Valley champagne! Tomorrow's regime is Pax Californiana! As a bright and shining city on a hill, we, the last best hope of mankind, are pulling the planet's ashes straight out of the stellar fire!"

"That's the truth!" crowed Lionel.

"Even when we golden Californians were mere American citizens, it was never that great an idea to bet your future against *us*. I mean, you *could* bet against us, but—where's the *fun* in that? If you try to beat us, even if you win, you have to lose!"

Lionel slapped his brother's two extended hands. "We rock! We rule! It's because we've got a shine on our shoes and a melody in our heart! We've got the rhythm!"

The brothers capered like utter fools as Sonja sat in heartbreak, and they laughed uproariously. It was the most glorious day of their lives.

EPILOGUE

WHEN INKE ZWEIG HEARD of the burial plans for her husband's deceased mother, she sensed that such arrangements could not possibly end well. Inke had been to a host of funerals. She had hated every one of them. Every celebration of death permanently drained Inke of some spark of her own life force.

Inke envied the dead at funerals—since the dead didn't have to endure the poorly arranged conclusions to difficult modern lives. The lack of any decent and comforting ceremony was the signature of a world in a near-fatal moral confusion.

What were the so-called Acquis and the sinister Dispensation? How had they vulgarly elbowed their way to the forefront of modern life? Why were people so anxious nowadays to pile on proofs of the stricken mourning on their electronic networks? As if the modern dead had no parents, no cousins, no children, no parishioners, no friends next door, no ties of citizenship. Instead there would be vulgar gold-wrapped bouquets from distant Moscow, remote-control acquaintances burning heaps of Chinese paper cash for the departed on live video links above the coffin . . . A globalized travesty.

Inke begged George to allow her to stay quietly with the children in Vienna. But, as was his method now—George began piling on all kinds of poorly linked "reasons" to sway her. George had become the addict of some new game he called a "correlation engine," and, since it had caused his business to prosper, he had begun to rely on it in his personal life.

She should see Mljet, George argued, for it was his birthplace and also remarkably beautiful. There was money to be made on the island.

John Montgomery Montalban, his firm's biggest business partner, was coordinating the funeral. The great man would certainly take things amiss if Inke did not show up.

All the sisters—Vera, Radmila, Sonja, even Biserka, the crazy one— they had all agreed to come see their mother buried. Inke had always nagged him (as George put it) about meeting all of his sisters. Here, at last, was the golden chance that she should not forgo.

The sisters were asking for her by name. They were also asking to see the three children. It was unthinkable that she not go to the funeral. She had to go.

None of this bullying convinced Inke. It only made her sense of a gathering catastrophe more gloomy and keen. These four harsh, implacable women, so tall, statuesque, blond, and icily identical—they all had high brainy foreheads, big beaky noses, and big flat cheekbones, like the female statues supporting Vienna's Austrian Parliament building—had they really agreed to step from their four separated pedestals? To really meet with one another, in the flesh? To eat at the same funeral wake, to talk together in public, as if they were women instead of demigoddesses?

They would claw each other's eyes out. There would be nothing left of them.

It had taken Inke years just to learn to manage George. George was the manageable one of the group—and George had a streak of true ferocity in his soul. George was cunning and devoid of scruples.

When she'd first met George, he'd been a teenage illegal laboring in her father's river shipyard, sleeping in there, probably eating the wharf rats. George scared her, yet he had a genius for putting the workshop in order. Her family's fortunes were collapsing and the world was violently spinning out of control. Inke had sensed that George might be capable of protecting her during the coming Dark Age. At least, he often darkly spoke of such necessities.

It would certainly take someone like George to protect her, in that murky world of slaughter that awaited everyone in the future: the seas rising, the poles melting, coral reefs turning to foul brown ooze, droughts, floods, fires, plagues, storms the size of Mexico: nothing was safe anymore. Nothing was sure, nothing was decent. Her world was horribly transformed, and this man who seemed to want her so much: he was also different, and somehow, in much the same way as the world.

She was just a common Viennese girl, round, brown, small, not the prettiest, no man ever looked twice, no one but George was fiercely demanding her hand, her heart, her soul. Since anything could happen to a girl whose father was ill, Inke had given in to him.

In the years that followed that fateful choice of hers, people had indeed died in unparalleled numbers and in awful, tragic circumstances, a terrible business, the whole Earth in disaster, a true calamity, a global crisis, enough to make any normal, decent woman tremble like a dry leaf and tear out her hair in handfuls . . .

Yet not all that many people had died in Vienna. As George rightly pointed out—George always had an eye out for the main chance—life in Vienna was rather good.

Because—as George said—the world couldn't possibly fall apart, all over, at the same speed, at the same moment. There simply had to be lags, holes, exceptions, safe spots, and blackspots—even if it was nothing more than a snug attic room where Inke could curl up with a good Jane Austen novel.

Even when the whole Earth was literally bathed in a stellar blast straight from the surface of the sun itself . . . an insane idea as awful as the black dreams of some of her favorite book authors, Edgar Poe and Howard Lovecraft—even in a natural catastrophe *literally ten times bigger than the whole Earth*, there were some people on Earth who hadn't much noticed it. They couldn't be bothered.

The passing years had taught Inke to count her blessings, rather than the innumerable threats to her well-being. She had three loving children, a handsome home, a relatively faithful husband. In the past few months—as his sisters had all collapsed, one by one, into abject puddles of misery—George was becoming a pillar of the global business community. George had been traveling the world, mixing with much better company than usual. He was better dressed, better spoken, suave, and self-contained. George had matured.

The death of his mother had been a particular tonic for George. Suddenly he was calling *her* "Mother." There were handsome new gifts for Inke, and, when George was at home, he was markedly kind and attentive. Even the children noticed George's improved behavior. The children had always adored George, especially when he was at his worst.

"You only have to bury a mother once," George coaxed, "it's not like

I'm asking you to bury my damnable sisters." This was a typical fib on his part because, in all truth, his mother and his sisters were cloned bananas from the same stem. Inke held her tongue about that, though. Everybody knew the truth, of course: the Mihajlovic brood were the worst-kept "secret" scandal in history. Everyone who loved them learned not to say anything in earshot.

Then George further announced that his mother's burial was to be a traditional Catholic ceremony. Not the kind of ceremony George preferred: those newfangled Dispensational Catholic ceremonies, with ubiquitous computing inside the church. No: George was firmly resolved on proper committal rites, with a vigil, a Mass, and a wake. Conducted in Latin. The Latin was the final straw.

At this overwhelming gesture, Inke had to give in. Her surrender meant the tiresome chore of shopping for proper funeral clothes for herself, George, and the children. For George wanted no expense spared.

Inke soon found, from the unctuous behavior of the tailors, that this was no ordinary funeral. It was to be a famous funeral. A world-changing funeral, a ʼglamorous climacteric. In particular, everyone asked if George's children were going to meet "Little Mary Montalban."

There seemed no use in Inke's obscuring the fact that her children were the cousins of Little Mary Montalban. Lukas, Lena, and even baby Ivan would personally meet the simpering, capering Little Mary Montalban, the "girl with the world at her feet" . . .

Mljet proved a keen disappointment. The island looked so mystical and lovely from the deck of a ferry, yet the landscape was a fetid, reeking wilderness, swarming with insects even in November, a rank place like an overgrown parking lot, and with scarcely any civilized amenities.

Inke's little German guidebook made a great deal of pious green fuss about the returning fish and the swarming bugs and the glorious birds of prey and so forth, but—just like the "Treasure Island" of her older son's favorite book author, Robert Louis Stevenson—Mljet must have been an excellent place to be marooned and go totally mad.

Inke remarked on this to the older boy but, although Lukas was not yet eight, and huge-headed, with missing teeth and spindly schoolboy limbs, Lukas already had his father's wild look in his eyes. "Marooned and going mad!" Lukas thought that was wonderful. He would maroon his little sister Lena and make her go mad, by stealing all her dolls and leaving her without any playmates.

Construction work was booming at the island's new tourist port, which was named Palatium. Someone highly competent was sinking a great deal of investment money here. Given that George was so deeply involved in those logistics, this was a heartening sight to Inke. It almost made up for the fact that the sea trip had badly upset the baby.

Palatium's newly consecrated Catholic church seemed to be the first building formally completed. It was certainly the first decent place of worship consecrated in Mljet since who knew when. The church had a proper crying room with a trained nursemaid in it, a quiet American girl. This girl was Dispensation—it was annoying how many of them dressed themselves to show their politics—but she loved babies.

Nerves jangled, Inke dipped at the holy water, led the older children up the aisle, genuflected, and slipped into a front pew. Peace at last. Peace, and safety. Thank God. Thank God for the mercies of God.

The coffin was candlelit with its feet toward the holy-of-holies. Inke and the children shared the shining new pew with an old man sitting alone. Some threadbare Balkan scholar, by the look of him.

The poor old man seemed genuinely shaken and grieved by the death of Yelisaveta Mihajlovic.

Inke could not believe that Yelisaveta Mihajlovic had been any kind of decent Catholic. If she had been, she would have trained her children in the catechism, instead of stuffing their cloned heads like cabbage rolls with insane notions about how computers were going to take over the world. Yelisaveta Mihajlovic was nobody's saint, that was for certain. That dead creature in the elaborate casket there was the widow of a violent warlord, a Balkan Lady Macbeth.

Still, there had to be some redeeming qualities to any woman lying dead in church. After all was said and done, Yelisaveta Mihajlovic had created George. Inke knew well that George wasn't quite human, but she considered that a distinct advantage in a husband.

Just look at that weepy old man over there; his blue-veined hands were clenched before his face, he was clearly Dispensation yet sincerely praying as a Catholic. Life wasn't about being perfectly consistent, was it? Mankind were miserable sinners. If they didn't know they were sinners before their whole Earth caught fire, they certainly ought to know that by now.

Inke rose from the pew to attend to the casket in the mellow candle-light. This was the most expensive, elaborate coffin Inke had ever seen. She'd thought at first that it was a properly open coffin, but no. The casket had a bubble top of thin, nonreflective glass. The dead woman's coffin was hermetically sealed.

And that corpse inside her bubbled sphere of death . . . what brilliant undertaker had been set loose there? The more one stared at those gaunt, painted, cinematic features, the more she looked like some brilliant toy.

There was just enough graceless authenticity left to the corpse to convince the viewer that the undertaker's art concealed an actual dead woman. Or a dead creature anyway, for the war-criminal fugitive had been living for years up in orbit, where human bone and muscle wasted away from the lack of gravity, where the air was canned and the skin never felt healthy sunlight . . . How many "days" had this waxwork creature seen, with her dead silent-actress eyes, those orbital sunrises, sunsets, as she bounded off the walls of her tin home like a fairy shrimp . . .

She didn't even have legs!

A shroud covered her lower body. Thin, cream-colored, silky fabric. Enough to veil her abnormalities, but enough to show the ugly truth to those who—somehow—must have known what she was doing to herself, to her body and soul, way up there.

She was sickeningly strange. Yet at least she was truly dead.

A reflective shadow appeared on the glass bubble. It was one of the clones. The clone took a stance at the far side of the coffin. She stared into the bubble, fixated, gloating.

She was dressed in elaborate, lacy white, with a long stiff bodice but a plunging décolletage, like some bulging-eyed bride, drunk at a Catholic wedding and burningly eager to haul the groom to a hotel.

Inke had only met one of the cloned sisters: Sonja, the strongest one. She knew instantly that this one was Biserka. She knew that in her bones.

"I'm Erika Montalban," Biserka told her.

Inke did not entirely trust her own English. "How nice. How do you do?"

"And you're Inke, and those are your kids!"

Lukas and Lena were sitting placidly in their pew, heads together over a silent handheld game. Inke knew instantly that Biserka would cheerfully skin and eat her two children. She would gulp them down the way a cold adder would eat two mice.

"Where's the baby?" Biserka demanded, scanning the church as if it sold babies on racks. "I love babies! I want to have lots of them."

Inke touched her scarf. "You should wear something . . . on your head. We are in a church."

"What, I have to wear a hood in here, like a Muslim girl or something?"

"No, like a Catholic."

"Do I get to eat those little round bread things?"

"No, you're not in a state of grace."

"I put the holy water all over myself!"

"You're not a Catholic."

"It is *always* like that!" Biserka screeched, wringing her hands in anguish. "What is with you people? I did *everything right*, and you're not having any of it? I'm going to find John. John is going to fix this, you wait and see!"

Biserka stormed out of the church.

"You told her the proper things," said the old gentleman. He had stepped from his pew to the coffin, without Inke hearing his tread. He spoke English. "You were kind and polite to her."

"Thank you, sir."

"My name is Dr. Vladko Radic. You do not know me, Mrs. Zweig, but I know a little of you. I am a friend of Vera Mihajlovic."

"I understand. How do you do?"

"I also knew Yelisaveta Mihajlovic. I knew her rather well. Yelisaveta was a great patriot. Of course she committed excesses. God will pardon her that. Those were very excessive times." Radic was drunk. Drunk, and in church.

"If I may ask you a favor," slurred Dr. Radic, "if an old man may ask you one small favor . . . the dead have to bury the dead, but my dearest *domorodac,* my dearest *Mljecanka,* Vera Mihajlovic . . . A very beautiful, very sincere, very lovable girl . . . for all the infernal machines that cover this island, it has never been the same without her!"

Radic began sobbing, in an unfeigned, gentlemanly fashion, wiping at his rheumy eyes. "I sit here praying for Vera . . . praying that she will come here to see this unfortunate woman, and that Vera can return to this place, and that life here can be made right again! Have you seen Vera?"

"No sir, I have not seen her."

"Please tell Vera that all is forgiven if she will come back to the island! Please tell her that . . . yes, life will be different, life *must* be different now, but Dr. Radic has not forgotten her, and she has many friends here and she will *always* have friends."

The poor old man's distress was so deep and immediate and pitiful and contagious that Inke burst into tears. "I know that Vera is here. She must be here."

"She is a very noble, good person."

Overwhelmed, Inke fled to the pew to rejoin her children. Lukas glanced up. "Is that our grandmother dead in that bubble?"

"No."

"Okay!" They returned to their game.

Worshippers were quietly filtering into the church. The liturgy began. It was a small church but an impressive, full-scale performance, which might have suited Zagreb or even Rome. Lectors, musicians, altar boys—the ceremonial staff almost outnumbered the attendees.

Then there were cameras. Not the small cameras everyone carried nowadays. Large, ostentatious, ceremonial cameras with sacred logos.

There was no sign of George at the funeral service, which was entirely typical of him. Yet the young priest—handsome, bearded, deftly in command of the proceedings—was an inspiration.

It seemed impossible that anyone could properly bury a creature like Yelisaveta Mihajlovic: yet she had to be buried somehow, all things had to pass, and this priest was just the man to do it. Each soothing element of the ritual was another wrapping round the creature's airtight coffin: the Introductory Rite, the Liturgy of the Word, the Intercessory Prayer, the Office of the Dead from the Liturgy of the Hours . . .

This priest was nobody's fool about the goings-on here either, for he chose to speak from Wisdom, Chapter Four:

"But the numerous progeny of the wicked shall be of no avail; their spurious offshoots shall not strike deep root nor take firm hold.

"For even though their branches flourish for a time, they are unsteady and shall be rocked by the wind and, by the violence of the winds, uprooted;

"Their twigs shall be broken off untimely, and their fruit be useless, unripe for eating, and fit for nothing."

Those who lacked a firm grounding in Scripture could not follow the priest's allusions, but those who grasped his meaning, grasped it well. Inke took satisfaction in that. She was suddenly glad she had come to the funeral. She always had a terror of preparing for a funeral, but as a funeral itself went on, there was always something right and good about it. When a funeral was over she felt profoundly glad to be alive.

Six pallbearers solemnly carried the creature's glassy casket to a hillside above the reviving city of Palatium. There was a neat hole in the soil there, chopped there as if by lasers. They conveyed the capsule into the Earth.

There was an impressive crowd at the graveside, much larger than the gathering inside the church. George had finally made it his business to appear. He looked solid and dignified.

The glamorous mourners at graveside were not seeking any consolation in the rituals of faith—on the contrary, it was entirely clear to Inke that they were there on business. They were all stakeholders in this process, somehow. They were cunning people. They all had good reasons to be here. They were burying the past so as to get a firm foothold on some ladder into tomorrow.

She was surrounded by handsome, self-assured, polished, gorgeous foreigners.

By the sound of their American English, Inke realized that these people had to be the Montgomery-Montalban clan. This was the famous Family-Firm, with its blood relations, its staffers, servants, investors, and trustees. How strange to think that Europe was so full of conscientious social justice, while America had its ruthless aristocracy.

There was a sudden jostling as a whole shoving crowd of Acquis cadres plowed through the crowd. These Acquis were unruly and ill rehearsed, for they had invited themselves to the proceedings. They had some right to investigate the proceedings, it seemed. Unwelcome yet inevitable, the Acquis were here like the police at a mafia wedding.

George was talking rapidly to one of the Acquis spies; for some reason, George was abandoning the decent suit she'd bought him and borrowing the man's white jacket.

There was another trampling surge past the grave—how had the crowd grown so large and unruly, so suddenly? A host of bodyguards and paparazzi.

Little Mary Montalban had appeared upon the scene.

The child actress, whose skyrocketing fame had the world in such a tizzy—she seemed just another child to Inke, rather neatly and soberly dressed in gorgeous mourning clothes. The child walked serenely through the crowd, breaking a wake through them, as if she parted adult crowds every day.

The little girl drew nearer.

Suddenly, she turned her face up to Inke. The girl's beauty was astounding. It burned and dazzled, like being hit in the face with a searchlight.

The child recited two lines, loudly, in a well-rehearsed German. *"How do you do, Tante Inke? I'm so glad to see you here with us."*

Inke found herself bending to kiss the child's delicate cheek. It was an irrevocable act, something like swearing allegiance.

Her children were thunderstruck to meet their famous cousin. It was as if someone had given them a toy angel.

Inke realized that the male stranger at her side was John Montgomery Montalban. She had met him once. John Montalban looked older now. And shorter, too—somehow, world-famous people were always much shorter in real life.

"George has asked me to say a few words after the interment," Montalban said. "My little Synchronist eulogy . . . I hope you won't mind that, Inke."

It was as if he were pouring warm oil over her head.

"Are you nervous?" she asked him, the first remark that fluttered onto her tongue.

"Yes, I'm worried," Montalban lied briskly, "I always hate these formal presentations . . . Inke, you married George. So you're our expert on the subject at hand here. What on Earth can I properly say about Yelisaveta? At the end of the day, it seems that I knew Yelisaveta best. Yet she was—of course—a monster. What can I say about her that isn't completely shocking to propriety? The world is listening."

Inke considered the world—the poor, imperiled world. "Did the old woman ever tell you that she would come back to the world, down from orbit?"

"She did. Sometimes. She was stringing us on, from her lack of anything else to do with herself. It was like a long hostage negotiation. Please give me some good advice here, Inke, help me out. Tell me what I should say about this situation. The world needs closure on the issue. She was our relative, you know."

Why was he talking to her in this confiding way? In the past, he'd always talked to her with the hearty exaggeration of an English lordship treating one of the little people as his equal.

"I think," she said haltingly, "I think Yelisaveta was just . . . a dark story made by her own dark times."

"That makes some sense."

"She tried to build something and it broke into pieces. The pieces could not hold. So she lied, cheated, and killed for nothing . . . but the truth is . . . she believed in every last horrible thing that she did. She fully believed in all of it. She was sincere, that was her secret. It was all her sacrifice and her grand passion."

Montalban was truly interested. "That is fabulous. How well put! And George is one of the remaining pieces, too! Yet George is the piece that is least like the rest of the broken pieces. He's not much like them, they really hate him for that . . . Why is that, can you tell me that?"

"George is a man. Men take longer to mature."

"I see. That may indeed be the case . . . in which case, may I tell you something important now about your George? George has always led a dodgy, improvised life . . . between the Dispensation and our good friends the Acquis . . . he was cutting corners, making connections . . . After this funeral George will have a changed life. Because those two great parties are finding a bipartisan consensus. We have found the powers necessary to defeat the climate crisis . . . And in doing that, we have let so many genies out of bottles that our Earth is becoming unimaginable. Do you see what I mean here? Instead of being horribly unthinkable, the Earth is becoming radically unimaginable."

Montalban was so solemn and passionate in this assessment that all Inke could do was blink.

"Inke, I aspire to see a normal world. A normalized world. I have never yet lived in any normal world, but I hope to see one built and standing up, before I die."

"A 'normal' world, John?"

"Yes. 'Normal.' Like you, Inke. To be normal is a very conservative business. Your husband is going to become a conservative businessman. That is necessary, and I'm going to help him."

"You're *not* a conservative businessman?"

"No, Inke, alas, I'm a hip California swinger from Hollywood who has multiple wives. But I do need a conservative businessman, rather badly. And since your George is part-and-parcel of a Relinquished experiment, he is perfect for that role. I foresee a leadership role for George. He will become a modern captain of industry and a pillar of a new world consensus."

"My husband admires you very much," she told him, "and he would like to trust you, but really, John . . . Biserka. Why Biserka?"

"Yes," he said wistfully, "I know. 'Biserka.' "

"Why?"

Montalban looked at the gathered children—they were plunging through the crowd, bobbing like corks. "My little daughter Mary . . . she lacks for playmates. Mary doesn't have much of a peer group. Why don't you and the kids come and visit us this Christmas? We'll all go to Lily-Pad. Up in orbit. It's very quiet up there. It's private. We'll have a good long chat about certain matters. You and I, especially. We'll iron some things out."

"Why do you want to fly into outer space? That is dangerous."

"The Earth is dangerous. And the sun is also disquieting. If the sun grows seriously turbulent—then Mars wouldn't be far enough away for us. I commissioned some speculations on that topic. We've made some interesting findings. Should the Earth's sun become unstable, it turns out that, with the Earth's present level of industrial capacity, we could escape to the Oort Cloud with a biosphere ark of maybe a hundred, a hundred and fifty people. Carrying our ubiquitous support machines, of course."

Montalban seemed to expect an answer to this extraordinary declaration. "Of course," Inke told him.

"The Earth would become a cinder. Mars would be irradiated. Hot gas would be blasting off the surfaces of Jupiter and Saturn. The only spark of living vitality left in the solar system would be a shiny bubble containing us. Us, a whole lot of our maintenance machinery, and mostly, microbes."

" 'Us,' John."

"Yes, I mean *us*, Inke." He waved his hand at the funereal crowd. "You, me, the kids. People. There wouldn't be much of us left, but we would be what there was."

"You really think that way."

"Yes, I have to think that way. It's necessary."

"You're not a conservative businessman, Mr. Montalban."

"No, I'm what people call a 'Synchronic realist.' We choose to look directly at the stark facts of science and history." Montalban sighed. "Of course, whenever one does that in an honest spirit, everything becomes visionary, abnormal, and extreme."

There was a bustle at the graveside. Somehow, amazingly, George had assembled his sisters into a public group.

Since they violently loathed one another, Vera, Sonja, Radmila, and Biserka had all been determined to stand out during the funeral. Rather than wear proper dark mourning clothes—as everyone else was doing—they had each, independently, decided to mark themselves out as free spirits by dressing entirely in white. So the sisters were all in white, identical, grim and chilly and marbled, pale as statues.

Making the most of this misstep, George had hastily borrowed a white jacket from an Acquis cadre. He'd ripped off the jacket's political tags, pips, and braiding. So George was also in white.

Gathered there at the monster's graveside, two by two with George standing at their head, the women were intensely romantic and pretty. Five siblings holding up the autumn sky.

"This is George's finest hour!" said Montalban, his dark eyes wide. "Look what he's achieved! I could *never* do that! Never! He's got them publicly holding hands! Like when they were kids!"

Inke knew fear. "This is not going to work."

"Of course it will work! He's finally got them burying their primal trauma here! Even though they're a broken set, they're violently off-kilter . . . they're letting go of their past! Everybody's watching! The whole world adores them."

Inke knew that the women could not bear up. Flawed from birth,

scorched by murder, their hearts were broken: they had failed comprehensively. They were strong and resolute and intelligent women, but
they could not possibly support the roles that fate had forced upon
them. They were broken statues for a broken world.

"They cannot bear it," she told him.

"Well, I'm not claiming that this is a perfect solution for them—
peace never lasts forever in the Balkans—but come on, Inke, they're not
stupid! Look, he's giving them the ceremonial shovels!"

It was a local tradition to distribute short-handled shovels at a graveside, for the convenience of mourners casting dirt.

George was the first to pitch in with his fancy shovel—without another
word or gesture, he began heaving damp clods straight into the open
grave. He looked thrilled, overjoyed. George meant to finally conceal a
lifelong embarrassment. He might have filled that grave all by himself.

George was so gleeful and eager about his work that the women, as if
helpless, fell into line.

Soon they were all throwing dirt into the Earth, earnestly, tirelessly.

When each saw that the others were sparing no effort, they really set
to. Their arms and legs in ominous unison, the clones labored like identical machines.

Inke stared at the uncanny spectacle. Every spectator was silent and
astonished.

Vera was the best at the labor. As an engineer, Vera understood dirt
and digging. Vera had a pinched, virginal quality—Vera was a fanatic,
the kind of woman who had never understood what it meant to be a
woman. Vera was efficient and entirely humorless, a robot.

Radmila made it all look so effortless. She handled her shovel like a
stage prop. Radmila was the world's most elegant gravedigger. It was as
if every woman in the world should aspire to spend her evenings filling
graves.

Sonja had filled many graves already. Sonja was the one who best understood what she was doing. It was a moral burden to see Sonja at her
deadly work. It made one sweat.

"Biserka isn't doing much," Inke said.

"We call her 'Erika' now," said Montalban. "She broke her ribs. She's
still in a lot of pain."

"Your Biserka is up to no good. Biserka has never been any good. She would never hold up her own part of anything."

"I like to think of my Erika as a troubled girl from a severely disadvantaged background," said Montalban. "But, what the heck, yeah, of course you're right, Inke: Biserka is evil."

"Why *her*, John? The other one is the mother of your child."

"Well, I love them all so very dearly, but . . . they're so fierce and dedicated and selfless and good! They frankly tire me! Biserka considers herself a cauldron of criminal genius, but since she's so completely self-absorbed, and so devoid of any interest and empathy for others—motivated entirely by her resentment and always on the make—well, Biserka's certainly the easiest to manage. There's something abject about Biserka. I don't have to negotiate that relationship all the time. Biserka is the one that I fully understand. And she needs me the most. Left alone in a room, Biserka would sting herself to death like a scorpion. She will always need her rescuer. She'll always need a white knight to save her, she'll always be in trouble, and she will always depend on me. That's why I love her the best."

"To love an evil woman means that *you* are evil."

Montalban shrugged. "I like to think of myself as a deeply fallible man who is healthily in touch with his dark side."

Biserka cast a shovelful of dirt over Radmila's beautiful shoes. Radmila resolutely ignored her.

"Hey, I think I'm getting a blister!" Biserka whined, straightening and sucking at her fingers. "Why don't we stop all this hard work and let the servants do it?"

"Get out of the way," said Vera.

Biserka stabbed her shovel into a loose mound of dirt and departed the grave in a huff.

"You shouldn't have said that to her," said George mildly.

"Oh, so *she* has a hard life?" snarled Vera. "I've been digging up this island for ten years! Do you smell that fresh air from the hills? I *built* that fresh air."

"You thought *that* was work?" Sonja demanded, incredulous. "Your ten-year vacation on a tropical island? I fought and I suffered! The air was black! The air killed people!"

Radmila was silky. "I hope you don't expect us to praise you for worming your way into the bowels of a totalitarian regime."

"Listen to *you*," shouted Vera. "You're famous and rich! Even your *daughter* is famous and rich."

"Vera, is it *my* fault that you missed out on life by dressing up like a skeleton?"

"At least I'm not like *her*," shouted Vera, "a soldier's whore who lifts her skirt for any man with a gun!"

Sonja scowled. "Like a *Hollywood actress* is the pillar of chastity? I don't think our dirty skirts are any of your dirty business, Vera."

"They're going to kill each other now," Inke told Montalban. "Those spades can be turned into weapons."

"Any technology is a weapon. Go and stop them now, Inke."

"What, me? I'm a nobody."

"That's what I treasure about you. You're a normal human being, and you've even got normal kids. Go and stop them, Inke. You must. We've got only a few seconds left. Go intervene, make them more normal. Hurry."

"You do it."

"I can't. Don't argue with me. Do it, go." Montalban squeezed her shoulder, gave her a little push.

Inke somehow tottered into the midst of the sisterhood. They'd stopped heaving dirt into the grave and were hefting their shovels to batter and slash.

Everyone in the crowd was silently watching the tableau. Even George was staring at her intervention. Yet George seemed unsurprised to see her jumping into the quarrel. He was even daring to hope for the best.

AFTERWORD

THE CARYATIDS: AN INTERVIEW WITH
AUTEUR DIRECTOR MARY MONTALBAN

. . .

MARY MONTALBAN: So, yes, clearly, the funeral was a great cathartic moment. My grandmother died twenty-six years ago. The death of that oldest clone freed the Caryatids to take on different lives.

ENTERTAINMENT INSIDER: We do know a lot about the Caryatids, but we rarely hear much about your aunt Inke.

MM: Well, no, of course not. Inke's family, but she's not in the Family-Firm.

EI: So: What on Earth did Inke do for them?

MM: Inke did something they could never do for themselves. Those of us who know them and love them best—we all know that they're not individuals. The Caryatids are a matched set—a broken, damaged set. Inke knew that, she sensed it. So—there at the funeral, in public—Inke convinced them that they should exchange their burdens. They could choose to abandon their own roles, and play the roles of the others instead.

EI: Because Radmila was heartbroken. Sonja was defeated. Vera was hiding in some forest . . .

MM: Yes, they were miserable, but since they weren't quite human, they did have other options. If they could see beyond despair, they could hold up *one another's* burdens instead of breaking under their own.

EI: Cooperating. Like caryatids changing positions as they hold up some building. "Caryatids" being female sculptures that support buildings on their heads. From ancient Greek architecture.

MM: I can see you've been studying.

EI: *Caryatids*, that's not exactly a common title for an artwork.

MM: I know—but it all goes back to the ancient Greeks, doesn't it? The Greeks were the first to write "history."

EI: Ancient history seems to mean a great deal to your Family-Firm.

MM: It means everything. It *is* everything . . . Those ancient Greeks, they would never give women a vote, but piling a building on a woman's head, that was classical behavior for them.

EI: So the Caryatids collapsed, and yet, after that . . .

MM: They were all such capable, energetic, serious-minded women. Doing their impossible jobs in unbearable circumstances. Once they changed positions, they revived.

EI: As long as each clone was doing the impossible job that *someone else* should be doing, they each felt like they were on holiday.

MM: Well, of course that is part of their mythos: that elegant, neat solution. They rotated their roles, smooth and easy, without ever missing a beat. But that was a neat solution for us, not for them. We who loved them—the various communities who took them in—in many ways, we made them behave in that way. We forced the issue. We all felt much happier when a new Caryatid arrived to save us from the ugly wreck of the old one. People insisted that they could do the impossible. Because we needed the impossible done. Obviously, it was impossible for them to switch roles without our collusion, but we gave them that because we benefited by it. It was our happy ending, not theirs.

EI: Critics say that Sonja was much better at playing Mila Montalban than the actual Mila Montalban.

MM: That's a cheap shot at a fine actress, but . . . Well, Mila had no trouble running an Adriatic island resort. Vera blossomed inside a Chinese high-tech research camp. The Chinese much preferred her to Sonja. Sometime later Radmila went to China, while Sonja went to the island . . . Once in rotation, they didn't simply bear their burdens in suffering, they were able to thrive.

EI: It seems so simple that they could trade existences and end happily.

MM: Oh no, no—believe me, nothing *ended.* And *happiness*? It's sheer arrogance for any outsider, any normal person to think that we could solve their problems ... Nobody ever imposes a solution on those women. It's all I can do just to describe them.

EI: As the scriptwriter, you mean.

MM: Well, as a contemporary media creative, I always wanted to do a classic biopic about my mothers. I mean, to make a cinematic artwork with a linear narrative. A story line with no loose ends, where the plot makes sense. I enjoy that impossible creative challenge. It's impossible because only history can do that for us. Sometimes it takes twenty-five years, even two hundred years to crush real life into a narrative compact enough to understand.

EI: They say that to end with a funeral is the classic sign of a tragedy. Your latest project, *The Caryatids*, concludes with a funeral.

MM: Well, that's a mother-daughter issue . . . Look, can I be frank here? That narrative is supposedly about my mothers, but as a pop-entertainment product, *The Caryatids* is the ultimate Mary Montalban star vehicle. It's not about them: it's all me. Obviously it's me. I produced it, I directed it, I wrote the script, and I play all of them. I play every major part: I play Radmila, Vera, Sonja, the bit villain part of Biserka, I even play the dead grandmother in the glass coffin.

EI: Why did you make that creative choice, Mary?

MM: Because I'm a guaranteed draw and I can get big financing. But . . . well, I'm the only actress I could trust to inhabit those roles. Because I'm the only woman on Earth with any hint as to what's going on in their heads.

EI: "To understand all is to forgive all."

MM: I know that sounds corny, but, well, once you have a child of your own, like I do, you come to realize that the world's oldest, dumbest nursery maxims are the keys to reality.

EI: Surely somebody else understands the Caryatids. What about their other children?

MM: You mean Erika's brood? Give me a break!

EI: How about John Montalban? He often said the Caryatids were all one organism. Was he right about that?

MM: He's a clever guy, my dad. That big scandal that wrecked his career, people need to overlook that. He couldn't help himself—he was ruling-class in a planet that was ungovernable. If you just leave my old dad alone, he just reads his Synchronic philosophy and collects twentieth-century fine arts.

EI: I never quite got it about that so-called Synchronic philosophy.

MM: Well, that's the true genius of Synchronism; it's a futurist's philosophy, so it's permanently ahead of popular understanding.

EI: Synchronists seem to worry a lot about giant volcanoes. And the sun blowing up.

MM: Okay, look, you're baiting me here, but . . . Yes, the Caryatids are passionate about solar instability. That's why they all live in orbit now. That, and the fact that their own mother lived in orbit . . . They all have a very strong rapport with ubiquitous systems. They always did. And an orbital habitat really needs ubiquitous computing. Because a space habitat is a completely defined pocket ecosystem, it's a little toy world where you have to trace every mineral, every energy flow. They were born inside a scene like that, so they all ended up in flying glass bubbles. You'd think they'd be at peace with that by now, at peace with us down here on the planet's surface . . . But no, they've got the sun's troubles on their backs.

EI: Will the sun blow up, Mary?

MM: Someday? Absolutely it will! All you have to do is look at the Hertzsprung-Russell diagram. But personally, I think . . . if the sun's misbehavior is serious . . . well, I'm a performing artist. I need my public. I'd prefer to stay here inside this local planetary ecosystem, busted up as that is, and be fried with my fellow bacteria.

EI: And it's the same with those supervolcanoes?

MM: One of 'em is bound to blow, that's inevitable. It's just the truth.

EI: You recently said that "the structure of space-time is rotting."

MM: It's true, but do you really want to get into that issue? We don't have all the time in the world here.

EI: No. You're right. I don't think we need to get into that issue, Mary. But tell us, why do you think actresses are so interested in entropy and physics these days? Some of them even write science papers. You, for instance.

MM: I think that was inevitable. One of those "black swan" things. You can never predict a black swan, yet it happens anyway, and then everybody justifies it and rationalizes it after it's done. That's very much my own story . . . I am a black swan, I was born one, and that's why I have always been both a monster and a major pop star.

Now I'm trying to make sense of the experience of my mothers. History passes. And some important pieces of major evidence are just plain gone.

EI: "Major evidence"?

MM: The part that's missing is the work they cared most about. Those ubiquitous systems, what they used to call the "mediation," the "sensorwebs." The Caryatids were brought up inside a crude and primitive "smart house"—some incredibly invasive surveillance scheme . . . there is nothing left of that technology nowadays. Those were the technical structures the Caryatids were born to support, but . . . Those technologies advanced so fast that they vanished. The languages, operating systems, frameworks of interaction, the eyeball-blasting laser-colored neural helmets . . . all that stuff is more primitive than steam engines now.

I mean, you can tell how a steam engine works by just looking at it, but a complex, distributed, ubiquitous system? There's no way to maintain that! That all became ubijunk! Those cutting-edge systems are gone like sandcastles. A rising tide of major transformation threw them up on the shore, and then the whole sea rose and they are beyond retrieval.

EI: That sounds so sad . . . But there's very little any of us can do about that.

MM: All I know is that the Caryatids were passionately into that, fanatical about it, yet time passed and now it is *gone*. It's the one aspect of their experience almost entirely closed to me as an artist.

Futurism is prediction. We all know that's impossible. But history is retrodiction, and that's impossible, too. So we have to paper over those black holes with sheer imagination.

EI: So you tell stories.

MM: Well, yes. That's what I do.

ABOUT THE AUTHOR

BRUCE STERLING is the author of ten novels, three of which were selected as *New York Times* Notable Books of the Year. *The Difference Engine,* co-written with William Gibson, was a national bestseller. He has also published four short-story collections and three nonfiction books. He has written for many magazines, including *Newsweek, Fortune, Time, Whole Earth Review,* and *Wired,* where he was a longtime contributing editor. He has won two Hugo Awards and was a finalist for the 2007 Nebula for Best Novella. He lives in Austin, Texas, with frequent side jaunts to Turin, Italy; Los Angeles; Belgrade; and Amsterdam.